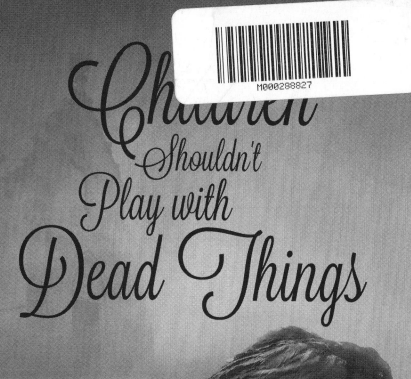

Children Shouldn't Play with Dead Things

Children
Shouldn't
Play with
Dead Things

Martina McAtee

Children Shouldn't Play with Dead Things
Dead Things Series Book 1
by Martina McAtee

Cover Design: Nathalia Suellen

Dedication

This book is dedicated to my mom and dad. I wish they could have been around to see this.

Acknowledgements

There are so many people I want to thank for helping me along the way that I don't even know where to start. To my daughter, Mikyla for putting up with me living with my head in my laptop for six months. To my sister, Susan, and my nieces, Shannon and Dani for holding my hand, reading terrible drafts and basically just listening to every freak out. To my best friend, Melissa for reading this book not once, not twice but three times looking for my numerous grammar errors (I have a comma problem). Thank you to Lee Ann for reading this book and encouraging me along the way when you were under no familial obligation to do so. To Kathy, who was as proud of me as my own mother would have been. Also, thank you to Nathalia Suellen for taking my cover design ideas and turning them into the most beautiful design ever and Atmosphere Designs for designing the perfect website in such a short time. And, finally, thank you to Google, you've always been there when I needed you, even when I didn't quite know what I was looking for. You're the best.

"Thus strangely are our souls constructed, and by such slight ligaments are we bound to prosperity or ruin."

~Mary Shelley, Frankenstein

Chapter 1

EMBER

"You know, Ms. Landry, you have the best skin I've ever seen on a corpse," Ember Denning told the body lying before her. "I would know; I'm a professional." She dusted powder across the older woman's cheeks, Ember's whisper conspiratorial as she added, "But if you see your sister up there, don't tell her I said so, since I may have said the same thing last month."

Her latest client was predictably silent on the matter. She sighed. She needed livelier friends.

"Ember?"

Ember squeaked in terror, spinning around, makeup brush brandished before her like a weapon.

Her boss chuckled. "What are you going to do, rouge me to death?"

She dropped her hands and shrugged, defeated, going back to her task. "It's a powder brush, actually."

He looked at his watch. "What are you doing here, Ember?"

She furrowed her brow, hoping she looked suitably confused. "I work here?"

That got her the eyebrow. Miller Hammond was a lot of things—including the owner of the funeral home she stood in—but he wasn't stupid, and he wasn't buying it. He folded thick arms across his chest and fixed her with his best, hardened stare. He was trying for threatening, but with his dark freckled skin and kind eyes, he looked like he should be playing God in every movie.

"You know exactly what I mean. I thought you were going to the cemetery today?"

She shrugged, eyes sliding away. "The day's technically not over yet."

"Girl, do not play games with me," he said. "You need to go see your father. You missed his wake. You cannot miss his burial. You need to see him before…" He trailed off, letting his words go unspoken.

He didn't have to say it. She needed to see him before social services came to collect her. She didn't see the point of shoving a seventeen-year-old into foster care for one year, but the social worker had assured Ember her opinion didn't matter.

"Why do you even care?" she asked, tone casual as she slammed her brushes back into their proper containers. "He didn't care about me when he was alive. Why should I care about him now that he's dead? It's not like he knows I'm there."

He glanced at the old woman lying on the table. "Who are you trying to convince? You spend more time talking to the dead than the living."

Her face flushed. She didn't really have a good answer, so instead she said, "The difference is these people just died." She snapped her rubber gloves off. "My father has been dead for years. Somebody just finally laid him down."

"Ember," he said, his voice soft with…something, sympathy, maybe pity. "Your dad was troubled, he—"

"Was a drunk," Ember finished.

"He loved you." He moved towards her, but she held up her hand. He stopped, palms raised in surrender.

She hunched in on herself. She had a thing about personal space. She gave him a ghost of a smile. It wasn't his fault she was weird. Miller was just trying to help. He was always trying to help.

"I..." she started, apology dying on her lips.

"No. Nope. You don't have to believe me, but you do have to listen to me. Not another word. Take your skinny behind out of here and go do what's right. Now. I'll have Alice finish up with Ms. Landry."

I do not have a skinny behind, she thought with a huff. "Fine," she said, snagging her sweater from the hook by the door. "But don't blame me when she ends up looking like one of those queens on Bourbon Street."

"Uh huh." He waved a hand at her. "And you go straight home after the service. It's going to be crazy in the quarter tonight. I don't want you getting caught out in that."

She rolled her eyes but nodded. "Yeah, yeah."

"I mean it."

"Okay!" Jeez, it's not like it was her first day living in New Orleans. There was a festival in the quarter pretty much every day, especially this close to Halloween.

"Oh, and Ember."

She turned with an exasperated sigh. "Yes?"

"Happy birthday."

She gave him a lopsided smile. "Thanks."

The walk to the cemetery was quick. People were already celebrating. Men wore skull masks and top hats, and women wore elaborate face paint and beautiful dresses in honor of Dia de los Muerta. She stared longingly at a dark-haired girl with a huge red rose in her hair and sugar skull face paint. If Ember were a normal girl, she'd be preparing for the event with her friends. Yet, despite sharing her birthday with the day of the dead, she'd never celebrated it.

She smiled at the girl as they passed, but the girl dropped her eyes and moved far away on the narrow sidewalk. People avoided Ember as if a force field existed around her. It didn't hurt her feelings anymore. It was why she usually ignored Miller's fatherly warnings about being careful. Nobody wanted to be near her. People were afraid of her. She just didn't know why.

It was cold even for that time of year. Swollen grey storm clouds marred the afternoon sky, casting the landscape around her in shadow. She pulled her sweater tighter, hoping her arm hid the

 3

largest hole. She shivered as the wind picked up and swirled the fallen leaves around her feet.

She wasn't the first to arrive at the service. A sea of strangers, all gawking at her with undisguised interest, stood before the large mausoleum housing the remains of her father. Those gawking were mostly his students and other colleagues from the university, there to satisfy their morbid curiosity. Her father had no friends. It was hard to make friends when you spent your whole life as a barely functioning alcoholic, there weren't many friends at the bottom of a whiskey bottle.

She could feel their scrutiny, like tiny daggers, piercing her skin. She hated when people stared…and they always stared. She was strange looking, her hair too orange, too wild, and her wide violet eyes too strange. New Orleans was a superstitious place, and something about her triggered people's paranoia.

She set her jaw, grinding her teeth until the muscle in her jaw popped. She just wasn't herself since he died. Maybe she was getting sick. Thunder rumbled overhead, and she squinted into the sky, inhaling deeply. It smelled like rain. Of course, it was going to rain. She hadn't brought an umbrella.

As the minutes ticked by, she became restless. She hated waiting. Couldn't they just start this useless ritual already? People whispered to each other, their gazes heavy on her back, their hushed voices like tiny insects scuttling in her ears, making her skin crawl.

She glanced at the gates. She could go. She could just turn and leave. But everybody would see. She chewed at her thumbnail. What did she care what a bunch of strangers thought about her? She could do as she pleased. She had nobody to answer to. Her breath caught on the thought. She had nobody. She stayed where she was, frozen at the thought.

A dark-skinned man in a long black robe ambled his way to the front of the crowd, smiling and shaking hands with the people, clasping them warmly on the shoulder like a visiting dignitary. The group quieted, and Ember watched as the woman closest to her smoothed her hands over her blouse as if there would be an inspection after the service. Ember rolled her eyes.

 4

"Brothers and sisters," the man's voice boomed in the silence, echoing off the surrounding stones. "We are gathered here to say goodbye to a dear friend."

She couldn't help the snort that escaped, covering it with a cough as eyes swung towards her. It was his job to spout off platitudes about the dead, she reminded herself.

What was he going to say? 'Dear friends, we've gathered to say goodbye to a man who was a lousy professor and an even worse father. A nasty, neglectful jerk that spent his days trying to decide if he would ignore his only child or verbally abuse her to the point of neuroses. He spent most nights passed out in his vomit and none of us are sorry he's gone."

This crowd would love that.

As he spoke, her anxiety grew. She felt feverish, a heat overtaking her body, starting at the soles of her feet and crawling higher with each passing moment. Beads of perspiration formed on her lip, despite the cool air whipping around the stone mausoleums. She had to be coming down with something.

She tuned out the preacher, her eyes fluttering as she swayed on her feet, vision swimming. She blinked hard several times and dabbed at the sweat at her forehead with her sleeve. Was she going to pass out?

A wave of black umbrellas swung into the air as the sky opened up. People huddled together, trying to ward off the frigid cold and the sudden torrent of rain.

She made no move to protect herself from the deluge, all her energy focused on remaining upright. Her hair stuck to her face, her sweater and black dress clinging like a second skin. She should be freezing, but she was in flames, her mouth dry and head stuffed with cotton. What was happening to her?

The preacher droned on despite the weather, the woman in the blouse rushing forward to shield the good reverend with her obnoxiously large black umbrella. What was this lady's deal? Was she trying for extra grace in heaven? Ember's fingers buzzed like she held a live wire, the sensation growing until she was sure a million fire ants writhed beneath her skin, scratching and biting.

 5

Her eyes swept the crowd, noting how people inched even farther away from her. Could they see what was happening? Maybe they just questioned the sanity of a girl who didn't have the sense to get out of the rain?

Her eyes scanned the perimeter, looking anywhere but the crowd. At first glance, she thought him a statue, an apparition in the deluge of rain. He sat perched on top of a mausoleum, crouched like a gargoyle with his elbows on his knees, a hood shrouding his face. Three stone crosses rose behind him, giving him the appearance a post-apocalyptic monk guarding a sacred shrine.

That feeling beneath her skin intensified, and she fought the urge to tear at her flesh with her nails. How could anybody not see something was wrong? She balled her hands into fists, clenching until her nails pushed tiny half-moons into her palms. The pain brought the tiniest bit of relief, as she focused on it and not the razor blades beneath her skin.

It hit her then, pain like a lightning bolt, ripping through her skull. She would have hit her knees, but she was paralyzed, hanging like a marionette doll controlled by some unseen puppet master. Her limbs wouldn't budge, cement heavy and useless. She tried to scream, but no sound came. Nobody looked her way. Could they not see there was something wrong with her?

Dread clung to her as real as the fabric against her skin. She was on fire. She needed to cool down, but the rain was as hot and thick as the blood pounding in her ears. She was going to die like this, standing at her father's funeral, drenched and in agony.

Her eyes found the figure in the distance. If he was a monk, maybe he'd hear her prayers. Maybe he could end her misery. He tilted his head, and she stupidly thought maybe he'd heard her somehow. Maybe he could sense what was happening.

He stood then, rising from the top of the mausoleum like another spire. He pushed his hood back. She wished she could see his face. She needed him closer. She needed to see him, to know he saw her. She was going crazy. He was too far away to help. She was going to die there, and he was going to watch.

She found the idea weirdly comforting. At least she wouldn't be totally alone in the end, not like her dad. Another shot of pain seared

 6

through her, her vision whiting out. She hoped it happened soon. She welcomed losing consciousness, anything to make the pain stop.

Her panic ratcheted. If she closed her eyes, if she succumbed to this…feeling, she wouldn't just pass out…she was going to die. She didn't want to die.

She felt it then, a slippery coolness washing over her; icy fingers pressed against her temples, working their way under her skin and soothing the searing heat like ice water through her veins.

She wasn't sure how long she stood there, eyes closed, breathing deep, letting the break overtake her, but by the time the sensation began to fade, the rain was gone and the people were drifting away. She shook her head, trying to clear the frosty cobwebs clouding her brain. She timidly took a step forward, relieved to find her limbs working.

She looked to the mausoleum in the distance, but there was nobody. Had he ever really been there? Was this what it felt like to go crazy?

Chapter 2

MACE

Mace kept his head down and his sopping wet hood up. It may not have protected him against the weather, but it afforded him some anonymity. She had seen him in the cemetery, forcing him to hang back farther than usual. He wasn't afraid of losing her. The girl only had three destinations: the funeral parlor, the cemetery, or that ramshackle apartment she called home. The greater concern was her getting home in one piece.

He weaved through the crowd of drunken revelers, doing his best to keep her in his sights. She paid no attention to her surroundings, drifting along in a daze. She stepped in front of a cab, earning her a honk and a shout in Creole. She didn't even acknowledge him. He was unsure if the girl had left her father's funeral with a death wish or if she still suffered from the effects of the incident in that cemetery.

It mattered not to him, either way. He'd spent the last seven days bored out of his mind. It would be a shame if a bus hit her just when her life was getting interesting. He couldn't fault her for his boredom, he supposed. It wasn't as if she knew he followed, and it seemed unreasonable and somewhat impolite to task somebody with keeping their stalker entertained.

Entertaining him was an impossible task, really. Immortality sounded great in the brochure, but after the first hundred years, everything seemed redundant. His life had become a tedious loop of stalk, kill, repeat. He had to eat, but it didn't make hunting any less monotonous. He was famished, but when he looked at the crowd, not one of them seemed more appealing than following the girl. He'd rather go hungry. Besides, cleanup in a crowd like that would be messy. People shouldn't let the media fool them; murder wasn't that exciting after the first fifty bodies or so.

His eyes landed on the group of drunken college guys harassing one of the street musicians, his eyes lingering long enough that one of them might mistake his intentions. He glanced at his charge, still wandering through the crowd like a ghost, before looking back at his meal options. He shouldn't have, not in that crowd. Really, though, would the world even notice one less douchebag in boat shoes and a backwards ball cap? It would practically be a public service.

He shook his head as one of the boys tried to snatch the wig off a female impersonator, getting a right hook to the face for his trouble. Call it what you wanted, natural selection, Darwinism, top of the food chain; some people just didn't make the cut. He rarely went after humans. They didn't provide much of a challenge, but sometimes he was willing to make an exception for the greater good.

With one last glance, he shook off his hunger and went back to following the girl. He was certain those boys would be around later. The rain started once again, just as the girl made it to her apartment. Mace pulled himself further into his damp hoodie, grateful the cold didn't affect him. If he weren't immortal, he'd likely die of hypothermia. Instead, he was just very uncomfortable.

He settled himself on the roof across from her building, tugging his sleeping bag around his shoulders, grateful for the overhang that shielded him from some of the rain. He tucked his knees against his chest, resting his elbows there as she came into view in the window. She flung off her wet sweater and moved out of view only to reappear in her bedroom window. When she yanked her dress over her head, he dropped his gaze to his phone, glancing at the time. It was almost time for check-in. He was to call every six hours, no exceptions. It was part of the reason he'd almost declined the offer. He wasn't much for deadlines. He felt it stifled his...creativity.

They were quite insistent he be the one who watched the girl, despite his taste for exotic cuisine and his penchant for homicide. It made no sense. Mace knew where he ranked among his kind. He was very much a last resort. He wasn't a babysitter or a bodyguard. They didn't hire him to follow humans, no matter how bizarre they appeared. They didn't even hire him to kill humans.

He pulled a granola bar from his bag and tore into it. It didn't satisfy his hunger, but it gave him something to do with his hands. As he watched, she stopped to answer the phone. She became more agitated as the call went on, finally slamming the phone down in its cradle and ripping it from the wall. She smashed it on the floor. His brows knitted together, she was acting quite strange since the funeral.

He wanted to talk to her. He needed to know what she was, but his orders were clear. Observe her behavior. Report what he sees. Do not interact with her. Do not kill her. They stated the latter explicitly...twice. He was to report anything unusual immediately.

The term unusual was subjective, it would seem, because everything about this girl was unusual. She had no friends. She interacted with very few people. She'd only attended school once in the last four days and while there, she'd kept her head down and hadn't spoken a single word. Her classmates hadn't been so kind. It seemed not even the death of a parent could stop people from being people, but she hadn't acknowledged them in any outward way.

She hadn't returned since. Instead, she chose to hide in the cemetery. He'd first thought she was there to visit her father. He'd been wrong. She was far too familiar with the cemetery for a girl her age. She knew everybody. Literally, every single body. She spent hours putting single flowers on the graves of the deceased. She lit the candles often left as tribute. She carefully righted trinkets friends and family left behind. She wasn't just respectful of the dead; she was reverent.

When she wasn't tending the dead, she was talking to them. Before that first day in the cemetery, he'd thought her mute. Then, he'd watched her have a forty-five-minute conversation with a mausoleum with the name ARSENAULT etched across the top. As she carried on her one-sided chat, she drew, pencil flying, sketching an old man dressed in his Sunday best and a beat up fedora.

It was safe to say his new charge had a singular preoccupation with the dead. Perhaps they were speaking to her. Even so, it wouldn't explain why he was watching her; his employers rarely concerned themselves with the special humans. But after what he'd just witnessed in the cemetery, he supposed it was safe to put her firmly in the non-human column—breed undetermined.

Given her fascination with the dead, he would almost think Valkyrie or reaper, but power didn't seek them out. That power in the cemetery had come for her, swirling up from the ground and swallowing her whole. She'd stood, paralyzed, helpless to do anything. Had she unwittingly called that power to her, or had it come for her of its own free will? He wasn't sure which was worse.

He supposed she could be a witch, but she hadn't been in control of that power. If she was a witch, she was very new or completely incompetent. Perhaps if he could get near enough to see her mark, it would give him a clue as to her origins, but that would mean getting closer. He'd already gotten too close. He'd already interfered. He'd disobeyed his direct orders.

He wouldn't feel bad about that…couldn't even if he'd chosen to. They'd known what they were getting into when they'd picked him for the task, so the fault lay entirely with them. He had no idea why he'd approached her, other than just to see what would happen. He was curious by nature. They had to know he wouldn't be able to leave something so tempting alone. So much energy surrounded her, how could he not try to tap into it?

Theoretically, it shouldn't have worked. His magic should have had no effect on hers. Very rarely could you temper somebody else's magic by adding your own. If anything, he ran the risk of creating a much bigger complication, such as killing a large crowd of people at a funeral and rendering himself unemployed.

It had worked, though. Her magic had practically rolled over and purred at his, and his magic had responded in kind, wrapping itself around hers and making itself at home. Witch magic didn't do that. It was maddening. He felt like he was missing something, something important. It gnawed at the corners of his mind, just out of reach.

 11

A flash of color caught his attention at the window. She had changed into jeans and a bulky sweater, a tattered purple duffle bag in her hands. She stuffed clothing, her sketchbook, shoes, and anything else she could fit into the bag. She went to the kitchen and pulled out a coffee can from the top shelf, pulling out cash and stuffing it into her jean pocket.

Interesting.

His phone vibrated in his hand, startling him out of his thoughts.

"Mace," he answered.

"It's like you're trying to piss him off."

"Echo." He grimaced at her tone, picturing her pinched face. "To what do I owe this pleasure?"

"Check your watch. You're late checking in."

He glanced at his phone. "Ah, right you are, luv." He'd lost track of time.

"So, anything to report?" Echo prompted, annoyance creeping into her voice.

The girl flitted around the apartment, a rare smile blooming on her face. The rain began to fall harder, coming in sideways. She rushed to the window, hands on the frame when she looked up and froze.

He did too.

There was no way she could see him, not from this distance, not with the rain. He squinted as she turned away just a bit before looking back, worrying her bottom lip between her teeth. Maybe she could see him. She'd observed him in the cemetery earlier. He couldn't help but stare back. Her cloud of orange hair was billowing in the chilly air, and even with the rain gusting in her face, she looked...captivating, like some vengeful spirit out of a gothic novel. She stared for another second before slamming the window shut hard enough to rattle the glass in its frame.

He blinked, spell broken.

"Hello?" Echo questioned through clenched teeth.

He opened his mouth to tell her what he'd seen but faltered. If he told them she was a...well, a not human, there was an excellent chance his next assignment would be to kill her like the others. It had to be why they'd chosen him. Nothing else made sense. They'd obviously wanted him to ensure she was supernatural before they put her down.

He wasn't quite ready for that. He had to know what she was. He'd been around a long time, and he'd never seen somebody who appeared to leach power from the ground they stood on. His fingers flexed. His magic wanted to know too.

He cleared his throat. "Sorry, bad reception up here. Nothing to report yet. The girl is dismally boring. I should charge him triple for forcing me to endure this type of torture." He lowered his voice, attempting a flirty tone. "Any chance you feel like telling me what he wants with her? Since when did we start concerning ourselves with humans?"

She snorted. "That's hardly any of your business, is it?"

"No need to get snippy, luv. It was a fleeting curiosity."

"He doesn't pay you to be curious; he pays you to do as you're told."

"Well, somebody has her sassy pants on today. What has your knickers in such a twist?"

The girl's voice dropped to a whisper. "Please, please, don't do anything stupid, Mace. Just watch the girl and report what you see. A trained monkey could do it."

"Yes," he said. "That's the thing of it. He could have assigned anybody to watch the girl. Why the homicidal maniac? Why hire a killer to babysit one tiny human girl? Seems like a terrible staffing choice, really, like hiring an alcoholic to tend your bar."

"Just mind your business, do your job, and don't do anything that is going to get you in trouble."

"What's he going to do? Kill me? I'm immortal."

She made a grunt of frustration. "Yes, well, there are far worse things than death, as you well remember. Whatever she is, she's got him on edge. Don't make him mad."

He sighed. "I'll be in touch."

He ended the call just as the girl opened the old laptop on the coffee table. She sat on the floor, typing furiously for the next few hours, her attention never wavering. The rain had disappeared by the time she hoisted her bag over her shoulder and headed for her front door. She didn't even bother to lock it behind her.

"Now where are you headed?" he asked the empty rooftop.

  13

Chapter 3

KAI

Kai Lonergan hated math. You would think being a supernatural creature in a supernatural town would make you exempt from mundane chores, like math and econ, but no, the authorities forced shifters, witches, and even reapers like him to endure the horrors of high school. The town claimed they had their reasons; keeping up appearances—blah, blah, blah—but as far as he could see, it was just good old-fashioned torture.

He dropped his chin to his hand and sighed dramatically. "I hate this," he told his sister. Tristin didn't even look up from her notebook. He leaned forward to peer past the waterfall of her dark hair. She sat hunched over her desk, tongue poking from the side of her mouth. His sister was no artist, but he could see she was doodling dismembered stick figures with pools of black ink at their feet. Great, as if people didn't already think they were freaks. The school therapist would have a field day with that.

He continued his conversation despite his sister's lack of participation. "Hate's not even a strong enough word," he decided. "I loathe math. Detest it. I hate math more than I hate asparagus, more than I hate that weird fruit thing Isa makes us choke down every Christmas. I hate math more than I hate"—he shuddered—"marshmallows."

His sister shook her head and grunted but didn't otherwise acknowledge him. If Quinn were there, he'd understand. Quinn understood Kai's hatred of squishy weird foods because Quinn was the best, best friend ever. But Quinn was in smart-people math where they started throwing in hearts and hieroglyphics and alchemical symbols, most of which Kai was sure they just made up. Quinn assured Kai it wasn't so, but no good could come from putting math and chemistry together.

"Come on, Tristin, commiserate with me. Be my sister. Let us band together over a mutual hatred of math."

A desk chair scraped behind him, and a shadow loomed over his desk. Warm air puffed against his skin as an angry werewolf rumbled, "Shut. Up."

Kai grimaced. He'd managed to forget Rhys's annoying presence for almost ten whole minutes. That was a new record for him. In Kai's defense, it was hard to forget a six-foot-six slab of muscle that shadowed your every move. It was especially hard when they wore their shirts tight enough to count their abs and smelled like rain and sex and poor life choices. He closed his eyes, attempting to regulate his teenage hormones and wildly thumping heart before Rhys smelled it on him.

He needed a distraction. He decided on the easiest course of action, annoying the wolf. It was a win-win. He leaned back until his head was resting on Rhys's desk and grinned up at his perpetually grumpy face. "From this angle, it looks like you're actually smiling." Kai laughed softly. "It's like an optical illusion."

Rhys growled low in his throat. "Get off my desk."

Kai schooled his expression into a pout. "Now you're just hurting my feelings. Tell me I'm pretty, and maybe I'll relinquish your desk." He batted his eyes, satisfaction warming him as Rhys turned an unnatural shade of purple. "Come on," Kai coaxed. "Use your words."

Rhys started to partially shift into wolf mode, eyes glowing, the light bringing out the gold flecks in his brilliant green eyes, his canines elongating dramatically. Kai snorted a laugh. "You're so easy to rile up. One little joke and you go all flashy eyes. Those stopped working on me when I was like seven, dude."

The wolf moved closer until his face hovered just over Kai's, a lock of mahogany hair falling across his forehead. Kai's mouth went dry, and he swallowed convulsively, definitely not imagining the epic upside down Spiderman kiss they could be reenacting. Rhys made a choked noise that was as close to a laugh as he got. Kai knew it was because he heard his heartbeat stutter. Stupid werewolf hearing, it was such an invasion of privacy.

"Pay attention or I'm going to tell Isa you requested that weird pickled herring recipe she made last year, and I'll ask her to put that clotted cream sauce on it too."

Kai shuddered at the memory of the alpha's attempt at foreign cuisine and stuck his tongue out at Rhys, relinquishing the desk. "You suck."

"You wish."

His sister snorted at that, glancing up long enough to laugh at her brother. She thought Rhys was hilarious. They were two peas in an emotionally constipated pod.

Their teacher, Mr. Keller, appeared, looking as thrilled to be there as the rest of them. He took one last slug from his Styrofoam cup before throwing it in the trash. He dropped his bag on the floor loud enough to cut off the low murmur of restless students, waiting until all eyes were forward. "Okay, who wants to get us started on last night's quadratic equations homework?"

Crap. Kai knew he'd forgotten something. He dropped his head onto his desk with a loud thump.

"Has math finally killed you, Mr. Lonergan?" The teacher asked, sounding far too hopeful to Kai.

He heard the snickers of his classmates and lifted his head just enough to make eye contact with the aging witch. "No. Unfortunately, I'm still here, but I think my brain is literally melting." He dropped his head back on his arms.

"Tristin," Mr. Keller said. "You seem to be working rigorously on what I'm sure are your notes. Perhaps you could share them with your brother?"

Kai rolled his head towards his sister with a smirk, brow raised, eying her morbid drawings. "Yes, Tristin, you take the best notes, perhaps you could share with the whole class." Her pen slowed, and she looked up from her grisly masterpiece long enough to scowl at her brother and shoot him the finger from her lap.

She forced her face into some semblance of a smile. "Of course, Mr. Keller. I'd be happy to."

"I guess your sister absorbed the brains and the manners in the womb. Did she leave anything for you?" Keller asked.

Kai leaned back with a grin, tapping his pencil against his notebook. "She got the brains and the manners, but I got the looks and the personality."

"Whatever helps you sleep at night, sunshine," his sister retorted as she flipped to a clean sheet of notebook paper and started anew.

The teacher eyed him. "Mr. Lonergan, do you think I can get through the rest of class without you further derailing my lesson?"

Kai looked pained, the tapping of his pencil increasing. "Hard to say really. I can't help it, dude. Math physically hurts me."

"Don't call me dude." The teacher's eyes dropped to the pencil, warning clear as he gritted out, "Mr. Lonergan."

Kai opened his mouth to promise his best behavior when Rhys's hand appeared, snatching Kai's pencil and snapping it in half, before dropping it on his desk.

Kai's mouth fell open. That was his only pencil. He went to say so but went temporarily mute as he felt a familiar burning at his wrist. He didn't look at first, just rubbed absently at the spot, dread pooling in his stomach. Why did collections always seem to come on a Friday? Nobody should have to die on a Friday. It was the best day of the week. Whoever made these decisions should reserve deaths for awful days like Monday. People shouldn't have to work all week long just to kick the bucket just before things got good. Not that anybody cared about the opinion of one novice reaper.

He glanced at his sister, wondering if he should tell her he wouldn't be at work that night. He pushed the sleeve of his shirt up just enough to peer at the name, his curiosity getting the better of him. He skimmed over the name, letting his sleeve drop back into place, before yanking it up again in confusion. The hitch in his breathing sounded loud in the sudden silence.

There was no way that was right.

Rhys sat forward enough to whisper, "What is your problem now?"

"Can I help you?" Kai snapped, yanking his sleeve down to cover the name, sounding scandalized.

Rhys stared at Kai for a good thirty seconds before the wolf opened his mouth. Whatever scathing retort he had planned was lost as Tristin's pen fell from her fingers. She looked at her brother, eyes bleeding red as a shriek ripped from her lips. Everybody whipped around in their seats, hands covering their ears, cringing away from her.

Goosebumps erupted along his skin. Tristin covered her mouth with her hand, eyes wide as she looked at him. Kai's heart slammed against his chest as he stared at his sister.

"Well, that was unexpected," he said, to nobody in particular.

Chapter 4

TRISTIN

Tristin sat on the wooden bench outside the principal's office, staring at her hands in her lap. She refused to look up, knowing she was the reason for the whispers and the laughter of the students moving between classes. This was so embarrassing.

Kai sat next to her, quiet for once. She could feel the empathy rolling off him in waves. Her brother hated to see somebody miserable. He would sit and stare, radiating love like a sad-eyed golden retriever until she placated him. "I'm fine, really. You don't have to keep me company. I'll just tell them I...saw a spider...or something."

Kai arched a brow at her. "Tristin, two months ago, you ripped out a wendigo's jugular with your bare hands." He pulled a face, like he could still see it. "Nobody will believe you."

He was right. There was no way anybody was going to believe anything she said, maybe not even the truth. She wasn't sure she believed the truth. She'd spent the last twelve years as a banshee who couldn't banshee. She'd finally started believing she wasn't ever going to get her powers back and wondering if she'd ever really had them at all.

She had no memory of ever screaming. Allister swore he'd heard her scream as a child—and Allister wasn't really one to make stuff up—but the kids in town hid too much, and she just didn't trust them. Her brother was the reaper, so she had to be human. That was just the way it worked. Yet, suddenly she wasn't and everybody knew it. Her face burned at the thought of more attention on her.

"Why now?" she asked, mostly to herself.

Kai took a deep breath and looked at her. "I think I may know why."

She glowered at him, eyebrow raised. Of course he did. How long would he have sat there giving her puppy eyes if she hadn't said anything? She said as much, earning her a hurt look and a deep breath.

"Okay, I need to show you something, and you can't freak out," Kai said.

Tristin blinked at him slowly. "Bro, I'm not the drama queen in this particular duo."

He shrugged. "True." He turned to shield himself from the passing students and pushed the sleeve of his plaid shirt up. "Look."

Her gasp was audible even in the crowded breezeway. Kai's eyes widened and Tristin glanced up to make sure nobody had heard her before dragging her gaze back to the name. She ran her hands across the letters and numbers.

November Lonergan

29° 59' 8.2644" N

90° 6' 40.2552" W

She fought to get a grip on her heartbeat. She was freaking out. Holy crap. She was *definitely* freaking out. She breathed in and out slowly. She stared at the name. This made no sense at all. November was dead.

"What the hell is going on?" she whispered.

Kai thought about it for a while, his thumb rubbing absently over the words on his wrist. "Maybe it's a coincidence?"

She glowered at him. "You think it's a coincidence that my abilities return the exact same moment our dead cousin's name shows up on your arm to be collected? Really?"

"Well, it is our birthday," he said, cheeks flushing.

"Happy birthday, here's your reaper powers and your dead cousin?" she asked. "Nothing about this makes any sense."

"I don't know, Trist, Allister said your powers would resurface eventually."

"Let's just forget my freaky banshee powers for five minutes and focus on our dead cousin."

"Our technically undead cousin," Kai supplied.

"Not for long if she's on your arm," she reminded him. "This feels wrong. It feels like a trap. We should tell Isa."

"No way," he snapped, immediately looking apologetic. "I just mean we don't even know what we'd tell her."

"Um, how about our dead cousin's name popped up on your soul collecting to-do list?" Why was he being so stupid about this? "Come on, Kai, you have to admit this feels wrong. November is dead, and even if she weren't, they wouldn't send a family member to collect her soul. It's creepy."

"So maybe they're sending me a message. Maybe I'm not supposed to collect her. Maybe I'm supposed to save her."

She stared at him for a long minute. "Have you lost your mind? Do you know what the Grove will do to you if you actively interfere with a collection?"

She clenched and unclenched her jaw until her teeth hurt. They had to tell Isa; they couldn't *not* tell the alpha. They needed somebody with more information than they had. Besides, they had to go home sometime.

She looked away, asking, "What about Rhys?" She didn't want to see the look of betrayal on his face. If they couldn't talk to Isa, her brother had to be the next best thing.

"Have you suffered a recent blow to the head?" he asked. "He hates me. He would probably tell me to go, just hoping I'd get killed or do something stupid so he could turn me into the Grove himself."

She rolled her eyes. "You are ridiculous."

He waved off her comment. "Maybe, but that's not important. What is important is figuring this out without involving the others."

Tristin had no idea why he was so desperate to leave the pack out of this. "Why? Kai, this is crazy. We can't just run off chasing a ghost. We don't even know where we're going."

"New Orleans," he said, showing her the GPS coordinates on his phone.

"Are you freaking crazy?" she shouted. "Isa would never let us do this. We've never even left this town, much less the state. We have no idea what's out there."

"Could it be any worse than what's here? Tristin, this town is Disney for the paranormal. New Orleans couldn't be any worse."

"How would you know? All your knowledge comes from the human internet and television shows."

He looked at her funny. "Um, that's where most people get their information, Tristin."

"No, that's where humans get their information, you're not a human."

He arched a brow. "Right back at ya, sis."

Her sigh was longsuffering, her look withering. Before she could retort, he held up his hand. "Look, I have no idea what this means or what's out there, but I'm not going to just ignore November's name appearing on my arm, not when your powers magically resurface at the same time. I'm going to New Orleans, and I'm going to save her. Are you coming with me or not?" She stared at him balefully until he said, "Wonder twin powers, activate?"

He held up his fist.

"You're such a loser," she muttered, as she bumped her fist against his.

"Really?" he said, eyes bright, grin spreading across his face. "We're doing this?"

She made a frustrated noise, startling the few stragglers in the hallway. "Fine, we'll go, but when Isa finds out, I'm one hundred percent blaming it all on you."

He jumped to his feet and kissed her forehead sloppily. "I'd expect nothing less." His smile looked positively evil when he asked, "Now, whose car are we stealing?"

     22

Chapter 5

EMBER

Ember headed to the bus station on autopilot. She wasn't going to foster care. She just couldn't. She'd rather be homeless, sleeping under bridges, than be at the mercy of somebody who thought she needed a parent. She just needed to get on a bus and forget about this town, forget about her father. Her life would be different somewhere else. It had to be.

She walked, eyes down, hands shoved in her pockets to ward off the cold. She was far enough from the quarter that the noise level was tolerable. The festivities hadn't picked up just yet, but the crowds were increasing. Parade floats parked along the side streets, getting ready for the procession to start. The sky was on fire, painting the sky orange and yellow, as the sun sank out of sight, signaling revelers that the celebration would soon begin.

The sounds of jazz poured out into the streets, as people made their way in and out of bars and restaurants. She wouldn't miss that. She'd seen the inside of every bar in the quarter, knew that distinct scent of alcohol, sweat, and stale air. She'd spent her whole life retrieving and reviving her father just enough to drag him home and help him collapse on the couch.

Her father.

Every time she thought of him it was like a blow to the diaphragm, leaving her winded and aching. He was dead. He was dead, and he wasn't coming home. No more rescuing him. No more cleaning up after him. No more abuse. She should be relieved. It shouldn't hurt. He didn't deserve her feelings. He didn't deserve anything. This was all his fault.

She stuffed down the gnawing ache. She didn't need him. She paid bills. She had a job. She'd dealt with his bill collectors. Hell, she'd dealt with his bookie, a hard assed woman named Shelby. Between Ember's father's drinking and gambling debts, they'd practically lived in squalor. She couldn't do much worse on her own.

She swallowed hard, forcing back the icy panic before it could take hold. She'd be fine. She would. She didn't need anybody. She couldn't remember the last time her father had done something even remotely maternal. She'd last seen him passed out in front of the kitchen sink, still clasping an empty bottle. Her boot had found his ribs as she stepped over him to get to the fridge. He had grunted and called her a selfish brat. She'd laughed at him. She'd called him a loser.

A burst of icy air hit, and she tried to burrow deeper into her sweater. She'd thought there would be time, time to fix it all. He would get sober and explain what it was she'd done to make him hate her so much. Then they'd get past it; they'd move on and finally be a family.

Instead, he went and died on her without a will or a cent to his name, leaving her at the mercy of the state, at the whole world really. Father of the year.

She noticed the quiet first. When she looked up, she wasn't at the bus station but back at the cemetery, standing before the closed iron gates. She looked around, disoriented. She glanced over her shoulder, eyes scanning the suddenly quiet streets for any sign of movement.

There was nothing but the sound of dead leaves, rattling on the trees and scurrying across the sidewalk. Even this far from town, there should be people, partygoers just starting their nights or the early birds looking to get home before the party really picked up.

She shivered, unable to shake the feeling she was being watched. She pushed her duffle bag between the bars and scaled the fence, suddenly needing to put as much distance as possible between her and her phantom observer. Once over, she slung the heavy bag across her shoulder and trekked her way past two-hundred-year-old mausoleums.

The wind howled like a wounded animal. The sky transitioning from fire to indigo to inky black, the moon rising in the sky behind shreds of silver clouds. She used the pale sliver of light cutting across the ground to navigate her way, but she didn't need it. This was her playground. She spent more time here than her own home.

She easily found the gaudy mausoleum housing her father. Somebody kept the place in pristine condition, but the name of the crypt's benefactor was a mystery she'd never solved. Her father couldn't afford to pay for the upkeep, and to her knowledge, her only other family lay behind the walls.

She set her bag on the ground and laid herself along the bench, arms behind her head, watching the clouds play hide and seek with the moon.

The cold marble leached through her sweater but she didn't care. It felt good. She tipped her face upwards, towards its light, letting the moon's rays fall upon her face. Was moon bathing a thing? If not, it should be. It made her feel charged up, like it gave her superpowers.

Most people found it spooky out here, surrounded by the dead; she found it peaceful. There were many graveyards in New Orleans, most brimming with tourists hoping to catch a funeral or perhaps a voodoo ritual. She liked this one because it was off most tourists' radar, too far to walk from most hotels and not famous enough to make the added effort.

She lay there for what seemed like an eternity, breathing in and out. She had to go soon. She should say her goodbyes. That's obviously why her Jiminy Cricket conscience pulled her there, to try to say something nice to her father.

She swung herself into a sitting position, frowning at the doors of his mausoleum until she was cross-eyed. She opened her mouth to talk at least a dozen times, but the words wouldn't come. She swallowed the lump in her throat.

 25

This shouldn't be so hard. It wasn't as if he could talk back. She could finally tell him how much she hated the way he treated her. How she hated the lies, the half-truths, the general lack of interest in her existence. How it seemed he was constantly punishing her for something. It's not like he could yell at her anymore. He couldn't call her names. He couldn't tell her how much he wished she'd never been born. He couldn't walk away this time.

She blinked the wetness from her eyes, swatting at her cheeks. He didn't deserve her tears or her attention. She stood, reaching for her bag.

"A bit late for a girl your age to be traipsing around the cemetery."

She gasped, spinning to locate the disembodied voice echoing off the stones. There was movement to her left as a shadow broke from the rest and moved into view, head down and hands in his pockets. He wore the same black hooded sweatshirt, still pulled low, hiding his face from her.

It was the boy she'd seen earlier. It had to be. She doubted there were two people wandering around the cemetery in mysterious black hoodies.

"You," she said.

"Aye, me." That voice. She wanted to curl up in it and take a nap.

"You scared the crap out of me," she said, hand fluttering over her pounding heart. He was still scaring her if she was being honest. She squinted, trying to make out his face inside the shadows of the hood. He made no move to reveal himself, but she could feel him watching her all the same.

As seconds ticked by, her imagination went wild, picturing everything from a horrible deformity to a monster with no face at all. She shook her head. The holiday was getting the best of her.

She shifted her weight. "Are you going to just stand there in your creepy hood and stare at me?"

There was only a slight hesitation before he slowly pushed back the fabric of the sweatshirt. Her eyes went wide. No matter how slow his reveal, it wasn't enough time to prepare her for what she saw.

He was stunning, all high cheekbones and perfect lips. His brows were just this side of too thick, the same color as the stubble on his perfectly chiseled jaw. It wasn't like she hadn't seen hot guys before. New Orleans was full of them. Some even shared his chiseled-out-of-marble features…but his eyes…they were like nothing she'd ever seen.

They glowed. There was no other way to say it. Perhaps it was a trick of the … the light—or maybe she was going crazy—but his eyes…his eyes were a swirl of liquid mercury framed by long dark lashes. She supposed they could be contacts; it was the day of the dead. Either way, she couldn't stop staring. When his hood dropped, she realized his hair was silver as well, long on top and messy, shot through with strands of white. If she'd ever thought to draw the moon in human form, she imagined she'd have drawn him.

She almost stepped closer. His grin pulled her out of her trance. He was obviously used to this reaction. "Better?" His voice was a low murmur in the quiet, and his faint accent—English, maybe Irish—made her stomach swoop in a funny way.

Her cheeks flushed. "Jury's still out."

He tilted his head, smirking like she amused him, but it didn't reach his eyes. "I'm sorry to hear that, luv, I was hoping we could be friends."

She took a step back, wiping sweaty palms on her jeans. Her heartbeat sounded loud in her ears. Concrete surrounded her on all sides. If he wanted to hurt her, she'd made it easy for him. He took a step forward, but she stood her ground. There was really nowhere to go.

His eyes raked over her but not in a sexual way. It was methodical, unemotional, like a scientist reviewing a specimen. Her mouth went dry at the thought. She was the specimen. He arched a brow, his voice conversational. "It's really not safe for someone so young to be out here all alone, far from anybody who could help you."

She couldn't help the look she gave him. "What are you, nineteen? Did they drop you off from the senior center?"

He huffed out an amused sound, his smirk bleeding into a predatory grin as he prowled closer. Goosebumps erupted along her skin. She didn't buy his amusement, but that look—the cold, calculating way he moved—that she believed.

"Oh, I'm older than I look, luv."

She believed that too. He looked like a teenager, but he carried himself with a confidence most boys her age didn't possess. She pushed her hair out of her face, mind racing. She felt restless, skin crawling in a way that was too much like what happened at the funeral for her peace of mind.

"What do you want from me?" she asked.

He stopped, tilting his head, eyes icy and so beautiful. "I told you, I want to be your friend."

That look did not scream friends. She took a moment to wallow. Seriously, what karma was she working off? Some girls get to be prom queen; she got orphaned and murdered before graduation. She snorted at the thought, unable to stop the giggle that escaped abruptly. She jammed her fist against her mouth to stop it, but it was too late.

The laughter bubbled out of her, as unstoppable as the tears streaming down her face. She was losing it, burning from the inside, angry and scared, fear jolting along her skin like electricity.

She wasn't an expert, but she was pretty sure this was what her therapist would call an inappropriate fear response. An image of her last therapist popped into her mind, the image so clear in that moment: Her stupid horn-rimmed glasses, her constant sour expression, that morally superior tone as she'd lectured Ember. "You don't take anything seriously, Ember." "Therapy only works if you work it, Ember."

You shouldn't laugh at your killer, Ember. Ever the disappointment, she was.

Mr. tall, light, and scary looked put out, as if her mental breakdown was inconveniencing him. She swiped at her cheeks, pulling herself together, sniffling loudly. "I'm sorry, but I don't think you understand the kind of shit day I've had." Though he had been there earlier. "Well, maybe you do, but I mean, you have to appreciate the irony. Ten minutes ago, I was leaving to start a brand new life, and now I'm going to be killed standing five feet away from the man who swore my smart mouth would get me killed someday."

She went lightheaded as the enormity of her words hit her. "Oh, God. This is like the part in the movie where you try to kill me, right?

You're going to try to kill me, and I feel too crappy to even try to run."

She was talking more to herself. She leaned back against the rusted mausoleum gates behind her, enjoying the cool metal against her skin. Her head was swimming, the stars above blurring in the sky. *No, not now.* Whatever had happened earlier was happening again. She could feel it rising up in her, that weird feeling like her insides were melting and liquefying while she could do nothing to stop it. Was it a panic attack? Could a panic attack cause what happened in the cemetery earlier? Maybe it was some kind of fight or flight adrenaline response.

She felt caged, trapped by her own body. It was all in her head. The ground wasn't vibrating at her feet. There was no way she was really burning up in forty-degree weather. Even in her haze she could see him watching her. Maybe if she just held still, he would be quick about it. Her head lulled on her shoulders. She was going to pass out. It would serve him right.

Then he was just there, in her space, fingers cupping her face. She moaned at the feel of his cold hands against her overheated flesh. "And if it is, luv? If this is the part where I try to kill you? What then? Are you going to pass out and take all the fun out of it? Or will you fight back?"

There was no mistaking the threat of his words, but he whispered them against her skin like a promise. She couldn't think straight. Her head filled with a sound like angry bees. She pitched forward, dropping her forehead to his shoulder, her eyes drifting closed.

He was so cold; even through the layers of his clothes; his body seemed to emit a pleasant icy radiance that soothed her feverish skin. She wrapped herself around him, locking her arms. She buried her face against his throat, her nose rubbing against his skin.

His body went rigid in her arms. She didn't blame him; sane girls didn't try to cuddle their killers. But nobody ever accused her of being sane. She was a girl who played in cemeteries and talked to the dead. She was a girl with three therapists before she was twelve. She was a girl in flames, and he was ice water. If she were going to die, she was going to have this first.

They stood there, bound together by her forced embrace, those strange vibrations increasing, growing inside her like a living thing.

His panting breath was ragged against her ear, he writhed within her grasp, but she refused to let go, she couldn't let go. Could he feel it too?

If she let go, this peculiar energy would overwhelm her. So she stood there, breathing him in, letting him anchor her, trying to guard herself as that feeling inside her grew, stretching and building until she was certain her skin might split trying to contain it. She gasped as that power left her like a sledgehammer to her diaphragm. The boy grunted like he'd received a physical blow, sagging against her heavily.

Almost instantly, the world seemed to right itself. Her blood ceased to boil, the vibrations stopped. It was only then that she became aware of what she was doing. She let go, shoving him back. Despite his size, he stumbled, blinking hard. They stared at each other, his confusion mirroring her own.

"What are you?" she whispered. "What are you doing to me?"

He rushed her, shoving her against the concrete hard enough to knock her teeth together. "What did I do to you? What game are you playing? What are you? What was that? What did you do?"

She whimpered, heart thundered in her chest, feet scrambling for purchase as she realized he'd lifted her from the ground. He was fit but not nearly big enough to haul her off her feet with just one hand. She shoved at him uselessly. "Put me down."

He didn't so much put her down as simply let go; her abrupt descent left her heart lodged in her throat and her legs fighting to keep her on her feet. His eyes narrowed, hands tangling in her messy hair, tilting her head to the side. "Come on, luv, you can tell me. I'm sure it's eating at you, keeping this secret."

He was insane. She opened her mouth to say so, but her brain short-circuited as his nose traced along the column of her throat. "I promise, this will be so much easier if you just tell me," he purred, lips pressing the words into her skin. She moved closer to him. In her defense, she'd never been this close to a boy before; especially not one who looked like he did.

He inhaled deeply. "We can do this one of two ways." He pressed his mouth to the shell of her ear. "I promise one is infinitely more pleasurable than the other."

Ew. Oh, God. What was she doing? What was *he* doing? Seducing her for information? Threatening her? It really bothered her that she didn't know the difference.

She needed to get it together. This was not how she was supposed to die. She'd had a plan. She'd written it down obituary style for a morbid ninth grade English assignment. She would die of obscenely old age in her enormous—but tastefully decorated—plantation home surrounded by her beautiful and ungrateful grandchildren.

He huffed out a laugh. Had she said all that aloud? She was too scared to be embarrassed. Instead, she slapped at his hand.

He stepped away swiftly, and then he was pacing before her. "You're really not going to tell me? You're only hurting yourself on this one."

"I don't know what you're talking about," she said. "You're crazy."

He sighed heavily, his tone shifting from annoyed to chiding, as if speaking to a rather stupid child. "I'll figure it out eventually," he said, pointing at her. "You don't smell like a witch. You certainly aren't a shifter." Then he was back before her, gripping her chin, turning her head side to side, like he was examining livestock. "But you most definitely aren't human." Tiny hairs rose along her skin at his touch, a shiver slipping along her spine. "You're trying my patience. What the hell are you?"

She pushed away from him, head throbbing with his words. "Stop with the grabby hands."

She needed to think. He was clearly unhinged. She had few options. She could run, but could she outrun him? Her gaze raked across broad shoulders and a flat stomach. He looked like he did a lot of cardio. She could scream, but who would hear her? Instead, she did what she always did when she was nervous—she babbled.

She'd watched a million documentaries on serial killers and the mentally ill. Netflix was her friend. She could totally figure this out. If he was a killer, she had to make him see her as a person, tell him about her life, say her name a lot, make him believe people would care if she died. *Even if that was a lie.*

But what if he was schizophrenic? He thought she wasn't human. What was she supposed to do then? Orient him to reality? Play along with his fantasy? Why hadn't she paid closer attention?

 31

"What's your name?" she heard herself say, voice breathless.

He arched his brow, tsking softly, his expression bored. "I'm asking the questions here, luv."

"Just tell me your name," she demanded, panic creeping back in.

"Mace." The answer tumbled from his lips unbidden. He looked mystified, like his own mouth had betrayed him. He absently rubbed a spot on his chest.

"Mace," she repeated, with a nod. Okay, it was a start. "So um, here's the thing, Mace, I'm only seventeen and I don't want to die."

He gave her a look and a fair-enough shrug and gestured for her to continue, clearly amused by this turn of events.

She frowned, but soldiered on. "You can't be much older than me so…let's just think about this for a minute, okay?" She raked a hand through her damp hair. "I'm not really sure why you want to kill me, but my life has pretty much sucked up until now. Like so much suckage. I can't even explain the level of suck." She risked a glance in his direction. "But I feel like, statistically speaking, that's gotta change, right? I'm not trying to sound like a motivational poster, but it's supposed to get better. I'd very much like to have a pulse when it does."

He narrowed his eyes at her, brow furrowed as he took a step towards her.

She held up her hand, palm out. "Stop. Just listen."

He stopped, looking at his feet and then at her again.

"I'm a nice girl." She promised, before frowning. "But maybe you don't care about that. I mean, if you're, like, a murderous psychopath, you probably aren't super interested in my feelings, but what about yourself?" She reasoned, gesturing spastically to all of his… self. "You seem like the kind of guy who thinks a lot of himself."

He cocked an eyebrow but said nothing. She was in turbo babble mode and couldn't stop. "If you kill me, your life is over. You will definitely go to jail. I mean, look at me." She gestured to her face. "I look like an ad for facial cleanser and girls who eat yogurt. Juries eat that stuff up. You'd probably get the chair."

He looked a little dazed. "You make a passionate yet confusing plea, luv."

Her heart sank as he took a tentative step towards her, then another, grinning as he advanced.

"Come *on*. I'm sure you don't want to go to prison," she whined. "You are way too pretty for prison. You'd make a lot of the wrong kind of friends in prison." *Stop saying prison, Ember.* "Do you want those kinds of friends? Of course you don't. We could be friends?" she finished lamely, face flushing with shame. Maybe he should just kill her. It would be less embarrassing.

He blinked at her, cheek twitching. "Aw, are you asking me to be your friend now? One might question your judgment."

Her hands fell to her hips, swaying on her feet. "Wow, not to put too fine a point on it, but I've only seen you twice and both times you were here." She gestured to their surroundings. "You hang out in cemeteries because you have so many friends? Is this where your book club meets?"

"I can see why you have no friends," he said drolly.

She squinted as something glinted in the air above his head.

"I—" was all he managed before the object made contact with his head, sounding like a hammer hitting an overripe melon. He hit his knees with a groan, whatever he was going to say dying on his lips.

She looked at his crumpled form, unreasonably disappointed.

She'd really wanted to know what he was going to say.

 33

Chapter 6

EMBER

She stared, not even surprised anymore. Behind Mace's prone body stood a boy and girl about her age. The girl still held the shovel, holding it like a ballplayer choking up on a bat. The two were eerily similar in looks; tall, tan, dark hair, almond-shaped eyes, and long, lean muscle. They had to share DNA.

The boy hugged himself, bouncing on his heels, staring at his companion in exasperation. He had to be freezing with just his jeans and thin long-sleeved shirt. Truthfully, she didn't know how they weren't both freezing. The girl wore denim shorts, a striped crop-top, and a long-sleeved flannel shirt with combat boots. Ember supposed the flannel and the beanie cap slouched on her head might provide a modicum of warmth, but not much.

"*That* was your plan?" the boy asked.

The girl heaved a sigh, pulling a small packet from her back pocket. "No, that was just step one." She poured a smoky-colored powder into her hand and knelt next to Mace. She slapped his face and he groaned, trying to get to his feet. "Ah, ah," she chided, kicking his legs out from under him. "None of that. Don't want you standing, just breathing."

She blew the powder into his face, smiling in satisfaction as he coughed once and passed out. "And that was step two."

The boy fixed the girl with a withering look. Ember flinched; his bitch face was strong.

"What?" the girl snapped. "We don't have all night? I couldn't watch anymore of…whatever that was." She tapped her wrist. "We gotta go."

He turned his attention to Ember then, wincing as if he was used to having to apologize for his companion. He took a deep breath, steeling himself. "Listen, this is going to sound crazy, but you have to come with us if you want to live."

Ember blinked at him stupidly. She had no idea what to do with that.

The girl dropped her face into her hands. "*That* was *your* plan? Come with us if you want to live? We drove four hours so you could hit her with a line from *Terminator*?" She looked pained as she whispered, "This is why nobody takes us seriously."

Ember shook her head. They looked so normal. Well, they looked like hipsters but certainly not your run-of-the-mill straitjacket-needing crazies. Her stomach felt slippery. Maybe this really was all some sort of fever dream. Maybe she'd passed out at the funeral and slipped into a coma. Maybe she was dead and this was hell.

The guy rubbed his hand across the back of his neck, gesturing with his head to Mace. "I'm ever so sorry if I offended your delicate sensibilities; next time I'll just hit her over the head with a shovel."

They ignored Ember's indignant, "Hey."

"Honestly, I would have respected you more," the girl said.

"Can we get on with this, or do you wanna lecture me some more?"

Yep, they were crazy. She looked around, searching for anything that would make sense of any of this. This *was* New Orleans. Maybe she'd stumbled into an elaborate dinner theatre production. Maybe she was on candid camera. Maybe this was some sort of weird live role-playing game. That was a thing. She'd seen it on the internet.

She glanced at the boy on the ground with renewed interest. It *would* explain his bizarre look. Was this all part of the game? Was he faking being unconscious? Was there another girl out there waiting

35

to be *fake* attacked? Mistaken identity made a lot more sense than her being a supernatural creature, and it came with the added bonus of making her crush a bit less pathetic.

She used the toe of her shoe to gently shove at the boy's— Mace's—shoulder, content to ignore the two squabbling before her. He really was pretty. His eyelashes fanned shadows over his cheeks. His face was peaceful as if sleeping. She sighed. She finally met a boy willing to have a conversation with her—albeit a strange one—and two crazies ambushed them. She'd been making progress with him.

The two continued their argument, oblivious to her. "I wouldn't need to lecture you if you would stop lacing *every single* conversation with stupid pop culture references that nobody gets but nerdy comic-con dweebs like you."

Cute-movie-guy's jaw dropped. "How dare you. *Terminator* is a classic. James Cameron is a—"

The girl threw up her hand. "One word, bro, *Titanic*—"

She could try to just slip away…but they were blocking her exit. "Um, guys—"

"*Titanic?*" the guy interrupted. "That movie was epic. Let's talk about how the last movie you liked featured vampires who sparkled like bloodsucking pixie strippers. Sparkly vampires? When was the last time you saw a vampire glittering like a disco ball? Hell, when was the last time you saw one who didn't explode in sunlight?"

Ember sighed, staring at Mace forlornly. It was a testament to how screwed up her life was that she just wanted him to wake up and sniff her threateningly. He still wasn't moving. She glanced surreptitiously at the two before, again, toeing at him. This time nudging his chin with her boot. She cringed as his head flopped like a ragdoll.

Her stomach lurched. Was he dead? Ember's mind raced. What if he had just been some actor? But what if he really was a serial killer? She glanced at the two, chewing on her lip. What if *they* were serial killers? Did mass murderers hang out bantering after they killed people in anything other than Quentin Tarantino films?

"Hey!" she shouted, startling herself as her voice echoed in the silence.

They both turned to her at exactly the same time, fixing her with identical expressions.

Creepy.

"Uh, not that I'm not grateful for the…rescue, I guess, but"— she pointed at Mace—"is he dead? And, if so, does that make me an accessory to murder?"

Movie guy sighed, raking his hands through his hair. "Despite my sister's best efforts, he'll live. It's apparently not his time to go…but it was almost yours."

Ember's eyes went wide, and the girl whacked him on the arm. "You should really look up the word tact, bro." She stepped forward then, smiling like it physically hurt her. "My name is Tristin, and this is my brother, Kai. Do you remember us?"

She didn't. "Um…"

"We're your cousins," the girl—Tristin—said.

Ember frowned at them. The three of them couldn't have looked more different. Where she was pale, they were dark, her orange hair wild and crazy next to their gorgeous board-straight dark locks. Her wide eyes looked nothing like the tip-tilt eyes of the two before her. There had to be some mistake. "I don't have any cousins."

The two exchanged looks, before Kai said, "Listen, I know this sounds crazy, but I swear we're telling the truth. It's been a long time. Maybe you've just forgotten about us. It's been twelve years."

Even if what they were saying were true, she wouldn't remember them. She'd spent years in a therapist's office trying to remember her past, but she didn't think there was a way to explain dissociative amnesia in a sound bite. "I don't—"

Tristin cut her off. "Our last name is Lonergan, like yours."

Her heart sank. It really was a case of mistaken identity. "My last name is Denning. My name is Ember Denning."

The two exchanged a look for a full minute, and Ember had the uneasy feeling they were having a conversation she couldn't hear. Kai gestured emphatically at Tristin in a sort of go-ahead motion, and the girl pulled out her cell phone. With the push of a button, her flashlight blazed, blinding them all. When her vision cleared, Tristin held her cell phone to her face and waved Ember forward. "Come here, look." The girl's pupils contracted in the light, revealing the same brilliant violet eyes that Ember looked at in the mirror every day.

 37

"But my name is Ember Denning," she repeated.

"No." Kai smiled at her like she was a simpleton—the second time she'd gotten that look in one day. "Your name is November Lonergan. We're your cousins. That thing was going to kill you, and you need to come with us."

She was getting a migraine. There was no way she was going anywhere with these people just because they shared the same eye color. This was completely nuts.

"You guys are all crazy."

From his spot on the ground, Mace's hand flinched spastically, and he groaned.

"What did you hit him with?" Kai asked his sister.

She shrugged. "Hellebore. Quinn gave me some stuff just in case we ran into any baddies that were immune to everyday violence."

Mace was making another valiant effort to rise from the ground. She was secretly rooting for him.

Kai leaned into his sister, his whisper carrying. "It's getting late. Isa is going to kill us." He gestured towards Ember. "We can't leave her here."

Tristin eyed her up and down. "Can't we?" she asked. "Right now we can still walk, Kai. It's her choice."

Kai tugged his sister aside, but she could still make out their conversation. "Seriously? We already talked about this. She's family, Trist."

Tristin's gaze fell to the ground before she said, "Once we do this, we can't go back. Everything changes. This is a really bad idea, you get that, right?"

Ember wanted to believe they were just two lunatics, but something about them nagged at her like a hazy picture she just couldn't get into focus.

Kai shoved his sleeve up. "I don't think we have a choice. Look."

Tristin looked at his wrist, eyes widening. She paled beneath her tan skin. She eyed Mace. "Screw it." She held out her hand, resigned. "Come with us if you want to live."

Kai sighed, clearly relieved. "Yeah, what she said."

 38

She could run. She could go back to the funeral home. Then what? A year in foster care? She just wanted to go home. Except she didn't have a home anymore. All she had was a skull-splitting head-ache, a fever, and absolutely nowhere else to go.

"No—"she started.

Tristin clenched her teeth. "Get in the car, or I swear to whatever deity you believe in, I will knock you out and drag you there."

Kai's brows shot up. "Wow. What was it you were saying about tact, Trist?"

"I'm done being nice," Tristin vowed. "This is the stupidest thing we've ever done; forgive me if I'm not in the mood to humor anybody."

"When were you being nice?" Kai asked.

Tristin ignored her brother, looking at Ember. "Well, what's it gonna be?"

Ember rolled her eyes. "Well, when you put it that way...why not?"

Chapter 7

KAI

The walk back to the car felt like a death march. He should feel pretty good about himself. After all, he'd saved a life. He'd saved a family member. Saving people was much better than watching them die and crossing them over. Whenever he risked a glance at Tristin, she glowered at him. She was mad. Isa would be furious at them, and for all her talk, his sister liked to follow orders. She was the good soldier.

They tried to keep a quick pace, but November—Ember, he corrected—kept craning her head behind her. He opened his mouth to reassure her she was safe. That grim would be down for a while. He didn't know what type of creature that was, but the hellebore seemed to be keeping it down, at least for now. But before he could reassure her, the corners of her mouth drooped downward when she saw nobody followed.

He sighed. He really hoped that guy was an incubus, or his cousin had even worse taste in men then he did. She tried to slow her walk, but he took her upper arm, dragging her along—gently, of course. A slow, painful death already awaited him at home; the only thing to make it worse would be accidentally damaging a human. She stiffened at his touch, trying to pull her arm away. He loosened his grip until they were barely touching but didn't dare let go entirely.

When they reached the Toyota, she just looked at him, sulking. He reached around her and opened the door, gesturing grandly for her to get in. She gave one more look towards the gate.

"Get the hell in the car," Tristin snapped.

Ember sighed, flopping into the backseat and crossing her arms like a preschooler on the verge of a major tantrum. It was strange to look at her. She looked like their mothers. The similarities were uncanny, really. She had the same ivory complexion and fiery orange curls, the same freckles. She even had the tiny space between her front teeth.

Kai and Tristin favored their father's Thai side. The only thing they'd inherited of their mother's was her reaper gene and her violet eyes; the same eyes as Ember. Even if he hadn't trusted Ember's name popping up on this arm, he would have trusted her eyes. How could he not save her?

They'd only driven a short distance when she said, "I'm pretty sure kidnapping is a felony offense."

Tristin took her eyes off the road long enough to fix him with a look that screamed *she's your problem*. Kai sighed. He would rather be doing literally anything but this, even dealing with Rhys. "Technically, you agreed to go."

She stabbed a finger in Tristin's direction. "Only because she threatened me. That's coercion."

What was she, an attorney? "I'm almost positive that is not what coercion means," Kai said, risking a glance at his sister. Tristin didn't even acknowledge her this time, focusing instead on the miles of pavement stretched before them.

Kai rapidly tapped out a text, letting Isa know they were on their way back, promising he would explain everything when they got there. His stomach swooped as he hit send. He was so screwed. While he considered saving his cousin a win, he had failed in every other conceivable way. He had failed to show up for his shift at the diner. He'd failed to tell his pack about Ember. He'd failed to inform his alpha of his epically stupid plan.

His phone vibrated, signaling a text. A single question mark popped onto his screen followed by ten exclamation points. It was the most hostile question mark he'd ever seen. Isa clearly wanted more information, but there was no way he could explain it all by text.

Besides, he preferred to delay the litany of abuse for as long as possible. She was going to kill him slowly and with pain. If she didn't kill him, Allister would, and then they'd both let the Grove have him. He didn't respond. Instead, he put it on silent and settled it screen down on his leg, determined to ignore all future messages.

Tristin took one look at his face and muttered, "We should've just left her to die."

Kai shuddered. "Tristin, that's a bad way to die."

"There's a good way to die?" Ember asked, voice dripping with sarcasm.

He looked at her over his shoulder. "Yes, in your big fancy home surrounded by your snotty grandchildren."

Ember narrowed her eyes. "You jerk. How long were you creeps there listening to us?"

"Long enough to know that you suck at flirting, but under different circumstances, you may have made an excellent motivational speaker?" he said.

"Different circumstances? As opposed to my circumstances now when I'm…what, exactly? Marked for death?" There was a slight edge of hysteria beginning to creep into her voice, and she looked even chalkier than before. He supposed it was only a matter of time. Nobody was so cool they didn't care they almost died.

She wiped the sleeve of her sweater across her brow. "Could you maybe turn up the AC?" she asked. "I wish you people would just tell me what's happening."

He did as she asked, pointing the jets at her. She shivered in response, perspiration running in rivulets down her temples. That wasn't good. Was she sick? Had that thing done something to her they hadn't seen?

"Listen, you said you don't remember us, but do you remember growing up in Florida? Do you remember our mom?"

The girl's face went pale…well, paler. "I don't remember anything before my father and I moved to New Orleans. My therapists say it has something to do with the trauma of my mother's death."

Tristin looked at him and mouthed, "Therapists. Plural?"

He gave her his angriest eyebrows. It was not the time. What happened twelve years ago had traumatized everybody.

Ember kept going, missing the exchange between them. "This makes no sense. I feel like I'm going crazy. That…guy, Mace, said I was something but not a witch and not a shifter. Was that for real?"

Kai sighed. "I don't want to overwhelm you, Ember."

"Oh, that ship has sailed. I'm whatever is worse than overwhelmed."

"Flabbergasted?" Tristin said dryly.

Ember wiped her hands down her face. "Come on, give me something. What's happening?"

"Maybe give her the Cliff's Notes version so she stops whining?"

Ember glared at the back of Tristin's skull. "You're kind of a bitch."

"It's true," Tristin agreed mildly.

Ember's head thumped lightly against the glass, her lashes fluttering against her cheeks in the dim light.

"Are you okay?" he asked, reaching into the center console. "Water?"

She eyed it suspiciously but drank it down anyway. "Thanks. I don't know what's wrong with me. I feel so…weird."

Glancing at Ember and then him, Tristin telegraphed annoyance with just her eyebrows. She cut her eyes at their cousin again and then the roadside. He gave a subtle headshake. They were not ditching her on the side of the road. How had it escaped his attention his sister was a soulless monster?

A light illuminated the interior, and Ember's eyes cut to his as her fingers flew over the screen of her cell phone. *Smart girl*, he thought. "Shit, Ember, wait—"

Tristin glanced sharply in the rearview mirror. "Seriously?" she questioned, reaching back with one hand to pluck the cell phone from Ember. You've had this the whole time?" Tristin glared at him. "Why didn't you check her?"

Tristin powered down the window and flung the phone into the night.

Kai made a face at his sister. "Was that necessary?"

"You want people tracking her back home?"

For a moment, everything went silent, Ember gaping at Tristin. Kai tensed, feeling the power shift in the air just before Ember screeched in fury and launched herself at Tristin.

The car swerved across the line as Ember attempted to use Tristin's hair to yank her into the backseat. Kai scrambled, trying to untangle himself from his seatbelt to pry Ember's hands free of his sister. Ember wouldn't let go. She was strong and—Ew!—so sweaty.

"Ember, calm down. Jeez, it's just a phone. We'll get you another one." Her gaze shot to him and he jerked back, releasing her. Her eyes were wild, all pupil and black veins. "Holy Exorcist, Batman."

Her grip on Tristin tightened over the squealing of the tires. Tristin fought to keep them on the road as cars swerved out of their way and horns blared. "Oh my God, get her off me and shut this down before she kills us all."

"I'm trying," he shouted, fishing his fingers into his back pocket and snagging a little packet of powder. He tried to shield it as he dumped the powder into his hand. If he tried to blow it in her face, it would go out the window or worse. He groaned as he realized what he had to do.

He shoved his hand over her nose and mouth, praying she didn't chew his fingers off. She gasped as the powder hit her lungs, letting go of Tristin. Ember clawed at her chest like the powder was searing her from within. She looked slightly betrayed but also grateful.

"I'm sorry," he said, wincing as her eyes rolled back, her head thudding against the door.

Tristin waited a good mile before she rolled up the window, breathing hard, her hands shaky on the wheel. "What the hell was that?"

Kai waited for the adrenaline rushing through him to calm down. "I have no idea, but I'm going to guess she's not a human."

"No shit, Sherlock. I see you've been shopping in Quinn's stash too."

"I've been keeping it just in case," he said smugly.

"Just in case we were attacked going seventy miles an hour on the freeway?"

He grinned. "Exactly."

"So now what do we do with her?"

"Excellent question," he said. "And I have no idea."

"Here's a better question. How are we going to explain why she's not enjoying the great hereafter? How about what are we going to tell Allister? Or the Grove? Oh and what are you going to tell Isa?"

"Yeah, about Isa…" He turned to his sister then, smiling with too many teeth. "I need a favor."

Chapter 8

TRISTIN

Tristin stood outside the restaurant for way too long. It wasn't like the wolves didn't know she was out there. If anything, she looked guiltier by lingering beneath the neon lights of the restaurant's sign, instead of just stepping inside as she usually would. It was useless to just sit out there. They'd heard her the moment Kai dropped her off. They'd probably even smelled the unconscious girl in the backseat. Keeping secrets from werewolves was almost impossible.

Isa wouldn't hurt Tristin, not really, but she still felt like she was going to puke. But she couldn't stay out there all night; they'd come looking eventually. It always went easier if you surrendered instead of being captured. She took one last deep shuttering breath and went inside.

They'd closed the diner two hours ago, so she went in through the employee entrance. The wolves stood in the back in the midst of closing down the kitchen. Donovan smiled at her as he sprayed across the floor with a garden hose. Isa, who was sitting in her office, glanced up at Tristin's appearance.

The alpha smiled, eyes predatory, at the sight of her. She clicked out of whatever she was doing on the computer and rose. Despite being just twenty-eight years old, Isa moved like somebody much older. She was dressed casually in jeans and a tank top, her tawny hair unbound.

"Tristin," she hummed, "I cannot wait to hear why you missed your shift and took an impromptu trip to, where was it again, oh, that's right, New Orleans?"

Tristin wasn't afraid of much. She'd worked hard to make herself strong. She was well versed in Krav Maga and mixed martial arts. Wren had taught her advanced weapons training. Yet, standing before her angry five foot two alpha made her stomach feel squishy. "There was a, um, situation."

"Oh, I see. Let's sit down and talk about it," Isa said with a smile that Tristin knew was just luring her into a false sense of security. Isa wrapped her hand around Tristin's upper arm. Tristin winced as sharp claws pierced her skin just enough to let her know her statement wasn't a request.

Isa pulled Tristin into the front, the door separating the kitchen from the dining area swinging wildly in their wake. Isa shoved Tristin towards the large booth in the back corner. Tristin slid onto the red vinyl seat, looking around.

Neoma stood at the counter, refilling ketchup bottles. The little blonde looked up, smiling at Tristin and giving a slight wave before ducking her head back down to the task.

Just as she was about to speak again, Wren slid into the booth next to Isa, sliding his arm across her shoulders. Tristin stared at the alpha's mate awkwardly.

"What?" he asked. "Did you think I was going to miss this? I don't know what you did, but your brother is clearly wetting his pants in fear, so it must be pretty good."

She gave him a baleful look and began to speak but was interrupted again when the kitchen door swung open and Donovan sauntered out. He'd removed his chef's coat, revealing his bare torso and a wide expanse of muscled copper-colored skin. He wore only his checkered chef pants. Donovan was always half naked. He had no shame. Quinn tumbled out behind Donovan. Tristin sighed. What was Quinn even doing there? It was his day off. She couldn't get away

 47

from him for even one day? He pushed his glasses up the bridge of his nose, giving her a grin.

"Did we miss anything?" Donovan asked.

She glared at the two of them.

"Sorry, Dagger," Quinn said. "We aren't missing this. If Isa is going to kill you two, we want to watch."

She bristled at the nickname, smiling tightly at her brother's best friend. "Then make sure you stick close so I can take you down with me."

He winked. "Aww, I knew you couldn't stand to be without me."

"Enough," Isa said. "What happened?"

"Well…" Tristin stumbled, searching for where to start. "It's not that I don't want to tell you, I just feel like Kai should be the one to tell you."

Wren looked at her, confused. "Then why isn't Kai here to do that?"

"Because he is a dirty coward," Quinn laughed. "He totally sent her to plead his case."

"Is that what this is?" Isa asked, gaze piercing through Tristin's soul. "Are you here to beg for your brother's life?"

Tristin shrugged, looking anywhere but at the alpha. "Sort of."

"Fear not," she told Tristin. "Like any good parent, I'm not going to kill him. I am, however, going to put the fear of God in him." Isa exploded across the table then, less than an inch from Tristin's face, causing her to reel back. "What were you two thinking? Running around? Leaving the state without telling us? You went into territories belonging to other wolves. You could've started a war. You could've been killed." Her breath hitched, voice wavering. "We wouldn't have even known where to start looking for your rotting corpses."

Wren tugged her back, rubbing her arm as her eyes flashed gold. Donovan and Quinn snickered until Isa cut her eyes at them, growling low in her chest. They looked away, Donovan whining.

"I'm sorry," Tristin said, meaning it. "We just didn't know what else to do. A name appeared on Kai's arm, and then it all just…got away from us."

Isa's face pinched in confusion. "So, Kai had a collection?"

She could only nod.

"Was it a child?" Isa asked. "Those are the hardest on him."

"No, not exactly." She was stalling, but what came next was going to set the wolf off…again.

Isa's mouth tightened, and Tristin could feel the woman's eyes boring into her.

She took a deep breath to calmly tell her exactly what happened but couldn't stop the words falling from her lips. "Kai was supposed to collect somebody, but the name was the name of somebody that he knew, and that couldn't be right because…well, just because… there was no way, but he had to go because you can't refuse a collection but…he couldn't do it."

"Couldn't do it?" Isa repeated quietly.

Tristin swallowed hard. "He couldn't collect her."

"Are you telling me that there's some girl lying dead on a slab who is still in possession of her soul? Trapped inside her body?" Isa sounded horrified.

Tristin forced her mouth to move, her words barely a whisper. "She didn't die."

They all exchanged confused glances, Wren finally saying, "What do you mean?"

Her mouth was desert dry, her tongue sticking to the roof of her mouth. She hated her brother for this. "She was family, Isa. It didn't even seem possible. Like so impossible. But, Isa, the name was November Lonergan. What could we do?"

Silence stretched as they waited for her to continue. She didn't know what to say. Quinn finally broke the standoff, asking, "What *did* you do?"

Tristin looked at her alpha with dread. "We saved her."

The entire group looked poleaxed. Isa's golden eyes bled red, and the noise that escaped the alpha was inhuman.

"You what?" Wren shouted, slamming his fist down on the table so hard the Formica cracked and a salt shaker fell over, rolling to the floor with a crash. To his credit, Quinn stepped closer, placing a hand on Tristin's shoulder. She cowered against him, heart jackhammering in her chest. Quinn retrieved the fallen salt shaker, throwing a pinch of salt over his left shoulder before returning it to its place on the table.

"Let's hear her out," Quinn suggested. Isa turned her furious eyes on him, and he quickly abandoned her plight. "Or, I'll just shut up and not speak. That works too."

"That'd be a first." Neoma laughed where she now spun on her stool at the counter.

Isa continued to stare Tristin down as she lifted her phone and called the only person besides her brother who wasn't there—Rhys. She spoke in clipped tones, explaining the situation to the other wolf as succinctly as possible.

"I'm going to call Allister. No. We have to tell him. We have to try to get ahead of this." She listened intently before saying, "Rhys. Calm down. We will handle this. No, I will handle this, and you will calm down. Everything will be fine." Again, she listened, nodding as if he could see her. "We'll be there as soon as we can," she said, clicking the button on her cell. "I'm going home. You guys finish up here and meet us back at the house."

"Impromptu pack meeting?" Donovan joked.

"More like crime scene cleanup," Wren ground out. "I'll be right behind you." Donovan hit Quinn in the face with a spitball, and Wren closed his eyes as if searching for inner peace. "And I'll bring the children with me."

"You," Isa said, jabbing a finger in Tristin's direction. "You are not in the clear, so don't get too comfy. I see a lot of cleaning grease traps in your future."

Tristin grimaced. She wasn't sure who she felt sorrier for, Kai or their cousin. Either way, she was pretty sure this was going to end badly.

Chapter 9

EMBER

When Ember came to, the world was a blurry swirl of color, her world out of focus like she was viewing it through a dirty window. Her head throbbed, and her tongue felt like she'd dragged it across a dirty carpet.

Despite her aching head, she noted the rather comfortable couch beneath her and the sound of agitated voices carrying from the other room.

"So you thought you'd just disregard *everything* we've ever been taught and bring her here without consulting any of us, without consulting our alpha?" asked a male voice she didn't recognize.

"What should we have done? Left her to die?" That voice was clearly Kai.

"Yes!" the other male shouted. "You are a reaper. That is your sole purpose for existing, remember? That is the textbook definition of what you were supposed to do, dumbass. You help people who are going to die to…die." Ember winced at the lame ending to what had started out as a scathing comeback.

"You don't get it, Rhys. Tristin screamed. She screamed for her. That means something." Kai sounded almost frantic as he pleaded. "It has to mean something. Besides, she's family, man."

There was a snort of disgust. "We have no idea what your sister's screams mean. We don't know anything at all about banshees. How could you be this stupid? You brought her here, and you don't even know who she is. You don't know what she is. Do you ever think before you act?" There was a sigh of exasperation. "It's not always about you. You don't get to just make your own decisions and let the rest of us clean up after you."

"Oh, screw you," Kai snarled. "I'm sorry I care about people. I'm sorry I wasn't able to stand by and watch my family member get slaughtered. I'm sure you would have just grabbed some popcorn and enjoyed the show, but we can't all be heartless robots. I'd say it must be a wolf thing, but since the rest of the pack have feelings, I'm guessing it's just a *you* thing. You're such a dick."

"And you're too reckless. Where is this girl going to stay? Here? We aren't an orphanage for homeless paranormal teens. There's not a lot of room here at the inn as of late. You're lucky the pack lets you two stay here. Isa is going to kill you when she finds out."

"We have six bedrooms, and your sister will understand," Kai said. "Ember's my family. You don't abandon your family. Even someone like you should be able to get that. There aren't many of us left."

Having heard enough, Ember risked sitting up, unable to stifle the groan that slipped from her lips as the world tilted on its axis. They both glanced at her sharply. Kai grimaced and looked at her with apprehension.

The other boy glowered at her, a sneer pulling sharply at one overly pouty lip. He was one of the largest guys she'd ever seen. His eyes were bright green and shone like they were lit from within. He was all heavy brows and squared jaw. She supposed he was good looking if you liked that Spartan warrior look. Despite the fact that he was currently looking at her like he had homicide on his mind— which was apparently her new type—he wasn't really doing it for her. Maybe it was the skull-splitting headache pounding behind her temples. Maybe it was because he looked like he wanted to murder her newfound family member.

  52

Rhys cocked his head to the side, like a German Shepard, and smirked at Kai. "Hope you know what you're going to tell my sister. Because she just pulled up."

He pushed past her cousin, body checking him into the bannister as he passed. Kai stumbled but recovered, having braced for the impact. How often did the wolf shove him around? He glanced at her, smiling in a way that was probably meant to be reassuring but instead looked like terror. He walked out of her line of vision, likely in the direction of the door.

The door opened and closed in rapid succession, confirming her suspicions. "Hey, Isa—" Kai began. There was a muffled oomph, followed by a squeak, and then the blur of a body flying past the doorway, followed by another fast moving shadow.

A crash erupted along with the sound of splintering wood and shattering glass. She was on her feet before her brain even registered the decision, carrying her to the next room. The crash was the coffee table, currently crushed beneath her cousin.

On top of him was a woman. Well, she was definitely female, though the elongated teeth currently at his neck were undeniably not human.

She felt herself nodding to nobody in particular as she made peace with the realization that her cousins weren't crazy, the supernatural was real, and there was, given the conversation she'd overheard, a werewolf about to tear her cousin apart.

"Isa, I can explain," Kai panted, his hands held up in surrender, his throat bared in submission. She'd seen that on Animal Planet. "Please, please, please just let me explain."

Isa growled—she honest to goodness growled—low in her throat. "Oh, too late for that, buttercup, your sister already filled me in."

He looked dismayed at this new information. Isa didn't wait for further explanation; she slammed him once and then again against the wood remnants. He sucked in a pained breath. "Careful," he grunted. "I know you're mad, but I don't heal like a wolf; fragile human-like physique here."

Another snarl. "You're not a human," she hissed. "You're a reaper and an absolute idiot. Do you have any idea what you've done? Give

 53

me one reason why I shouldn't just tear you apart and feed you to the rest of the pack like reaper tar-tar?"

"I'm probably really gamey, like free range rabbit," he joked. The low rumble that emanated from the wolf made Ember's blood run cold. Kai whimpered.

Ember's heart rabbited against her ribs, an entire drum line pounding against her skull. If this wolf killed Kai, she was probably next. Perspiration trickled between her shoulder blades and beaded at her hairline. Why was it so hot in here? She pulled at her dampening sweater, desperate for any kind of relief.

Kai's hand was on his neck where a tiny bit of blood dotted his skin. "Come on, Isa. I know you're mad, but you're not going to kill me. If you want to kick my ass, just do it so we can move on."

The girl leaned back a little, still straddling his waist, arms folded across her chest. Kai sat up slightly, resting his weight on his forearms. "Aren't you even a little curious how she popped up on my list when she's supposedly been dead for twelve years?"

At that, the wolf turned to glance in Ember's direction.

Embers gasp was reflex. There was no other response when faced with glowing gold eyes, a slightly elongated nose, and a low drooping brow. She felt her mouth fall open. She prayed she didn't do something completely uncool like wet her pants. She fought to keep her hands to herself and not reach out to touch the creases that marred the girl's heavily furrowed brow. She was equal parts terrified and fascinated.

As she watched, the wolf tossed her head back, shaking her head like an ad for fancy conditioner. Her long hair flowed, slightly obscuring her face, but it didn't hide the way her features shifted, bones sliding under skin, righting themselves until her features looked entirely human.

"Awesome," Ember whispered, before she could stop herself.

She dropped heavily into the high backed chair behind her, gawking at Isa. She was stunning when she wasn't shifted and snarling with murderous rage. She wasn't tall like Rhys. She was tiny even, but Ember could see the resemblance. They were both gorgeous, with dark hair, impeccable bone structure, and insanely long lashes.

 54

They also shared the same startling green eyes. Ember's hands itched to sketch them.

Isa cocked her head in that same canine way Rhys had earlier, though she didn't appear to be listening for something; she seemed to be concentrating. Ember fought not to shrink under the wolf's weighted gaze. Dogs could sense fear, she reminded herself. She bit down on her lower lip. She didn't think they'd appreciate a dog joke.

"So," the older girl began. "You're claiming that *you* are November Lonergan."

Ember floundered, not sure how she should answer. She opted for the truth. "Um, I never claimed to be anybody." She shrugged apologetically at Kai, wondering absently where Tristin had ended up. Had Isa killed her? "I was minding my own business when I was assaulted in a cemetery."

Isa snapped her gaze to Kai, her look mutinous. Kai's eyes widened, and he shrank from the wolf.

"No, not him," Ember clarified quickly. "Kai didn't attack me... they didn't attack me. Some hot, sullen guy with major bedhead did." Her heart did a weird little flip-flop as she pictured Mace. If that was even his real name. She tried to explain. "Well, he was going to… attack me, that is. He, um, well, he talked about attacking me. Actually, first he just insulted me a lot…then he talked about killing me, but like in a weird flirty way." The she-wolf was looking progressively more confused. "I guess that's not really important. Kai and Tristin found me and saved me."

"She's definitely one of them," Rhys muttered as he appeared in the doorway. "She rambles as bad as he does."

She flipped up her middle finger in his direction, with a glare, hoping it wasn't the last thing she ever did. He snorted, rolling his eyes.

There was a clatter from the front room, and all eyes swung for the door. Ember was prepared for almost anything but what she saw.

  55

Chapter 10

MACE

Mace wasn't sure exactly how long he lay on the ground, clutching his throbbing head. He wasn't sure about much really. He didn't know how they'd found her, he didn't know where they'd taken her, and he didn't know which one had wielded the blow that felled him. He did know, however, that he'd happily beat them to death the next time he saw them. If he could just get off the ground. He stared at the stars overhead as they swam in and out of focus. It was his own fault for indulging his curiosity.

His phone rang in his pocket, which felt miles away from his hand for some reason. Whatever the girl had hit him with—hellebore, he suspected—was potent. Ember had been worth it though. She was something. He groaned, attempting to right himself before thinking better of it and lying back down.

If he didn't answer, there was an excellent chance they would send somebody else to follow the girl. Possibly somebody with even looser morals than himself. If such a person existed, he didn't want said person anywhere near his newest hobby.

He'd met plenty of fascinating girls over the years. He wouldn't be so trite as to say she was different. They had all been unique in some way. This girl, though, she was a bit of a mystery. He should've known better than to make assumptions, but he'd thought she would be meek and quiet. His intentions had been pure. He simply wanted a conversation, but when she'd asked if he'd planned to kill her, he just had to know how she'd respond.

She surprised him. He wouldn't let her surprise anybody else. She was his. He had to know more about her. His magic wanted hers, and it seemed the feeling was mutual. If he wanted to keep her, he didn't have much choice. With great effort, he pulled his phone from his pocket.

"Mace," he said.

"What did you do?" He held the phone away from his ear, wincing at the pain that shot through his skull at Echo's definitely-not-flirting tone.

"What?" he asked, feigning innocence.

"You had one job, Mace. Watch and report."

"I'm sorry. I realize I'm two hours late with my check-in, but I assure you there was nothing to report," he lied smoothly.

I just disobeyed a direct order, threatened a girl, got hit with some supernatural pepper spray, and was left for dead in a cemetery. Nope. Nothing at all to report.

"We happen to know otherwise."

"Do you?" he asked. "Fascinating. What is it you know?"

"Do you think this is a game?" she whispered.

"It's all a game." He grunted as he pushed himself into a sitting position, reclining against the stone building at his back.

"It isn't a game to some of us. I get that you get some sick thrill out of flirting with a lifetime of torment, but some of us would like to keep our skin on our bodies."

His eyelid twitched. "I'm not interested in any of us losing our skin, least of all myself. I just don't like secrets, and you and I both know there's no reason for him to have chosen me for this job unless he has something else in mind for this girl."

"So what?"

His eyebrow shot up. "So what? It doesn't bother you that he might want to kill an innocent human?"

Echo snorted. "Oh, please. Since when did you care if humans are innocent? You lived off those innocent humans for over a century. Are you suddenly developing a conscience?"

"I'm simply saying I don't understand why I'm being kept out of the loop. Shouldn't I have all the information if I'm going to keep tabs on this girl?"

"This isn't a loop. It's a ladder, and you're on the bottom rung, so just do what you're told before you get us dead, yeah?"

"Wow. Time has made you bitter, Echo."

"Listen to me, you go find that girl. You do exactly as you're told and not one thing more. Do I make myself clear?"

"Mm, no. I don't think so, m'dear," he said, happy that she couldn't see him grimacing. "New plan. Tell the man upstairs I want to speak to him directly."

She laughed, hard and loud. "That will never happen."

"Tell him I want to speak to him now, or I'll just rip the girl's throat out and be done with it. I am, after all, the only one who knows her whereabouts."

"Are you crazy?"

He felt a little bad. The poor dear sounded near panic-stricken.

"Do it, Echo. This conversation is starting to bore me, and we both know what happens when I get bored. I promise you, the girl didn't go far. Tick tock."

"Hold," she said, leaving him listening to surprisingly jaunty music. He always expected the bad guys to have darker taste in music, but he supposed that was stereotyping.

Time seemed to creep by as Mace listened to all the hits from the classics to today. He stared up at the stars, the shapes still bleeding in and out of focus, hoping that his supernatural hangover would soon dissipate. His eyelids were starting to droop when a voice came on the line.

"Mace," the other man said, voice hissing Mace's name like a snake. "I knew giving you this job was a mistake. I knew you were reckless, but I didn't think you were suicidal. You will not touch that girl unless I say. Is that understood?"

He rolled his eyes. "Yes. Yes. I'll be tortured, maimed, and you'll cut out my heart, rend the flesh from my bones. Blah. Blah. Blah.

Just tell me what she is, and I'll go back to being creepy lurking-in-the-shadows guy until you let me off my leash."

"Excuse me?"

"What is she? You must know. That's why you've been waiting for her powers to show, right? I've never seen anything like it."

There was a long pause. "So she did come into her power? I knew it," the other man muttered under his breath. "Were you planning on telling Echo this?"

"I wanted to tell you directly. I'm not really one for middle management. Too much room for error. I think if this arrangement is going to work, I should just speak directly to you."

"I'm not entirely sure where you got the idea that you were somehow the one making decisions around here, but I assure you that is not the case. I will just hire somebody else to watch the girl. Somebody who knows how to take orders."

"What do you think that somebody will do when they get a taste of her magic? I can tell you, whatever she is, she's powerful and a bit out of control. It seems like she might be quite a weapon with a little bit of training. Do you really trust anybody else with her? Besides, she and I really hit it off quite nicely." He thought back to their brief interaction. "I think she likes me."

"So you disobeyed a direct order and talked to the girl?"

He smiled at that. "Oh, come on. You know me. You had to know I would. You can't dangle a hunk of meat in front of a lion and not expect it to at least give it a sniff."

There was a snort from the other end of the line. "I can't figure out if you're a genius or one of the stupidest people I've ever met."

"It varies from day to day," he reasoned. "But I'm not wrong. We wouldn't want your fancy new toy falling in with a bad crowd, would we?"

There was a long pause on the other end of the line. "I want you to make friends with her. Get her to trust you. Do nothing else until I say. Nothing, Mace. Until further notice, that girl is your new best friend. Are we clear?"

"Crystal, sir. Crystal."

Chapter 11

EMBER

A rather disheveled looking, pale boy fell through the doorway as if gravity itself was working against him. Rhys shook his head, using just one hand to right the boy, sighing as if this was something that happened all the time. The boy glared at the doorframe as if it was the culprit. He then righted the navy blue beanie cap perched on his longish shaggy brown hair and pushed up his black-framed glasses with one finger.

His eyes widened as he took in the scene before him. Kai gave a half-hearted wave from his position beneath Isa. The new kid gave a confused one-fingered salute back, moving to the side of the room where he would be out of the line of fire.

Behind him, another boy followed. He walked with every bit of grace and confidence the first one lacked. He had the build of an athlete and biceps the size of her head. His hair was close cropped, and his complexion was the same melted copper of some of the creole kids she grew up with in the French Quarter. He had the palest blue eyes Ember had ever seen. He wore a pair of baggie jeans and a sleeveless grey hoodie. He sort of hovered at the edge of the room, hands buried deep in his pockets like he was cold.

She was no expert on the supernatural, but from what she could tell, the wolves' eyes all seemed to glow slightly. Which meant the paler boy was not a wolf. His eyes were amber behind those square frames, beautiful but human.

"Where are the others?" Isa asked, tone sharp.

"Harpy," Donovan said as if it explained everything.

Clearly it did because Isa huffed an aggravated sigh.

Hoodie wolf's gaze fell on Ember, and a huge smile split his face. "Is this her?"

He rushed forward. She shrank back, bracing for an attack. Instead, he leaned forward, nose pressing against the space where shoulder meets neck, inhaling deeply. Her skin crawled, her muscles tense. His hands braced on either side of her head, boxing her in as he took his time snuffling at her like an overeager puppy. People really needed to stop smelling her.

"What *is* she?" he asked wondrously, to nobody in particular.

Her head was pounding. Was he kidding? What was *she*? What the hell were they? What was she doing here? She was not a pet. She shoved hard, only briefly admiring the wall of his chest muscles as she pushed him. He didn't even budge, though he did grunt a bit.

"Uh, dude," the pale boy said. "I know we've never really lived in the outside world, but humans out there don't like being sniffed. They think it's strange."

The guy in front of her laughed with a shrug, like that was the weirdest thing he'd ever heard, but he backed off. She glared at him. "Yeah, that's right. We don't." She pulled her legs to her chest, wrapping her arms around herself and wiping her sweaty forehead on her sweater sleeve. "Here's a short list of other things we don't like. Being kidnapped. Being driven over state lines. Being the only human in a room full of supernatural freaks. Being stared at by said supernatural freaks like they are contemplating whether she's their next snack or a nifty science project."

As her last sentence died off, silence filled the room, growing awkwardly until Hoodie McSnifferwolf turned to Isa earnestly and said, "I like her, Isa. I like her so much. Please tell me we can keep her. This place is so boring and she's"—he sighed—"awesome."

 61

He suddenly seemed to remember his manners. He thrust out his hand. "I'm Donovan."

She stared at him blankly, brain fighting to keep up with his odd behavior. She took his hand before dropping it, his skin scalding against her already overheated skin. "You're hot," she gasped.

He winked at her. "Thanks. You too."

"That's not wh—" she started.

"Ignore him," Black Glasses said. "He has no manners at all." He walked forward, clumsily sticking his hand out for her to shake. He flinched when she took his hand. "I'm Quinn, and given the way everybody in this room is reacting to you right now, I'm about ninety-eight percent positive I'm the only everyday human in this room."

There was a shuffling outside the room, and two more people hurried through the door, Tristin trudging along behind them resentfully. "Did we miss it?" a male voice asked, sounding more curious then disappointed.

Ember gaped, more stunningly good looking people. A petite girl with long platinum hair and huge pixie like eyes stood just inside the doorway, leaning herself against Rhys, her back to his chest. They were a striking couple, like the kind you'd see on a romance novel cover. He wrapped an arm around the girl's waist and used his other thumb to wipe at a weird green substance on her cheek.

"Harpy?" he asked.

"Harpy," she confirmed in a soft bell-like voice.

The guy who arrived with her cousin and the pixie didn't venture far from the door either. He stood, arms crossed, leaning against the wall, taking in the scene. He was tall and lean, hair the color of wheat. A rather impressive tattoo snaked up his right arm and disappeared under the sleeve of his t-shirt.

"Oh, come on," Ember moaned, clutching her temples. "Do all wolves look like they escaped from a movie? Are you like supernatural models?"

Quinn snickered, crossing his arms over his chest, mimicking the older male. He moved to lean against the wall as well, flailing as he realized he'd miscalculated the distance.

 62

She didn't think this was funny at all. Did being supernatural make you supernaturally hot? Were they just genetically gifted? Was it years of breeding out flaws? Would she somehow get hotter since they thought she was something not quite human?

Maybe she could finally get rid of her freckles or that weird birthmark on the back of her neck or the slight gap in her front teeth. That would be awesome. There had to be some perks to being kidnapped by werewolves and, well, whatever her cousins were.

Isa finally left her perch on top of Kai, kneeing him in the diaphragm as she did, most likely on purpose, judging by the small smile playing at her lips. She walked over to the older guy with the spiky blonde hair and planted a hard kiss on his lips. "Hey, babe."

He smiled, wrapping his arms around her. He buried his face in her neck, growling softly. Ember knew she was staring, but she couldn't look away. The man rubbed his cheek against Isa's and made a strange sort of snuffling sound. Ember risked a glance at the others. Nobody seemed to think this was strange at all. Kai dusted wood and shards of glass off his butt and cracked his neck. Ember tried to school her features into a look that didn't scream "what the hell" but knew she was failing miserably. Finally, she couldn't take it anymore.

"Will somebody please, please tell me what's going on?"

Isa untangled herself from her boyfriend, dragging him to the sofa across from Ember's chair. She shoved him down roughly and sort of draped herself across his lap. He just smiled dopily at her.

Jeez, these people didn't care at all about personal space. Isa looked at Kai and Tristin each in turn. "Gather round, children." Isa commanded the room, her voice daring somebody to argue. "It seems it's story time. And, since Kai decided he can make decisions without his pack, he gets to be the one to fill us all in." Kai at least had the decency to blush.

Tristin stayed against the wall, near Quinn. Donovan sat in the mate to the chair Ember was sitting in. The pixie girl peeled herself away from Rhys and settled herself on the floor in front of Donovan. The boy began to run his hands along her back and shoulders, not even looking as he did so.

Kai sat on the couch next to Isa, like he wanted to be close to her but wasn't sure if he was still in trouble. From the corner of her eye, Ember watched Rhys watch Kai. What was the story between those two?

Kai looked at his sister, clearly hoping for help. She smirked viciously instead. "Go ahead, brother, seems the floor is yours."

Chapter 12

EMBER

"I hope you weren't planning on starting without me," a voice asked from the doorway.

A man of about fifty sauntered into the room, casual in khakis and a button down shirt. He had familiar eyes and hair greying at the temples. He had a big fake smile on his lips that made Ember think he should be selling life insurance or used cars.

She didn't know if he was friend or foe as his arrival sparked several different reactions. Isa looked relieved. Quinn's mouth turned down at the corners. Tristin shuffled closer to Rhys, who tucked her into his side, his bored expression never changing.

Kai looked like he might vomit.

Isa smiled. "Of course not, Allister. You're just in time. We were going to introduce ourselves to our new friend here, and then Kai was going to tell us exactly how screwed we are."

"Excellent," the older man said, smiling benevolently at her, earning a glare from Quinn.

Kai took a deep breath and blew it out slowly before nodding. "Uh, right, introductions," he mumbled to himself. "So, um, this is

Isa…Isa McGowan, she is the alpha werewolf of the Belladonna pack." His voice shook as he continued, "This is her mate, Wren." He gestured to the man beneath her. "Um, they're like werewolf married…kind of."

Isa slapped Kai's arm and then stroked a hand through his hair. He leaned into the touch. "That's Rhys," he said, gesturing half-heartedly toward the broody wolf in the corner. "He's Isa's douche-bag brother. He says he's in charge of keeping everybody safe, but mostly he just scowls and mopes and rolls his eyes."

Everybody chuckled at Kai's assessment except Rhys, who growled low at Kai. The alpha raised a brow at her brother and the sound died with another eye roll. Ember wondered if it was possible to sprain an eye muscle.

"You've met Donovan; he's an omega," Kai said as if Ember knew what that meant. Donovan nodded towards her. Kai pointed to the blonde girl with the wide hazel eyes. "That's Neoma. She's an elemental; she came with Wren."

Ember tried to keep up, she really did, but this was a lot of information for her foggy brain to digest. She'd seen enough movies to get the werewolf part. The last introduction stymied her. "Elemental?"

"She's fae," Kai said.

Ember smiled weakly, at least she'd been right about that. "I thought you looked like a pixie."

Neoma's face fell, and Quinn laughed. "Oh, no. Faeries and pixies are not the same thing. Pixie's are nasty, violent little things… like Tinkerbelle with fangs." He crooked his fingers like snake teeth for emphasis. "Neoma is a faery, an elemental from the Orhenthral Court."

"Oh, sorry." Ember looked to Quinn. "What about you?"

It was Rhys who spoke up. "Oh, the human? Near as I can tell, his job is to eat all of our food and distract him"—he gestured to Kai—"from providing any useful contribution."

"So, you're really just human?" Ember blurted.

They all gaped at her. Her face flushed, not what she'd said to deserve that look. Allister sneered at Quinn. Quinn glowered back. The Allister guy seemed like kind of a douche. Tristin glared at Ember, gravitating towards Quinn like a magnet. The room seemed

 66

to be turning hostile. She tried to correct herself, wiping her brow. "I'm sorry, I didn't mean it like that. It just seems like there's not a lot of humans around here."

Staring down Allister, Quinn shrugged and said, "The town has been cloaked from the humans for their own protection. We get too many supernatural creatures roaming through town. We have many humans here, but they're all born to magical families. Mine are witches. Talbot witches, actually. Now, that doesn't mean anything to you, but we're kind of a big deal in the supernatural world." She wasn't sure if he was joking. His face would suggest no.

"So, supernatural people are cool with humans?" That sounded promising. If she was a human. Of course, she was human. God, she hoped she was still human. Didn't she? She didn't know anymore.

"Most supernatural families don't care what their children are as long as they're healthy. But some, say, from prestigious bloodlines like mine, tend to look down on humans."

Ember nodded, but Quinn, still staring at Allister, didn't notice.

"Despite what my brother thinks, Quinn contributes plenty around here, human or not," Isa stated, eyes on Rhys, her tone denoting it as the end of the matter. Rhys was too busy glaring at Kai to notice. As far as Ember could tell, Rhys's full time job was watching Kai.

"So, yeah, that's everybody," Kai finished lamely.

Allister cleared his throat, and Kai looked embarrassed. "Oh, yeah and this is Allister Talbot. He's the head of the witches' council and Quinn's dad."

"Oh," Ember said. Well, that explained the hostility. She smiled sadly at Quinn. She could relate. She could write a book on daddy issues.

Isa spoke up, watching the older man. "Allister, this is the girl Kai saved. November Lonergan."

  67

Chapter 13

KAI

Kai almost laughed at the look on Allister's face. Almost. The older man stumbled forward, stopping just in front of his cousin. "I..." Allister started. "How is this even possible? I mean, we all thought you were dead."

"Nope, alive and well," she said, her head lulling a bit on her shoulders. "Well, alive, anyway. Sort of."

Allister studied her. "You do look just like them. Nobody could miss Seraphina or Samara when they were in the room. That hair..." He reached out a hand but caught himself. "Are you all right, my dear? You look...unwell."

Unwell is generous, Kai thought. Her skin was chalk. She was sweating again, like in the car, her pupils so dilated he could no longer see the iris. The girl was definitely sick. Had she been bitten?

"I just feel shaky," she promised. "It's been a long night."

"Yes, it has," Isa said. "So why don't we let Kai tell us what happened?"

Kai couldn't help it; he slid towards Isa before speaking. He needed her to not be mad at him. "I was in class this morning when

I got a name for collection." He shoved up his sleeve, tapping the blank space where Ember's name had been just hours before. Ember leaned forward, her brow wrinkled in concentration. From a distance, his tattoo was a swirl of black ink starting just above his elbow and winding around his bicep. If you looked closer, though, the image consisted of names, all crammed together to create a pattern. The names of his collected.

"Hello?" Ember raised her hand as if she was in kindergarten. "Newbie, remember? What does that mean?"

"So, I'm a reaper, a collector, to be exact. I cross people over." He felt his face flaming with embarrassment, though he didn't know why. He thought about his next words. "When it's somebody's time to go, I collect their souls so that they can move on to the otherworld. The names appear on my wrist, kind of like a tattoo. Once they've been collected and passed through the veil, the name moves to its place in the design." He gestured towards the swirl of names.

"That's so cool," she said, her eyes glassy but her tone reverent.

"This morning, it was Ember's name. Her real name."

"Where did you find her?" Allister said, as if Ember wasn't sitting right there.

"New Orleans," Tristin said.

"This whole time?" Allister asked Ember. She nodded, frowning. "And your father, he's…" He trailed off.

"Dead, since last week," Ember mumbled.

He felt the mood of the room change. The wolves shifted, moving closer to each other and his cousin. They found comfort through contact.

"We're very sorry for your loss, Ember. That's terrible," Isa said, giving her a sad smile.

His cousin nodded, shifting uncomfortably.

"Okay, I'm going to need you to backtrack a bit," Wren said. "You're in the middle of class and find a dead girl's name on your arm and you don't question it. You didn't think to call us?"

Kai's mouth tightened. "Of course I questioned it. She was dead. I knew it couldn't be possible," he told the room. "But her name was there."

  69

He looked at Ember, wincing at the words, explaining further. "As far as this town knew, you died twelve years ago with our moms and the others."

She seemed to take the information in stride. Maybe she was in shock. "I didn't even know you existed, so I guess that makes us even," she said.

He plunged on. "I was going to say something to Rhys," Kai said, hoping his already erratic heartbeat would mask the lie. "But then, Tristin screamed."

All eyes swung to his sister, whose eyes dropped at the weight of everybody's stares. She slid herself to the floor, drawing her knees to her chest.

"Is that true, Tristin?" Allister asked. "Did you scream?"

She froze, looking to her brother for help.

"She did," Rhys supplied. "I was there. She scared the crap out of our sixth period math class."

Isa looked like she wanted to skin Rhys alive. "If you were there, why am I only just hearing about this now?"

Rhys's nostrils flared. "I was going to tell you, but then I was sent a text four pages long about the supplies for the twin's birthday party this weekend. I figured they would tell you at work."

"Wait," Ember interrupted. "Your birthday is this weekend?"

"No, our birthday is today, like yours," Kai said, glancing at the time on his phone. "Well, technically yesterday now."

"We share the same birthday? How old are you?"

"Seventeen, like you."

"Our moms had us on the same day?" Ember shook her head. "That's really weird, right? Like, even in this world that's gotta be weird."

"We'll get to that in a minute," Isa said. "Tristin, you screamed... for Ember?"

"How should I know what I screamed for?" she grumbled, her posture defensive. "It's not like I know what I'm doing or have any control over it."

"Well, now. That *is* interesting," Allister said, looking at Tristin with a smile that made Kai's stomach feel squishy.

 70

"The screaming is important because…why?" Ember prompted.

"Because Tristin is a reaper as well," Allister supplied, his gaze still on Tristin. The added attention had Quinn sliding down the wall to put an arm around her.

"Are you a soul collector thingy like Kai?"

"There are many different types of reapers," Quinn explained.

"Oh, so what type are you?" Ember asked.

"Banshee," Tristin mumbled.

"Banshee?" Ember repeated. "Really? I thought banshees were old women who would wash the clothing of the soldiers destined to die in battle."

Tristin narrowed her eyes at Ember. "You seem to know a lot about the supernatural for a girl raised with humans."

"My father was a professor of Celtic mythology and occult studies. I grew up in New Orleans. I know more than you think," Ember said, "Though, up until ten hours ago, my knowledge was entirely anecdotal."

Isa gave her an assessing look before saying to Kai, "Continue."

Kai looked like he was struggling to decide how to proceed. "I figured if Tristin screamed it had to be something, right? Tristin hasn't screamed since…well, in a really long time." He cleared his throat. "Banshees are rare," Kai supplied to Ember.

"How rare?" Ember asked, looking to Tristin.

Tristin's jaw tightened in a grim line, her eyes fixed on the floor. "Like as far as we know, I'm the only one still in existence." Quinn squeezed her tighter. She half-heartedly tried to shake it off, but he held on until she deflated against him.

"That just makes you more special," Quinn said. Tristin hmph'd but said nothing.

"My son is correct. You're unique. That makes you special. You screaming is a good thing. It means you didn't lose your powers; they were just dormant."

"You thought you lost your powers?" Ember asked.

Tristin shrugged but said nothing.

 71

Ember looked puzzled. "But even if you are the only one, some-body must have information on your powers. On what you are. There have to be records, books, databases."

Kai watched as Allister puffed out his chest. "Of course, the council has records, and she can petition them to give her access to information concerning banshees when she is eighteen."

Ember's forehead furrowed, blinking like she was trying to clear her vision. "I don't get it. Why does she have to be eighteen? Can't you just go to your local library and google information on banshees?"

Allister's eyes narrowed. "I'm sure this all seems confusing to you, but you have to understand, Ember, information about our kind is highly sensitive and dangerous in the wrong hands. As such, the Grove has restricted access to any information concerning our kind until adulthood."

Quinn snorted. "Adulthood? You mean if you're an adult witch. Even then, it's not likely to get you anywhere. Requesting informa-tion from the Grove is like asking the government about Area 51. You'll get back a bunch of papers covered in black sharpie. Every-thing's classified."

Kai felt for his friend. It physically hurt Quinn not to have access to the thousands of years of knowledge hidden in the Grove library.

"Okay, I understand it's dangerous, but how do you ban books. I mean, they're books. Don't people have a right to that information?"

There was no hiding Quinn's bitterness. "You would think that, this being America and all, but no, not in our world. If you aren't a witch, you are a second-class citizen. Only the witches can be trusted."

"But that's crazy? How can that be possible?" Ember asked.

She was right. It was crazy. It hadn't always been like this. There was a time when information was free. Back when his mother and aunt ran the council. Back before whatever happened to cause the council to close ranks and shut out all supernatural creatures but the witches.

Allister shifted uncomfortably. "It's a long story, Ember, and it's getting late. The Grove keeps the information well hidden for the protection of all," Allister said, as if he rehearsed the line in front of his mirror at night. "Can we please focus on what brought you to us?"

"Weird," was her only response.

Kai cleared his throat, startling the room back to attention. "So, after Tristin screamed, I showed her Ember's name. We both decided we should go to New Orleans and see for ourselves. We had to know if it was really her."

"Isa," Allister said. "It seems you are not keeping a close enough eye on your pack. Should I be concerned? The consequences of this little excursion could've been catastrophic. They still might be."

Isa flinched like he'd slapped her, before she steeled her spine, looking at Kai then Tristin. "He's right. You should've come to me first. You know we can't travel through another alpha's territory without permission. You could've caused a ton of trouble for the pack," Isa scolded. She looked to the others. "Nobody is to travel outside of this town without my express permission. I thought that was clear, but it seems I was mistaken."

Kai wouldn't make eye contact with the alpha. "I never had to clear a collection with you before. And besides, like I said, we didn't really know if it was real."

Rhys shook his head. "That just makes it worse. You don't think it's weird that your dead cousin's name pops up for a collection in another state? You didn't stop to think it might be a trap? When have you ever had to travel this far for a collection? Nothing about this made sense, and your first instinct was to say, 'Screw it, let's just see what happens?' That's not how the pack works."

Kai set his jaw. "Well, as you like to tell me all the time, we're not really part of the pack, are we?"

"Enough," Wren barked from beneath the alpha. "No more distractions. Just finish telling us what happened. This is giving me a headache."

"When we got there, she had attracted the attention of some kind of grim."

Eyebrows shot up all around the room. "What kind?" Neoma asked, crawling closer to Kai, like a child excited the teacher was finally getting to the good part of the storybook.

Kai shrugged. "Not sure, vampire, maybe an incubus, random demon of unknown origin?"

"Whatever he was, he was certainly interested in her, and it looked like the feeling was mutual." Tristin supplied.

Ember looked embarrassed, ducking her head. "Grim?"

"It's just our code word for anything supernaturally bad. We made it up; it's not in the official handbook," Kai explained.

"There's a handbook?" Ember asked.

Kai smiled. "I was kidding."

"Oh," Ember said, disappointed.

Isa jerked forward, and Wren hissed in discomfort. "Let's get back to the grim. Was he looking for her? Or did he just happen upon her?" When Wren moved her, she patted his face. "Sorry, babe."

"I don't know," Kai said, shrugging helplessly.

Isa's eyes shot to Ember. "Have you ever seen this creature before?"

Ember shook her head, goosebumps erupting over her skin. "I don't feel s'good," she said, the words sloppy like her tongue was refusing to cooperate with her brain. She tugged at the collar of her sweater.

Kai looked to Isa, not sure what was happening or what they should do about it. Ember was drenched in sweat, a near impossibility in a house that kept its air conditioning set to seventy degrees to offset the wolves' elevated body temperatures.

Donovan moved closer to his cousin, putting a hand on her forehead. She didn't try to move away. In fact, she swayed closer. "Isa, she's burning up."

"It's so hot in here," Ember mumbled, yanking off her sweater, leaving a wet black tank top that emphasized her corpse-like pallor. "S'anybody else hot?"

"Ember?" Isa pushed Donovan out of the way, clasping Ember's face in her hands. "Ember? What's happening here? Are you okay? Did that thing do something to you? Did it bite you or scratch you? Ember, honey, stay with me. This is important."

 74

Ember blinked unfocused eyes at the alpha, looking at her like she'd never seen her before. Suddenly, Ember bolted forward, surprising Isa and causing her to stumble back.

Ember lurched to her feet, her head swiveling in every direction before she clutched her stomach, looking at Isa with dread. "I'm so sorry," Ember managed before vomiting a foul black sludge onto Isa's ancient and expensive Persian rug. The alpha had just enough time to look dismayed before she caught Ember's limp body in her arms.

Chapter 14

EMBER

Ember was in the ocean. All alone in frigid black water. She floated upon gently cresting waves, eyes narrowed against the blinding white sky above. Water filled her ears until the only sound she heard was her own steadily thudding heartbeat. The chilly water was lovely, a balm to the scorching heat of her skin.

It was a dream. It had to be. It couldn't be anything else. But she'd stay like this forever, happily floating in a vacuum of silence and nothingness. But the universe had other plans. Frantic voices, muffled and far away, shattered her peace. She tried to protest, but a heavy weight descended on her, sucking her under the surface. She gasped, arms thrashing, as water filled her nose and mouth, scratching and fighting her unseen attacker.

Each time she broke the surface for a much needed breath, she was shoved back down. Her dreams never felt this real before. Panic clawed at her chest. She had to wake up. She had to wake up, or she was going to die.

She forced her eyes open, viewing the world from beneath a foot of water. She wasn't dreaming. Amorphous shapes moved above her, and a large hand at the center of her chest held her under. She began to struggle anew, her screams bubbling through the water.

Then it was gone.

Arms flailing, she scrambled to gain traction as she broke the surface, coughing and sputtering, choking water from her burning lungs. Her brain was swimming, and she fought to stay conscious.

Were they trying to kill her?

She looked around, trying to visualize her attacker. She was in a bathtub. She was in her underwear. She wasn't alone. Kai, Tristin, Quinn, and Rhys were against the far wall, arms akimbo, limbs entangled as if thrown across the room. Three of them stared at her in horror, but Quinn smiled like he had a secret. She opened her mouth to ask why they were doing this to her, but she only choked up more water. Her world started to go black at the edges, narrowing as she started to slip beneath the water.

The last thing she heard was Quinn saying, "Take her out. She's had enough."

When she woke again, she was in somebody else's clothes and tucked into an unfamiliar bed. Quinn sat in a wooden chair next to her. He was pouring powders into a steaming cup. "Oh, good, you're awake. Drink this."

Ember narrowed her eyes at him, sitting up with effort. Her whole body ached. "What is it?" She sniffed the cup suspiciously. "Is this some kind of potion? I thought they said you were human?"

"It's true. I am but a simple, useless human." She arched a brow in his direction. He sighed. "Sorry, it's not witchcraft; it's just herbs, some yarrow tea with a few other things thrown in. I'm hoping it will help with your fever—even though I'm pretty sure this isn't the flu."

She sipped the tea, wincing at the taste. "You don't seem useless." As far as she could tell, Quinn was the only one with any real information.

"Sorry," he said again, blushing. "I'm not always this annoying. My father tends to put me in this mood."

She nodded. "I can relate."

"Anyway, since we don't have a hospital around here, and our healer sort of parted ways with her grip on reality eighteen months ago, I do what I can."

 77

"Did she train you?"

"I trained me. I have an IQ higher than Einstein and an eidetic memory. I could probably teach myself open-heart surgery with the right YouTube video."

"So you take care of everybody?"

"I don't know about that. I keep them alive. It's not like we can go to the local hospital with a werewolf scratch or a vampire bite."

He sounded a little defensive, like he was used to having to justify himself and his usefulness. She didn't say anything, watching as he jostled small bottles and vials in the box at his feet. His human brown eyes were almost luminous in the dim lighting of the room. He had freckles smattered across his cheeks, and he pushed his glasses up the bridge of his nose almost like a nervous tick. He had a sweetness to his face the others didn't.

"So, I had a fever? Is that why you tried to drown me?" she finally asked.

He grinned at her. "Technically, I ordered Rhys to try to drown you."

She couldn't help but smile back. "Awesome, thanks. All my future nightmares will be much more vivid."

"Normally, you don't plunge somebody into ice water to help a fever, but yours was so high I took a chance. There was no way we could take you to a hospital with a fever that high. Any human would have been dead."

"So I'm definitely not human?" It was weird to hear somebody say it aloud.

"It seems more unlikely by the minute."

She swallowed the last of the bitter tasting tea. "Does it bother you? Being human?"

He swallowed hard, his eyes meeting hers briefly. "Me? No, not really. I mean, if I really wanted to be supernatural, I could have somebody bite me. A shifter, vampire."

"They can do that? That's a real thing?"

"It's illegal in our country, but in other places, yeah. I could be... something." He took her cup. "Still wouldn't be enough to interest my father. If I'm not a witch, carrying on the family name, I'm nothing."

 78

She touched his hand. "If I know anything, it's that nobody should have to work this hard to interest their own father. Screw him."

He smiled, and Ember fell a little in love. "You sound like Kai," he said.

There was a knock on the door, and Kai stuck his head in, almost like he'd heard them. "Hey, can I come in?"

She nodded, feeling heat prickle along her skin. "Sure." To Quinn she said, "I don't think your tea is working, I feel sweaty."

He grimaced. "Sorry, that's how it works. It helps sweat out the fever."

"Gross, thanks again for that."

There was another terse knock at the door, and then Rhys barged in with wet hair, bare chested, and sweatpants riding low on his hips. Ember was pretty sure she was gaping, but she couldn't help it. Rhys's abdominal muscles had muscles. If there was such a thing as an eighteen pack, Rhys possessed it. Ember didn't even like him, and she was grudgingly impressed.

"Isa wants to see Ember downstairs when she's feeling better," he said. He looked at Kai. "And she said to tell you you're working a double tomorrow."

Her cousin openly glared at Rhys's bare torso as if it had offended him. Kai swallowed hard, dragging his gaze back to Ember, heat flaring in his cheeks.

Oh, Ember thought, that explained the weird tension.

Rhys waved a hand in front of Kai's face. "Hello?"

A strangled noise escaped her cousin. Rhys's lip twitched. He sniffed the air, frowning. She couldn't imagine ever getting used to this wolf behavior.

Kai crossed his arms over his chest, fixing a scowl onto his face. He kept his eyes to the floor. "Yeah, fine. Whatever."

Rhys slammed the door with more force than necessary.

After a few awkward minutes, Kai said, "So...how are you?"

"Considering my night? Okay, I guess. Embarrassed."

He flopped down on the bed next to her, crossing his legs at the ankles and snaking an arm under her pillow. "Why, because you

  79

threw up some horrifying black goop and then passed out in a rather spectacular display of melodrama. Happens all the time," he said, waving his hand like it was just another night at Casa-de-Werewolf.

"Really?" she asked, doubting him.

Kai laughed. "No, not really. It was really disgusting. And awesome."

She rolled her eyes at her cousin as he nudged her shoulder with his. She wanted to move over, feeling crowded by his presence. He didn't seem to feel the same. After a minute she asked, "What's happening to me?"

Quinn and Kai exchanged looks before Quinn conceded, "We don't know. Truthfully, this whole thing is weird. You aren't human but you aren't a witch."

"And I'm definitely not a reaper, like you and Tristin?"

Quinn thought for a minute. "It seems unlikely, but really, it's hard to say at this point. Witches and reapers both inherit their magic, but there is only supposed to be one reaper per family."

"Why?"

"The common theory is because it's a form of soul magic. It's a supernatural failsafe to make sure that no one family has access to that kind of power."

"But you and Tristin are both reapers."

She felt Kai shrug next to her. "The witches said it was a fluke because we're twins, they say our magic may have split in utero or something. They probably would've looked into it more, but then Tristin's powers disappeared so people stopped worrying about it."

"So, there can't be more than one reaper, but there can be more than one witch in a family?"

Quinn nodded. "Most supernatural creatures, including witches, inherit their magic only when another witch in their line dies. So when a witch dies, their magic passes to the next who bares the mark."

"The mark?"

"Sometime around puberty a mark appears signifying they are the next to inherit."

Ember sat up on her forearms. "What does this mark look like?"

 80

"It varies for different families. My family's mark looks like an olive branch. Kai's and Tristin's look like the moon. If both your parents are supernatural, the mark will signify whose magic you'll inherit."

Ember's heart rate sped up; she pushed her hair aside for Kai, showing him the full-moon-shaped birthmark at the base of her hairline. "Like this?"

Kai inhaled sharply. "How long have you had this?"

"My whole life, I guess. It's always been there."

She looked back and forth between her cousin and his friend, distress etched across their faces. The mark was obviously freaking them out. She started to panic. "Why? Is this bad? What does it mean? Oh God, did I accidentally murder somebody or something? Is that why I can't remember anything?"

Kai looked horrified. "No! Jeez, Ember. It's just that you shouldn't have that mark. If you were a witch, you would bare the mark of your father's house, not your mother's."

"Wait, my father's house? Are you saying my father was a witch?" Her laugh sounded harsh even to her own ears. "My dad couldn't be a witch. He was a drunk. He barely functioned as a college professor."

Kai looked away. "I can only tell you what we know about your family. Your mom was a reaper. Your dad was a witch, a witch from a pureblood family. That carries a lot of weight in the witch community. It's not that you couldn't be a witch; you just don't smell like one, and you bare the mark of our mothers. Plus, Quinn's dad would've been able to sense it. Other than that, we just don't know."

Ember fidgeted. "So, maybe the witches are wrong. Maybe more than one reaper can exist in a family."

"Or maybe the witches are lying," Quinn said, his voice bitter.

"Does your mark look like mine?" Ember asked Kai. "Is it a circle like mine?"

"Not exactly, it's a crescent moon. Tristin and I both have the same mark."

After a minute of Quinn staring into nothing, he looked at Ember, his brown eyes serious. "Ember, do me a favor, keep your hair down until we know more about your powers. I think it's better nobody knows about your mother's mark for now."

She nodded, her mind trying to process the ins and outs of magic. There was just so much she didn't know. "So, what about the wolves, do they have to inherit their powers?"

Quinn shook his head. "No. People in shifter families are either born shifters or humans. Humans born to shifter families can decide to take the bite when they are eighteen, or they can stay human. Occasionally, an alpha shifter will bite a human not born into a shifter family, but it's illegal here, and the Grove takes that sort of thing very seriously. Vampires can transfer the virus with a bite, but on rare occasions, vampires can be born."

"Pregnant vampires? Seriously?" Ember rubbed her temples. "This is so confusing."

"Magic is fluid. It's not something we can explain scientifically. People aren't born ghosts, poltergeists, or furies. Same with the harpies, they are turned that way due to circumstances; it's usually vengeance driven. Demons are demons because they sold their souls. Wendigo, selkie, and chupacabra aren't really even necessarily supernatural, just rarely seen hybrid creatures with bad attitudes. It would take me days to explain everything, and even that wouldn't help because the real information is being kept from us, guarded by the witches and hoarded by the Grove."

"What is this Grove you keep talking about?"

Kai scoffed. "Depends on who you ask. The witches will tell you they are the supernatural system of government in charge of keeping the balance. But that's because the Grove put them in charge, forcing all other supernatural people to answer to them. Who would think it was smart to put humans in charge of the super humans?" he finished, almost to himself.

"Wait, the Grove is human?"

"No, the Grove was human," Quinn said. "They're druids, humans who sold themselves to the gods in exchange for magic."

"So, you can buy your way into magic? Why wouldn't everybody do it?"

Quinn's mouth twisted. "They are slaves. They spend hundreds of years in servitude before they can call themselves one of the Grove. They endure years of torture at the hands of their brothers. They are taught to speak all languages, forced to know all things.

 82

A wrong answer to a question asked by the Grove can lead to a fate much worse than death. When they have proven themselves, the Gods release them to serve as mentors and tormentors to those stupid enough to want to follow their example. They start out as humans, but they end up monsters."

Ember shivered. "They can't be the only people with information. Isn't there anybody who would know? There has to be more than three adults in this town. Somebody willing to talk." Then a thought occurred to her. "This isn't like that movie where the kids kill all the adults and pray to that creepy little demon kid in the corn field is it?"

Kai smiled, nodding in admiration. "*Children of the Corn*. Stephen King." Quinn nodded in agreement, and the two knuckle-bumped over her without looking. "But no, we didn't kill any adults."

Quinn cleared his throat. Kai rolled his eyes but said, "Okay, well, not any good adults."

"And never any humans," Quinn supplied.

Ember wanted to scream in frustration. They talked in riddles. She needed answers. She needed to know if she was going to keep vomiting black goop and feeling like people were trying to tear her brain apart with meat hooks. She needed to know she wasn't going to keep passing out like some paranormal overheating engine.

Quinn must have sensed her frustration. "Listen, anybody who knows anything won't talk about it for fear of having to deal with the witches' council or worse, the tree huggers. I'd love to say we saved your life and brought you to a magical place where everything is going to be okay, but it's not true. In many ways, this town is like an entirely different world. The only law that matters is the Grove, and they have a lot of laws. More than we could explain to you in a hundred years."

She felt sick, her chest tight. There was no guarantee they'd find out what she was. Tristin had been living there her entire life and still knew nothing about being a banshee. What were the odds they'd figure out what Ember was before it was too late?

"If you're feeling better, you should get downstairs and talk to Isa. She's in the kitchen stress-baking."

Quinn's eyes lit up. "What is she making this time?"

"Pumpkin muffins, I think."

Ember frowned. What did you say to an alpha werewolf after you puked on their carpet?

Chapter 15

EMBER

She padded barefoot down the stairs. It had to be well after midnight, but everybody was still awake. After a few wrong turns, she found herself in the kitchen, which was bigger than the apartment she'd shared with her father. Isa had changed into a pair of leggings and a slouchy looking t-shirt and was sliding around the kitchen in… leg warmers?

It *was* freezing in there. She didn't know what the temperature was like outside, but the air conditioning hummed along at full blast, causing condensation on the many windows. Ember shivered, freezing after her ice bath.

Isa stirred a bowl of something orange as music played softly in the background. Ember hovered in the doorway, waiting for the other girl to acknowledge her. Isa bobbed her head, hips swaying, lost in the music or her thoughts.

Ember took a step back, feeling like she was intruding, and turned to go.

"Get your butt back here," Isa said, not looking up.

Ember did as she was told, taking it all in as she walked. The kitchen was decorated in cool greys and blues, the cabinets and countertops white. The appliances were stainless steel and probably cost more than a car. To her left was another set of stairs and, to her right, a set of French doors that led to the backyard. How could they afford a house like this?

She slid onto a stool at the center island, and Isa handed her the bowl. "Stir."

Ember stared at the spoon thrust into her hand for only a moment, before she began to stir, watching the older woman carefully. She moved with grace and efficiency, the kitchen clearly her domain. The hazy windows and soft music created a cozy pocket of calm, putting Ember at ease.

She pulled a tray of muffins from the oven and replaced it with one waiting to go in. Ember watched, mesmerized, as the alpha burned herself transferring twelve still hot muffins from the tin. She clutched them by their little decorative papers, each relocation punctuated with a whispered, "Ouch."

Isa placed new cups in the tins and slid them over to Ember with a small ladle. "One scoop each. Don't overfill."

Ember did as she was told, dropping the batter into the paper cups, content to take instruction if it meant she could stay there, hidden in the kitchen with Isa. Isa in the kitchen was its own kind of magic. There was something about the tiny wolf Ember found comforting.

Even in their bubble, Ember was aware there were literal wolves outside the kitchen door. Sounds traveled throughout the house, muted but ever present. Wren and Donovan watched something in the living room, the low murmur of the television dotted by their occasional laughter. Neoma was singing from somewhere at the top of the stairs but never revealed herself.

It was just the sounds of people existing together, but it made Ember edgy. Most of her nights were spent at the funeral home or alone on the couch waiting for the phone to ring and tell her she needed to pick up her dad from the bar or find a way to pay whoever he owed money to that week. She didn't know how to be a person somebody liked. Her default setting was sarcasm. Isa said Ember could stay, but what happened when they realized she was awkward and socially inept? How long before she wore out her welcome?

 86

"Ember."

Her name startled her out of her thoughts.

Isa smiled apologetically. "I know this must be weird for you. I can't imagine what all of"—she gestured vaguely around the room—"this must seem like to you. I don't want you to worry. Nobody is going to kick you out. You are now part of our weird little family. Our parents were friends. They would never let you live on the street and neither would I."

"Even if I keep passing out and redecorating all of your rugs with Satan's vomit?" Ember asked, trying for a joke but flushing with embarrassment.

"Listen." Isa dropped her voice down to a whisper. "Rhys turned for the first time when he was seven and shredded my great-grand-mother's hundred-year-old sofa and three hand sewn pillows, and then he peed on the carpet under the dining room table. His fangs would drop so often without his permission he talked with a lisp for two years. He was so embarrassed he stopped talking for weeks at a time. It's why he barely talks today."

Ember winced. She didn't want to feel sorry for the wolf, not when he was so hostile towards Kai. Isa went on, "When I first turned, I forgot to bring clothes with me and had to walk home completely naked. Kai botched his first soul collection and the poor dead guy almost got a front row seat to his own autopsy. The stuff that happens to us…it's no different than puberty for humans, embarrassing and inevitable. You're just a late bloomer."

Isa was sweet, trying to make Ember feel comfortable, but she didn't know how to share space with so many people. She didn't know how to be part of a family.

"I know we are overpowering. If you think this is too much… if you think *we* are too much…I can talk to Allister about maybe contacting your father's family. You were born here, Ember. You have people in this town. Your dad didn't really get along with them, but I can't imagine they'd turn you away, even if you aren't a witch."

She was starting to think the alpha could read minds. Ember wasn't entirely sure what that meant, but from what she gathered, the witches weren't real fond of non-witches, which put her squarely

 87

in the middle of a fight she couldn't even remotely begin to understand. She didn't think she could handle that kind of anxiety.

"Ember, I'm not going to lie. We're a huge family. On a slow day, six people live here. Donovan has his own place, and technically, Quinn lives with his dad and sister across town, but they sleep here more than there. We are loud. Rhys, Kai, and Quinn are always bickering. Neoma sings like she's in a musical. Tristin is often super-aggressive and snotty for no discernable reason. Wren wants to fix everybody's problems, and I've been told when I'm stressed out I'm no Swiss picnic either. We fight a lot. We butt heads a lot. I'm in charge. I'm the alpha and ultimately what I say goes, and sometimes people have a problem with that. You don't have to like what I say, but you do have to do what I say. Some people can't handle that."

Ember struggled to see what she was getting at. Before she could ask, the timer beeped and the girl spun around, repeating her earlier process. With two trays cooling, the smell of pumpkin was overwhelming. Ember's stomach growled loudly. Color bloomed on her cheeks, but Isa just laughed. Ember hadn't eaten all day.

Isa placed a muffin on a paper plate and poured Ember a glass of milk.

"What I'm trying to say is we want you here, and you are welcome to stay, but you are free to go if you want. We just want you to stay close by until we figure out what's happening to you. You could hurt yourself."

"Okay."

Isa's face split into a toothy grin. "Okay? You'll stay with us?"

Ember took a deep breath, letting it out slowly, trying to temper the anxiety building in her chest. "Yeah, sure."

"Oh and this is now your house too. The kitchen, living room, library, and porches are all community space. We are used to a crowd. We are lucky enough to have a large house. We have six bedrooms. Two beds per room in all but the master. Quinn usually beds with Kai when he's here. Neoma prefers to sleep on the couch in the solarium, something about sleeping under the stars. You can have the last room at the top of the stairs. It's the most private. We will get you your own sheets and any clothes you need tomorrow."

Ember nodded, overwhelmed by everything. She broke off a piece of muffin and blew on it before stuffing it in her mouth. "Oh muh gaw." Swallowing, she said, "These are amazing."

Isa smiled. "Thank you." She placed her hand over Ember's. Ember snatched it back without thinking. Isa's eyes went wide. Ember felt her face flush. "Sorry," she said. "I'm just not used to all the touching."

Isa's eyes softened. "*I'm* sorry," she said. "I grew up surrounded by shifters. We scent everything. We want everything to smell like us. We are worse than actual wolves."

That explained all the touchy feely stuff. Ember felt like she had a lot to learn. Her knowledge of wolves consisted of information gleaned from Animal Planet documentaries, and her knowledge of werewolves came from old black and white movies.

"It takes a little getting used to," Ember admitted.

Isa's expression turned serious looked at Ember. "Nobody here has the right to touch you without your permission. Our...habits aren't your problem. If Donovan or anybody else is touching you—"

"I don't think—" Ember started.

"No, Ember," she said. "This isn't up for debate. You are new to the pack, so they are going to do anything they can to make you smell like them, to make you smell like home. If you are uncomfortable, you tell them no. Even me."

Ember nodded earnestly. "Okay."

"Your acceptance isn't conditional. I agreed to take you in. Allister agreed that you should be here."

They ate in silence for a while before Ember asked, "Isa, can I ask you a question?"

"Of course."

"Why do I have the same last name as Kai and Tristin? Our moms were sisters. Weren't my parents married?"

Isa shrugged. "In our world, you take the last name of the person whose family is more prominent. Not sure if it's a matter of safety or bragging rights, but it's always been that way. Your father came from a powerful witch family, and the twins' father was a human born to a large leopard pack out of Thailand; but in the case of the Lonergans, few names carried more weight. At least before the witches took over."

People respected her family. Ember thought of her life in New Orleans. Her dad had been a joke. A punch line his students used to amuse each other in the dining hall. She'd had no friends and barely showed up for school. Her heart squeezed. Her mother would've found her a huge disappointment.

Isa frowned, sensing Ember's shift in mood. She moved closer, hand hovering over Ember's before she caught herself. Isa looked bewildered on how to comfort Ember. She took a deep breath and grasped the other girl's hand; Ember needed to embrace her new life. Since the pack was touchy-feely, she would do her best to try.

"Allister is going to look into what's happening to you. He thinks it would be best if you try to get back to a normal routine. Tomorrow, I'll take you shopping for some supplies. You can take the weekend to get settled, and we'll get you registered for school on Monday."

Ember tried to take in all this information, her hand spasming around Isa's as the door between the kitchen and the dining room banged open, Kai and Rhys barreling through. Kai rushed towards the muffins, but Rhys swept a massive arm around Kai's shoulders, jerking him backwards, swinging him away. Rhys held Kai hostage with one arm, snagging a muffin with his free hand.

"Rhys." Kai whined, making grabby hands towards the muffins just out of reach. Rhys snickered, taking a bite of the muffin, paper and all, making exaggerated moaning noises. "So good," he told Kai around a mouthful. Kai's eyes bulged, staring at Rhys's lips, watching his tongue flick the crumbs from his lower lip.

Ember looked away, feeling like she was intruding on…something. Quinn came in and saw his captive friend. He whooped a war cry and hurled himself at Rhys's back but slipped on his own shoelace, toppling forward. A pained look flashed across Rhys's face as he seemed to try to decide whether to let Quinn fall or sacrifice the muffin Rhys had pilfered. He dropped the muffin and spun to catch Quinn's arm, saving him before he hit the ground.

"I'm going to put you in bubble wrap," Rhys grumbled.

Ember noted that he'd dropped the muffin but not her cousin. Kai was not letting that stop him with the muffins within reach. He

 90

stuffed one in his mouth and another in his pocket. He didn't take the paper off either. She pulled a face; she didn't get boys at all.

Kai tossed a muffin towards Quinn, but Rhys intercepted it, flashing green eyes at Quinn. Quinn made a sad noise.

Isa smiled at Ember, her back to the boys, and growled low. Rhys stiffened, huffing and giving the muffin to Quinn. Ember couldn't help but smile. Rhys couldn't even see his sister's face and he'd obeyed. What it would be like, to have that kind of quiet control. Quinn groaned as he took a bite. Rhys consoled himself with another muffin still in the tin, eating it one-handed out of the wrapper.

Isa smiled fondly at the chaos. "Welcome to the circus, Ember."

Ember pointed at the boys. "They must be the clowns."

Three males glowered at Ember around their muffins.

"Uh, we on a date here, dude?" Kai asked, eyeing the arm that kept him snug across Rhys's chest.

The wolf snorted and shoved him away.

 91

Chapter 16

TRISTIN

Tristin slipped left and hit the bag with a hard right cross. She grunted as she threw two jabs before circling left. She couldn't believe she'd been so stupid. Sweat drenched her clothing and burned her eyes, but she still threw punch after punch. The adrenaline had long since worn off and reality was creeping in.

She wanted to scream. She wanted to cry. Instead, she hit the bag with her left knee hard enough to rattle the chain from which it hung. She was just as responsible for this mess, maybe more. She never should have let her brother intervene. They should have told the pack. They should have told Isa.

She kept moving, kept circling the bag. Every time she stopped moving, dread crept up her spine, creating a sick feeling in the pit of her stomach. She hated uncertainty. She liked facts. She liked orders. Everybody was so preoccupied with keeping Ember's mysterious powers under control that the real danger hadn't occurred to them yet. They couldn't see that the real danger wasn't the girl puking up black goo but something far more sinister.

Footsteps approached, but she didn't stop, instead throwing a left roundhouse at the bag before faking left and coming in hard with a right elbow. It was Quinn. She knew his walk, the way he breathed. She ignored how the knot in her stomach loosened at the sight of his shadow against the wall.

He set something down and came around the other side of the bag, holding it in place as she pounded away until her muscles screamed for relief. He made sure he stayed out of the way of her fists and feet and said nothing, just watched her with those endlessly curious eyes.

"I brought you a muffin."

She didn't acknowledge that he spoke. She couldn't. Not yet. When she just couldn't bring herself to throw one more punch, she let her arms fall.

He clung to the bag. "What's eating you, Dagger?"

She set her jaw, trying to decide whether she wanted to talk it out or not. Quinn always wanted to talk. He wanted to know all of her thoughts and feelings. He'd never met a thought he didn't think needed expressing. That was why he and her brother were such good friends. Every thought flew out of their mouths without them worrying about consequences.

She just wasn't like that.

She sighed, almost wishing Rhys had come to find her. He understood not wanting to talk about feelings. They could just sit in a room and be, without having to fill the silence. He understood what privacy meant. However, Rhys wasn't there and Quinn's whiskey gold eyes were so earnest. How could she not tell him?

"Everybody is so preoccupied with Princess Power Surge upstairs they seem to be forgetting we have a bigger, more pressing problem." She put her hands on her hips, just sucking in air and catching her breath. He handed her the water bottle on the table. She poured it over her head.

She didn't miss the way his eyes followed the drops of water as they rolled down her throat.

"She was supposed to die, Quinn."

"Okay," he said, voice hoarse, distracted.

"She was supposed to die but is, instead, upstairs eating pumpkin muffins and bonding with the pack."

Quinn's eyes scanned her face, looking for a clue.

"Kai didn't complete his assignment."

Quinn's eyes widened. He stuffed his hands in his jeans pockets and licked his lower lip. "Well, yes, but…there have been cases of reapers who failed to collect the souls they were assigned."

"Those reapers left the soul in a dead body. They still died. They go back and finish the job, collect the soul, and that's it. Crossed over, no problem. That's a slap on the wrist; a rookie-with-nerves mistake. This is different. This is much worse. You know I'm right."

She took a deep breath, trying to stave off the panic building in her chest. "He didn't just keep her from crossing over. He actively prevented her death. She's not supposed to be alive. Her name disappeared from his arm. That's never happened, Quinn. That's never happened."

Quinn pulled her into his arms. "Have you ever met another reaper? We don't know if it's ever happened before or not. Let's not worry until there is something to worry about, okay?"

She didn't answer him. It was true; they hadn't met other reapers. Allister said they existed. He talked Kai through his first collection. That was the thing about this stupid town, nobody came in, and nobody went out. The same people had been here for as long as she could remember.

"Don't, I'm all sweaty." She squirmed against him, but she wasn't really trying to get away.

He rolled his eyes, loosening his grip, giving her the chance to move away. She pretended not to notice.

Quinn was lame. He had terrible taste in movies, and he was the most uncoordinated person she'd ever met. He wore stupid beanie hats pretty much every day and those stupid black framed glasses he didn't even need because he thought he looked like Clark Kent. She inhaled deeply; but he smelled like home, his arms always felt really good, and he was just tall enough for her to put her head on his shoulder.

"Do you know what they could do to him, Quinn? Do you know what they might do to all of us?"

She chewed on her bottom lip, rubbing her cheek against his flannel shirt. Quinn didn't say anything for a long time. He just stood there, holding her but she knew his mind was working over a hundred different scenarios, mentally rereading every word he'd ever scanned in any human book.

She didn't need extra-special senses to know he was afraid. He looked to the door, dropping his voice to almost a whisper. "What if she died now? What if the next time she spikes a fever we do nothing?"

He sounded sick at the idea, but it wasn't as if they hadn't committed horrible acts to protect this town and the people they loved. His hands fidgeted idly with her hair, combing through the wet strands.

She smiled weakly, shaking her head. "Are you just going to sit there and watch her die? Do you think Isa and the others will do the same? Just sit and watch her self-destruct?"

"If it comes down to her or Kai, yeah, I think we'll do what we have to do."

"You're wrong. Kai would happily die for somebody else, even a stranger. The damage is done. Besides, Isa and the others are already in love. You like her too, I can tell. Isa loves an orphan, and that girl just screams love-me-I'm-tortured."

Quinn snickered. "Maybe they won't find out. Maybe her name disappeared for a different reason. Maybe he was supposed to stop it?" Quinn was grasping at straws, and they both knew it.

"The Grove will never allow that to go unpunished. He literally just altered the fabric of the universe. We must maintain the balance. How long do you think before they find out? How long before they figure out what he's done and come for him?"

"Tristin. You're freaking out over nothing. We don't even know anything will happen. If something happens, I'll figure something out. I always do. I promise. There has to be a way to keep Ember alive and the tree worshippers off our backs. We just need more information."

She smiled into his throat. He believed that you could solve any problem in the world with an internet connection and the right password. She shivered as she felt his lips graze across her forehead, letting her eyes close for just a second.

"Dagger."

Her eyes fluttered open. "Huh?"

 95

"I love you, but you should probably take a shower."

She hid a slight smile against his shoulder. "Are you saying I stink?"

"Yeah, but in like a super sexy I'm-a-badass kind of way."

She snorted. "It's no wonder you're single."

"I'm single because my future wife refuses to acknowledge that we are fated to be together."

She burrowed closer to him. "Wow, she sounds like a real bitch. Maybe you dodged a bullet. She doesn't really sound like wife material."

He stepped back, smiling that dopey smile as he rubbed his thumb across her cheek. "Oh, I don't know, underneath that knife-wielding ass-kicking exterior, she's gotta really soft heart."

She shifted her eyes to the ground. "That scar on your thigh would beg to differ."

"So she stabbed me. Think of the story it will make at our wedding reception."

"You are impossible and annoying, so I'm going to go shower before I stab you again."

His smile split into a grin, and he wiggled his brows. "Good, I'm going to bed with the images of you showering fresh in my mind."

She snickered at the grunt he made when her water bottle connected with his shoulder, snagging the muffin as she walked past. Despite Quinn's assurances, she couldn't shake the awful feeling that things were going to get worse. She couldn't lose her brother. She *wouldn't* lose her brother. It didn't matter what she had to do.

Chapter 17

EMBER

Ember sat in the window seat of her new room, steadfastly ignoring the noise below. She sat knees to chest, staring out at the moon. She'd been in the house for two days, and she still couldn't believe this was real life. She ate pancakes with werewolves. She went grocery shopping with a reaper and a faery.

Florida was weird, so like Louisiana in some ways but different in others. She was used to the noise of the city. She craved it. Screaming drunkards, jazz music, and police sirens normally sang her to sleep, but here the noise was different, wrong. There were feet pounding up and down the stairs, music playing in the kitchen, Kai and Quinn clutching controllers and screaming at people through headsets while playing imaginary black ops soldiers.

It wasn't like she hated it there. Isa was great. She didn't give Ember a hard time for escaping to her room when everything got to be too much. Isa even pretended not to notice Ember was still awake long after she told the others she was going to sleep. Everybody was nice.

Well, except Tristin. She hated Ember, but Ember wasn't about to send her any cookie baskets either after what she did to Ember's cell phone. Isa had replaced Ember's phone with something much nicer. She'd also replaced Ember's holy sweaters and beat up boots too. She'd even given Ember an allowance that was far more generous than anything her father could have given.

Isa was like Ember's werewolf Godmother, always trying to make her comfortable. Everybody tried so hard, but it was so much. It was too much. Ember didn't want to be ungrateful; she just didn't know what to do with all of the attention.

Besides, something just felt...off. Her cell phone came with all kinds of fancy features, but she'd been unable to sync her contacts. When she'd asked Isa about it, she'd said she didn't really understand the technology stuff and said Quinn could look at it. Ember had access to the internet, but her email password suddenly didn't work. She was probably just being paranoid.

As promised, her room sat at the end of the hall, giving her as much privacy as a house could holding this many people. It overlooked the woods to the south side of the property so she didn't even have to worry about passing cars. She was completely isolated.

It was kind of spooky at night, the way the moonlight cut through the trees, making even the mundane look more ominous. Leaves shook on swaying branches, sounding like a pit of angry rattlesnakes. From inside, it gave the strange illusion of it being cold and breezy like it would be anywhere else in November. It was just a trick, though.

The humidity in Florida was a thousand percent, maybe higher. It sucked the breath from her lungs and made her already unmanageable hair impossible.

There was a light knock on her door.

"Yeah?"

Kai poked his head in. "Can I come in?"

She smiled at him. "Sure."

It was weird to look at somebody and see her own strange eyes looking back. On her, they looked eerie, but on her cousin, they were attractive. Kai flopped down on her bed and made himself comfortable. She glanced at the vacant twin bed sitting opposite her own and sighed. It seemed even reapers wanted things to smell like them.

"So, just checking in. Are we driving you crazy? Is that why you hide up here?"

She smirked at him. "No, that's not it. I just don't know how to deal with so many people. I'm like a Martian. I don't understand your ways."

Kai laughed. He grabbed one of the small ornate throw pillows from her bed, tossing it in the air and catching it. "I'm sure we can be annoying. We annoy each other, and most of us have lived together forever."

"Why is that?" Ember asked. "How did two reapers end up living with a pack of wolves, a human and a…faery?"

Kai thought about it for a while. "I don't know, really. It was such a long time ago. I just remember Allister bringing us here and telling us this was our new home."

"But who took care of you? Isa couldn't have been much older than we are now."

"Younger. She was sixteen when she became alpha. She didn't even get to finish school. She took care of Rhys, Tristin, and me. Allister found somebody to help run the restaurant, but other than that, Isa was on her own." He smirked. "Well, until Wren came courting."

"What about Quinn and Donovan? What about Wren and Neoma?"

He laughed. "Quinn and I met in class. He was the only one who would talk to me. Since our moms ran the council when everything went down twelve years ago, they were still blaming reapers for what happened back then. Tristin and I didn't have any friends. The kids who did acknowledge us just made fun of us, but not Quinn. He just sat down and started talking."

"Everybody keeps talking about this thing that happened twelve years ago. What is it? I don't understand. What happened to all of your parents? What happened to my mom? Why don't I remember anything?"

Kai shook his head. "I wish I could tell you, but nobody knows. Well, maybe people know, but they won't talk, especially to us. Everybody is always telling us we will understand when we're older, but I

 99

think it's a lie. I don't even know if they know what happened here. All I know is everything changed when it did."

"Do you remember me? Cause I don't remember you."

He thought about it for a long moment. "It's strange. My memories of my life before everything changed are…I don't know how to explain it." His eyes narrowed in concentration. "Okay, like, when I remember events that happened to me after, they play like a movie. I can replay it in my mind. But everything before…the people…the events…are like photographs. Just single still moments. I can see your face, but I don't remember us playing together. I can see my mom, but I don't remember hugging her or her voice." There was a hitch in his breath as he finished.

She hadn't meant to upset him. "I don't remember my mother at all. I've only seen one photo of her. I don't know what's worse."

"I don't know either."

He blinked rapidly, and she couldn't handle the sad look on his face.

She changed the subject, realizing she didn't want to talk about her mom either. "Tell me about how you met the rest of the pack."

"Donovan showed up about eight months ago. He stumbled over the county line, and we found him bleeding out in the woods. He was barely recognizable. We didn't even know he was a wolf at first glance."

"That's awful."

"We don't normally let outsiders into our territory, but he was so injured Isa didn't think he'd survive the night. When he finally woke up, he told us his pack was forcing him to fight other wolves for sport. That was it. He never left. Isa never met a stray she didn't like."

Including me, she thought. "What's an omega?"

"Omega's are sort of loners, I guess? In some packs, they are the lowest in the pack, but they are also wolves that are part of a pack but like their space. Donovan disappears a lot. He doesn't go far, but he'll full shift for a few days and live in the woods. He doesn't like to be tied down."

 100

She nodded as if it made any sense at all but didn't press further. "And Wren and Neoma?" Ember asked, almost afraid to know. Each story seemed more horrid then the last.

"Neoma came with Wren. As for how she met Wren, that story is hers to tell. It's…intense. She may tell you one day. As for Wren and Isa, they've been betrothed since before they were born. It's an arranged marriage."

"You're lying," Ember gaped at him. "No way, they are all googly-eyed over each other."

"Now." Kai laughed. "You weren't here when Wren showed up to say he was sent by his pack to enforce the betrothal. Isa punched him in the face, went full shift, and tried to rip his throat out in the doorway, almost succeeded too. He's been in love ever since."

"But, an arranged marriage? Really. Isn't that sort of old fashioned?"

Kai tossed the pillow, reaching out and snatching it from the air as it went wide. "It used to be common in packs years ago. It's such an antiquated notion nobody really cares about enforcing them outside of pack politics. Most betrothals are for show, a way to honor traditions and let other packs know two packs are allied. Sometimes when packs are small like ours, they are perceived as weak, and sometimes an alpha will agree to follow through for the good of the pack."

"So, they are only married because his pack wants them too?"

Kai barked out a laugh. "Hah, no. After Isa was done whipping Wren's butt all over our front lawn, she stopped long enough to listen to his side. He wasn't trying to stake a claim as alpha of our pack. He doesn't even want to take over as alpha of his own pack. Wren prefers to take orders, which works out well because Isa prefers giving them."

Ember could see Wren wanting to take orders. He was tough and smart, but he wasn't a strategist. He was more a kill-first-ask-questions-later type. Isa seemed to think everything through to make the best decisions for the pack.

"Couldn't they just rule together?"

Kai arched a brow and gave her a look. "It's a nice theory, but somebody has to have the final say."

"So, what happened?"

 101

Ember listened as he talked, telling her the story of how Wren and Isa fell in love. His voice was soothing, and the steady rhythm of him throwing and catching the pillow was luring her into a trance. She let her head lull to the side, her gaze falling to the edge of the property. She sat up with a gasp at the figure standing below. She looked to Kai and back, but the figure was gone.

"What? What is it?" Kai was on his feet and staring out the window.

"Nothing," she said, her cheeks going red. She didn't know why she lied. "I guess I just caught my reflection."

"It's the woods," he said. She stiffened as he put a hand on her shoulder. "It makes you see things."

There was a stilted knock before Rhys stuck his head around the corner, looking at Kai. "Hey, we gotta go. Somebody spotted something weird out in the woods."

Kai frowned looking out Ember's window. "Where?"

"Somewhere off of Highgate Road. Why?"

Kai just shook his head, giving the woods outside her window one final glance.

He sighed, gently setting her pillow back in place. "Sorry."

"It's fine," she said. "I think I just need some sleep."

"Okay," he said. "See you in the morning."

Ember sighed. The group seemed to disappear at least once a night to investigate something weird. Kai said it was the price of pack admission, something about protecting their borders.

"Thanks for keeping me company," she said.

"You could come downstairs. We don't bite. Well, you know what I mean."

She smiled, but her mind was racing. "I know. I will."

As soon as the door closed, she flipped her lights off and returned to the window seat. She snagged her pillow and comforter, setting up her post at the window. There was no way it was possible, but it had to have been him. She chewed at her thumbnail, scanning the property for any sign of movement. He was out there. He was watching her just like at the funeral. She could feel him like an invisible cord tugging at her center.

Mace was in Belle Haven.

Chapter 18

KAI

"Are you sure she said it was Mrs. Carlton?" Rhys asked Kai for the tenth time.

"Yes," Kai snapped, shoving back an errant branch and slapping at a mosquito on his neck. Rhys's boots beat out a steady cadence behind him as they crunched through beds of pine needles.

Kai stepped on a tree branch, and it cracked loud enough to make him jump.

"Could you make a little more noise?" Rhys muttered.

Kai flung a glare over his shoulder. "Oh, right, we might spook it. How well do zombies hear?"

He didn't get why he had to be traipsing around in the woods with Rhys while Tristin, Wren, and Quinn got to hang out at home. Isa was sending them out on a wild zombie chase all on the word of a disturbed old lady. Everybody knew Sylvia Goode was crazy. She called at least twice a week claiming to see the craziest things. Six months ago, she claimed she'd caught a unicorn. The whole thing was ridiculous.

"We don't know it's a zombie," Rhys grumbled.

Kai's footsteps fell with more force as he thought about it. Mrs. Carlton had been dead for eight weeks. Isa was obviously still mad at him. This was a punishment. It had to be. She could have sent him out there with anybody. But no, as usual, it was Rhys. It was always Rhys.

"No, there's an excellent chance it's a delusional fantasy created by a demented old witch," Kai said, letting go of a branch, smiling as it smacked hard against Rhys's chest.

The wolf grunted. "But what if it's a revenant?"

Kai rolled his eyes at the fancy term. "*Zombies,*" he emphasized. "Don't exist because we only have five registered reanimators in the world, and none of them are permitted to use their magic."

"What if one of them went rogue?"

Kai couldn't help but snort. "A reanimator went rogue and turned my third grade teacher into a flesh-eating zombie? What would be the point of that exactly?"

"What is the point of any of the things these grims do? Evil things do evil-like things, it's sort of their…thing."

Kai snickered before he could catch himself. He risked a glance back at the wolf, hoping the slip up wouldn't have Rhys dropping into embarrassed silence. Kai lived to mock Rhys—he considered it his life's work really—but he tried not to mock Rhys when he fumbled for words. He'd gotten enough of that when he was a kid.

"Even evil things have to have a reason to evil. No matter how random it may seem to us. I can't imagine some random reanimator wandering through town and deciding to raise some old lady's body for kicks. It just seems…farfetched."

Rhys scoffed. "Last week, Quinn had to disinfect a wound on my side caused by a manticore, but a rogue reanimator seems farfetched?"

Kai cringed at the thought of that bite on Rhys's side. That thing had been nasty. It seemed some new creature was wandering into their territory almost every day lately, like they had turned on a vacancy sign. Kai turned to snark back a reply but instead found himself abruptly yanked back against Rhys's chest. "What the f—" Rhys clamped a hand over Kai's mouth.

"Shh," Rhys said against Kai's ear. "Listen."

Kai froze, eyes drifting closed. It was faint, a strange scraping sound and then something clanging softly, like an old ship's bell. "Where's it coming from?" he asked, his lips moving against skin, his voice inaudible to human ears.

Rhys's muscles tightened, dropping his palm from Kai's mouth. Kai could practically feel him concentrating. "I think it's the old school. It sounds like the flagpole."

"Isn't it condemned?" Kai asked, trying to focus on anything but the feel of Rhys plastered to his back.

"What does that matter?" Rhys asked.

It didn't really, but how was he supposed to concentrate with Rhys that close? He was glad it was dark so he couldn't see the heat rising under his skin. "Let's just go," he muttered.

They crept closer to the noise, scanning the trees as they went, not entirely sure what they were looking for. It could be an animal, but the cold feeling in his gut was telling him otherwise. If there was one thing he'd learned, in this freaking town they could be dealing with anything.

They stopped at the edge of the tree line butting up to the school property. The bell sound they heard was indeed the flagpole, a metal loop clanged at the top where it still held the tattered pieces of an American flag. The place looked like a construction zone. Yellow caution tape wrapped around the columns of the school's entrance, and tiny red flags stuck up from various parts of the ground, warning of danger that Kai's eyes couldn't make out in the dark. Several pieces of equipment sat on the property, including a bulldozer that had seen better days.

He found the source of the scraping noise and recoiled. "Oh, that is so wrong," he groaned.

The metal spikes on the bottom of the bulldozer's bucket pierced what had once been Mrs. Carlson through her abdomen, holding her hostage in front of the dilapidated school. She was still moving. Her hands scraped uselessly against the rusted metal bucket, though it didn't appear she was trying to free herself. It didn't appear she was doing anything. She was just...there.

"What was it you were saying about zombies not existing?"

 105

"Don't gloat, it's unbecoming." Kai squinted, noting the way her mouth opened and closed like a fish out of water. Her skin looked grey and sloughed off in places. So gross. "What do you think she's doing all the way out here?"

Rhys shrugged. "Don't know. Maybe she was trying to get back to the school?"

That was the most depressing thing Kai had ever heard. He couldn't imagine coming back from the dead and trying to go back to work. "This doesn't make sense. Don't you think your wolfy senses would have picked up a reanimator?"

"Why didn't your reaper senses pick up a reanimator?" Rhys snapped back.

"I don't have super awesome hearing or X-ray vision. You're the superhero," Kai said.

"Then I'm putting in for a new sidekick. A quieter one," Rhys snarked, his tone conversational.

Kai rolled his eyes in the dark. "Whatever. The only thing that really matters is what do we do with her?"

"It's not a her; it's an it. It's not alive."

"She looks pretty alive to me," Kai said.

"Semantics. What do we do? How do we kill it?"

Kai shrugged. "Text Quinn?"

Rhys nodded once.

Kai dutifully reached for his phone. *Mrs. Carlton is a zombie, how do we ice her?*

The response came immediately. *Seriously? Take a picture.*

Kai snapped a picture and sent it because he was a good friend.

"Really?" Rhys asked, exasperated.

So cool. How do you think it happened? Is there some kind of rogue reanimator roaming around Belle Haven?

Sometimes Kai felt like he lived in a real life episode of Scooby Doo.

You too? I don't know. Focus. How do we stop her-it-her, dammit.

I don't know, not a lot of hands on experience with zombies. In the movies, you sever the brainstem.

 106

Aww, come on, man. She taught me how to multiply my nines, and you want me to stab her in the head?

I don't want you to do anything. I didn't even know zombies were a possibility. My only reference materials are The Walking Dead, comics and some very outdated human google references.

K. Keep you posted.

Rhys leaned against a nearby pine tree, massive arms folded across his chest. "Well?"

"Sever the brainstem."

Rhys pulled the knife strapped to his leg and handed it to Kai handle first.

"Why do I have to do it?"

Rhys's mouth hitched at the corner. "She was your math teacher; given how you feel about math, I thought you might be feeling vengeful."

Kai rolled his eyes. Mrs. Carlson was nice. He had no interest in stabbing her in the head. He snatched the knife anyway, marching forward with determination. As he got closer, his resolve flagged.

She didn't look like somebody who'd been dead for two months. She looked…well, dead and rotting, but not as much as he would have imagined. Up close, her skin was grey in some places and black in others. She looked at him with vacant eyes, jaw snapping and hands reaching for him. Her nails were torn and jagged, caked with dirt. He shuddered. She'd crawled through six feet of dirt and rocks and roots only to be thwarted by an errant piece of construction equipment.

He stood, frozen; he'd never killed anybody he knew before. After a minute, Rhys pulled him away and tugged the knife from his hand. His mouth was a hard line as he held her head still; Kai looked away as Rhys drove the blade into the base of her skull. Kai still couldn't escape the slick scraping sound of the blade dragging through flesh and bone.

Her body went slack. Kai didn't know if he was relieved or disappointed she'd gone so easily. Rhys wiped the knife on his pant leg and shoved it back into its sheath.

"Now what do we do with her?" Kai whispered.

Rhys's brow furrowed. "Why are you whispering now? She can't hear you."

He was whispering because he was spooked. He couldn't shake the feeling he was missing something.

Rhys pulled her from the blades of the bulldozer as if she weighed nothing and laid her on the gravel patch where the grass had long since given up. He pulled the lighter fluid from his back pocket, dousing the body.

"Dude, what are you doing?"

Rhys looked at him as if he was nuts. "What do you think I'm doing? I'm burning the body. We don't know if she's dead, dead. No body, no reanimation."

Kai nodded; Rhys wasn't wrong. There was a reason so many residents chose cremation. Nobody wanted their graves robbed for spells or their bodies desecrated for any other nefarious purposes. It was the smart thing to do; Kai just hated the smell of burning flesh.

He sat on the step of the school's porch, as flames engulfed her body. Rhys leaned against the railing, testing it first to make sure it could hold him.

"I feel like we're missing something," Kai finally said aloud.

"Everything feels...different since Ember got here. Not bad but...am I crazy? Can you feel it too?"

Rhys nodded but said nothing.

"You don't think..." He let the idea die on his lips. It was impossible. There was no way Ember could do this. Except there was Tristin, his brain argued. Maybe Tristin wasn't a reaper because of the twin bond. Maybe it was their family. Ember did have the mark. Could Ember be a reanimator?

"You smell like anxiety," Rhys grumbled, his hand shooting out to touch Kai. He knew better than to read anything into it. Wolf DNA made Rhys's need to comfort override his loathing of Kai.

"We need to find out what's going on with Ember," he said finally, trying not to dwell on how pathetic he felt as he pushed into Rhys's touch.

Chapter 19

EMBER

Monday came faster than Ember anticipated. It turned out enrolling in high school in a mystically charged town was surprisingly easy. They didn't seem too concerned with the proper paperwork and documentation. Ember was almost disappointed. The idea of school made her stomach turn. She wasn't sure she could handle it if things went badly there too. Isa assured her she had a built-in clique. She'd never be alone here.

"I can't believe they didn't at least ask for my ID or a social or anything," Ember remarked to Tristin.

"Well, when everybody here could easily conjure up whatever documents they ask for, it doesn't really seem worth worrying about," Tristin said. They waited outside the office for Ember's schedule.

Kai and Quinn stood nearby at their lockers, deeply engrossed in what was probably a conversation about video games, comic books, or obscure eighties movies. It seemed to be the only topics the two of them ever discussed. Kai's eyes cut to a stocky blonde guy, words dying on his lips as the guy strode down the hall. He had too many muscles and a smirk on his face. On his way past, he gave Ember a leer so invasive she wanted to go home and shower. Before Ember could even think to respond he was turning his attention to Tristin, winking at her. She made a gesture that implied she was vomiting.

When he saw Kai, he sneered and said loudly, "Hey, Lonergan, made your sister scream lately?"

Kai smirked as all eyes in the hallway rolled towards him. "No," Kai said. "But your brother looked pretty satisfied when he left the other night."

The guy's face contorted in rage, and he launched himself sloppily at Kai. To her cousin's credit, he didn't even flinch at the large fist heading towards his face. It never hit its target. Instead, Rhys was there, eyes flashing, a deep growl rumbling from his chest as he held the boy's fist in a crushing grip.

Ember's heart pumped double time. Where did Rhys even come from? Did he just lurk in the shadows waiting to fight with somebody? How old was he?

"Walk. Away," Rhys rumbled in a tone no human could match. He used the boy's own fist to shove him backwards, hard enough for him to fall on his ass.

"Your bodyguard won't always be here to protect you, bitch," the other boy told Kai.

"Big talk from a guy named Eugene," Quinn piped up from where he stood just out of the way.

"It's a family name," the boy spit, rubbing his bruised hindquarters as he walked away.

Quinn smirked, pleased with the outburst.

Kai's chest was heaving, but it seemed to have more to do with his proximity to the wolf than the excitement of the confrontation. He punched Rhys's chest, flinching as his fist made contact with the solid wall of muscle. "I could've handled that myself."

He glared at Kai, nostrils doing that weird flare thing he did whenever in Kai's presence.

"Really? Cause you looked like you were about to handle it by getting punched in the face."

Kai flushed from his neck to his hairline. "Nobody asked for your help," he whispered.

The wolf placed a hand on Kai's chest, pressing him back to the locker. "My sister will kill me if I let anything happen to her pet."

  110

He leaned forward, his lips inches from Kai's ear. "Stay. Out. Of. Trouble," Rhys snarled, before turning and walking away.

Ember didn't get what his problem was. He was such a jerk. He had about Kai's crush, right? Her cousin stared down the hall before straightening his bunched-up shirt.

"Whatever, douche," he muttered to the werewolf's retreating back. Rhys's shoulders stiffened, but he kept walking.

Well, so far, it appeared super powers didn't make high school suck any less. She had government first period, which meant separating from her cousins.

Kai smiled at her encouragingly. "Don't worry, Donovan and Neoma are both in that class. They'll keep an eye on you."

Tristin rolled her eyes. "It's not her first day of preschool. She doesn't need a babysitter." She grabbed his arm. "Come on."

Walking into the room actually felt exactly like her first day of preschool. These people all knew each other. She could already feel herself starting to sweat. Nice, that's attractive. She straightened the skirt of her new dress and took a deep breath. Maybe she could just make a run for it.

"Hey, hot stuff."

The squeak that erupted from her was both mouse-like and embarrassing. This delighted her attacker all the more. He kissed her cheek before dancing away.

"Donovan!" She wheezed in exasperation, narrowing her eyes at him. He was wearing yet another sleeveless hoodie, a royal blue one that made his Husky blue eyes even lighter. Did this school even have a dress code? She was positive that his biceps were going to distract her from learning about their government.

A dark-haired man, who she could only assume was the teacher, sat at the front of the room. He didn't look like the teachers at South Oleander High. He wore jeans and a red-checkered shirt. He'd rolled his sleeves to his elbows, revealing tattoos running all the way down to his fingers. They resembled runes she'd seen in her dad's books on alchemy. He wore black-framed glasses, and he was, objectively speaking, good looking...well, for somebody who was her dad's age. Gotta love that paranormal DNA.

"Excuse me, Mr. Bishop?"

He didn't look up. "Yes?" What was with the people in this town not making eye contact? "I'm new. Ms. Kelley told me to give this to you."

She slid the paper underneath his nose. He pushed it to the side. "Thank you. Take a seat."

She turned to scan the classroom. Donovan gestured grandly to the empty seat next to him in the second to last row. Neoma had taken a seat behind him, and she smiled shyly at Ember. She scowled at Donovan on principle but was relieved she didn't have to look for an empty seat. She smiled at Neoma as she settled.

The moment the bell rang the teacher looked up. He stood, smiling at the class. "Good morning, young people. It appears we have a new student."

All eyes turned to her. "Our new student is…" He faltered, looking apologetic as he struggled to reach the piece of paper he'd left on his desk. "November Lon—" he stopped abruptly, his eyes skittering to hers, startled. He recovered, clearing his throat. "Lonergan. November

Lonergan. Welcome, November." His voice died off, and he stared at her as if he'd seen a ghost.

"Ember," she corrected. "Just Ember."

He smiled tightly. "Of course, Ember it is." He shoved the piece of paper in his pocket. "I hope you're better at government than the other Lonergans I know. Okay, people, open your books to chapter six."

A girl in the front row watched Ember all the way to her seat. The girl had black hair, ivory skin, and an extremely nasty scowl on her face. If Snow White and Dracula had produced a child, it would have been this girl. Ember took her seat, giving the girl one last look before Ember opened her book.

The rest of the class was uneventful, though she could feel the eyes of the other students boring into her. As class ended, people filed out.

"Ms. Lonergan, may I have a word?" the teacher called out.

"See you at lunch?" Donovan asked, slinging an arm around Neoma.

She nodded absently before she walked towards the teacher. "Yes, sir?"

"You don't have to call me sir. Most kids just call me Alex."

"That's weird," she said, not entirely sure what to make of him. He seemed like he was trying too hard.

"Do you know who I am?"

She stared at him for a full minute before cautiously answering, "You are Mr. Bishop, my government teacher?"

"That's not quite what I meant."

Why was everybody in this town so enigmatic? "Should I know who you are?"

"I would hope so. I'm your uncle."

Ember felt herself go numb to her fingertips. Tiny little sparks licked up her arms like she stuck a fork in a light socket. She took a few deep breaths. She couldn't get all charged up at school. There was no ice water to hose her down.

"I'm pretty sure my cousins would have mentioned my teacher was also my uncle."

He laughed humorlessly. "I'm almost certain you are wrong about that. I suppose you're staying in that makeshift boarding house with those wolves?"

She thought of the six-bedroom house with its insanely large bathrooms. "I'm hardly staying at a youth hostel."

"Your father wouldn't want you there," he snapped. Ember flinched, taking a step back. His tone softened. "Listen, Kai and Tristin didn't have any choice about where they lived. All their family is gone. You have choices. You aren't like them."

"You're telling me I'm a witch?"

"Kai is a reaper. Only one exists at a time in a family. He inherited the gift…" He looked like the word stuck in his throat. "When his mother died. You certainly aren't human. I can feel the energy coming off you."

That really didn't answer her question. He talked like a politician. This information only made the energy tingling over her move faster. "I don't even know you."

"You don't know them either," he reminded her.

"No, but they came to find me. Why didn't you ever come to look for me? Why didn't my dad ever mention you? If you and my dad were so tight, why were we living in Louisiana under an assumed name? Did you know I was alive?"

The older man paled at the barrage of questions, but Ember didn't care. She could feel her anger building. "If we were such a close family, where were you while my dad was drinking himself to death? While our family was unraveling?"

"Ember, please calm down. I promise, if I would've known about you, I would've come to find you. I thought you were dead," he said beseechingly. "We *all* thought you were dead."

"So, I guess the question is, why didn't my dad trust his own brother to know we were still alive?"

He heaved a sigh. "Ember—"

"I'm fine where I am," she said numbly. She grabbed her bag, walking quickly through the door. She jumped as she came face to face with Donovan. She slapped one of his arms. "Stop scaring me. Were you eavesdropping on my conversation?"

He shrugged, not denying it. "Listen, I'm not going to tell you what to do, but I will tell you the witches lie. They lie about anything. They will do or say anything to maintain the balance."

He pulled his hood up and shoved his hands deeper into his jacket pockets. He looked ridiculous.

"And not for nothing," he said, walking backwards away from her down the hall. "But your uncle just lied to you."

 114

Chapter 20

EMBER

Every class put her more on edge. Each teacher greeted her with the same dropped jaw fascination as her fellow students. She was a ghost returned from the dead and the entire school seemed intent on treating her as such. By lunch, she was starving, and her head was pounding.

Quinn knocked into her shoulder gently in the lunch line, guiding her along and joking about nothing while she piled food onto her plate. He offered to carry her tray, but given his ongoing struggle with gravity, Ember declined.

Once he paid, he guided her to a table. She felt the knot in her chest come undone. For the first time in her life, she didn't have to search for some place to sit at lunch or hide in the bathroom.

Everybody was there but Neoma. Quinn said she'd left early to help Isa with a catering job. Even Rhys lurked at the end of the long table, brooding over his pizza like it wronged his family. Kai and Donovan parted for her to sit between them as Quinn dropped down next to Tristin. She smiled gratefully. She started shoving fries into her mouth, moaning obscenely at the taste of salt and carbs. She barely stopped to chew.

"God, I'm starving all the time lately," she said to nobody in particular.

The wolves all nodded in understanding. She noted the massive quantities of food piled on their plates as well. Not that it stopped Donovan from trying to steal her fries. They must expend a lot of energy. Even Kai seemed to be eating more than the average human.

The only person who seemed concerned about caloric intake was Tristin. She ate a spinach salad and salmon. There was no way she bought that at the cafeteria. She must have packed her lunch. For some reason the idea of her badass cousin carrying a lunchbox was amusing, not that she'd ever dare say so.

Once she'd finished her pile of fries, her cheeseburger, and three bites of her pizza she asked Donovan, "What did you mean after first period? You said my uncle lied. How would you know if my uncle was lying?"

Kai and Tristin looked at each other, so she addressed them too. "Yeah, I know you didn't tell me about my uncle. Did you really think I would somehow make it through his class without him saying anything about the return of his long lost *dead* niece?"

They looked sheepish. "It was Allister's idea. We wanted to catch him off guard. See how he responded. We knew Donovan would be there to watch his reactions. This whole town thought you were dead. They thought your dad was dead. We just wanted to see if he'd known the whole time," Kai said.

"Granted, it was a poorly executed plan," Quinn said, shrugging. "But we tried."

"So…how do you know he lied?" Ember gestured to Donovan.

"Wolves have excellent hearing, and our sense of smell works differently. When Alex told you he didn't know you were alive, his heartbeat told me he was lying, and he smelled weird, kind of sour. He smelled like a lie."

"So, I'm not a witch?" she asked. Donovan's gaze dropped down to his plate before he looked to Tristin and Kai.

Quinn spoke first. "That's a little more complicated. Witches usually have a really obvious scent. You can smell their magic. The wolves say you don't smell like a witch. You don't smell like anything they've scented before, right?" Donovan and Rhys nodded.

"It's not like you can trust anything your uncle says anyway. We all know the witches are dirty liars," Tristin grumbled, snatching one of Quinn's fries.

"Wow, little brother, are you just going to sit there and let your girlfriend slander us like that?"

Quinn glanced up to the girl standing behind Rhys giving her a flat smile. She shared his same dark brown hair and golden eyes. She wore her long hair braided down her back in a complicated way that looked like it took hours, and she dressed like she'd stepped out of a fashion magazine. She couldn't be more different than her brother.

Every muscle in the wolves' bodies tensed. If they'd been in wolf form, hackles would've raised all around. "Aww," he pouted. "The truth hurts, sis."

She snorted, glancing around the table with disdain. "I'll never get why you hang out with these…orphans when you have a family at home who loves you."

"Hah," he said. "That's rich, coming from you, Astrid. Dad barely tolerates me and treats me like I'm useless. I have a place in the pack. They treat me like an equal."

Kai threw his arm around Quinn's shoulders, squeezing affectionately. "Aww, you're an equal, man. Even if you are a smooshy human." Kai's leg jerked, and he hissed in pain, looking at his sister with hurt eyes. "Ow. What the hell?"

She smiled, eyes glittering meanly. "Just reminding you that you too are a smooshy human."

"It was the sentiment…" He grumbled, rubbing at his shin. Quinn beamed at Tristin, winking at her. She rewarded him with a bored expression and an epic eye roll.

The girl who had been watching Ember in class came to stand next to Astrid. Ember supposed one might find her pretty in a gothic horror movie kind of way.

"Alex is right, you know," the girl said, trailing one too long red nail across Rhys's shoulder. "You should be with your own kind, not this ragtag band of losers."

Quinn glared at the girl.

"Aww," she pouted. "Truth hurts, doesn't it?"

 117

Beside her, Kai tensed, eyes following the girl's hand along the wolf's shoulder. "Settle down, Cruella, no need for name-calling. Isn't there a fresh batch of puppies for you to skin?"

"Mmm." She grinned, leaning into Rhys to simper sweetly. "There's one puppy whose skin always looks yummy."

Rhys looked pained, swatting her hand away. "Go away, Stella."

The girl shrugged, like she was used to Rhys blowing off her advances, and walked around the table slowly until she stood behind Ember. Ember stiffened; she couldn't help it. She didn't like having Stella so close. She leaned down, closing her eyes and inhaling deeply.

Her magic rippled along her skin, bristling at the intrusion into her personal space. "I'm getting real tired of people sniffing me."

The girl pushed her hair behind her ear, batting her clearly fake lashes. "Let's go, Astrid. She's not one of us. You can practically smell the stench of reaper on her. That's almost as bad as people who breed with animals."

Astrid snickered, but Ember let her eyes go blank, making sure she met the girl's gaze with laser focus. At first they laughed, but it only took about forty-five seconds of awkward staring before Stella cracked. "What are you staring at, freak?"

"Sorry, you two were being so melodramatic. I was waiting for one of you to scream, 'Filthy mudblood' in a horrible British accent." Ember made sure that she said the words with her own obnoxious version of an English accent, drawing the attention of the surrounding tables.

Kai and Quinn smirked at the two girls. Even Rhys almost smiled.

The two turned on their heels and returned to a table across the cafeteria. Ember asked the group, "So my dear Uncle Alex shares family business with students? That's sort of weird, right?"

Quinn shrugged. "Alex took over as head of the Red Oak coven when Allister became head of the witches' council. Since most of the coven is underage, he's mostly just a glorified babysitter." He glanced over at the table where Stella and Astrid sat huddled together with six others, whispering and pointing in her direction emphatically. That wasn't good.

"When Alex is on campus," Quinn said, drawing his attention back to Ember. "He has to treat all of us students equally. Once he sets foot off campus, he's just another witch that hates everybody but other witches."

Ember sighed. "My life was easier when I was putting makeup on dead people." She looked up to five blank stares. "What? Don't judge me. This place is exhausting."

Chapter 21

EMBER

Ember was dreaming. In her dream, she was a child, her little hands clenched in front of her, her tiny toes buried in the sand of the beach where she stood. She couldn't be older than five. Overhead the sky was a mass of thick black clouds backlit by the moon hidden underneath. Lightning snaked across the sky, and thunder boomed loud enough to rumble the ground beneath her. The sea was blood red, and the waves in the distance immense and rolling towards her. Her heart hammered in her chest, the wind whipping her hair into her face, plastering her nightgown to her body.

She held her hand up to see better, blinking against the sand blasting her skin. She knew what she had to do. She could feel it. She stumbled towards the water; she just needed to be closer. She needed to touch the water. Her fingertips tingled, and she breathed heavily, trying to contain the power suddenly itching for release. It slithered under her skin, pulsing in her hands.

She had to do it. Just like the bird. "Mommy!" she screamed, her voice sucked into the void of the storm.

The sky opened up, the rain plastering her nightgown to her body and matting her hair to her face. She was filthy, but she didn't care. She had to fix this. She could fix what she'd done.

She thrust her little hands into the air, feeling the power rip from her, her fingertips burning like it took the flesh with it, but she didn't care. Not if it worked. It had to work. The power flowed through her, pulling in through the soles of her feet and pouring out through her fingertips.

As her power dwindled, so did the rain, until all that remained was the warm wind that had started the whole thing. In the distance, a silhouette moved towards her.

"Mommy?" she called again. It was definitely a woman. Ember could see the dress, the hair, long and messy. As she grew closer, she could see the fabric of her mother's favorite dress, tattered and askew. Ember jumped up and down, pumping her tiny arms over her head as the figure lurched closer. It was her mom, but something was wrong; she didn't sway her hips or swing her arms like Ember's mom. Her motions were awkward and jerky, as if unseen strings pulled her limbs askew like a broken marionette.

"Mommy?" Ember whispered. She'd broken her mommy.

Ember yelped as thick arms yanked her backwards off her feet. She struggled to break free until she realized she was in her father's arms.

"Ember!" her father cradled her against him, eyes fixed on the figure in front of him. "Sera?" he whispered. "Oh God, Ember, what did you do? What did you do?"

"It's like the bird. I fixed her like the bird. I want mommy," she cried. "Let me go."

"Ember, stop. That's not your mother."

"Put me down," she begged, wriggling in his arms, trying to escape. "I want mommy!"

Her father pulled them down the beach and into a tiny clapboard house, closing and locking the door. "Stay away from the windows, November Isabel. That's an order."

She collapsed on the floor in tears. "I hate you. I hate you!" she screamed.

Her father paid her no attention, snatching up the phone and smashing in somebody's number, and then taking the phone into the next room. She heard the off kilter thumping footsteps as they made their way up the steps.

Step. Drag. Step. Drag.

She could make out the outline of her mother behind the thin white curtain, her hand slapping the glass and dragging down with methodical repetition. She looked to the hallway, where her father had disappeared, quietly crawling towards

the door, mouth dry and heart pounding so hard she could barely hear anything else.

She pulled back the curtain. Eyes wide, she took in the creature on the other side of the glass and screamed.

Her screams woke her. They woke everybody. Heavy footsteps pounded towards her door, and six spooked people stumbled into her room, clearly expecting something more sinister than a nightmare.

"What is it? What's happening?" Isa asked, eyes scanning every corner.

Ember was drenched in sweat, her sheets a crumpled mess on the floor. "Nightmare. God, I'm so sorry. I didn't mean to wake everybody. It was just..." She tried to get her shaking under control. "It was just so real."

Isa sat on her bed while Ember tried to get her bearings. She tried to explain her dream, but she was grasping at bits and pieces, fragments of fleeting memories. She remembered her mother and rolling seas. Ember remembered her fear. The storm. Her mother's bloated and distorted face.

"Sounds apocalyptic," Neoma said from the doorway, one delicate bare foot perched against her calf like a music box ballerina.

Wren nodded. "Sounds pretty terrifying," he agreed, sympathetic.

"Dreams of the apocalypse are often caused by a feeling of having no control over your personal life. They can also be caused by adolescent hormones, the death of a parent, or any significant loss. Given everything that's happened to you, it stands to reason you'd feel a bit out of control, and your brain would dredge up some scary end-of-days chaos. The end of the world is the ultimate way to avoid your problems." All eyes swung to Quinn.

"Did you memorize a dream dictionary?" Kai asked seriously.

"Eidetic memory, dude." Quinn winked at Ember. "I'm not completely useless."

Ember winced; that was the third time she'd heard Quinn say that. Ember blamed his dad, and she was almost positive she wasn't just projecting.

"You're not even a little bit useless," Isa assured, fondly. "Hell, lots of other people aren't pulling their weight around here." She glared at her brother.

"What?" Rhys asked. "What am I not doing? Do I not babysit your children? What would you like me to do? What the hell does he contribute?"

He thrust his head in Wren's direction. There was a flash of anger on the alpha's face before she pulled herself back. "It doesn't do well to question me, brother. But, since you are in such a helpful mood, I have a task for you." She smiled and Rhys's face fell. "You are going on a field trip, and you're going to take one of the...children."

She looked around the room as if she hadn't already made her decision. "I think you should take Kai." She smiled beatifically.

Rhys clenched his jaw so tightly that Ember could swear she heard his teeth grinding. "We have school today," he grunted.

"Well, guess what?" she snapped. "You're both sick. I'll write you a note tomorrow." She stared him down, flashing her wolf eyes at him, daring him to defy her.

He dropped his gaze. Kai looked miserable.

"Okay, kiddies," she joked. "Since it's almost five a.m., why don't we all just get up and get dressed? I'll make everybody waffles."

Quinn gazed at Isa with such love. Ember hoped their enemies never offered Quinn waffles or Wi-Fi; they'd never see him again, and she suspected his brain was more of a weapon than anybody imagined.

Chapter 22

TRISTIN

As always, chaos ensued. People were fighting over who would shower first, who needed to pee, who needed to brush their teeth. Bodies squeezed past each other in the hallway, and doors slammed with unnecessary force. Tristin was already dressed and ready to go. She didn't waste time with makeup; she just threw on her clothes, pulled her hair into a ponytail, and made for the stairs.

She wasn't trying to eavesdrop, but Isa's voice carried in the sudden quiet of the hallway.

"Allister, I'm doing the best I can."

Tristin assumed Isa was on the phone.

"Of course, I'm keeping an eye out, but I can't be obvious about it." There was a pause and then, "That couldn't be helped. No— It's been years. Nobody's ever— Yes, I get that, but it's delicate. They're dangerous. You know it's not that easy. They don't know they are prisoners."

Tristin's mouth felt sour. Had Allister created some kind of temporary prison there in town? The idea made her cringe. The pack patrolled nightly. Most of the creatures they found ended up dead, but what about the ones they turned over to the council? Were they the prisoners Isa referred to? How did somebody not know they were prisoners? Quinn was right to hate his dad; there was something so wrong about him. Isa only associated with Allister because it was necessary, but Tristin wished there was another way.

She was being unreasonable. Isa was their alpha. She always did what was good for the pack. She took care of them.

"Yes, I know what I'm doing. Everything is being handled."

Isa's cell beeped as the call ended. Tristin thought Isa was alone until Wren asked her, "Are you sure you know what you're doing?"

There was a groan. "I have literally no idea what I'm doing."

"Do you think sending the boys to Josephine is a good idea?" Wren questioned.

"I'm not sure, but she sent me that letter a year ago. She said she had a vision where Kai made a terrible mistake and Tristin's banshee powers returned. She told me when it happened I needed to send word to her. At the time, I wrote it off. I mean, she's so old. But Kai did screw up and Tristin screamed. Something bad is happening here, and clearly, Josephine has some idea what it is. I can't ignore it, Wren. She knows things."

"Why not tell Allister then?"

Isa sighed. "Because I don't trust him. I just don't."

"What if he finds out we're keeping things from him? Allister works for the Grove, Isa."

"We work for the Grove, Wren," Isa hissed back.

Tristin's breath caught, and she slapped a hand over her mouth and made for the stairs. What the hell did that mean? Isa had to answer to the witches' council, but Tristin didn't work for the Grove. The Grove didn't really get involved in shifter business. There was an agreement in place. None of it made sense. Why was Isa sending her brother and Rhys on some super-secret mission? Who the hell was Josephine? Why did she care about Tristin's banshee powers?

There was only one person who could help her with this. She needed to talk to Quinn. Tristin went downstairs and ate breakfast with everybody else, throwing elbows over waffles and bacon like everything was fine. She couldn't help but look at Isa every few minutes.

Whenever Isa caught Tristin staring, she stuffed another bite of waffle into her mouth and slid her gaze to Quinn. Quinn smiled and winked. She panicked and smiled back. Quinn's smile faltered, looking at her with a deeply honed suspicion. She stuffed another piece of bacon in her mouth and spent the rest of breakfast making pictures with the butter and syrup. By the time breakfast ended, she'd eaten her body weight in waffles. She felt sick, but she had a plan.

Guilt and bacon burned a hole through her belly as she lay in wait for him at the foot of the staircase, hoping to snag him in his waffle-induced bliss. He'd do it. He'd do anything she asked of him. That was the problem.

When she snagged him by the arm, he jumped a foot.

"What the hell, Dagger?"

"I wanted to talk to you."

He looked at her dubiously. She rarely initiated conversations with him, or anyone really.

"Um, well, if you wanted to talk, we just ate breakfast together. You sat less than a foot away from me for over an hour."

She stared him down.

"Oh," he said, frowning. "You don't want to talk to me; you want to talk at me. I should have known when you smiled at me." He sighed morosely. "Why didn't you just say so?"

"Let's go outside."

His face crumpled and he whined, "No. Not outside. Outside means that you're not only going to ask me to do something horrible, but it's so horrible you don't want the pack to know about it."

She shushed him, grabbing his hand and pulling him towards the door. She said nothing when he laced their fingers together. She dragged him all the way to the edge of the property where there was no chance even the wolves could hear.

She stood awkwardly, trying to decide the best way to ask for a favor.

"So, talk," he said. She looked down at their entwined fingers. She was going to hell for this. She took a deep breath and told him everything she'd heard. The whole thing. Quinn stared at her, blinking owlishly behind his lenses.

"So…?" she asked.

 126

"So…what?"

"So, you don't think it's strange Isa saying she works for the Grove?"

"Everybody works for the Grove, Dagger, if they want to stay on their good side."

Okay, she'd thought the same thing, but still, she had other questions. "Okay, then what did she mean by prisoner? Who's being held prisoner and where? And what does it have to do with me, Kai, and Ember? Why are my banshee powers coming back now? Why does this crazy psychic know anything about us? Can any of this save my brother from the Grove?"

She was out of breath by the time she was done and Quinn looked fascinated and, well, a little turned on. "Focus," she said, shaking their joined hands to get his attention.

"Oh, I'm focused."

Tristin rolled her eyes. "Focus on the problem at hand."

"Which is what exactly?"

"What is Isa up to, and can it help save Kai from the Grove?"

He looked sick. "Listen, Dagger, you know I love your…everything—so much—but I'm not investigating our alpha. Not even for you."

"But what if she knows how to help Kai?"

"Do you think if Isa was worried about Kai and the Grove she wouldn't do everything to protect him? He's her favorite, more than Wren, more than her own brother."

"Nobody's even talking about it. They're all too focused on helping Ember. I need you to focus on helping me help Kai."

"Help Kai?" Quinn echoed. "How do you propose we do that?"

"Quinn, your father is on the council." His eyes widened at the mention of his father. "Hell, your father *is* the council. If anybody would have information about what happens when a reaper actively prevents the death of a collected, it would be him. This can't be the first time this has happened. It just can't be."

"My father knows what Kai did. If he had any plans of addressing it, I'm pretty sure he would've done so the night Ember got here. Do you want me to point out that he hasn't pursued notifying the

Grove about what he did? You want me to casually ask my father—my father who hates me—for a favor for my friend, who he also hates?"

Tristin played with Quinn's fingers. "I didn't say I wanted you to talk to your dad."

He pulled his hand back, exasperated. "Then why did you even bring him up?"

Her eyes slid away.

"Tristin, just tell me what you want me to do already."

"Remember last summer when you hacked into your family's grimoire?"

Quinn's mouth fell open. "You mean the time my father disowned me, threw me out of the house for months, and threatened to kill me himself if I ever did it again. Yeah, I vaguely recall that."

"Last time you were trying to break into your dad's personal records. What we need is more general. We need access to the library."

"The Grove library?" Quinn asked. "Are you kidding me? Where would we even begin? The Grove holds all records. If I could even get in, which I'm sure I can't, where would we even begin to look?"

She slid her eyes away guiltily. "There has to be information on reapers. If we went in looking for that specifically…"

"Are you kidding me?" he shouted. "Do you remember how difficult it was last time, and that was just my family's personal grimoire. It took me two days, and I barely managed to read three pages before my dad shut me down. He increased not only his firewall and encryption, he maxed out the wards too."

"You are the smartest person I know. If anybody can do—"

"Tristin. Are you listening to yourself? It would take an entire coven of neo-pagan hackers to get past all the enchantments on that database. The Grove has texts dating back over a thousand years."

"It used to be public record," she pouted.

"Well there's no way we can hack into that computer. Not unless you have a coven in your back pocket I don't know about."

It wasn't worth asking if any witches would help. He was a traitor as far as they were concerned. He had defected to align himself with

 128

shifters and reapers. There was no greater sin in his father's eyes, and his father was the voice of the witch community.

Something occurred to her then. "It used to be a matter of public record."

He frowned, looking at her like she was crazy. "Yes, I heard you the first time."

"No, you don't understand. It was in a library. People checked out books, photocopied them. Took home pages to study."

"Yes, and the Grove ordered all copies destroyed."

"They ordered all non-witches to destroy their copies. Not every witch could have gone digital. Somebody has to have a copy of whatever text we need."

"Dagger, that is like looking for needles in a bank vault full of needles; poisoned needles that could turn us into toads. Where would we even start? I can promise you nobody in this town would be stupid enough to leave valuable information lying around."

"But if I could find somebody, and we could get access to the information…could you memorize it?"

He ran his hands through his hair. "If—and that is a big fat freaking if—I was to see the book, I would be able to memorize whatever I could read, but it's way too dangerous. They'd have us killed—or worse."

"What do you think they're going to do to my brother when they find out what he's done? Or me, for helping him?"

His silence was chilling. Nobody disobeyed the Grove.

"Even if we find somebody who has this information, do you think they are just going to let us see it? I'm a human, and you're a banshee; we are hardly capable of going up against witches or anything crazy enough to keep forbidden documents in their house."

"Leave that part up to me."

"Tristin, you're being crazy. You're going to waste a lot of time chasing your tail."

He used her real name. That was never a good sign. "I'd rather put my energy towards saving my brother than watching everybody else fall all over themselves trying to save the reason he's in danger in the first place."

 129

He didn't say anything for a while. "So, you need to find another reaper?"

"I need to find somebody who can help us protect my brother, ideally somebody who understands his power. We can't trust the witches to help."

"We literally have no idea what we're looking for. This is a terrible plan."

"It's the only one we've got."

"Okay," he said with a smile that didn't reach his eyes. "But if I die, you better write me the best eulogy ever."

She punched his arm. "Shut up. Let's get back before anybody notices we're gone."

"I'll just tell them we were making out."

"You might want to come up with something they'll believe."

"Someday, Tristin Lonergan, you will regret not locking this down when you had the chance."

She snickered as his strut off was ruined by a poorly placed tree root. She stepped over him as he sprawled in the grass. "I'm sure my devastation will be endless."

Chapter 23

KAI

Kai couldn't believe he was back in the car again. This time he wasn't making the four-hour drive to Louisiana. Nope, this time Rhys was dragging Kai out to the swamps of the Florida Everglades. He hated the Everglades. It took forever to get there.

He couldn't think of anything worse than Isa trapping him in the car with Rhys for almost eight hours just to visit the land of mosquitos, gators, and pythons.

"I *hate* the Everglades," he told the wolf, Kai's voice gunshot loud in the silence.

Rhys snorted. "Not exactly my dream destination, either." Kai cut his eyes at Rhys and he shrugged. "What? This wasn't my idea."

As the silence stretched on, Kai assumed the wolf had nothing more to say on the matter. Good, it sucked trying to carry on a conversation with somebody who was monosyllabic at best. Kai leaned the passenger seat back. It wasn't as if his highness was going to let Kai drive anyway. Nope, Captain Control Issues never let anybody drive his baby.

Kai closed his eyes and tried not to think about the fact that Rhys was close enough to feel the heat of his body. Stupid werewolves and their stupid body temperatures. Kai turned his face towards the window, not thinking about how good the other boy smelled, or the way his shirt stretched too tight across his shoulders. Kai scrunched his eyes closed and pulled his cap over them to block the strobe of the passing streetlights.

It would be light soon. He was just drifting off when a large finger poked his ribs. "Hey. No sleeping. We need to talk about what we're going to do when we get there."

Kai blew his breath out through his nose. "Fine," he said through clenched teeth. He fixed his hat and let his chair rocket back into the upright position hard enough it shook behind him.

"Hey, careful," Rhys admonished. "This car is a classic." He stroked the steering wheel like he was soothing a child.

"Yes, my liege," Kai said drolly, flicking his hand in a sort of flamboyant salute.

"You're such a dick," the wolf grumbled.

After five minutes of total silence, Kai prompted, "So…are you going to tell me what this mysterious super-secret assignment is? Because for now, all I know is we're heading to the Everglades. The only reason people go there is for a body dump."

Rhys paused enough for Kai's heart to start pounding. Oh, God. He could not handle a body dump.

The wolf must have heard the uptick of his heart. He rolled his eyes at Kai. "Calm down, there's no body in the trunk. Like I'd put a dead body in this car. That's what the truck is for. Isa wants us to reach out to the wolves in the Glades. There's an elder out there who she thinks may have some information about Ember."

"Why would an elder wolf have knowledge of a kinda-sorta-maybe-if-you-squint-hard witch?"

Rhys stared at him balefully. "I didn't say she was an elder wolf."

"So she's a…?"

"Witch, really old and really powerful."

Kai looked at him in disbelief. "There's a super powerful witch living in wolf territory? Surrounded by her enemies? That's ballsy."

Rhys set his jaw, cutting his eyes at Kai for a moment. Rhys's constant sour disposition must be hard on his teeth.

  132

"Like…I…said," Rhys started, drawing Kai's attention back to the conversation at hand. "She's really old. She has been the pack's witch for a long time. She chose to stay with the pack rather than deal with all the…politics that erupted when everything fell apart."

"So she's living with the pack?" That was unheard of. He was surprised the higher ups let her get away with it. She must have some kind of mojo if the tree worshipers weren't getting involved.

"Isa says these wolves have cut themselves off from the world. They revere Ms. Josephine. They aren't going to want to let us talk to her. If you think the witches are secretive, you haven't seen the Glades shifters. They are highly suspicious of others, especially non-shifters." He eyed Kai pointedly.

"Yeah, I get it, non-shifter here." He moved in his seat, pressing his hand against the glass of the window, following the drops the condensation made on the outside of the pane. "So, how dangerous is this little mission?"

Rhys contemplated the question before saying, "Not as bad as the succubus this summer but more dangerous than the baby vamps in April."

"Great." That succubus had infected a visiting wolf from another pack and mind melded him into almost killing Isa and Rhys. Rhys had ended up with a broken clavicle, a shattered pelvis and a really large dagger shoved through his spleen. Luckily, it was wood and not silver. To date, it was the worst night of Kai's life. He was pretty sure it wasn't Rhys' best memory either. The baby vamps had put up a fight, but they were too new, all bitten, no born. They had eventually left quietly with the pack, sustaining only minor injuries.

"If this pack won't trust me, why did she send me and not Wren or Donovan? Or why not just come herself?"

Rhys looked his way, expression guarded. "You know alphas don't go into another alpha's territory without permission. It's not like we could shoot them a text or an email to let them know she'd like a meeting. Besides, Isa wouldn't leave the others, not until we know what Ember is. As for why she sent you? That's easy. To annoy me, obviously."

Kai's insides twisted. "Wow, such a charmer. Sometimes I'm shocked you're single."

Rhys nostrils flared, his look going from smug to constipated to expressionless.

Rhys fell silent again, so Kai chose to pass the time the usual way, by irritating the wolf. "So, Isa sent me out into the middle of the swamp with a guy who finds me annoying. I'm having a hard time thinking you'd have my back." Kai did his best to look leery. "I mean, if I'm so annoying, maybe you'll just let one of these wolves solve your little problem once and for all. You'd never have to worry again."

Rhys gave a longsuffering sigh, like he was onto Kai's plan but couldn't help but take the bait. "I just said you annoy me. I didn't say I wanted you dead."

"Oh, well, in that case…" His hand flailed uselessly.

"I've never not had your back."

"Maybe you've just never had the opportunity to get rid of me." He had started the conversation to be funny, but he was getting irritated, though he couldn't pinpoint exactly why. The silence stretched for so long, he figured Rhys considered the conversation done.

"I wouldn't let anything happen to you," he said, so softly Kai almost missed it.

Kai knew Rhys could hear his heart flip-flop in his chest, but he couldn't help it. It was the nicest thing Rhys had ever said to Kai. How pathetic was that? It was like Rhys said, "I hate you, but I wouldn't let you be slaughtered by backwoods werewolves." Swoon. Not. How did humans deal with crushes?

"So," he asked, changing the subject. "What's the plan? We go in and ask nicely, or you go in all 'grrr, arghh'?" He made his hands into claws and baring his teeth.

Rhys bit his bottom lip, and Kai was almost positive Rhys was trying not to laugh.

"Um, I'd say we at least try to ask nicely. Besides, these shifters aren't—that is, they are slightly…"

"Oh my God, just spit it out? They're what?" Kai said, exasperated.

Rhys flushed. "Feral, Okay? I'm not sure I could take on more than one at a time."

Kai's stomach rolled. "Feral like they don't wear shoes or have running water? Or feral like they tend to rip your throat out first and ask questions later?"

Rhys risked a glance Kai's way. "Possibly both."

Kai stared at him incredulously. "So your sister sent us into the woods alone together to ask invasive questions to a pack of feral wolves on the off chance that an old witch might remember something about Ember? She really hates me now, huh? I mean, she's always disliked you, but now she wants me dead too?"

"I don't question my sister."

Kai snorted. "Uh, yeah, you do. All the time."

"Look, I don't know why she's sending us out here. I have no information other than what I told you. She wouldn't send us out here if she didn't think we could handle it. Besides, I do have a gun if it comes to that."

Kai huffed out a laugh. "Dude, that doesn't make me feel better. I've seen you shoot. You have the aim of a storm trooper."

The wolf stared at him. "I have no idea what that means, but I'm assuming it's an insult."

Kai smirked, staring at the wolf before he caved and barked, "What?"

"Don't even pretend you don't worship *Star Wars*. I've seen that stash of action figures you keep in your closet. If *Star Wars* were a person, you'd marry it."

Rhys kept eyes forward, but Kai had the pleasure of watching the color flush up his neck to his face. Kai couldn't tell if it was embarrassment or fury in the dim haze provided by the passing streetlights. "Stay out of my closet."

"No problem," he said. "It's not like there's enough room for both of us anyway."

Rhys's mouth fell open before he snapped it shut hard enough for his teeth to clack together. "Just go to sleep," Rhys sniped, reaching for the radio. "I'll wake you when we get there."

"Fine," Kai sniped back.

135

Chapter 24

EMBER

Ember supposed things had been going far too well. Even after the horrible nightmare that woke her, she'd let her easy morning lure her into a false sense of security. Breakfast was nice; she'd never really sat around a table family style and listened to people bicker cheerfully. She managed to avoid another uncomfortable conversation with her uncle, though he still stared at her creepily, like he was trying to send her messages telepathically. Maybe he was. She really had no idea how any of this witchy stuff worked.

Lunch was quiet but still painfully awkward. Kai and Quinn usually ran the conversation. With Kai and Rhys who knows where, Quinn's conversation attempts were thwarted by Tristin's pointed stares and glowering. Her cousin really was awful. Neoma was always pleasant, but she didn't talk much.

Things eased up a bit when Donovan slid into the seat next to her and started talking about something the triplets did in physical science that might have gotten them suspended.

"The triplets?" Ember asked. Why was everybody in town related to everybody else? "Who are they?"

Donovan pointed to the witches' table, where seven kids, including Stella and Astrid, were sitting. The three in question, two boys and a girl, stood out for their unnecessary closeness. They were all very…handsy. "Um, if they are related, that's gross."

"Naw," Donovan said around a burger. "We just call them that because they look alike."

She narrowed her eyes. They did look alike. Platinum hair, pale skin, cheekbones you could etch glass with. "They aren't related?"

Donovan laughed. "No. You have to wonder if dating somebody, much less two somebodies, who looks that much like you isn't sort of like the height of narcissism."

Tristin shrugged, bored. "I read an article that said lots of people get involved with people who look like themselves; it's called the mirror effect or something like that."

Quinn pushed his glasses up. "Actually, the mirror effect—"

"Don't care," Tristin snarked, her eyes still on the three.

Ember had no idea what was going on with those two, but it seemed strangely hostile. As she watched, the female triplet looked up at Ember and winked before feeding a fry to the guy on the right.

"Okay," Ember said aloud, though more to herself. The girl laughed as if she heard Ember. "Is she a witch?" she asked.

Tristin rolled her eyes. "They're all witches." And that was the last anybody said about the strange triad.

Tristin and Ember both had French for fourth period, but Tristin somehow found a way to not walk to class with Ember. In fact, Tristin took so long the bell was already ringing when she slid into the seat next to Ember. The teacher, Madame Krug, who was oddly enough a German werewolf, not French, glanced sharply at the clock and then pointedly at Tristin. Tristin dropped her eyes, slumping further into her seat. Ember was about to ask Tristin where she'd been when there was a palpable energy shift in the room.

All eyes swung to the door.

Her breath caught, her skin tingling. He stood, leaning casually along the doorframe as if waiting for her to notice, his silver eyes cold as he smirked at her. There was a low murmur as students tried to figure out if he was there to cause harm. He didn't look like he was there to fight. In fact, he looked serene; casual in jeans and a

 137

black t-shirt, grey hair messy in a way that made her want to run her fingers through it.

"Mace," she whispered.

His gaze fell on her. "Hello again, luv," he grinned. "It's nice to know I made an impression."

"Can I help you?" Madame Krug asked, her face pinched in displeasure.

"Absolutely." He walked towards the teacher, seeming to enjoy the way the students leaned away from him. He produced a square of paper from his pocket. "The rather unpleasant woman at the office said I should give this to you."

She perused the note, eyebrow cocked. "Well, class, it appears our quiet little town is becoming quite the hotspot, meet our latest new student, Mace." She looked at him suspiciously. "Do you have a last name?"

He smiled wanly. "Smith."

The teacher sighed like she was contemplating early retirement. "Have a seat."

He slipped his hands into the pockets of his jeans, sauntering through the aisle. He stopped between Ember and Tristin. Ember thought he was going to say something to her, but instead, he looked at Tristin. "I can't be certain, but I am almost positive you're the one who knocked me out in that cemetery."

"Guilty as charged," she said, her smile cold.

He arched a brow. "I'll have to return the favor sometime."

"You can try," she said, voice saccharine sweet.

He grinned, clearly enjoying how feisty her cousin was. He slung his bag down next to the chair directly behind Tristin, making sure he kicked one booted foot against the bottom of her seat, jostling her.

"Real mature," she muttered.

Madame Krug started the lesson, but Ember wasn't listening. She could feel his eyes burning into the back of her head. It felt like somebody had switched off the air conditioning. Beads of perspiration formed on her upper lip and slid down her spine. Her skin crawled with energy, slithering through her veins like tiny insects.

 138

"Knock it off," Tristin whispered. "You can't use magic on school grounds."

Ember couldn't use magic anywhere; she had no idea what she was doing. She clenched her fists, letting her nails dig into the tender flesh of her palm. She was positive this was Mace's fault. She had been okay the last couple of days.

"It's not like I can control it," she shot back.

Tristin handed her a bottle of water. "Here, drink this and calm down, before you get us both in trouble."

Ember didn't know how this could negatively affect her cousin but took the offering anyway, drinking down the whole thing. It didn't help. If anything, the energy licking along Ember's skin seemed to be taking root, moving from her arms to her torso—even her toes tingled.

Dread sat heavy against her chest. She couldn't start vomiting up black goop again; the witches would never let her live it down. She had to get out of there before she humiliated herself.

Just as she was about to ask to use the restroom, she felt it. Tendrils of cold pooling into her bloodstream, soothing the fire licking through her veins. She slumped lower in her chair, letting her head fall forward in her hands as she bit her lip, biting back a groan. There was a low chuckle from behind, but she couldn't care about him, not at that point. The feeling was too good; her toes curled in her shoes, as a full body shiver rolled along her skin. She needed to control herself, or this was going to get embarrassing for an entirely different reason.

The cold leeched out of her system as slowly as it came in but took the fire with it. Ember sighed in relief. She looked at Tristin. "Thanks," Ember said.

The girl looked at Ember, confused eyes staring at the empty water bottle. "You're welcome?"

Nobody noticed her little episode. Mace's presence seemed to be overwhelming everybody's senses, like a supernatural signal jammer.

When the bell rang, she headed for the hall, relieved her next class was across campus. She walked away from Mace as fast as her legs would carry her. She should text Kai or Isa about Mace, though Tristin was probably all over it. What would Ember even tell them?

He wasn't doing anything really. He wasn't actually hurting anyone. She just needed to get through the day and she'd tell Isa tonight.

Ember had really believed it was Mace standing outside her window that second night, but after three days passed without another sighting, she'd just assumed it was her mind playing tricks on her. She sighed as she took her seat for fifth period. She just needed to pull it together.

She felt his presence before she actually saw him. He slipped right into the chair behind her. "So we meet again."

She tried to look bored as her heartbeat tripped over itself. "Stalking is illegal, you know."

He just laughed; that same smug chuckle from earlier, as if she amused him. It made her want to punch him in the face. He leaned back, lacing his hands behind his head. This was the only class she didn't share with a single member of the pack. She took a deep breath, trying to channel some inner peace. It was just fifty minutes. She could survive that.

It was not just fifty minutes. He'd somehow maneuvered his way into every one of her classes, forcing her to endure his presence for the rest of the day. He was a menace. He caused mayhem wherever he went, students and teachers giving him a wide berth.

He enjoyed the chaos, knocking her book off her desk, so he could brush his hand against hers, letting his arm bump against hers in the hallway, casually brushing his hand against her hair, saying he thought he saw something in it.

It was making her crazy, those shadowy touches, the subtle invasion of her senses. She should be repulsed—her cousins said he was a demon, something evil—but her body wouldn't get the message. When he touched her, she fought the urge to lean into it. His presence made her jittery in the weirdest way. Every time she looked at him, he grinned at her like he knew a secret, like he knew *her* secret, like he knew she wanted him to touch her.

By seventh period, she was climbing out of her skin. Her leg jittered, and she tapped her nails on her desk just to try to find a way to keep herself in one piece. She couldn't catch her breath, lungs burning like she was breathing in some kind of noxious chemical. She had to get out of there.

   140

When the teacher finally dismissed them, Ember bolted, almost knocking over one of the triplets in her wake.

"Sorry," Ember mumbled, as the taller of the two boys stared her down. When she saw the others waiting at the lockers, she called over her shoulder, "I'll meet you at home."

Four confused faces stared back at her.

"But you rode with us," Neoma said.

Ember didn't stop to explain, making her way around the side of the main building and collapsing on the bench under the huge cypress tree. The air outside was oppressively hot, but she sucked in grateful breaths anyway. How was she going to do this? She couldn't spend every day like that.

"There you are, luv."

She scrunched her eyes closed for a moment before turning her eyes towards him. "What are you doing here? How did you even find me?"

"I missed you," he deadpanned.

She looked around, realizing they were alone. "How did you find me?" she asked again.

He arched one thick brow. "That is a long and boring story. The good news is I'm here now."

Her forehead furrowed. "Back to try to kill me again?"

"I'm hurt you think I would travel all this way just to kill you."

"I'm terribly sorry if I've hurt your feelings. You didn't strike me as the sensitive type when you were threatening my life."

"I would never. I only eat to survive," he said.

"So, you were going to...eat me?" she asked. "Are you some kind of cannibal? Oh, God, is that a real thing? Cannibalistic demons? Wait, don't tell me."

"I just said I wasn't trying to harm you. This is how misunderstandings happen. Lack of communication. We should work on that."

She ignored that. "Seriously, what are you? I know you aren't human. Kai says you're a demon."

 141

He dropped down beside her on the narrow bench. She swallowed hard. His eyes were spectacular in the sunlight, liquid pools of mercury, with flecks of black. She flushed.

"That's quite personal. I didn't realize we'd reached that level of...intimacy...so quickly." He slid an arm around her shoulders, his voice a low murmur, making her shiver. "Very well, luv. I'll show you mine, if you show me yours."

She fought the urge to run her hand along his leg. What was wrong with her? She shook her head.

"Stop calling me that," she snapped, dropping out from under his arm and moving to stand a safe distance away. She crossed her arms, glaring. "I'm not telling you anything."

He smiled then, that slick predatory grin. "You don't know what you are, do you?"

She slid her eyes to the ground.

"That's all right, lu—"

She shot him a dirty look.

He held his hands up in mock surrender. "Sorry...November, it is."

"Ember," she mumbled automatically.

"Appropriate."

"Ember!" She turned to find Tristin staring them down. Donovan, Neoma and Quinn at her back. "We need to go."

"Don't let me keep you," Mace said, standing and bowing with a flourish. "I'll be around."

Her body's traitorous reaction scared her more than the intended threat of his words. She watched him leave, that energy pooling inside her sad to see him go. Maybe she was sad to see him go too, just a little.

Chapter 25

KAI

Kai came awake with a squawk, face to face with glowing eyes and fangs. His fist flew, connecting with its target. Rhys grunted at the impact, rubbing his jaw and glaring.

"Dude, what did you expect was going to happen. You could have just called my name. No need to Edward Cullen me. What kind of creeper gets that close to somebody's face?"

"I did call your name," Rhys griped. "About ten times. You didn't even flinch. I was checking to make sure you were still alive. You *sleep* like Edward Cullen."

"Clearly you never read the books because the vamps didn't sleep in those books."

"Literally nobody cares," Rhys said.

Kai rubbed the sleep from his eyes, cracking his neck. "Why are you all wolfed out?" he asked.

"We're here. They have this place warded. Can't you feel it?"

Kai went still, pushing out with his senses. Yeah, he could feel it. Somebody had set up an elaborate barrier spell. They had just tripped a mystical alarm. Was it wolves at the receiving end of the signal or was something else lurking out there. He wasn't sure which was worse.

They exited the car, closing the door softly. Rhys scented the air. He growled low as ten or so fully-shifted wolves broke through the tree line, eyes glowing and teeth snapping. Rhys was right about the Glades wolves being anti-social.

They advanced, watching Kai with intent. So much for attempting to play nice first. The sound of cracking bones and slick skin made him ill as Rhys went full wolf. Kai shuddered. He'd never get used to that sound, not ever. He let his hand run over the fur on Rhys's side.

If Rhys was intimidating as a human, he was terrifying as a wolf. He stalked forward, positioning himself between Kai and the Glades wolves, crouching low and returning the snarls, eyes flashing in warning. Rhys crowded Kai back against the passenger side door, with a clear message. Rhys wanted Kai in the car so Rhys could fight ten savage wolves by himself.

Kai allowed himself a moment to bask in the heroic stupidity of the wolf. It was somewhat hot that Rhys was willing to be torn apart for Kai, even if it was just so Rhys didn't have to face the wrath of his sister.

The wolves advanced, spreading out to surround them. Rhys snarled, jaws snapping ferociously, saliva flying everywhere. Rhys pressed against Kai again, but he knew if he got in the car, Rhys wasn't coming home. Kai couldn't stand by and watch Rhys die.

Rhys made to leap into the fray, so Kai did the only thing he could think to do. He took a deep breath and stepped between Rhys and ten undomesticated werewolves. Kai dropped to his knees, baring his throat, eyes fixed to the ground.

God, he hoped this worked.

Everything stilled. The wolves froze, whining their confusion, looking to the wolf standing before them for their cues. Kai tried to keep his trembling under control, but this was, by far, the stupidest thing he'd ever done.

The enormous brown and white wolf at the front skulked forward. Fetid breath huffed against Kai's neck, saliva dripping on his t-shirt. He swallowed, feeling like he had a baseball lodged in his

 144

throat as an icy sliver of terror stuck in his ribcage, constricting his lungs. He was so stupid. He was so, so stupid. Canines closed around the thick tendon of his neck. He scrunched his eyes shut tight, waiting for the wolf to tear out his throat. Rhys rumbled, inching forward to Kai's side. The wolves growled back, moving back into a defensive stance.

"Shut. Up," Kai managed through clenched teeth.

From the corner of his eye, he watched as Rhys bent low on his paws, lowering his eyes. The pressure at Kai's throat ceased, and he looked around in confusion. The wolf shifted, and suddenly there was a naked man standing there. Kai bolted to his feet, his eyes looking anywhere but forward. Wolf nudity was always awkward.

"Who are you?" the older man grumbled. "You're trespassing."

Kai stuffed his hands into his pockets. "We're here on behalf of the Belladonna pack. Isa McGowan sent us. We were hoping you'd allow us to speak to your witch, Ms. Josephine."

The alpha eyed Rhys warily. Kai elbowed Rhys in the flank and he whined before shifting back into human form. The two men stared each other down, the alpha looking back and forth between Rhys and Kai, puzzled.

When the alpha took a step forward, Rhys wrapped his hand around Kai's bicep and tugged him back towards him. Kai kept his eyes forward, much more at ease with the idea of seeing a random stranger naked than feeling a naked Rhys behind him. Nope. That was a thing that was definitely not okay.

The alpha tipped his nose into the air, leaning in to smell him. Rhys's hand tightened and loosened spastically, and the alpha arched a brow at Rhys. Kai looked between the two, watching them somehow have an entire conversation with only their eyebrows. Finally, the alpha came to some conclusion, nodding at Rhys. Wolves were weird, Kai decided.

"Ms. Josephine doesn't take kindly to strangers, especially reapers," the alpha warned.

"Oh pipe down, Edgar."

Kai and Rhys looked to the sound of the new voice. A tiny, dark-skinned woman with shock white hair hobbled her way towards

 145

them from the woods. She wore a flowery housecoat and clutched an intricate wooden cane. She looked to be in her late seventies, but witches didn't age like others, so she could have been well past a hundred. There was just no way of knowing.

"Ms. Josephine, we don't know these people," Edgar objected. "We don't know their intentions."

She waved her hand. "Please, they are children."

Kai bristled at that. She wasn't wrong, but he had seen some stuff. He'd almost died more than once.

"Oh, don't get your knickers in a twist, young'un," she said. "I don't mean no disrespect, but you truly are no risk to me." He didn't miss the threat in her tone. "So, if you're here, the little alpha must have sent you."

Kai looked to Rhys, who nodded. "Yes, ma'am."

After a minute, she said, "You can ask your questions, but that don't mean I'm gonna answer, understand?"

"Yes, ma'am," Kai promised.

She patted his cheek, and another growl rumbled from Rhys. Kai swiped backwards at him without looking. What was wrong with him?

She laughed at Rhys's bizarre behavior, clearly tickled by the wolf. She was close enough for him to see her deeply wrinkled skin, a lifetime of experience road-mapped across her face. Just how old was she?

She moved to stand before the wolf. "Relax, child, I'm not gonna hurt him." She crooked her finger, forcing the wolf to stoop deeply so they were close to eye level. She placed her hand on his cheek, her eyes closing, deep in concentration. After a moment, she opened her eyes and smiled. She ran her hand through Rhys's hair, and his eyes fluttered closed in what appeared to be ecstasy. Kai shook his head. It took everything in his power not to laugh. The dog jokes practically wrote themselves. He was so using this as blackmail later.

"I like this one," she announced.

"Edgar, bring the boy some clothes. I know y'all don't mind being naked, but I can't concentrate." Kai gawked at the old lady as her eyes roamed Rhys's naked form before winking at Kai.

 146

They walked back through the woods to their camp. Two wolves left to find clothes for Rhys. Kai scanned his surroundings, distracting himself from the naked wolf to his left. Twenty or so mobile homes sat in a circle around a manmade lake. A fire pit sat crumbling in a ring of dead grass surrounded by logs and folding chairs. Children ran wild everywhere, ranging in age from toddler to teen, all in various stages of undress.

When he finally turned around, Rhys was clothed. The sweatpants were baggy, but the t-shirt was clearly a size too small, stretching too tight across the shoulders. That suited Kai just fine. They sat on the porch of Ms. Josephine's old trailer, crowded together with barely enough room for her rocker and two folding chairs. The wolves hovered on the stairs and around the railing, insisting on protecting their witch.

"Ms. Josephine," Kai began. "Our alpha says you once lived in Belle Haven. Do you know what happened there twelve years ago?"

The old woman's brown eyes closed, and for a moment, Kai feared she'd dozed off. With brows raised, he looked at Rhys. He gave him the what-do-you-want-me-to-do eyebrows back. He was about to gently nudge her when she opened them again and said, "A lot of things happened in that town." She snorted. "You'll have to be more specific."

"My cousin, November, died. Do you know anything about it?"

"So many people died that day. You would have been, what, five years old?" she asked. "The better question is why don't you remember what happened?"

Kai stopped, dumbstruck. It wasn't that he didn't know what happened…except that he didn't, not really. He knew he'd had an Aunt Sera and a cousin, November. He knew they'd died. He just had no recollection of how. It was like he'd told November; he had no real recollection of them at all. No family dinners. No holidays. No play dates. Why would that be? The witch's knowing look told him she thought it was strange as well.

She seemed to sense his shifting mood as much as the surrounding wolves. She reached out and snagged his hand, clutching it tight enough that Rhys tensed too. Kai used his other hand to keep the wolf from acting like…well, a wolf. Her brown eyes bleached white

   147

and a string of Latin poured from her lips. Kai shuddered. Witches were freaky.

When her eyes came back to brown, she looked at him hard. "There is some powerful magic at play here, boy." She snatched Rhys's hand and repeated the whole little ritual. "You both been hexed. I'd venture to say you ain't the only ones. I can feel the link, like plinking on a string on a spider's web. When I push on your strings, I can hear the echo of the spell on the others."

Kai looked at Rhys, bewildered. "So, you don't know anything about how my cousin died?"

She gave him a measuring look. "I don't *know* anything." Kai felt his heart squeeze; they'd come for nothing. "But I can tell you the rumors."

Kai nodded. He'd take any information. Something to indicate what was happening to Ember. "If your cousin was November, you must be Christopher and your sister, Tristin." He again looked to Rhys, startled that anybody would know who Kai was. "Yes, I know you, child."

"My dad was Christopher. I go by Kai," he said.

"You look like your daddy. I was there when you were born."

He felt like he was visiting an old neighbor, not really sure where she was going with her train of thought, if anywhere at all.

"Did you know all three of you were born with the mark of a reaper?"

His heart stuttered. Rhys glanced at Kai sharply, probably hearing the uptick of his heart. Sometimes the mark came early, but nobody was born with the mark. "What?"

"Mm, all three of you came into this world with a mark meant for just one." Her fingers fiddled with the end of her cane. "That fear you're feelin', imagine how the town felt? Three children, born to one family, possessing the potential for soul magic. Some folks thought it was a dark omen, given the town's history with death magic and the curse."

"What history? Death magic?"

"That's a story for another time, child. Just know that your birth was significant enough to make a great deal of powerful people nervous." She looked to the sleeve of his t-shirt, where the names of his collected peeked from underneath his sleeve. "You're a collector. It seems fitting. You had a sweet disposition as a child, perfect for helping folks cross over." Kai just shrugged, but she continued. "Isa tells me your sister is a banshee."

"Well, kind of. Until the other day, she hadn't screamed in…"

"Twelve years?" she asked.

"Yeah, Allister says she screamed the day our mom died."

She nodded.

"So Em-November…she's—she would have been a reaper? Like us?" Kai prompted.

She smiled sadly. "No, child, she was nothing like you."

Kai grunted in frustration, agitating the wolves. "Ms. Josephine, what happened to our parents? What happened to my cousin? What happened to the town?"

She held up a hand. "It started with a meeting. Your Aunt Sera was the head of the council then, but your mama worked with her. That was when the council had more than just witches. But it was the witches of the Red Oak coven who put forth the petition to preemptively bind your magic. They were spooked. They said Sera wasn't taking the threat of three active reapers in one family serious; that she was too reckless with her authority on account you was her kin. They said she needed to let the coven bind your powers before she got herself killed and you three came to power all at once."

Dread pooled in his stomach, thick and heavy, but he said nothing, letting the witch tell her story—their story. "Your mama and your aunt Sera were livid. They knew binding your powers was only the first step in the coven's plan. She coulda rejected the idea outright, but she didn't. She listened. She put it to a vote. She sent everybody home and said the council would meet the next day. Your aunt was a good girl, always fair."

The old woman squinted. "Here's where things get…muddy. I got a visitor that night. They told me Sera needed me to leave. Said he couldn't say why, but she needed me to come back here and stay put until she sent for me."

"My Aunt sent you away? Why? Weren't you friends?"

The old witch tightened her lips, nodding. "The why isn't important yet. I wasn't there for the vote, but I sent my vote back letting them know I stood with Sera and Samara. I didn't think it necessary to mess with babies. The council got their vote. The shifters, the fae, and even a few witches sided with your aunt. It was close, but in the end we had the votes. The council would do nothing 'til one a you showed some signs of coming to power. Sera figured even if all three of you came to power after she died, she had years to teach you restraint and to hide that power if need be. She was wrong."

She looked sad. "People were angry; they knew better than to argue a vote. They say everybody almost made it out unscathed. If it had only happened three minutes later, who knows how different things could have been. If people hadn't heard…"

"Heard what? What happened?"

"Your sister screamed."

Kai sucked in a breath. "What?"

She eyed him gravely. "Your sister foretold the death about to take place in that town. The death of your Aunt."

Kai frowned at that. That would mean his sister predicted the death of his aunt and his mother. It wasn't possible. Even if they all bore the mark, none would inherit their power until Sera was dead. The old lady had to be confused.

"But my aunt was still alive."

Ms. Josephine looked right at him. "Yes, but not for long."

Kai tried to digest the information. He'd always assumed his Aunt Sera died the same day as the others.

"Seraphina died that night. Murdered, I 'spect, though there ain't nobody left to ask. I shoulda gone back to see…to check…but she told me to go, and I trusted she had her reasons. We don't know who done it, but I still say it was a council member. We didn't know her body was in the water, but sweet little November did."

Goosebumps rose on Kai's skin, and his stomach rolled as he remembered the dream Ember shared just that morning. "What did she do?" he asked, not really wanting to hear it.

"They say she called her mama straight from the water. Pulled her broken body from the ocean, and brought a dead woman straight to her own front door." Kai glanced quickly at Rhys, his expression horrified.

"She was a reanimator," Rhys said, more a statement than a question.

She looked him dead in the eye. "Oh, child, she was so much more than that."

"What does that even mean?" Kai asked, reaching out beside him, not sure what he was looking for until Rhys's hand circled his wrist, and he could breathe a bit easier.

Ms. Josephine looked at each of them in turn. "Before I tell you the rest, I need you to remember she was just a baby, she couldn't know what she was doing."

Kai and Rhys both nodded, but Kai wasn't sure he wanted to know what was worse than turning your own mother into a zombie.

"They managed to put Seraphina down and burn her body, but it was too late. The council was in chaos. Your sister's scream foretold the death of the head of the council. November raised her mother's body from the dead. Two of three reapers were showin' powers in the same family, much too early; people were scared. Reaper powers wasn't supposed to work like this. The coven was in a panic. They confronted your mama and November's daddy now that control of the council fell to them, least 'til they could elect another. They said they'd taken a new vote without them and agreed binding your powers was for the best. Your mama refused. The witches threatened to get the Grove involved. She said it wasn't what Seraphina woulda wanted. They said she shouldn't get a vote on account of her being human. People were yellin' and screamin' with no end in sight." She sighed. "I 'spect you three saw these screaming people as a threat. They were attacking your family. That is when your sister screamed again."

"Predicting the death of my mother?"

"Perhaps. Some say she wasn't predicting a death but sounding an alarm."

"An alarm to who?" Kai managed.

"To November, of course."

 151

Kai thought he was going to puke. Tristin had screamed twice, once for his aunt and now for...who knows...his own mother? The town?

"What did she do?" Rhys asked, voice dry, emotions raw.

"She did what reanimators do, child," she said. "She raised an army to fight."

Kai went cold all over. The kind of power it would take to raise an army of the dead... it took people a lifetime to develop that kind of power. It couldn't be possible. Stories of reanimators having that kind of power were the stuff parents told their kids at bedtime. Fantasies.

"An army? She started a war?"

The old lady looked a million miles away. "She started a bloodbath."

Rhys sounded shaken when he said, "She is the thing that annihilated our town? She killed our parents?"

Kai could feel Rhys's agitation without looking and so could the other wolves. Rhys's fingers tightened around his wrist. "Is that true?"

She waved her hand in a vague gesture. "I told you, I wasn't there. Who's to know who killed who?"

"She started it though?" Rhys prompted.

"She was a baby," Ms. Josephine admonished, "If a child found a gun and shot somebody, would you call 'em a killer? There was no way she was ever gonna to be able to control the army she raised. She didn't know what she was doing." She looked at Kai, and there was no mistaking the challenge in her words when she said, "She died too remember?"

Kai swallowed hard, praying his stress levels masked the lie. The last part was untrue; he'd seen his cousin just this morning, eating waffles and conjugating verbs in French, but that didn't stop him from picturing the scene in his head. Why was Ember suddenly starting to remember these things? Why weren't they?

"Ms. Josephine, I've been having...weird dreams. Dreams about this. Could this spell be wearing off or breaking down?"

 152

She stared at him hard for a full minute, her mouth twitching at the corner. "I suppose there could have been a spell that would wear off at a set time. Or…maybe if the caster of the spell died, the spell would break down over time."

"Could a spell make an entire town forget something huge like this? Can a spell make somebody forget they had abilities?"

"Could a witch create a spell to make people forget? Mayhap, but if you are talkin' an entire town, you'd need a whole lotta magic. That kind of magic would take more than one witch. It would take a coven. A powerful coven to erect the spell, and at least an extremely powerful witch to constantly reinforce the magic," she said, a shudder running through her. "As for makin' somebody forget they had a gift? Simply makin' 'em forget wouldn't be enough. Their abilities would start to come out even if they didn't know they had 'em. You'd have to bind their magic."

"If—" She eyed him pointedly, like she knew exactly what he was asking. "If, there was a coven that powerful and a witch who was constantly vigilant, they could bind somebody's magic, but it would be at enormous risk to both the witch and the person whose powers were bound."

Kai's mind raced with the possibilities. There was only one coven in Belle Haven. Could the Red Oak coven have been big enough to erect a massive spell like that? Could it have been the Grove?

"How so?" he heard Rhys ask.

"Binding a person's power takes energy. Even a powerful witch would have side effects. He'd constantly need to recharge his power supply. That kind of energy requires dark magic, blood magic. Playing with dark magic ain't never done nobody no good in the long run. Eventually, the devil come to collect and the spell will…" She made an exploding motion with her hands.

Kai just sat there. He couldn't help it. He didn't want to think about the implications of the witch's words. He'd grown up in Belle Haven. He knew every person in that town. He couldn't imagine anybody meddling in blood magic.

"What happens to the person whose powers were bound?"

Kai glanced up at Rhys's question. Kai should have thought of that.

 153

"Think of it like cracks in a dam. That spell, all it did was build a wall 'round all that magic. Once the spell breaks, cracks will form, tons a power all trying to escape through those tiny little cracks. A body ain't made to contain that kinda energy, child. Eventually one a two things will happen. That person will either implode from the crazy, or those cracks will shatter that wall and unleash hell on the world."

Kai lurched forward, clutching the woman's withered hand. "That can't be the only two possibilities. There has to be a patch to block the leaks or a way to disarm this...energy bomb?"

The wolves bristled at his abrupt shift, but she shushed them. "I don't know what you're playing at, child, but believe me when I say you and your pack ain't prepared for this."

"Is there?" he pushed.

"If the...person...whose powers were bound could find a anchor or a filter, somebody who could channel all that power or temper it maybe 'til they could learn to control it, they may be able to keep from imploding."

He nodded, making to stand. "Thank you for your time, Ms. Josephine."

She clutched his hand, pulling him back down. "Whatever you're thinking, boy, don't meddle with things you don't understand. This will only end badly."

He nodded again, jerkily.

They were halfway off the porch when the old lady spoke one last time. "Boys." They turned to see her leaning forward in her seat, hands folded across her cane. "I know you won't heed my warning. I've seen what's to come, and believe you me, I don't envy you. I'll be seeing you boys real soon though."

Kai frowned, but she nodded then, dismissing them.

He bowed his head to Edgar as he walked past. "Thank you for allowing us into your territory. Sorry if we almost caused a... problem."

The older man clapped Kai on the shoulder and shook Rhys's hand. He took a card out of his back pocket and handed it to Rhys.

 154

"Next time just text me and let me know you're coming. My cell's on the back."

Kai glared at Rhys, contemplating murder. He held his tongue until they were in the car. "So much for feral backwoods hicks. We could've been killed."

"But we weren't, and we got what we came for."

"Did we?" he asked.

"Yeah, we know that your cousin is a witch doctor with wonky powers and no off switch. We also know she killed our parents and about thirty other people. Serial killers get jealous over those kinds of numbers."

"We don't know that for sure. She said it was just rumors."

"She knows," Rhys warned quietly. "I don't know how she knows, but she does. She also knows you were lying about Ember being dead."

"We also can't tell the pack," Kai said fiercely.

"How do you suppose that's going to work? What? We go back and tell them she didn't know anything? I'm not lying to the pack."

"I'm not saying lie to the pack. I'm saying we just omit certain things from the newbie witch doctor with the wonky powers. What do you think would happen if we were to tell her she not only raised her mom from the dead like she dreamed, but she is also responsible for the death of a few dozen people? What would that do to her control problem, you think?"

"So, we tell the others but not her?" Rhys's tone implied that this was not okay with him.

"We just go home and tell Isa and Wren about Ember's control problem, but we tell everybody else the rumor was Ember was a reanimator and that somebody erected a spell to make the town forget and bound her powers, but the spell is wearing off."

"So…we just leave out the zombie mom, the mass homicide, and the part where she is a ticking time bomb who could kill herself or us at any moment?"

"Yes, exactly."

"We have to tell the pack."

155

Kai growled in frustration. "They will send her away. They won't accept her. I don't want to abandon what's left of my family. What if it was Isa?"

"We don't abandon pack." Kai opened his mouth to protest, but Rhys put up a hand. "We don't abandon family either, but we don't lie to our pack. We will find another way."

Rhys's tone implied the conversation was over, but Kai wasn't giving up. There was no way the pack could know what Ember did. If Rhys wouldn't agree with the plan, Kai would find a way around him.

Chapter 26

EMBER

Ember glanced at the clock for the hundredth time before going back to her sketchbook. She shaded the cheekbone of a young man's face, before moving to emphasize the fullness of his bottom lip. Like most sketches, the face before her was unfamiliar, just an image in her head, a distraction. He was all gaunt angles and full lips. He screamed lead singer in a rock band. She used a finger to shade just below his chin and wondered if he was a real person.

Her eyes wandered to the clock again. Kai and Rhys had been gone for hours. Isa and the others didn't seem worried, but Ember couldn't help but think something was wrong. She didn't know why Isa cared what some old witch had to say about her, but Isa said she trusted Josephine. What if they learned horrible things about her? There had to be some reason her father hated her. Whatever she had done was so bad her brain literally blocked it from her memory. How long before they found out the truth and kicked her out?

Tristin wandered into the kitchen with Quinn hot on her heels, carrying his laptop open in front of him.

"Somebody as clumsy as you really shouldn't be tempting gravity like that," Tristin warned, pulling open the fridge door.

Ember snorted, and Quinn gave her a hurt look. "Turning on me so quickly, Ember? And after I brought you back from the brink of death...no loyalty these days."

Ember laughed, but it died when she saw Tristin's death glare.

Wren poked his head into the kitchen. "Tristin, I need you. We got a call. Donovan and Neoma are still closing the restaurant, so you're up. Allister wants us to check out something weird over on Lexington Street."

Tristin stared at him balefully. "He'll have to be slightly more specific in this town."

Isa walked in, giving Ember a look. "Actually, Wren, why don't you take Ember?"

Wren's eyes widened, dropping his voice to almost a whisper, "On a hunt?"

Isa rolled her eyes. "No, out for ice cream. Yes, on a hunt," she said, loud enough for all to hear.

Quinn looked from Tristin to Wren to Isa. "Um, I mean this with the utmost respect, oh alpha mine, but do you really think Ember should be going out on a hunt with her little...control problem? What if she, ya know?" Quinn mimicked her vomiting and passing out.

Ember narrowed her eyes at him, and Isa's smile bled into a snarl. "If I didn't think it was a good idea, I wouldn't have suggested it. But, if you would like to go as well, to provide guidance or moral support, you are more than welcome to accompany her."

Quinn blanched, clearing his throat. "I'm more of a behind the scenes kind of guy. Planning, healing, general research... I'd just get in the way. Besides, Dagger and I were sort of in the middle of something."

Isa arched a brow. "Mm, then why don't you leave the decision making to me?"

"Of course," Quinn said. "Good idea."

"I'll go too," Tristin said, "I don't mind. Somebody who knows what they're doing should be out there to cover Wren."

She looked at Ember with contempt. Ember couldn't say she disagreed. She had no idea what she would do if faced with something paranormal. She felt the others were far more qualified to deal with those things given her control problem…especially now that Mace was back in town. Tristin had at least kept her mouth shut about that, though Ember didn't know why.

Isa nodded at Tristin, and that seemed to be the end of the discussion. Tristin bolted upstairs and returned with a knife strapped to each wrist and one strapped to her thigh. On the way out, Wren pulled a gun from the hall closet, checking the clip and making sure there was a round in the chamber. He holstered it and slid it onto his belt. Ember's stomach rolled. What could they possibly be worried about fighting that Wren couldn't defeat with his razor sharp teeth and claws?

They took the SUV for the short ride to Lexington, Ember letting Tristin ride shotgun. The street wasn't crowded, but a few stragglers were leaving a dimly lit bar aptly named The Witches Brew. *Witches are really full of themselves*, Ember thought.

"So what are we looking for again?" Tristin asked.

"Not sure. Allister asked us to check out a complaint made by Addison Leary. Said she saw some weirdo lurching down the alley, and she couldn't tell if he was drunk or something else."

Ember didn't know many people yet, but Addison worked at the coffee shop Kai made them stop at every morning. She was a shy pretty human girl with bad acne and a sweet disposition. She always gave Ember extra cinnamon.

"So are you like the cops around here?" Ember asked as they slid from the Suburban.

Wren grinned. "As close to cops as you get in this town. Now, be quiet and stay close." They crept slowly down the alleyway, Ember feeling silly, Tristin and Wren sweeping back and forth in what seemed like total darkness. They reached the chain-link fence at the end of the alley with no sign of Addison's weirdo.

There was another street to the left and an abandoned two-story building to the right. Wren began moving towards the building, when the sound of glass rolling across pavement caused him to freeze. Ember's chest tightened. She willed herself to calm down. It could just be a stray animal.

 159

He gestured for Tristin to check the building and for Ember to follow him. He put a finger to his lips, though she hadn't said a word. Her thundering heartbeat was probably getting on his nerves.

They crept closer towards what looked like an old storage shed. A dumpster with peeling green paint sat to her left. Her stomach lurched at the smell of rancid food and dirty diapers. She had no idea what store they stood behind, but she was making it a point to never go there.

By the time they reached the warped door of the metal shack, Ember was sure her heart was in her nose. She took a shaky breath as tiny little jolts of electricity pulsed along her skin, whimpering as heat rushed over her faster than anything she'd ever felt before. She held her hands before her, positive she'd see flames.

Wren turned, nostrils flaring. "Ember? What's wrong?"

She opened her mouth, but the door slammed open behind Wren. A shadow staggered forward with a groan, and Wren yelled as the thing bit into his shoulder.

Her eyes widened as the thing tore at him. It was almost human, but the pupils were white, the flesh rotting. On some level, her brain supplied words like *not human* and then *zombie*. She registered the sound of Tristin's boots on the pavement and willed her to move faster.

"Wren!" Tristin's frantic scream echoed in the empty alley, breaking whatever spell held Ember frozen. Her hand shot forward, her fingers knotting into its hair, trying to pry its mouth from Wren. Skin slipped loosely over bones as part of its scalp came away in her hand. She screamed, dropping the flesh and swallowing hard to keep her dinner down. The thing didn't seem to notice its scalp missing. She hesitated, afraid to try again. If its face came off, she might actually vomit and die as Quinn predicted.

The thing yanked hard, and Wren hollered, trying to dislodge its grip as it tore through muscle. Ember screamed again, light exploding from her fingertips with enough force to rock the thing back on its heels. Wren jerked from its grip, leaving her and the creature face to face. She could see it was a man, at least by the build. The flesh was missing from a portion of his lower jaw, revealing bloody teeth. He groaned and whatever was in his mouth fell wetly to the

 160

pavement. She didn't look at it. He looked so familiar, high cheek-bones, wide set eyes. She'd seen him before.

Wren wrenched her back just as Tristin's knife entered under its jaw and out the back of its skull. It jerked twice, a strange hissing sound escaping before it fell to the ground in a heap. Ember stood gaping. Tristin knocked Ember aside, tearing at the bottom of Wren's t-shirt with an ease born of adrenaline, inspecting the wound.

"Shit, that looks bad," Tristin said.

She wasn't wrong. The wound was deep and ragged, flesh missing and blood flowing freely.

Wren flinched as Tristin tied the scraps of his shirt tightly over the injury. When she continued to fuss over him, he shooed her off. "It's fine. We need to burn the body like they did the other night. I'm not taking any chances."

Tristin turned on her. "This is all your fault. You distracted him. You could've gotten him killed."

Ember's mouth fell open, more herself than a few minutes ago. "What? I didn't ask to be here. I didn't deliberately freak out."

"Tristin, enough," Wren said. "I'll be fine. Ember saved me. Whatever she did stunned it enough to let me get away." He looked at her. "How did you do that?"

Ember shrugged, not knowing what to say. "I really don't know."

Tristin sneered. "Shocking."

It took only a few minutes for Wren to get the gasoline and set the body ablaze. Ember wasn't sure what to think of them doing this enough to keep body-burning supplies in the car. After a while, she asked, "Not to be stupid but…was that a zombie?"

"Zombie, revenants. Whatever you want to call them," Wren said.

"We shouldn't be calling them anything. Zombies don't exist. Reanimation is forbidden," Tristin reminded him.

"Well, nevertheless, there it is. The second zombie in just over a week."

Tristin glared at Ember again, as if she was to blame. Seriously, what did she ever do to Tristin?

Wren slung an arm around each of them, wincing. "Ouch. Come on, let's get home so Quinn can disinfect this thing before it closes wrong."

"Yeah, I think you need stitches," Ember said, nose wrinkling.

He laughed. "Naw, I'm good."

When they arrived home, chaos ensued. Donovan jumped up from his spot on the sofa. "Holy crap, dude, what got you?"

Neoma crinkled her nose at the blood and looked at Ember with a sudden interest. Ember frowned at Neoma's interest and she looked away. Wren kept walking, everybody following in his wake, asking questions he didn't bother to answer. Isa met them in the kitchen from the back stairs, Quinn behind her with the first aid kit.

Had someone texted, or had Isa smelled the blood? Wren peeled the tattered remains of his shirt off, and Quinn untied the scraps of cotton from the wound. This clearly wasn't Wren's first fight. In addition to the new wound on his shoulder, a huge bite mark rested just over his heart, and another long scar ran just underneath his ribs on the right side.

While everybody fussed over Wren, Ember collapsed back into her seat from earlier, wishing she'd never left. She picked up her charcoal pencil, idly tapping it against her lip. Her eyes fell to her sketch from earlier, really taking in the details for the first time. High cheekbones, narrow face, and wide set eyes.

She gasped as recognition dawned, pushing the sketchpad away, like it burned her.

Tristin turned, her gaze zeroing in on the sketchpad. Ember reached for the book, trying to get it back before Tristin could see, but it was too late.

Tristin snatched it up, staring at the image for a long time before showing it to Wren. "I told you this was all her fault."

To his credit, Wren took the information in stride. In the picture, the young man was in much better shape than he'd been when he'd taken a chunk out of Wren's shoulder, but there was no doubt he was the same guy.

"Well, that is certainly an interesting turn of events," Wren said, handing the picture to Isa.

Ember closed her eyes, waiting for the other shoe to drop. There was no way they'd keep her if she was somehow conjuring zombies.

Chapter 27

KAI

It was way past midnight when they stumbled through the door, but the entire household was awake and an intense argument was well under way.

Isa loomed over Wren, who sat shirtless on a kitchen stool. "Just let him put in a few stitches so it heals properly. You could get an infection. We aren't bulletproof."

"Well, then it's a good thing I didn't get shot," Wren shot back with a grin.

Quinn stood by, preparing to suture a raw looking wound, silently waiting to see who would win the argument. Ember sat at the breakfast nook looking miserable.

"What's going on?" Rhys asked. "What happened?"

Wren spoke first. "I took Ember and Tristin to check out a call. Things got…complicated."

"You took Ember on a call?" Rhys shouted. "Why would you do something so stupid?"

Wren smiled, kissing Isa's flushed cheek. "Because my alpha told me to."

"Do you have something you'd like to say to me, brother?" Isa asked, folding her arms and gazing up at the wolf.

He huffed. "No."

"So, what was it?" Kai prompted, pointing at Wren's wound.

"Revenant."

"That she conjured," Tristin said, pointing at Ember.

Kai and Rhys looked at each other. "What do you mean?"

Tristin snatched away Ember's sketchpad and showed them the picture. "She was drawing this before we left. This zombie got Wren. She created him."

Rhys sighed. "I know that guy." He looked like he was wracking his brain. "Mike—yeah—Mike Hutchins. He was the guy who worked at the body shop."

"How could Ember have conjured a zombie in what...minutes? It would have taken him a while to climb out of his grave, don't you think? Maybe she's just psychically linked to them?" Neoma said from where she lay inexplicably on the kitchen floor.

They looked at the picture with more interest. Kai suddenly had an idea. "Can I see that?"

He took the book and flipped back a few pages, looking at face after face until he found the one he was looking for. There she was, Mrs. Carlson. He showed it to Rhys, who just grunted his acknowledgement.

Ember looked green. "What's going on?"

"We'll tell you, but first we need to talk to Wren and Isa alone. Ms. Josephine wanted me to give them a message privately."

Rhys set his jaw, eyebrows drawing together, looking like he wished he could strangle Kai with his bare hands.

"Porch, now," Isa barked.

Once they were safely away from the others, Kai told them about their visit with Ms. Josephine. He told them about the spell cast on the town, how somebody, more than likely Ember's own father, had bound her powers, and that, essentially, she was a ticking time bomb unless they could teach her to channel her energy.

"Is that everything?" she asked.

Rhys stared hard at Kai. "Th—"

 165

"Yeah, that's it. Isn't that enough?" Kai asked, cutting off Rhys while casually sliding out of his reach. Luckily for Kai, Rhys spent so much time glaring at Kai nobody seemed to catch his blatant lie. Rhys might trust the pack to overlook Ember's responsibility in the death of their parents, but he just couldn't risk it. Not yet.

She sighed. "Tell everybody to be in the living room in twenty. I'll call Allister."

Wren's brow furrowed. "He's going to want to know why you sent the boys without his permission."

She waved him off. "I'll tell him it was a last minute idea that I figured wouldn't turn up anything, and I didn't want to bother him."

Kai pulled a face, Isa might trust the witch, but he didn't. There was no way Allister could be unbiased despite his protests to the contrary. The distrust between witches and other supernatural creatures went too deep. Besides, the guy was a dick to his own son. Good guys didn't act like that.

The pack took the time to freshen up. Kai took a quick shower and threw on pajama pants and a clean t-shirt, running a towel over his damp hair as he padded barefoot downstairs.

People flopped wherever seating was available, impatiently waiting for answers. When the doorbell rang, Rhys stomped to the door and yanked it open, turning away from his guests before they could say a word. Kai smiled to himself. Rhys didn't like Allister either.

Allister entered, immaculately dressed as usual. Did Allister ever sleep? He wasn't alone. Astrid stumbled in behind him, dressed in a light yellow sundress and cardigan, clearly exhausted and wearing a sour expression.

Quinn sat up straighter in the armchair. "What is she doing here?" he asked, staring down his sister.

"Someday she will take over my seat on the council. I need to make sure at least one of my children carries on my legacy with dignity." His tone was jovial but his smile cold. Quinn flinched as his sister smirked. Tristin shifted to sit on the end of the armchair, not touching Quinn but positioning herself between him and his family. Astrid glowered at Tristin, but Allister just raised a brow.

Ember rubbed her eyes. "Is anybody going to say anything, or are we just going to stare at each other awkwardly? How do you

 166

guys stay up all night like this? I'm tired. We have school in like five hours."

Neoma giggled. The other's turned to her and she flushed at the sudden attention, covering her mouth with her hand.

Rhys filled in the pack with military precision. His tone clipped, embellishing nothing. Kai's heart knocked hard against his diaphragm, waiting for him to divulge the information Kai had kept from the others, but it never came.

"So, that's everything?" Allister asked. "She didn't know who was responsible for what happened to the council?"

Rhys stared hard at Kai before saying, "Yes, that's it."

"She said nobody lived to tell what really happened." Kai only half-lied. "I mean, she did tell us a lot, but she said it was just rumors. We know what Ember is now. We know that a council meeting started whatever happened. We know Tristin screamed at the council meeting." He glanced at Allister. "But I guess you already knew that."

Ember stayed silent throughout Rhys's explanation, chewing her thumbnail, feet tucked underneath her. She looked exhausted and confused.

"So, reanimators are just zombie makers?" Ember asked.

Quinn spoke. "Reanimators are a rare type of reaper. Their powers allow them communication with the dead, either by summoning an apparition or by raising the body from the grave. The raised aren't alive like people, just moving bodies with no thought process. It makes them easy to control. It's why reanimators have to register with the Grove. They don't want them creating an army of ravenous corpses, and that's why it's illegal to reanimate a corpse without the Grove's consent."

He looked pointedly at Kai when he said it, trying to relay a message. Kai's mouth went dry. All canine eyes turned to Ember. The color drained from her cheeks. He didn't know if the wolves smelled her anxiety or heard her heartbeat go wild, but he was grateful the witches didn't possess the same abilities.

Why hadn't he thought of that? Well, he kind of had. He'd talked to Rhys about it the previous week. He'd just been so relieved to know what Ember was that it never occurred to him what she'd done was illegal. She'd reanimated two corpses that they knew of, but there were three other pictures between Mrs. Carlson and the other guy, Mike. Had they come back too? If the Grove knew what she'd done, they'd come for them both.

Ember ran her hand across her face before combing it through her hair. "So, I can make zombies and conduct séances or raise an army of the dead but not really because it's illegal?" she asked, her voice flat. "That seems like a really lame super power."

Quinn shrugged. "Reanimators are not only rare. Their magic is so highly regulated because they are exceptionally powerful. It's actually really cool."

Ember didn't look convinced.

"And dangerous," Rhys added. "Nobody wants to be on the Grove's radar."

Kai glared at Rhys, but Allister said, "I'm afraid he's right. For now, I think it's best we say nothing. At least until Ember has gained some control. Since she hasn't actually reanimated anything, I think we are safe for now. We can control it."

The others looked to Isa. She hadn't told him about the revenants they'd killed. Isa had lied to Allister. Kai took a minute to digest the new information. Ember looked ill. There was a long pause before the alpha said, "He's right. Ember hasn't hurt anyone. We say nothing for now. We need to know more."

Ember looked shocked. Rhys's gaze bored a hole through Kai, but Kai had never been so proud of Isa in his life. It was official. Isa's lie told the pack Ember was one of them. Even if the Grove came for him, Isa would protect Ember so it wouldn't all be for nothing.

"So, now what?" Tristin asked.

"We need to know more about her magic, right?" Donovan asked.

"Couldn't you access the Grove library, Daddy?" Astrid asked, smirking at her brother. She had to know Quinn desperately wanted access to that information.

"I'm afraid that won't work. There is no way to access the library without alerting the Grove. We already have a big enough mess on our hands if they find out she's not really dead..."

  168

Ember yawned. "How do we know they don't already know? Couldn't they have sent me and my dad away?"

Allister tilted his head at her. "The Grove doesn't handle things that way."

Ember paled. "So, if they do find out I'm alive...that I'm a reanimator?"

Allister looked pained. "The Grove will do anything to maintain the balance. Imagine how unbalanced three reapers in one family may seem."

Quinn stared at his father with suspicion. Astrid looked uncomfortable at the attention on her father. She had to be questioning why her father would help them cover up what was sure to be a death sentence for all involved if the tree huggers found out.

"It's already risky. We weren't careful. People know you're alive. Your family knows you're alive. The Grove may already be aware. If people believe you're a reaper like your cousins, they may become scared. Things could get...ugly." Allister said.

Kai looked at Allister sharply. That's exactly what Ms. Josephine said. Had Allister been involved in what happened twelve years ago? Josephine said she'd been out of town, that's how she survived. How did Allister survive?

"It's going to be a bit hard to keep her powers under wraps if she can't control them. She is barely keeping it together on a regular basis," Wren said, subconsciously touching Kai's shoulder.

Ember blushed, tucking her feet under her further. Donovan turned and patted her leg comfortingly. She didn't flinch at his touch, just smiled. The knot in Kai's chest loosened a bit. She was warming up to their ways.

Tristin snorted. "Barely keeping it together? That's an understatement; she practically spewed magic all over us today in class."

Kai shot a glare at his sister. "What are you talking about?"

"Oh, that's right. You weren't there today. Ember's little friend made an appearance at school, and her magic went nuts."

Ember, her mouth hanging open, was staring at Tristin.

"Little friend?" Allister asked.

  169

"Yes, the grim from the cemetery, the one that tried to kill her. He followed her all the way from New Orleans," Tristin announced, smirking at Ember until Isa's eyes bled gold and she growled.

Chapter 28

TRISTIN

Isa looked at each of them in turn. "It seems my pack has forgotten who the alpha is around here. Is there any reason you four decided this information was unimportant to me?"

Tristin went still, and Neoma buried her face in Isa's shoulder, where she sat tucked under the alpha's arm. The others gazes slid to the floor.

"That...thing is here because of you? Of course it is." Astrid rolled her eyes. "We haven't had anything like that settle in this town in years."

"Yeah, and why do you think that is, sis?" Quinn questioned. "Oh, that's right. Because we run them out of town while you guys hide behind your sad Grove-approved spells and your huge egos."

"Quinn," Isa warned gently. "Enough."

He adjusted his glasses and slid his hand over Tristin's leg. She gave a shaky breath at the feel of his touch, running her palm over his but not looking at him. She ignored the raised eyebrow from her brother. She didn't need to explain their relationship to him.

"Right now," Kai said. "Our main priority needs to be figuring out how to get Ember's power under control so we don't have to worry about her blood boiling or her spewing her mojo all over us or anybody else."

"Tristin helped me in class," Ember supplied.

"Huh?" Tristin looked at Ember in confusion. Tristin doubted the water she'd supplied had helped her.

Ember nodded. "When we were in there, whatever you did helped."

Tristin looked around the room. "I didn't do anything. I swear."

"Interesting," Allister said, before adding, "So, how do we help November get some control over this power of hers?"

"What about trying to have her use her powers in a controlled environment?"

All eyes swung to Neoma. She blushed at having so many people looking at her.

Tristin watched as her brother looked to Rhys before letting his gaze skitter back to the faery. Rhys moved closer, hand sliding along Kai's lower back. What the hell was that about? Isa watched them too.

Ember looked flushed. Was she sweating? She really hoped this conversation wouldn't get her worked up. She didn't think she could handle another round of dunk the reaper in the bathtub.

"Ms. Josephine said she needed somebody who could filter or channel her magic," Rhys supplied.

"I could try to let her use me as a channel?" Kai shrugged.

Allister shook his head. "I don't think that's a good idea. From what I saw the day she arrived, that's a lot of magic. It may kill you. I think we need another way. Perhaps, Neoma is right. We need a controlled environment. Having Ember deliberately use her powers might help her gain some control."

"Okay, so controlled environment." Wren smiled at Neoma. "What did you have in mind?"

"We could go to the cemetery," she offered, picking at the flower detail on her robe.

"No!" Kai and Rhys both shouted.

What was going on with those two? Tristin looked at Quinn, knowing there was no way he was missing their strange behavior. He watched them carefully.

Neoma slunk further into Isa, who snarled at the two. Rhys moved to sit next to the girl. "It's a great idea," he said. "Really. It's just maybe we should start with something smaller. An even more controlled environment."

Isa and Wren still glared at them. "Such as?" Isa asked through clenched teeth.

"Morgue?" Tristin offered.

"God, no. An entire bay full of fresh corpses is probably a bad idea," Kai shuddered.

"He's right. Besides, it's hard to access and even harder to explain if we get caught," Quinn said. Tristin nodded.

Tristin looked at her alpha, who was extending and retracting her claws like a pissed-off cat. Cats. Yes. "What about the pet cemetery?" Tristin asked.

Rhys's hand partially shifted so his claws pricked through the fabric of her brother's shirt. Kai hissed but looked to Rhys. "It's actually not a bad idea. Worst case scenario, she raises an army of bunnies and really old cats."

Ember shuddered but said nothing.

"What do you think, Ember?" Isa asked.

Ember shrugged. "Sounds like a plan, I guess."

Tristin couldn't help feeling they were all going to regret this.

"Wonderful. Is that it?" Allister asked.

"No." All eyes swung to Quinn, who narrowed his eyes at his father. "I have some questions, Dad."

"Questions? For me?" Allister snorted. "Such as?"

"How did you know Tristin screamed at the council meeting?"

The witch flushed. "Excuse me?"

"Ms. Josephine said she heard Tristin screamed at the council meeting. You've been saying she screamed for years. I just assumed it was because Tristin was at home with us and you heard from whoever watched us. But Josephine says they were at the meeting, right?"

Quinn looked to Kai for confirmation. Kai nodded, hissing quietly as Rhys's claws pierced his skin. Yeah, they were definitely hiding something.

"You were on the council, Dad. You knew Tristin screamed. Sounds like you were there. I mean, somebody had to get the kids out of there, right? Everybody said you and Ms. Josephine were the only council survivors. She was out of town, so that leaves you. How did you know Tristin screamed if you weren't there like you've always claimed?"

"Exactly what are you accusing me of?" Allister sputtered.

"I'm not accusing you of anything, Dad. I'm just saying you said you heard Tristin scream, but Tristin was at the meeting. So you had to have been at the meeting too? Somebody rescued them from the conveniently unnamable evil that annihilated our town."

"What's your point, Quinn?" Tristin asked, nicer than she would have asked anybody else.

"You said you were the only council members to survive, but that's not true. Ember's dad survived. Ember survived. You said Tristin screamed, so that means you were there. You know what happened to the council, you know what happened to mom, to all of them. You have to know what happened. Have you known all this time and kept it from us? From all of us? If you know, you need to tell us."

Tristin put a gentle hand on Quinn, but he was too far gone. The tension between the two of them had been building for some time. If Quinn thought his father had lied to him about his own mother's death, there would be no going back for them. Quinn might be overreacting, but looking at Rhys and her brother, she didn't think so. Quinn was onto something.

Allister's mouth split into a sneer. "You ungrateful little bastard; do you dare to question me, to question my loyalty to this town? You think you're so smart, don't you?" Quinn said nothing. "You think I would lie about what happened to your mother? My own wife? My friends? I grew up in this town." He pointed at Ember. "Your father was my best friend." He shoved a hand through his hair, agitated. "That old witch is a troublemaker, always has been. She knows nothing. She wasn't even there. That's why she really refused to tell you everything. She had nothing to tell. Was I there? I don't know.

None of us do. They took it from us. They wiped my memories, just like the rest of the town and replaced them with whatever fake ideas they chose to implant. For all I know, they wanted me to know Tristin screamed. Maybe I did rescue you children. Maybe it was Ember's father or Alex. I'll never know. None of us will ever know. That's what they do. They fix things. The Grove always cleans up their messes."

He was breathing hard by the time he was finished. Quinn was blinking rapidly, and Astrid looked like she had invisible hands around her neck, but Allister wasn't finished. "You don't know shit about what happened back then, so don't pretend I'm the bad guy."

Quinn snorted. "That's convenient; you survive but the Grove Men-in-Blacks away your memories?"

"Quinn, please," Kai pleaded, looking back and forth between Allister and his friend.

Allister shook his head. "You've made your choice. Don't bother coming home. You don't live there anymore. I'll have your things delivered here since its clear where your loyalties lie. Let's go, Astrid." To Isa he said, "Let me know if anything changes."

Isa nodded, her eyes on Quinn.

Quinn sat, stunned. Kai moved to comfort him, but Rhys held him still. Tristin turned from where she sat on Quinn's armchair, sliding herself into his lap. She could feel him shaking. Quinn's arms went around her automatically, leaning his head against her chest.

"You okay?" she asked.

Quinn took a shaky breath, before shrugging, his tone more confident than he had to be feeling. "Whatever, I barely live there anyway. This is my home." His eyes darted to Isa. "I mean, if…that is, can I—"

Isa stood. "This is your home, Quinn." She clapped her hands together. "Now, everybody go to bed, we have to animate some corpses tomorrow."

The others drifted away, but Tristin stayed where she was, tucking herself across Quinn's lap.

"Are you really okay?" she finally whispered.

He shook his head against her shoulder. "No, but it doesn't really matter. He's lying. I know he is."

 175

"Yeah, he's not the only one. Kai and Rhys are up to something too."

"Maybe it's just all that unresolved sexual tension," he mumbled against her skin.

She snickered, sucking in a startled breath at the way his lips dragged across her shoulder. "Hey, I'm trying to comfort you here. You better not be malingering just so you can check out my boobs."

He laughed too, but it died just as quick. Finally, he looked at her and said, "He's never going to love me, is he?"

Tristin's insides twisted at the hopelessness in his eyes. She wrapped her arms around him awkwardly, not sure how to really comfort somebody hurting like this. She kissed his forehead. "Fine, you can look at my boobs for a little bit longer. Then it's bedtime."

"I like the sound of that."

She rolled her eyes. "Your bed, Romeo."

He groaned. "You're no fun."

"Ha, I could be lots of fun. You don't know."

"I'll wear you down eventually."

"Keep telling yourself that."

Chapter 29

EMBER

Ember shuffled off to bed with the others. The plan was to meet after school at the tiny pet cemetery located deep in the woods behind the house. The idea of raising mutilated corpses of long dead family pets made her already-difficult sleep impossible. She didn't understand the purpose of her power. It felt disrespectful. But what choice did she have? Isa and the pack had already done so much to help. They'd taken her in and given her food and clothes. So far, all she'd done is make their lives much more dangerous.

She lay in bed, staring at the ceiling. She'd memorized every tiny crack and divot. She thought having a name to put with this energy would make things easier, but she'd been wrong. Naming it wasn't the same as taming it.

Most nights, her powers were like a dull itch under the skin, annoying but manageable. Other nights it was like she was being slowly roasted alive, her magic burning her from the inside. Knowing it was a spell wearing off didn't make it better. If anything, it made it worse.

That evening the sensations were driving her mad, making her shake out her hands or dig her nails into her flesh to keep the feelings at bay. She tried her best not to think about it, to think of other things, but those other things always involved galaxy silver eyes, messy hair, and a cocky demeanor.

She was a terrible person for letting her mind go there. Sure, he was beautiful. Perfect, even. But he tried to kill her, and he was, technically, stalking her. Not the qualities one should look for in a boyfriend. Boyfriend? No, not a boyfriend. She wouldn't be that girl. *But he said he isn't trying to kill me*, her traitorous brain supplied. So, it was a what? A joke? Who jokes about that? Psychopaths. Crazy people.

It didn't matter that he smelled really good or that he looked at her with more interest than anyone else ever had. He was clearly insane, and smart girls did not fall for killers. They definitely didn't fall for people who specifically wanted to kill them.

If he'd wanted to kill her. Which he said he hadn't. She rolled over, shouting her frustration into her pillow. She flipped her phone on, looking at the time. It was almost six. She might as well get up. She threw back the covers and headed to the bathroom down the hall.

She rolled her head around on her shoulders, trying to breathe evenly as her magic decided to wake up too. She stripped her pajamas off and stepped into the cool water, like she did most mornings, biting her cheek hard not so scream at the feel against her suddenly overheated skin. She scrubbed quickly, hopping in place to keep the blood flowing to her limbs.

Her chest tightened, realizing they were going to make her call her power to the surface on purpose. She couldn't contain it now. She already spent half her time feeling like peeling her own skin off, so what would it be like if she just let the energy overtake her? It might kill her. Her life had gone from complicated to unrecognizable in less than a week. How could her father have done this to her?

She got dressed, throwing on a pair of shorts and a t-shirt. She could hear the others starting to stir, getting ready for school. She had a math test in first period. How could they expect her to do algebraic equations and then reanimate corpses? She couldn't do it. The idea of sitting through seven periods made her brain burn. She needed to relax.

She made a decision, grabbing her book bag and her sketchbook; she had to get out of the house for a while. She just hoped Isa wasn't too mad. Ember crept down the front stairs, praying the wolves were all preoccupied enough upstairs to miss her departure.

The heat engulfed her like a warm, wet blanket. It was barely seven o'clock, and it was oppressively hot. The humidity made her skin instantly damp. She dragged her hair off her neck and pulled it into a knot on her head just to try to get some relief. Living in Florida took some getting used to, but living in Florida with her power surges was a special kind of hell.

She made her way down the dirt road that led to the main street but turned off before she hit pavement following a tiny dirt trail. She'd never explored the town alone, only going to school and back or out with the others to the diner or for coffee. She had no idea where she was going, but she kept walking.

She cut through the woods until she hit the railroad tracks through the center of town. She walked along the railing. She'd never heard an actual train come through, so she figured she was safe enough. How had the witches handled the train when they cloaked the town?

She had never really been this far west before. It was a far cry from the center of town with its small cafés and charming Victorian houses. The woods to her right gave way to beat-up roads with old boarded-up shops and empty houses. It was so quiet. No people. No animals. Even the air seemed too still. Something was wrong. A sudden realization made her stop dead, rattled to her core.

Cars sat in driveways. A rusted bicycle sat outside a flower shop. One of the houses still had a swing set sitting in the front yard. There were still trash cans at the end of people's driveways. These people hadn't sold their houses; they'd abandoned them...or something far worse.

She looked over her shoulder, scanning the empty streets for any sign of life, suddenly spooked at the idea of so many people just...disappearing. The only movement was the single swing swaying empty in the slight breeze. Would they have wiped out a whole neighborhood to get rid of any humans not in the know about the supernatural? Everybody else seemed to think it was a possibility.

She shook off the thought, continuing on her way. She wiped her brow, spotting a gravel road that disappeared into a thick glade of trees. She probably shouldn't be wandering around in the woods in a town full of monsters, but she was a monster too, maybe more of one than the others.

She flinched as tiny shocks licked along her skin, almost like her magic wanted her to know it was there, just waiting for her to figure it out; like she needed reminding. Did they really think she'd figure her magic out in the middle of a pet cemetery?

She walked on, the road getting narrower until it was just a tiny trail of gravel choked by roots and overgrown with kudzu vines. She almost turned back but stopped when she saw the remnants of a small iron gate hanging by one rusted hinge.

It took her longer than it should have to reach it. She tripped over a rock, almost sacrificing a flip-flop to a thick knotting of plants. She shoved hard at the gate, the foliage too thick to go around. She squeezed herself through the tight space, grateful to find herself in a clearing of sorts.

The grass was overgrown, but it was like the vines and weeds just wouldn't grow there, instead climbing upwards, covering the surrounding trees, and creating a wall surrounding the space. In the center of the clearing, one enormous tree spread its branches across the expanse, enclosing it against the sun overhead.

Huge purple flowers hung heavy from the vines wrapping around the tree branches, and mushrooms of every conceivable type seemed to thrive around the base of the tree. Everything about this space seemed fantastical, like she was Alice in her strange new Wonderland. She hesitated; her magic liked this place, pulsing beneath the surface, but she felt like she was invading, encroaching on a sacred space.

She made it two steps before she saw the first stone, crumbled and half-hidden in the overgrowth. She knelt down, her laugh bubbling up before she could stop it. She'd found a cemetery…or maybe the cemetery found her. Maybe the dead would always find her.

She knelt before the stone, letting her fingers run over the rough granite. She could barely make out the name, but the rock vibrated beneath her fingertips as she traced the shallow grooves; something inside her shuddered in response. She pulled her hand back and stood, brushing off her knees. Power, like raw flame, burned along her palms, and her magic wanted her to go back, to touch the stone again.

    180

She rubbed her hands together, trying to appease the energy. She walked slowly, letting her eyes adjust to the way the sun filtered through the branches of the tree, creating a dizzying optical illusion of dancing shadows along the ground.

Was this the only cemetery in the small town? It seemed hard to believe. All the stones were weathered and old. It was more likely they'd created a newer more modern one years ago, leaving this one in peace.

Before, she would have found this place peaceful too. Before her father died, before she found out she had family, before she met a twisted demon who seemed to possess the power to make her forget he wanted her dead, before her magic found her. Yes, before all of that, this truly would have been a sanctuary from reality.

The closer she came to the great tree in the center, the more she could see it monopolized the space, thick roots snaking along the ground, displacing any stones in its path. She'd thought to sit under the tree and sketch, but as her hand brushed the trunk, an image flashed in her mind.

"November," her mother's voice said. "Put that down and come here."

She saw her. She saw her mother with her flame red hair and easy smile. Ember heard her mother's voice. She recognized the scent of lavender and something else, something entirely her mother. It was the first image of her as she was, before her imagination turned her into a vision out of a horror movie. Before. As quick as it came, it was gone.

"No," she said. "No. No. No."

She moved to the base of the tree and sat, tucking herself against it, just in case it was the cause for her vision. She closed her eyes tight. She had to remember. She needed an image of her mother that wasn't something weird and grotesque. Images swam back before Ember's eyes and she really saw her mother.

Her mother wore jeans rolled at the ankles and one of Ember's father's old button down shirts covered in blotches of color. She was painting on a canvas under a tree, under this tree.

Ember could hear children laughing in the distance and knew it was Kai and Tristin playing just beyond the stones to her left. Ember had been playing too, but she'd found something much more interesting. She'd found a bird; a tiny little

   181

bird with a grey belly and glossy black wings. She held it in her palms, belly up, presenting it to her mother like an offering.

"Mommy, it's got a owie," she said.

"No, sweetie. No owie," her mother said gently. "This bird has crossed over. It's gone."

Ember looked at her mother with confusion. "It's right here."

"No, baby. Its body is here, but its soul is gone. Somebody helped it across the veil. They helped to make sure it went safely. That's what we do."

Her face crumbled. "So it die?"

"Yes, sweetie," her mom said, kissing Ember's head and moving back to paint. "You should put it back where you found it or have the twins help you bury it."

"It should no die. Old things die. This widdle, see?" she stretched as far as her little arms could reach so her mother could really examine the bird.

"Ember, honey, sometimes things die even when they are little."

She scrunched up her face and carried the little bird back to where she sat on the other side of the tree. Kai and Tristin came to sit next to her.

"What happened to it?" Tristin asked, brow furrowed in concentration, stroking its belly.

"It's dead. See?" Kai said, poking it gently.

"That's sad," Tristin said.

Ember placed it on the ground and pressed her finger to its chest. It convulsed beneath her fingers. They looked at each other and giggled. She did it again.

"Do it again," Kai said.

She did. It jumped, squirming, eyes flying open. Kai and Tristin jumped back in surprise, but Ember scooped it up.

She ran to her mother, excited. "Look, Mommy, I fixed it."

Her mother gasped, dropping her paintbrush. "Ember, what did you do? How did you—"

"You are fond of cemeteries, aren't you, luv?"

Her eyes flew open, her jaw clenching as Mace's face swam into view and her mother's voice faded on the wind. Something flared to life low in her belly. Ember tensed, muscles and tendons straining as she gripped the roots of the tree, her vision bleeding red.

   182

She was on fire, her skin so hot she felt it might blister and peel from her, leaving nothing but the sudden seething rage. Her face contorted, lips pulling back in a snarl.

He took a step back, arching one brow. "Oh, I've made you cross with me," he said. "That wasn't my intention, lu—" She cut her eyes at him. "Ember," he corrected, pulling a face at his error. "My apologies. It's just not every day you find somebody meditating in a cemetery. I thought maybe you'd like to talk about it."

She tried to speak but found she was mute. Power poured into her, filling her up until her lungs felt scorched. She was drowning on dry land, and once again, she was helpless to stop it. Mace continued talking as if nothing was wrong, but he felt her struggle. She knew it like the sound of her own heartbeat, like the way it felt to draw breath into her lungs. Somehow, he was connected to her.

His voice hitched on a shaky laugh. "Come on, Ember, you can't stay mad at me forever."

She could. She would. She wanted to tell him, so but when she opened her mouth, it was not her voice. "Who are you?"

Mace recoiled, eyes narrowing. Ember watched it all, a spectator in her own body.

"Mace," he said. "And you are…?"

"We are infinite. We are everything and nothing."

Mace's eyebrow's shot upwards. "Ah, I see." He knelt before her, cupping her face before dropping his hands as if burned. He eased back. "Um, approximately how many of you are in there. No need to be exact, a rough estimate will do."

The cackle that echoed from her lips scared her, but the fear on Mace's face frightened her more. He didn't seem the type to panic easily. What if he left her? What would they do to her?

He didn't run. He looked her right in the eyes. "Ember, luv, I know you're in there. Whatever is happening, you have to fight."

She wanted to tell him he was right. She was right there, but they wouldn't let her. "She won't fight. She has no idea what she's doing. But you, you know, don't you? We know you. We need you. She needs you," the voice taunted in the singsong tone of a demented child.

 183

Mace had no idea what was going on. His smile was tight across his face. "I'm flattered, of course, but I'm afraid I will have to respectfully decline. I'm already gainfully employed."

The thing inside Ember screeched in fury. "You don't get to choose."

Her fists hit the ground, and it rumbled beneath her, tiny furrows forming along the surface. Mace looked alarmed. She was scaring him. Somewhere in the darkest part of her, she found his fear oddly satisfying, or maybe her magic did.

She did it again, her fists causing the ground to tremble, tipping over an already crumbling headstone.

"My apologies," he started, leaning back, hands in the air. "I'm at your service. Always happy to help."

"She's not strong enough for this. We'll burn her from the inside if you don't help. You know it's true, but perhaps you don't care about her?"

Ember felt herself gain control enough to stare at her hands, fascinated with the sparks arching between her fingers. She blinked heavily.

"Do you see this?" she whispered, watching as her fingertips blistered and blackened. She blinked hard against the sweat pouring into her eyes. She vaguely registered the pain in her hands.

"I do see it, yes. Um, I think it's important you relax, luv. Possibly try breathing?"

"I don't want to. I just want this. We just want this." She thrust her abused hands into the earth beneath her. Her relief was instant, like completing a circuit. All that power poured from her into the ground below; something like roots wrapped at her wrists, holding her to the earth. As the energy flowed from her into the ground, it felt like she was dying, her life draining from her, but she just couldn't bring herself to care.

Chapter 30

MACE

Mace stared at the girl before him, not at all sure Ember was even in there anymore. Her eyes bled black and her head fell backwards, looking up at nothing. Well that was certainly not good. Whatever had a hold of Ember was draining her. The ground trembled, headstones crumbling, tiny cracks appearing along the ground like lightning bolts, widening enough to swallow a chunk of concrete.

If he didn't stop this, they were going to swallow this cemetery and take the two of them with it. But he had no idea how to stop it. He could run. Nobody had ever accused him of being a hero, a benefit that came with having no soul. Even before he finished the thought, he knew he wouldn't go. He had no idea why. Maybe it was the way it taunted him. Maybe it was the way she'd looked so helpless. He wasn't ready to think about the why just yet.

"All right, luv," he said, inching closer. "I'm hoping you're still in there somewhere because you're going to have to help me out just a little. I think this is going to hurt like hell."

He plunged his hands into the dirt, just over hers. Whatever bound her hands below the surface loosened, allowing him to take hold, palm to palm.

The pain was instantaneous, like thousands of razor blades piercing his flesh. It punched the breath from his lungs. The bindings that once held Ember closed to embrace them both, sealing his fate. He was, once again, grateful for his immortality, as there appeared to be no escape.

"Ember, I need you to hear me." He could feel blisters forming where they connected. "Come on, luv. I know you're in there."

He did the only thing he could think of. He called his own magic to the surface. He'd channeled her energy in the cemetery; maybe he could do it again. He dropped his guard, letting her in. The magic running through her hit him like an atom bomb, wrenching him backwards. If not for their bound hands, she might have cast him out. He clenched his teeth as her magic felt his and fought back, chewing through his power and trying to replace it with her own.

He'd been in the world long enough to know his magic was powerful. This power—her power—was like nothing he'd felt before. It seemed like far too much for one person to hold.

"Ember," he said, grunting against the pain. "You have to work with me here. If you don't rein this in, you will hurt somebody." Most likely him. "I know you don't want to hurt anybody. That's not the type of girl you are. You are one of those do-gooder types. I know it."

He talked to distract himself from the pain and to find a way past her wall of magic. If he kept talking, maybe she would actually hear him from wherever it was she was hiding in there.

"Think of your pack. Ember, just look at what you're doing. Whoever's in there with you, don't let them win. Can you do that? Can you look at me? Look at anything? Do you really want to hurt somebody, Ember?"

Her head snapped forward, black eyes staring through him. He flinched. She lurched towards him, and it took a moment for his brain to register that she wasn't attacking him; she'd passed out, her head on his shoulder, body limp. The shaking stopped, the bonds that tied them together loosening enough for him to catch her as she toppled over.

He was soaked with sweat. His skin burned. He sucked air into his abused lungs, waiting for the pain to fade. He leaned against the tree, rearranging Ember so her head rested against his thigh.

He pushed her hair back from her face, tapping her cheek lightly. "Ember?" He slapped her lightly. "Ember, luv, just open your eyes and let me know you're...you? Please," he whispered the last part, embarrassed.

No response. He peeled open one of her eyelids, relieved to see those otherworldly violet eyes. This close he couldn't help but notice the tiny flecks of yellow around her pupil. He pressed his fingers against her neck. Her pulse was steady. She lived. That was something.

He held up her hand examining her fingertips. They were pink, the blistered black skin gone somehow. His hands hadn't fared quite so well, but he'd worry about that later.

He had no idea what to do with her. He pushed a stray curl from her face, letting his finger trace over the freckles on her nose. She was quite lovely, when she wasn't trying to peel the skin from his bones.

She sighed, turning her face into his hand with something akin to a purr. He swallowed hard, shoving down the strange feeling something had changed between them. He didn't have time for it. This power, whatever it was, would kill her or somebody else. He'd never seen somebody so consumed by her magic. She was an enigma.

The voice that spoke with him wasn't hers, but she showed no other signs of possession. She didn't hold any powers to suggest she was a witch or a reaper, but there was nothing else she could be.

"What the hell did you do to my cousin?"

Mace's head snapped up, grimacing at the intrusion. He plastered a smile on his face. "Well, if it isn't the boy reaper and his human sidekick."

"Get the hell away from her," the human said. "What did you do to her?"

"I didn't do anything. She had a little...outburst," he said, gesturing to the damage around them. "I took care of it. She's now comfortably sleeping it off. You're welcome."

They took in the fissures opened along the ground and then back to the girl in his lap.

"You're saying Ember did this?" Kai asked.

"You know she did."

The human looked startled. "Why was she out here?" he asked nobody in particular.

"I'm afraid when I found her she wasn't in the mood for chatting. I suppose I could've left her here and hightailed it out of town before she turned this place into a sinkhole, but I thought I'd at least try to help."

The other one snorted. "Right. You helped her."

He said nothing.

The human moved forward. "Wait. Did you help her?"

He raised an eyebrow. "Well, it's hard to help somebody when you don't know what they are but I did what I could. It would be helpful if you told me exactly what she is. Reaper? Witch? Hybrid?"

They ignored the question, the human asking, "So, what does that mean? What exactly did you do?"

"I just grabbed her hands and hung on. I tried to counteract her magic with mine. If I wasn't already dead, I'd say it very well may have killed me."

They took the information better than expected. The human stared at him for a long time, like he was examining him under a microscope, finally asking, "What are you?"

He contemplated not telling them, but really he had no reason to lie. "I'm sure you think I'm going to play hard to get, but since I can't actually die, I'll tell you. I'm sluagh."

The human's mouth fell open. "Lie," he said. "No way. They're extinct. They were wiped out by the Tuatha de Danaan centuries ago."

"Not all of us. You can't kill what's already dead, mate. It's true they managed to trap some of us in the in-between, but I assure you, some of us are still here."

"Uh, what is a sloo-ah?" the reaper asked, looking back and forth between the two.

 188

"Not what, who," Quinn said, never taking his eyes off Mace. "The sluagh were a race of dark fae, part of the Unseelie. Demons who flew in flocks like birds and stole the souls of the dying."

"Stole?" the reaper echoed. "He's a reaper?"

He scoffed. "He's a soul eater. In the hierarchy of supernatural psychopaths, it doesn't get much worse than him."

Mace raised a brow. "You're quite judgey, aren't you? I have to eat."

"A soul eater?" the reaper repeated.

"Some human scholars thought they were the fallen angels."

"Aye, that is true." Mace nodded.

"You're a fallen angel?" the reaper asked, voice dripping with disbelief.

He smiled. "I didn't say that. I'm simply agreeing with your mate. That is what they say about us."

The human's eyes closed as if he was trying to recall more information. "The sluagh were once human, but their deeds were so vile and repulsive they caught the attention of the Unseelie. The Unseelie took them, creating an army of creatures forced to sustain themselves on the souls of others. Sluagh feed on the weak and the sick before they can receive last rites. They prey on the broken and try to steal the souls of the dead before they can be carried across the veil by...well, by you, dude. They have the ability to steal any living soul and are immortal simply because neither heaven nor hell will have them."

Mace laughed. "That's a neat trick, mate. I bet you are a blast at parties, but I'm afraid most of that is simply propaganda."

The reaper bristled at the maligning of his friend. "Get away from my cousin. Actually, just stay away from my cousin."

He looked down at Ember with her face turned into his hand and sighed. He moved from beneath her, gently settling her head on the ground and brushing off his jeans.

The reaper's hand floated to the hilt of his knife.

"Easy, lads. I was just doing as requested." Neither moved, watching him. For his own amusement, he began to pace. "Now, I could, as you suggested, leave your cousin alone. But ask yourself this question." He came to stop before the two. "What if I hadn't

 189

been here? I don't know what she is, but I'm guessing you do. I think we can all agree she has no control over the amount of energy coursing through her veins."

The two looked at each other. He knew they knew he was right. He smirked at them. "So the next time she melts down, which of you will stand in and act as filter, hmm?" He looked back and forth between the two, palms up to show them the blisters. "I've been around for centuries, and it felt a little like she was trying to turn my skin inside out."

The reaper blanched. "Why would we ever trust you?"

"I've collected more souls than you will in ten life times." The human snorted at the term collected but said nothing. "I'm not interested in harming her. I just want to help her."

It was the truth. Sort of.

The human tilted his head, shoving his glasses up the bridge of his nose. "Why? Sluagh have no soul. You don't feel sorry for her; you can't care about her, what could possibly be in this for you?"

"I have my reasons. I'm afraid you'll just have to trust me."

Her cousin balked. "You basically just told us you are one of the world's most prolific serial killers, but you want us to trust you?"

"I'm certain the term you are looking for is mass murderer, but I see your point. So, allow me to put it another way." He grinned at them. "What choice do you have?"

The reaper bent down and picked up his cousin's limp form, grunting a bit at the effort. "I will discuss your *generous* offer with the pack and get back to you."

"Yes, do. I'll be around."

  190

Chapter 31

EMBER

Ember bolted upright, crawling towards the back corner of the sofa, her heart hammering. She scanned the room, trying to figure out where she was and how she got home. Seven faces stared back, shocked at her violent awakening.

"Welcome back," Wren smiled. "How are you feeling?"

"What? What happened?" She fought to make her brain catch up. Her head hurt, every muscle ached.

Tristin rolled her eyes. "You passed out...again."

Ember pulled a face at her cousin but said nothing, unable to deal with her irrational hatred. Ember looked at each in turn, taking in their grim expressions.

Her stomach sank. "What did I do? Why do you all look like I killed somebody?"

Donovan shook his head and smiled. "You didn't just pass out; you almost took out the entire town. Your magic is, like, out of control."

They all stared at him, incredulous.

It came back to her in a rush—her mother, Mace, the voice…that crazy voice from inside her, the power that seemed to rip through her.

"How did you find me?"

"The wolves tracked you for a while, but when they lost the scent, Neoma found you," Isa said, smiling at the girl.

Ember looked at the girl painting her nails in the corner. "How?"

Neoma just shrugged, not even bothering to look up from her task.

"Neoma has her own gifts," Isa said.

"I could've killed people," Ember said, almost to herself. Kai's gaze skated away from her to Rhys and then to the ground, and she felt sick as she realized the truth. "You knew, didn't you?" she asked Kai. "You knew something like this could happen. Who else knew?"

Everybody seemed confused by Ember's sudden outburst, everybody except Kai, Rhys, Isa, and Wren. "You knew too, didn't you?"

Kai scuffed his converse across the floor, not making eye contact with anybody. "It was my fault. I asked them not to tell you."

It shouldn't have hurt. It wasn't like Ember had been there long enough for them to have any kind of loyalty to her. They didn't owe her anything. They didn't know her. They didn't trust her. Why should they? She tried to ignore the sick feeling in her stomach. She should leave. She bit down on her lip, forcing back tears of frustration. She wouldn't give them the satisfaction. She just couldn't trust anybody. It wasn't like she hadn't learned years ago. She didn't cry for people.

From deep inside, she could feel that power stir, a slow tiny burn just looking for the oxygen it needed to burst free. She tried not to panic. Her legs shook, body trembling from the inside like her organs were shaking loose. She wanted to scream in frustration. She couldn't live like this.

Isa knelt down in front of Ember. Her skin burned as the alpha took Ember's hands in her own. "I know you don't believe this, but we thought it was for the best. You're being overwhelmed by your magic. You have no control. It's not your fault, and nobody's blaming you, but you need to try to take some deep breaths. Okay?"

Ember swallowed the lump in her throat, her first instinct to tell Isa to screw off. Ember drew in a few shaky breaths, in through her nose, out through her mouth trying to ignore just how stupid she felt.

"Why did you go to the cemetery?" Wren asked, once she felt a little more in control.

She shrugged, hands flailing. "I don't know. I wasn't consciously going to the cemetery. I didn't even know there was a cemetery. I just needed to get out of here. I just needed to leave."

"Leave? And go where?" Tristin asked, shooting to her feet and pointing in Ember's face. "Seriously? After Kai saved your life, you were just going to take off? You were just going to bolt and leave us to clean up your mess?"

Ember stared at her cousin. "What?" She wasn't moving out of state, she went for a walk.

Isa shot Tristin a nasty look, but the other girl was far too gone to heed the warning flash of gold eyes. Ember blinked at Tristin in confusion.

"You are so selfish. I can't believe you."

Heat prickled along Ember's spine, and then she was on her feet lunging for the other girl. Rhys caught Ember, arm around her shoulders, holding her back as she screamed, "What is your problem with me? What did I ever do to you?"

Tristin opened her mouth, baring her teeth, looking more animal than the animals surrounding her. Whatever she was about to say died with a single meaningful glance from Quinn.

"Nothing," she muttered. "Forget it."

"Forget it?" Ember shouted. Was she serious? "Seriously? Forget it? You are horrible all the time, you glare at me and roll your eyes, and you act like I killed your puppy. What did I ever do to you? What? Tell me, please."

Tristin dropped her gaze, but Ember's magic pulsed, barely contained. Rhys watched her closely, loosening his hold but not releasing her.

"Ember," Wren said, his voice soothing. "You need to calm down. We need to talk about some things."

 193

"Don't you think if I could calm down, I would? Don't you think if I had any control over this, whatsoever, I would do it? I can't control this. I can't stop this. What am I supposed to do?"

Power roared to life under her skin, and she opened her mouth to scream at the sudden pain, but her voice wouldn't come. She stared at the others helpless to stop it. Her magic was driving things, and she was going to kill them all.

Everybody in the room froze. The wolves bristling at the energy shift in the room. She didn't want this, but she was a hostage in her own body. Rhys looked to Isa as Ember's magic sparked from her fingertips.

"Um, guys?" Neoma called softly from the doorway, moving silently on her bare feet.

"Little busy, sweetheart," Wren said without turning around.

"I know," she said. "I'm pretty sure that's why he's here."

All eyes swung to the door. Mace sauntered in, taking in Neoma with interest. "Well, aren't you just the most adorable thing ever? I haven't seen one of your kind in a long while."

Wren and Rhys growled, eyes flashing, teeth elongating.

"Relax, boys, it wasn't a proposal of marriage." His eyes found Ember's, and he tilted his head. "Well, seems that I've arrived just in the nick of time."

Ember paled at his presence, but her magic purred, reaching out to him, trying to coax him closer.

"What are you even doing here?" Tristin asked, clearly confused by his arrival. "How do you know where we live?"

He cleared his throat, his grin smug. "Interesting development, mate," he addressed Kai. "While it appears Ember is unsure of her feelings towards me, her magic is a girl that knows what she wants."

Tristin snorted, rolling her eyes.

"So she…" Quinn prompted.

"Summoned me? Possibly? I'm not entirely certain, but I was just walking along minding my own business and found myself here, at your house. I can only assume she summoned me here."

"I did not," she managed to choke out indignantly, even as she moved closer to him. She held out her hand to him, horrified at her body's treachery. She didn't mean to do that. She didn't want to do that.

"Oh, come now," he said, linking his fingers with hers. Her whole body shuddered, the power inside her licking through her fingertips, circling his fingers. His brows lifted, looking down at their linked hands. He had to feel that. He looked mystified, staring intently, pulling his fingers from hers, only to have them drawn back into place like a magnet. He tried it again and then once more, an amused smile curving his lips.

She growled as she realized he was enjoying himself. This wasn't a game. She wanted to kick him, but she could only stand there at the mercy of this power coursing through her.

"Well, that's…disconcerting," Quinn said, breaking the strange bubble of silence.

"I have no idea what I'm even watching right now," Donovan voiced from his perch on the arm of the sofa.

"Ember might hate me, but her magic doesn't," Mace said, watching as her hands worked up his forearms, amusement in his tone. "So, I guess that means I'm sticking around."

"No way," Ember said, her teeth clenched so hard her jaw ached, willing her hands to stop moving over his arms. "There's no way that he's going to be around here all the time. He's the bad guy. He doesn't get to play hero."

"Fine, I'll go." He pried her hands away from him with a grunt of effort and turned to leave. He paused, a myriad of expressions playing across his face. He took a step, then another, looking progressively more pained with each step.

"Really?" He turned around. "Don't be ridiculous. You need me. You all need me. She'll take this house down to the rafters and after that, the town." He looked at Isa. "You're the alpha? I can keep her magic under control. I can help her channel it. You have to see I'm better than the alternative."

Isa sucked her bottom lip between her teeth and looked to Wren and then Ember.

"You can't be considering this after what Quinn told us? We can't possibly trust him," Tristin said.

  195

The walls of the house rattled, causing the pictures to shake. The wolves moved, and Kai grabbed Tristin's hand, pulling her out of the way as the chandelier swung precariously over their heads.

"Maybe he's doing that himself." Donovan said, looking spooked.

Mace looked equally spooked. "I assure you, I'm not. What exactly would I gain from this?"

"That's a great question," Wren asked. "What exactly are you getting out of this?"

"A sense of civic pride and a front row ticket to the show."

She didn't believe him, and she wasn't alone. It was Kai who spoke first. "Ember, what choice do we have? For whatever reason, your magic seems tied to his. Without him, you could hurt people."

Ember looked around, helpless. "Can't one of you do your wolf thing and tell if he's lying?"

"No heartbeat," Rhys grumbled.

Ember startled. "N-No heartbeat? He's dead?"

Mace looked at her imploringly. "Ember, just let me help you."

She hated this. She didn't want to be around any more people she couldn't trust. Nothing made any sense, but Kai was right. What choice did she have, really?

"Fine," she said, "but if you try anything…"

He held his hands up. "Best behavior, luv. On my honor."

Rhys snorted at his words, but her magic relented, curling back to sleep in that place deep inside her. She winced at the blisters on his palms. "Did I do that?"

"Don't trouble yourself, luv, I'll heal."

"Gosh, everybody is being so accommodating. Why don't you just have Quinn patch him up, since we obviously work with the bad guys now," Tristin fumed.

"Tristin, that's enough," Isa warned, glowering at Mace. "Sometimes we have to work with people we don't like…or trust. It goes with the territory."

"You're wise for one so young," Mace told the alpha. He then looked around, his face splitting into that smug grin. "So, who's going to tell me what she really is?" He grinned, triumphant.

Chapter 32

KAI

Kai slipped into the kitchen, abandoning Ember with a soul eater, a pack of confused werewolves, and his inexplicably hostile banshee sister. All and all, just another typical day.

He needed a minute to clear his head. He had no idea what to do about Ember magically tethering herself to a homicidal maniac. He also had no idea what to do about the fact that she might also *be* a homicidal maniac.

Her magic could blow up at any moment. What if tying herself to Mace only made her stronger? What if it made the soul eater stronger? Her magic and his together? They could annihilate half the population. He absently rubbed at the swirl of inked names wrapped around his bicep. He poked at the spot where Ember's name should have been. He'd never had a name disappear. He didn't even have anybody to ask what it meant.

His eyes fell on the plate of cookies on the counter, his stomach growling loudly. The only good thing to come out of this disaster was Isa's stress baking had gone to a whole other level. Like hall of fame amazing.

He was reaching for a cookie when a hand gripped his bicep, hauling him out the back door and onto the porch. The sadness over the loss of his cookie was cut short as two hundred plus pounds of werewolf slammed him against the side of the house. He grunted. He should be used to this by now. Rhys seemed to enjoy slamming him into things at every opportunity.

"Hello to you too," he rasped, attempting to suck air back into his abused lungs. "You know, you could just ask to talk to me like a normal person. At least *try* using your words."

Rhys just stood there, his forearm across his chest, all broody brows and intense eye contact. Kai licked his lower lip, trying to read something in the wolf's face. What Kai would give to know what was going on in that head of Rhys's. Kai swore the wolf did this on purpose. If you looked up enigmatic in the dictionary there was a picture of Rhys.

Kai's heart slammed against his ribcage. He hoped it read more as fear and less as god-yes-please-kiss-me. Rhys's gaze dropped to Kai's mouth before sliding away guiltily, like he was reading Kai's mind. Kai wanted to punch him.

"So…" Kai said, clearing his throat and tapping Rhys's forearm. "Air would be good here. You're sort of suppressing my diaphragm."

Rhys did his nostril-flaring thing and stepped back. Kai took a deep breath as he returned to full lung capacity. Rhys paced the porch but said nothing.

Kai flailed his hands. "Oh my God, just spit it out. Your inability to talk to me is literally killing me. Just open your mouth and speak."

"How much longer are we going to let this go on?" Rhys asked, his voice low but vehement. He parked himself against the porch rail, putting distance between himself and Kai, but not so much Rhys had to speak up to be heard. Everything about him was so calculated.

"What do you mean?"

His eyebrows shot up. "What do I mean? We have to tell them about her. We have to tell them everything."

"Why? I don't get why you think that we have to tell them everything. They know she's dangerous, and they know she can really mess things up. Why do we need to tell them that she was a homicidal

 198

preschooler? I see the way you look at her since we've been back. All you see is the girl responsible for killing our parents."

Rhys huffed. "That's not true."

Kai arched an eyebrow, crossing his arms.

Rhys glanced at a spot over Kai's shoulder. "Look, I know it's not something she could help. I look at her like she's dangerous, because she *is* dangerous. She's more dangerous than anybody knows because we're lying to them. We're lying to *her*. Even she doesn't know what she's capable of."

Rhys huffed as if he was trying to gather up the courage to keep going. "If you had raised an army of zombies, wouldn't you want to know? If you'd inadvertently hurt people with the same magic you can't control, wouldn't you want to know that? How do you think she's going to feel if she hurts somebody? Killing somebody is not quite as easy to shake off as bumping over headstones and knocking a couple of pictures off the wall."

"You are such a drama queen."

Kai's words lacked any real fire, but Rhys punched the wall next to his head, startling him. "Am I?" Rhys fumed. "We have a sluagh in our house babysitting our reanimator. Do you get that? Do you know what those things do? They feed on the souls of innocent people…without remorse. Hell didn't want him. Do you see where he falls on the spectrum of bad guy to sphincter-clenchingly evil? We've let two deadly creatures into our home. We've let them near our family, and we are leaving them defenseless because we are lying to them."

Kai's stomach did a weird flip-flop thing at Rhys's use of the word our. He didn't really know anything about sluagh except what Quinn had explained since the cemetery. There was no real solid research. None they could get their hands on anyway.

"Quinn said it's a legend, a Celtic ghost story Irish grannies told their kids to get them to behave. Like Keyser Söze in *The Usual Suspects*," Kai said.

Rhys rolled his eyes but otherwise failed to acknowledge Kai's movie reference. "That's exactly what the humans say about us in the outside world."

Rhys moved to the porch railing again, and Kai relented. "Fine, okay. She's dangerous. He's dangerous. They are both weapons of mass destruction. Why don't you say what you really mean, Rhys?"

"Which is what?"

"That this is my fault, that I should've just left her to die. That if I had just collected her and moved on none of this would be happening right now."

Rhys met Kai's gaze. "I'm not saying that."

"Actually you did say that. The night I brought her here, remember?"

Rhys's cheeks flushed. "I was mad. I was *concerned*." Kai could see Rhys getting frustrated. Kai waited, trying to be patient. "It's my job to take care of y—of the pack," Rhys said. "It is hard enough protecting us from vampires and trolls and the things we do know about. I can't protect us if I don't know what we're dealing with," he growled. "Why do you make everything so difficult?"

Kai said nothing, watching the expressions play across Rhys's face, letting him get it all out.

"Do you get what's happening right now? Do you really get it? We know that twelve years ago there was a witch here so powerful they forced a coven to cast a spell on an entire town, a witch that bound a girl's powers for years. We have a girl who can control the dead, and our only failsafe is a soul-eating demon."

Kai shook his head, gesturing helplessly. "Dude, our whole lives are dangerous. We fight monsters. We've almost died so many times. We always figure it out, and we always survive. We're good at this."

"No!" He balled his fists. "We are lucky. We are just…lucky. This is why you frustrate me…because you just don't get it."

"Then explain it to me. I'm right here," Kai fired back.

"I—" He turned away abruptly, suddenly fascinated with the yellowing grass.

Kai couldn't resist his own growl of frustration. "Oh, that's right. You don't talk about your feelings. You just grunt and shove and act perpetually pissed off. You think I don't get what we do is dangerous? Our parents are dead. All of our parents are dead, and they were good at this. They fought with all the information, and they still

 200

died, but I can't focus on that. If I did, I'd spend all my time broody and miserable like you."

Rhys looked over his shoulder, his expression unreadable. He was quiet for a long time before he asked Kai, "Have you thought at all about what's going to happen to you if they find out what you've done?"

He could play stupid, but he knew what Rhys meant. Kai hadn't thought about it. He'd actively been not thinking about it because thinking about it made him want to vomit.

Rhys was being kind by saying *if* they found out. It was only a matter of time before the Grove realized what Kai had done, and when they came, he would be punished. He spent every night trying to think of anything but what that punishment would be.

"What good is thinking about it? It's not going to change anything. Whatever they're going to do to me won't change by my freaking out about it."

He was sure the wolf could smell the fear, but Kai didn't acknowledge it.

"We can't lose you," Rhys said, quickly adding, "We can't lose any more people."

"Whether you guys lose me or not, you can't let it stop you from living your life."

Rhys looked at Kai like he was crazy. "Your sister would never get over it. Isa would be devastated. Quinn would try to find a way to get you back. The pack would fall apart. Why aren't you more afraid? You have to *want* to stay alive."

Anger twisted Kai's gut. "Yeah? I can wish myself alive now?" Kai asked. Why was Rhys so hell-bent on talking about this? What did he hope to accomplish? "Do you think telling me any of this is helpful? Do you think telling me my impending death will ruin the lives of everybody I love is in some way going to help the situation? Do you think making me feel guilty will somehow change what's going to happen?" He pushed forward, for once getting in Rhys's face. "Okay, let's play this game. Yeah, sure, why not. Tell me. How is Wren going to feel? Donovan? Neoma? Oh, I know, how are *you* going to feel?"

  201

Kai knew he was being a jerk, but he couldn't stop; panic gripped him like a hand around his throat, and he wanted to hurt Rhys for this, for making him think about this. "Come on, tell me. How are you going to feel when I'm not around to shove into walls anymore?" Rhys was silent. "What? You wanted to play this game. Tell me. Will you be happy to be rid of me once and for all? Will you admit how you feel about me when I'm long gone?" He was so close he could feel Rhys's panting breath on his face. "Will you regret not kissing me when you had the chance?"

Rhys's eyes flashed green, and they stood there, breathing in each other's space, neither willing to concede. "I—" Rhys swallowed, head dipping ever so slightly, but enough for Kai's heart rate to skyrocket.

"Hey, where'd you two losers take off too?" Quinn called out, the back door swinging open and shut.

Rhys blinked, looking to Quinn before pushing Kai gently out of the way and walking back into the house.

Quinn looked startled and then contrite. "Sorry, man. Didn't mean to, uh, interrupt."

"Can't interrupt something that was never going to happen." Kai shrugged, swallowing hard past the lump in his throat and dropping to the steps. He rubbed the palms of his hands against his eyes.

Quinn dropped down next to him, clapping him on the shoulder. "Friendly advice, man?"

"Sure."

"I think it's time you moved on."

Kai scoffed. "Like you and my sister?"

"Oh, I'm not saying give up entirely. I'm just saying maybe you should show him that you are a strong independent reaper who don't need no wolf." Quinn finished his statement with a head bob and a pointed finger.

Kai's eyebrows flew up, and he gave a startled laugh.

"You're ridiculous, man, but I love you."

"I love you too, buddy."

Chapter 33

MACE

Mace was rattled. He was an idiot. Ember glowered at him from the other side of the sofa. The others had cleared out, leaving them to stare awkwardly at each other. It gave the illusion of privacy, but in a house full of wolves, nothing went unheard. He should be trying to make nice with the little reanimator, but instead he just sat carefully contemplating his dilemma.

It was his own fault. It truly never occurred to him she could be a reaper, not with her cousins both possessing powers. In hindsight, it was the exact reason it should have occurred to him. It was now obvious why she was so valuable.

Except it wasn't.

There were other reanimators; they were rare, but they existed. So why was she so valuable? If she were simply a magical collector's item, they'd want to collect all three of them as a set or the rarest of the three. When it came to exceptional magic, there was no way to beat out the banshee. He'd never heard rumors of a banshee still in existence, much less one as young as Ember's cousin. She was the rarity.

He had to be missing something. Reanimators' powers were impressive but finite. They could reanimate and control corpses. The master reanimators could return a soul to corporeal form but, even then, for only a short period. The longest he'd ever seen a soul cling to this side was twelve hours. Reanimators could call the soul, but they didn't possess the ability to anchor it to a body. They didn't possess the ability to control an immortal...and yet she had.

Ember had been controlling him almost from the moment they met. Her magic had reached for him in the cemetery, it had forced his name from his lips, forced him to halt when he'd tried to come closer. At the time, he'd blown it off but moments ago, when he'd meant to leave, her magic hadn't allowed it. Every step he'd taken was agony, as if he'd been tethered to her by a million razor sharp hooks.

He was missing something, and he felt like it was there, just out of reach, waiting for him to put a name to it. In the cemetery, something had taken control of Ember's body. Somehow, Ember had been able to channel somebody else's magic. Whatever that something was had stupidly convinced him to link himself to Ember to keep her out of danger.

Reanimators couldn't channel the dead. There was no creature in the world who possessed the abilities Ember seemed to have. There was an excellent reason for that. If a creature existed who could do these things, they would be more powerful than any magical being in existence.

It would certainly make her a target. If word got out there was a creature with the ability to control all soulless beings, there would be no place safe enough for her. Every demon, vampire, sluagh, and fury would make it their mission to eradicate the threat. She would be a walking target. No, he corrected, they would be walking targets because he'd bound himself to this girl, and she now pulled his strings. He was a puppet, a walking, talking extension of her will.

Just like that, the word he'd been looking for, the only creature who could possibly possess all the qualities Ember did, came rushing back to him so quickly it made him dizzy. He risked a glance in her direction. She sat, legs crossed, arms folded, scowl locked in place, body language screaming do not cross.

  204

It seemed impossible to believe. There was no way for it to be true, but as soon as he looked at her face, he knew it was. Nobody else could know. She couldn't know. He had to be extremely delicate about this. The last thing he needed was her realizing she had the ability to control him.

It wasn't until she turned to look at him that he realized he'd been staring. As soon as they made eye contact, he felt her magic flare. It tugged at him, even as she tucked her hands in closer. She felt it too. She was in control again, her eyes laser focused on him. She didn't trust him. She certainly didn't like him. But her magic had decided he was useful.

There had to be a way to work this to his advantage. She had to think she still needed him. They all had to think she needed him. His current employer would probably give him anything in the world if he could deliver on this. Somebody like her. Power like hers. He could name his price. She was sweet and pretty, but he was immortal. He couldn't spend the next seventy years a slave.

How did somebody go about wooing a girl in this decade? More importantly how did one charm a girl into forgetting that he'd threatened to kill her?

It wasn't like he'd intended to harm her. He'd just wanted to rile her up a bit. Granted, it wasn't the most conventional way to flirt, but he wasn't a conventional guy. He supposed that maybe he could have found a better way to introduce himself, but it was too late to worry about that now.

He opened his mouth to say something, but she held up her palm. "Let's get one thing straight: just because my magic likes yours, don't think the same goes for me. I may have to tolerate you, but I don't have to like you, and I don't have to interact with you."

He fixed a lazy grin on his face. "Now, luv, I'm not trying to start an argument here, but if I'm to help you, you may have to interact with me a bit."

She looked murderous.

"Is this about the killing thing?" Her mouth fell open, trying to slaughter him with a look. "So, that's a yes. Okay, it's about the killing thing. It's perfectly understandable that you would be angry, even

 205

hold a grudge, but would it make you feel better if I told you that your life had never really been in danger?"

"Really? You were kidding? You threatened to kill me as, what, an icebreaker?"

He winced. "In all fairness, you were the one who asked if this was the part where I tried to kill you. I thought that maybe you wanted a bit of role-playing. You were out in the cemetery in the dead of night." She lunged at him, and he caught her wrists easily. "Careful, luv. Let's try to keep your magic happy, shall we?" He entwined their fingers. Her eyes skated downward. Her whole body trembled. It might have been her magic, but he hoped just a little of it was her.

"Truthfully, I just wanted to see what would happen. You can tell a lot about people by how they respond during stressful situations. You responded by making an excellent argument for my not killing you. Had it actually been a legitimate threat I probably would have let you go."

She blinked at him as if he were a crazy person. "You're lying."

"I'm not. I was merely in the right place at the right time. I saw you in distress at your father's funeral, and I helped. I just happened to still be there when you came back. I thought I should introduce myself." The lie was a gamble, but he was in damage control mode.

"By threatening to kill me?" she asked, flabbergasted.

"Again, you were the one who brought up the killing. I was just trying to chat you up. It was dark, and the moon was full. I saw a pretty girl, and I wanted to talk to you. My magic fancied yours... I just thought I'd see what happened. Perhaps my approach was unconventional, but I assure you, it was never my intention to hurt you."

"Do you know how my cousins found me?"

"What?" he asked, confused by the sudden change in conversation.

"Do you know how they found me?" she asked again, slower, like he was stupid.

"Google?"

She scowled at him. "My name appeared on his list."

"His list?" Ah yes, the collector. "Oh, *the* list. Really?"

 206

Interesting. She wouldn't have died by his hand. Had there been another threat that night? Had he deterred another attacker, or had she been fated to die in a natural way? Could her powers have killed her that night? She'd been pretty out of control in the cemetery. Had he prevented her death?

"Is your name still there?"

"No."

"So, that means someone or something prevented your death."

"My cousins prevented my death."

Mace grimaced. "Let's hope that's not the case."

"What? Why would you say that?"

"Do you know what happens when a reaper keeps his charge from dying?"

She shook her head, her face white.

"They upset the balance. It's the butterfly effect. It creates a ripple in the universe, and that is a capital offense in our world."

"What happens to people who do that?"

"I don't know, luv. As far as I know, nobody has ever been stupid enough to try."

"Never?"

"Not to my knowledge." Her fingers began to work over his hands, her thumbs massaging across his left palm, kneading him like a cat. She wasn't even aware she was doing it. "One thing at a time, Ember. Let's try to get your magic under control, and then we'll worry about saving your cousin. It won't matter if none of you is alive to face the consequences."

She nodded, her hands rubbing over his skin harder. "What's a soul eater?"

He couldn't even begin to know how to explain that in a positive light. "We are like reapers," he said vaguely.

"They help people cross over to the other side?"

"Sort of, but not exactly."

She set her jaw, her gaze determined. "So what, exactly, do they do?"

"Soul eaters do exactly what it sounds like we do. We consume the souls of the living to survive."

She looked like she was going to be sick. "You eat people?"

He couldn't help but be a bit offended. "I'm not a cannibal, Ember. We absorb the souls into ourselves so we may live."

"So you're like a psychic vampire?"

He sighed, taking both her palms in his, halting her fidgeting. "I realize this sounds bad, but I promise you, the souls I consumed were all truly terrible, horrible people."

He was sure on some level that was true. He didn't have to look far to find people whose souls he didn't mind robbing of their sweet hereafter. He rarely fed on humans…anymore.

She stared at him blankly. "You're a horrible person."

He conceded the point with a shrug. "Just think of all the time you'll have to teach me to be a better man."

She looked at him, warring with herself. "How are we supposed to do this?"

"We do as the she-wolf suggests and let you raise kittens in the cemetery until we're sure you won't blow a gasket and annihilate a small country."

"It's vile. The dead should stay dead. This power,"—she winced—"is revolting. How is this necessary? Why is it even possible?"

He sat quiet for a while. It wasn't like he really knew why they could do what they did; he just knew that they could. He pulled his palms from hers, watching their power fuse and roll between them.

"What would you give to talk to your mother one more time?" he asked.

Her gaze shot to his, startled. "What?"

"Just answer the question."

"Anything," she vowed.

"You can do that. You're a reanimator; that means that you could give somebody the peace of bringing a loved one back for a time. To say their goodbyes. To explain they're okay. To tell them where they hid the will."

She rolled her eyes but nodded. "I guess that part's not a terrible thing."

   208

"There's more, I'm sure, but we'll take it as it comes. Now, do you think your magic will behave long enough for me to go and make a phone call?"

She shrugged. He rose, truly hoping not to feel the flesh pulling from his bones. Her magic seemed to have acquiesced.

"Don't worry, luv, I'm not going far." Just far enough away for the wolves not to hear his conversation. He trekked to the farthest edge of the property line, and when he entered the tree line, he felt a painful tugging. He pulled up the number he was looking for and hit send.

"Well?" was the only greeting he received.

"Hello to you, as well. Yes, I'm fine. Thank you for asking."

"Mace," the man growled. "I haven't heard from you in days. I was starting to think you had abandoned your job. What's happening?"

He sounded stressed. He should be. He didn't seem to understand the ramifications of this girl's existence...or, perhaps he did. "I'm curious. Did you know what she was when you sent me to spy on her? Was it your plan all along to have me gain her trust?"

"What? What are you talking about?"

Mace smirked at the phone. He knew. Of course he did. "They think she's a reanimator."

"Hmm," he replied. "Yes, a reanimator. That would make sense."

Mace could hear it in the man's tone. "Cut the crap. You do know. You know she's not a reanimator." There was overwhelming silence on the other end of the line. "Did you not think it would be helpful for me to have all the information?" Mace asked. "Were you afraid I'd want to keep her for myself?"

There was a long pause before the man said, "When I think information is important, I'll give it to you. Not one minute before. You work for me. Now tell me, does she trust you?"

Mace clenched his teeth. He was used to dealing with all types in his line of work but the witch was seriously trying Mace's patience. "No, not at all, but it doesn't matter if she trusts me. She is forced to deal with me because, as it turns out, I'm the only one capable of filtering the thousands of years of energy pouring out of this girl."

"What? What does that mean?"

 209

Mace smiled. His employer didn't know everything then. "I couldn't put it together at first. But today, I watched the girl almost took out a city block with somebody else's words pouring out of her mouth."

"What are you talking about?"

"She wasn't possessed, but she wasn't herself. Then I realized she's channeling the old ones. The girl can syphon magic from the dead, or she could, if she had any way of controlling her magic. Instead, today, I'm pretty sure a couple of ancient witches decided to take the reaper for a test drive."

There was silence on the other end of the line, but Mace continued, piecing things together as he spoke. "I have no idea who thought to bind this girl's powers, but it was sort of like putting a cork in a volcano. Her powers are building, and just the energy leaking from the cracks could undo the universe if that's what they chose. Had I not been there, things would have ended…badly. So I think it's time to renegotiate."

The man snorted. "You aren't really in a position to negotiate."

"I'm living in her home. She needs me to survive. She doesn't know you exist. I know what she really is, and now I'm certain I know why you need her. I'd say that makes me in the perfect position to negotiate."

"I could just replace you."

Mace chuckled. "What are you going to do? We both know you can't kill me. If you lock me up, I'll eventually get out, and I don't think you want to spend the rest of your days worrying about the vengeance I will attempt to exact on you or your children or your children's children…blah…blah…blah."

There was an exasperated sigh. "What do you want?"

"I want her."

There was dead air on the line for so long Mace checked the screen.

"What?"

Mace smiled. "When all is said and done and you've done whatever magic you have planned to steal her power, I want her."

"Why would you want a powerless reanimator? She can't do anything for you."

 210

Mace snorted, not directly answering him. "You can have her power. I want her soul."

He had everything else. He had power, money, and immortality. What he didn't have was a reaper's soul—*her* soul. He wanted it so bad he could taste it. If he could have felt bad about it, he would have.

The man on the other end of the line laughed. "You can have the girl when I'm done. Her soul is no use to me. I'm going to need you to go to Georgia to pick up a package in a few days."

Mace flinched. "Ah, yes. That may be a problem."

"Why's that?"

"Seems her magic likes to keep us…close. Should I attempt to leave without her, there may be repercussions."

There was a chuckle on the other end of the line. "Does she know?"

"Not yet."

"Just be ready to go when Shelby texts you about the package. I can take care of the girl's magic, at least temporarily, but if this is more than a temporary problem, you may wish to speak to Shelby about a more permanent solution."

Mace closed his eyes; he had no wish to speak to Shelby about anything. She hated him. To be fair, she hated everyone, but especially him. Though, if anybody might be able to procure something to help sever this tie with Ember, it was Shelby.

"Just let me know when the package is ready. I'll figure out a way to get to Shelby if you figure out a way to make sure her magic doesn't flay the skin from my bones."

"I told you I'll take care of it. You just need to work on getting her to trust you enough to bring her to me."

He pulled the phone from his ear, putting it on speaker and firing off a text to Shelby about possible magical objects to help with his problem.

"I'm sure you can do that. Somehow, you seem to have no trouble getting girls to trust you."

"Perhaps, but she's not just any girl, is she? She's a necromancer."

   211

He hit end before the other man could form a denial. He was right. As impossible as it seemed, November Lonergan was a necromancer. Something akin to fear dripped along his spine as the enormity of it hit him. He couldn't allow her to know what she was capable of, not yet, maybe not ever.

After a moment, he sent another text to Shelby, asking about another matter entirely. Even as he hit send, he mentally kicked himself for his curiosity.

Chapter 34

TRISTIN

Tristin sat in the living room of the empty house. All the others were out at the pet cemetery watching Ember not reanimate ancient household pets. Tristin couldn't sit around inhaling the scent of fetid dirt and failure anymore, so she came home to beat her head against the brick wall of the internet. Even Quinn had abandoned her to see if Ember could actually channel all that wasted magic into purposefully reanimating one dead animal.

Tristin's lip curled. How had Ember ended up a reanimator? The power was truly wasted on her. She didn't even want to be a reanimator. She had this amazing, kick-ass gift, and she treated it like a curse? If Tristin had that kind of power at her fingertips, she would run with it. She'd be proactive; she'd train. Tristin had focus and drive. She didn't just sit around waiting for bad things to happen to her. She didn't wait for pillow-lipped demons to rescue her. She saved herself. She didn't get how anybody could live like that.

She hit enter on the internet search bar and growled in frustration as yet another set of human-run sites on mythology popped up. It was too hard trying to filter through what was real and what was fake information.

"What's going on here?"

She tensed, biting the inside of her cheek, glancing up at the soul eater. He'd been here for four days. "Why aren't you with Ember? Isn't that your whole reason for being here?"

"Everybody is taking a break. I heard your aggravation and thought I might be of assistance."

She arched an eyebrow and received that wide grin that made her want to hit him with another shovel. She saw the uncertain way Ember looked at him; like she wanted to have his demonically perfect babies but also worried he might one day eat those babies. Tristin supposed one might think he was good looking if you were into the fallen angel thing and supposing you could overlook the soul slurping evil demon monster part.

"Yes, I hear your kind is exceptionally helpful," she sneered.

"I may be more help than you think. I know what you're looking for."

She rolled her eyes. "What?"

"You're aiming to figure out a way to save your brother."

Her heart hammered in her chest. "What are you talking about?"

"Ember told me he saved her life. I know what that means for you do-gooder types. The authorities get involved. The punishment is swift, severe, and usually fatal. It stands to reason that you want to save him."

"What do you even care?"

"I don't really. It just seems like lately you do nothing but search the internet, beat up that defenseless bag in the attic, and make sad eyes at the human boy. It's irritating, really. You're kind of a sad sack when you're in a bad mood. So, for the sake of household unity, I thought I'd throw you a bone."

"Why should I trust you?"

"Why not?" he shrugged. "I mean, you haven't made any progress so far, or you wouldn't look so maudlin all the time."

"Well, it's not like I have a whole lot of options. The Grove keeps their library on lockdown, and no supernatural creature is stupid enough to keep copies of ancient magical texts lying around when it's a capital offense."

 214

He laughed then. She threw a pillow at his head. He caught it easily and set it back in the chair, fluffing it nicely before he sat. "I don't mean to laugh. But you have the answer right in front of you and don't see it."

"Then stop being so cryptic and freaking tell me." Why were bad guys always so in love with themselves?

"If I was a supernatural creature who wanted access to ancient texts anytime I needed them, would I keep them in my home?"

"Obviously not."

"Right. I would keep them where nobody would know what they are except me. I would keep them hidden in plain sight with people who have no use for them."

"Like where, my evil lair?"

"I would keep them with the humans."

"I've been through the human libraries and the internet; it's all misinformation spread by the witches. None of it's real."

He smiled then. "That is a vast overstatement. Skip the internet. It's too easy for the witches to follow the trail. You need to look for somebody who had a foot in both worlds, witch and human. A human who would need to be in possession of ancient texts...say for his job?"

He was clearly leading her somewhere, but, as long as it helped her brother, she didn't care.

"I don't know any humans who would need magical texts for their job."

"No, but you do know a witch who posed as a human for twelve years; a witch who would have no way of accessing the Grove library without letting on that he lived," he said, his frustration matching her own.

She gasped. "Ember's dad."

The answer had been there all along. He was right. Ember's dad had bound her magic. He had constantly reinforced the spell. He would have needed access to herbs and texts for the rituals. He was a professor of occult studies. Tristin had been so stupid.

"Seems you and the boy wonder should take a trip back to New Orleans."

"It's been weeks; there's no way they haven't cleaned out his apartment."

"I don't know anything about Ember's father, but if I were him, I wouldn't keep that stuff at my home. I'd keep it in my office. Start there. If the texts are ancient enough or interesting enough, a university would never get rid of them."

"Why are you doing this?"

Mace shrugged, palms up. "Relentless curiosity. I want to see what happens next."

She didn't say anything, warring with the desperate need to help her brother and her blatant distrust of creatures like him. He had no reason to lie or to even offer help. She didn't have any other options really. He had given her their only lead. She should have thought of it herself. It had been so plain to see. What else did Mace know?

"Can I ask you a question?" Tristin asked, suddenly.

He narrowed his eyes at her. "You can always ask."

Leaning forward and dropping her voice low, she asked. "Do you know where the Grove would keep prisoners?"

A strange expression passed across his face. "Depends on the type of prisoner."

Her shoulders fell. "I don't know what type of prisoners. It was just something I overheard."

It was his turn to drop his voice. "What exactly did you hear?"

"I heard somebody say, 'They don't know they're prisoners.'"

"Do you know who the prisoners are?" he asked.

She shook her head, defeated. "No."

"Well, can you tell me who said it?" he asked.

"I don't think so, no. I just wanted to know if there was any kind of containment center or prison maybe outside of town."

"The Grove isn't known for imprisoning people unless they plan on using them later. The Grove only tortures and kills, and you are better off with the latter, really."

Tristin paled at that. The thought of her brother being tortured by the grove made her queasy.

"Sorry, Banshee, that was…insensitive," he said. She said nothing. "It is curious, though, don't you think?" Mace asked, drawing back her attention.

"What?"

"Why Ember's name would pop up on your brother's arm?" Tristin bit down on her bottom lip. She'd said the same thing. "Have you ever heard of a reaper being asked to collect a family member?"

She hadn't. Ever. But they hadn't really heard much about reapers at all. That was the problem. Kai had learned reaping from Allister. But still, it just seemed weird to have a reaper collect a family member. It's why she'd thought it a trap. She said as much.

"I'm no expert, but either the universe has a perverse sense of irony, or there is something amiss with this whole situation. Either way, you should be careful. Something isn't right about this. It smells like a setup."

Goosebumps crawled along her flesh. He was right. There was something wrong about all of this.

"Hey, what's going on in here?"

They both turned to where Quinn stood in the doorway, looking back and forth between the two. He wasn't wearing his hat, so his chocolate brown hair was askew. He had dirt on his jeans and leaves in his shirt collar.

Tristin snickered. "What happened to you? Were you attacked by a tree?"

"Oh, slight incident at the pet cemetery." He held up a hand when she and Mace jumped to their feet. "Everybody is fine. Well, there is a hamster that will never be the same, but I think it's safe to say we really need Mace back."

"Sure." Mace sighed. "Remember what I said, though. I have no idea what's going on but be careful. Don't trust anybody here. Scratch that, just don't trust anybody anywhere."

He walked out, leaving her with a befuddled Quinn.

"What was that all about?"

"I got a lead on how to find the information to save Kai." She grinned at him.

He looked skeptical. "From him?"

217

She shrugged, moving forward, picking leaves and debris from his hair and his collar.

"Information is information."

"Or information from him gets us dead." He pushed back a strand of her hair with his finger. "Look, I want to help your brother too, but do you trust this guy?"

"What choice do I have?"

He sighed. "We, Tristin, what choice do *we* have?" He looked to the doorway. "We should carve it over the door like our new family motto."

Chapter 35

EMBER

Ember gave herself credit for keeping down her breakfast. There were small fragments of bone and hair everywhere. She didn't know how it happened. She wasn't even trying to do anything. One minute she was sitting there waiting for Mace to return, and the next...poof, exploded...hamster, maybe? There wasn't even enough left to ID the body. She didn't know how much longer she could keep this up. Her powers were useless. She was useless.

All around her, the pack stood and stared just as they had for four days. Isa looked nervous. Neoma was flitting about barefoot and filthy like a seven-year-old. Donovan had shown up on day two with no explanation for his previous absence. Rhys and Kai sat on the tailgate of the old pickup truck, just at the edge of the clearing. Kai's lip curled in disgust, and Rhys just looked, well, the way he always looked, broody and vaguely disappointed in everybody.

Ember's magic stretched within her, practically purring. Mace must be near. She hated the way the knot in her chest loosened ever so slightly. When he was close, her magic played nice, which meant no ice baths or interventions for Ember.

"So, luv, I heard you had a bit of a...setback."

She looked up at him from her seat on the ground, miserable, palms splayed towards the carnage. "How much longer are we going to keep at this? I can't do it. I can't make corpses move. I can't even keep them in one piece."

"Okay," he said. "Can we have a moment alone?"

"No way."

"Absolutely not."

Kai and Rhys spoke at the same time, all eyes swinging towards them.

Isa raised an eyebrow. "I'm sorry, I don't recall when I turned over the reins to you two?"

"You can't be serious?" Rhys asked, palms up. "You want to leave her alone with a soul eater?"

"What I want is for you to stop questioning me," Isa snapped.

Kai put an arm on Rhys's bicep and tugged. He took a step back and averted his eyes. They left slowly, each looking back in turn.

Isa looked at Mace and then Ember. "You can have a couple of minutes, but we won't be too far. We can hear her...and you."

When they were alone, Mace turned to her. "Well, they certainly don't trust me."

"Do you blame them?"

He shrugged. "Do you trust me?"

She stared up at him, squinting against the sun. It was on the tip of her tongue to say, "No, no way, absolutely not. There's no way I trust you." But, it wasn't true. Not exactly. She trusted in that moment he didn't mean to harm her, but she didn't trust him to tell her the truth. But that sounded like the beginning of a long conversation, too long to have in a pet cemetery, so instead she said, "My magic does?"

A strange expression crossed his face. "But not you?"

"I don't even know you, and given what I do know, trusting you is asking a lot."

He sighed. "Then I guess your magic trusting mine will have to do."

He sat down behind her, moving so that her back pressed to the muscled wall of his chest. Her breath caught as he moved close

    220

enough for his feet to snake underneath her legs and his hands to run along her arms, cocooning her in his embrace.

She went still, muscles stiff.

"You don't like to be touched, do you?"

"Don't have a lot of experience with it really," she countered, trying to force the tension from her body.

"Take a deep breath in and let it out. Try to relax. Let your magic use mine. Just lean your head back and focus on your breathing. Maybe let me drive a little."

She could feel the soft puffs of air against her cheek when he spoke. She sank back against him, letting her body curve into his. She tried to focus on the way his skin was cool against hers. The way she could feel his words vibrate against her back.

"That's it. Just relax. Try to sync your breathing with mine. In. Out. In. Out."

Her eyes fluttered closed, and she let her head lull against his shoulder, dropping her guard, just this once. She hissed in pain as her magic shot through her. She felt his hands wrap around hers, entwining their fingers. "Breathe, Ember. Just breathe in time with me. Focus only on that."

She could feel his grunt of pain as their power collided, and she fought to do as he asked. In and out, in and out. It seemed like such a simple request until somebody asked you to do it while they put you through a wood chipper. In. Out. She pressed deeper into his embrace, forgetting the magic, the cemetery, the pain and focusing instead on him.

She could feel his hands slip from hers, his cool calloused fingers moving over her palm, up her arms and down again. She focused on his breath against her ear, and the way his lips sometimes brushed her earlobe. She could happily live in the feel of him forever.

"Ember," he whispered.

"Mmm," she murmured, nuzzling her face against his neck.

His voice hitched. "Look."

She froze, acutely aware that she was again snuggling with Mace. She turned her head but didn't open her eyes. She didn't want to look. She couldn't imagine what she would see that would cause that

  221

catch in his voice. She cracked one eye open and then both, gasping at the enormous mutt standing before her.

He looked the size of a small pony. His once white coat was matted and caked with layers of dirt. He was missing an eye, but it appeared an old injury. He limped forward, favoring his front left foot. The flesh on his left paw was raw to the bone due to decay. He looked about, head lolling on atrophied muscles. She pushed back against Mace but realized there was nowhere to run. She could hear the blood rushing in her ears, her mouth dry.

The dog whined, hobbling closer to them. Mace tensed behind her, his arms still surrounding her. It wasn't possible. Had she really called that dog from the ground? She could see the disturbed earth of the grave, one of the newest in the tiny cemetery. He was probably the freshest thing in there. He didn't look like a ravenous zombie dog. The humans she'd brought back, they looked…well, like zombies.

"I did it," she whispered, her tongue sticking to the roof of her mouth.

"You did," he agreed, sounding both amazed and leery.

She held out a trembling hand, hoping she wasn't about to lose her fingers or worse. The dog limped forward, his one brown eye staring at her in earnest. He licked her palm and flopped down in front of her. "Is this normal?"

"I have no idea, luv. I've never met a reanimator. But don't get too attached. Your magic is new, and it won't last long. Reanimators can only call the soul back for a brief period. He will cross back over before the day is gone."

It hardly seemed fair. She let her hands run over the dog's matted fur, and he panted happily just like a normal living dog. She'd done that. She put both hands on his side, feeling his lungs expand and contract.

Mace unwound himself from her and stood.

"I'm taking him home with us."

"What?" Mace asked. "Absolutely not. Why would you want to do that?"

"Because we just ripped him back from the other side. He's had a hard day, and you're telling me it's temporary. We did this to him.

We have a responsibility to take care of him for as long as he's here. He should at least have a bath and a hot meal."

"Are you going to temporarily adopt every animal you yank from the other side? Because that could become an expensive and messy undertaking."

Ember stared up at him, not sure she was quite ready to get to her feet. "Listen, you might be able to help me channel my magic, but forgive me if I don't use you as my moral compass. You don't get to tell me what to do."

Mace looked much taller and even more intimidating when he towered over her, but she didn't care. She went along with everything they'd asked of her. She was sitting in the dirt, sweating her butt off and being eaten alive by mutant mosquitos; the least they could do is this. She stared up at him, crossing her arms. "He's coming home with us."

He threw his hands up, beginning to pace the tree line. "You're impossible."

She ignored his outburst. "Does everybody get that?" Ember yelled. "I know you hear us out there."

The others began to filter closer, faces grim, eyeing the dog warily. Ember paid them no attention, focusing on the only person who mattered. "Can I bring him home, Isa? It seems cruel to leave him out here?"

Isa knelt before the dog, who whimpered, coming to his feet, wobbling on his hurt paw to drop his head to the alpha. She smiled, petting his face and looking intently at his sore paw. "Of course." She easily picked up the dog and placed him in the pickup truck on the pile of blankets in the back. She eyed Rhys and Kai as she walked by. "It's nice to know someone recognizes my authority."

Ember wasn't sure if Isa was referring to Ember or the dog, but she didn't care because the dog was going home with them.

Mace wrapped his hand around Ember's wrist, pulling her to her feet. "This is a terrible idea."

The dog growled at Mace from the bed of the truck. Ember smiled. "It seems he doesn't like you either."

Chapter 36

KAI

"What should we name him?" Kai asked as they all trekked up the porch steps into the house.

"Why are we naming him at all?" Mace asked nobody in particular. "He's not going to live long enough for it to matter."

They all ignored him.

"It's Ember's dog; she should name him," Wren said.

Ember looked at the dog in Rhys's arms. "He belongs to all of us."

"Romero?" Kai suggested.

"Romero?" Isa asked.

"Yeah, you know, like George Romero, the father of all zombie movies?"

Ember grinned at him and nodded. "Yeah, seems appropriate."

"Seems a waste," Mace muttered.

Quinn came to stand in the doorway of the kitchen, eying the giant ball of fur. "Nice. Is that a dead dog?"

Kai grinned. "Nope, it's an undead dog. Brought back from the dead by our little reanimator." He pinched Ember's cheek. "We're so proud."

She slapped his arm. Quinn grinned at her, and she blushed before returning her attention to the dog.

"So, Isa," Quinn said, awkwardly propping an arm against the door. "Can Tristin and I borrow the Toyota? We'll be back by tomorrow night."

Kai bit his lip, trying not to laugh as his friend tried hard to seem casual about the enormous request. He should have left this to Tristin.

"I'm sorry, what?" Isa asked, eyebrows chasing their way to her hairline. "I'm sure you're kidding."

Quinn flushed, stumbling to say, "W-we just have a lead we want to run down on something. No big deal."

Tristin came to stand by Quinn, looking like she regretted trying to let Quinn handle the situation.

Wren wrapped his arms around Isa from behind and hooked his chin over her shoulder, staring at Tristin and Quinn hard. "Could you guys be any vaguer?"

Rhys gently laid the dog down on the rug in front of the door and turned to cross his arms over his chest, obviously not wanting to miss the show either.

Ember ignored them all, instead sitting next to the dog and placing his head in her lap, whispering to him. The two were clearly in love. She didn't seem particularly interested in what Quinn and Tristin were up to. Kai couldn't say the same. He was dying to know what scheme his best friend and sister were hatching. They had been together more in the last three weeks than their entire lives, and that was saying something.

"Yeah," Isa said, as if she were reading Kai's thoughts. "What's up with you two being all buddy-buddy lately? It's weird." She eyeballed them hard.

Tristin shifted, uncomfortable with the scrutiny. "Nothing. We just wanted to go check out some possible new information." His sister tried to smile, but it looked more like a pained grimace, bless her melancholy little heart.

"Do I look stupid to you?" Isa asked.

Mace clapped Quinn on the shoulder as he passed. "Don't answer that, mate, it's a trap."

Quinn looked at Tristin for a long time before finally saying, "We got a lead on somebody in New Orleans who may have some information on reapers. We just wanted to go check it out."

"Let me get this straight. You want me to let the two of you go to New Orleans, overnight, unsupervised, to check out a lead on reapers. Two seventeen-year-olds. Alone. In New Orleans. Overnight?" Isa asked slowly, waiting for them to understand the absurdity of their request.

"Why do you say it like that? What do you think is going to happen?" Tristin asked palms up.

Donovan laughed and looked at Quinn in sympathy. "Dude, if she doesn't know what Isa's worried about, then you got bigger problems than reaper stuff."

"Shut up." Tristin scowled at Donovan.

"I can't allow you guys to go traipsing around New Orleans alone."

"Please, Isa," Tristin asked. "This is super important."

Everybody froze. Tristin never begged. She pouted, she sulked, she snarked, but she never begged. Isa narrowed her eyes at his sister before saying, "That's it. Family meeting. Right here, right now. Everybody sit."

"In the foyer?" Rhys asked his sister, faintly amused.

"Sit," she barked. Kai saw Ember smile to herself as butts hit the floor. Wren moved to sit next to Neoma on the stairs. Rhys somehow ended up sitting just to his left even though he had to walk across the room to do so. Lately he always seemed to be right there. Maybe Kai just never noticed before.

"I'm getting real tired of feeling like I'm missing something," Isa said, gold eyes shining as she slowly prowled the room, staring down each of them in turn. "Now, I'm sure I'm just being paranoid, of course, because my pack would never be so stupid as to hide things from me, right?" Isa's teeth elongated, nails shifting to claws. She turned to look at Quinn and Tristin. "I mean, who would be stupid enough to lie to an alpha?"

Kai's hands trembled, his heart rate accelerating. Him. He would be stupid enough to lie to their alpha. She was going to kill them all, starting with him. Rhys's eyes darted to Kai, widening, silently begging him to calm down. It was too late.

Isa snapped her head around, just as Rhys's thumb brushed across Kai's cheek. Kai's heart rate quadrupled, the beat wildly off kilter, momentarily forgetting the alpha and the pack surrounding them. No one person should have that kind of effect on somebody. It was a health hazard. He licked his lips, blinking rapidly.

Isa zeroed in on her brother's hand and winced in what seemed to be sympathy. There wasn't a single person alive who didn't seem to know he was in love with Rhys. When she turned away, Rhys gave Kai a curt nod and arched brows that asked, "You good?"

Kai was so stupid. Of course, that was why Rhys touched him. Why not exploit Kai's ridiculous crush on the wolf to hide his and Kai's mountain of lies. Well, Kai's lies, really. For three whole seconds, Kai had thought Rhys was touching him because he was concerned. Kai pled temporary insanity brought about by the fear of death-by-alpha.

Kai slapped Rhys's hand away, focusing on Tristin and Quinn just as their alpha was. Isa stopped before Quinn, clearly sensing the weakest gazelle in the herd. "What is it you're going to look for in New Orleans?"

He shrank back under her weighted gaze. "We told you, we received information about some books on reapers that might give us some intel on, well...reaper stuff."

"One, who gave you this sudden information, and two, what exactly are you looking for?" Wren asked.

Mace spoke first. "I gave them the information. Well, I pointed out they already had the information."

"What information?" Isa asked. "What are you looking for?"

Kai watched his sister and Quinn exchange startled looks behind the alpha's back.

"Banshees," Mace supplied. "I saw Tristin attempting to research banshees using human websites to try to learn more about her magic. I simply pointed out she may be overlooking a great place to start."

 227

Wren clasped his hands together, leaning forward, curiosity getting the best of him. "Where?"

"Ember's father's office," Mace answered.

Ember's head snapped up, eyes narrowing on the soul eater. "What do you know about my father?"

"Only what I've heard around here the last few days, I'm afraid." He shrugged, apologetic. "But somebody bound your powers, luv. Somebody kept the spell juiced. The spell only began to dissolve when your father died. Your father was a powerful witch. It doesn't take a great deal of deductive reasoning to figure it was your father who cast the spell. Witches need spells, and spells mean books, especially to a witch hiding the fact they are alive."

Isa, focused on Tristin, expression softening. "I know you want to know more about your powers, but why now? Why when we are in the middle of all this?"

Tristin looked flummoxed. "I—"

Quinn cleared his throat. "Those books will only be in Ember's dad's office for so long before somebody else claims the office. If we don't get to them before they clean everything out, they may be gone for good. They could already be gone."

Kai hid a smile behind his hand. His sister looked like she wanted to kiss Quinn. Yeah, they were definitely up to something.

Isa tapped one manicured nail against her lips. "Okay, you can go, but I can't let you go alone. You are both my responsibility now. Kai and Rhys can go with you."

"What? No!" Tristin and Kai said at the exact same time, both looking at each other with hostility.

"Please, Isa," Kai begged. "I can't do it. I can't go back into the car with him." He pointed at Rhys. "Please. It's hell. It's just hours and hours of awkward staring and flared nostrils and emotional constipation. I don't want to go back to New Orleans. Why are you still punishing me?"

Rhys rolled his eyes but said nothing, clearly resigned to his fate.

"We don't need babysitters, Isa. We are just going to steal a few textbooks from an office on a stuffy college campus. We aren't going to go get hammered in the quarter," Tristin reasoned.

 228

Ember looked up then, a smile playing at her lips. "Actually, you're going to want Kai there."

Kai looked at Ember, betrayed. "Why's that?"

"Bait," she said.

"Huh?" Kai asked. "Bait for what?"

"Not what, who."

Rhys stiffened next to Kai. "Who, then?" the wolf asked, teeth clenched. It was Kai who rolled his eyes this time.

"Eric."

"Who's Eric?" Quinn asked, clearly amused by Rhys's weird reaction.

"My dad's TA. He's the gatekeeper. If you want in my dad's office, you're going to have to get past Eric, and Eric has a type."

"What type is that?" Kai asked, not sure he wanted to know.

"Pretty boys with pretty eyes," Ember said, still preoccupied with the dog.

"Aw, you are pretty," Donovan joked, winking at Kai.

Kai's face flushed under the pack's scrutiny, but Ember went on, "Even if there's a new teacher, Eric will know where the books are. I just don't know if it's a good idea for you to ask him. Maybe you can just get him away from the office?"

"Even if you find those books, you can't bring them back here," Wren pointed out. "Having those books is illegal. We are already skirting enough trouble. This would tip the scales safely into the gruesome-death-for-all category."

"That means Quinn has to be the one to get into the office," Kai said. "He's the only one who can memorize that much information."

"I can memorize what I can read, but I can't read an entire book in one sitting. I'm good, but I'm not that good."

"Enough," Isa said. "It's settled. You will be home by tomorrow afternoon. Tristin and Rhys have shifts at the restaurant, and I'm sure the others are tired of covering for you."

Neoma and Donovan nodded in agreement.

"Who's going to cover me tonight?" Quinn asked.

"I've got that covered," Isa said. "Mace is."

"What?" Mace choked, before regaining some composure. "I don't think so. I don't...do work. Do you really want me waiting on your patrons? I might get...hungry."

Isa stopped before the soul eater, using the claw on one hand to pick at another. "You're currently living under my roof. You will work just like the rest of the pack. Is that a problem?"

They all held their breath as Mace squared off against the alpha. "Put your claws away, wolf. You can't kill me, and I'm immune to any conceivable torture you could imagine."

Kai licked his bottom lip as the three other wolves shifted, flanking their alpha. Isa retracted her claws, halting her betas with a gesture. "I think you underestimate the levels of my imagination. Ember may need you, but you still answer to me. You will work at the restaurant, but so as not to...tempt you, you can work in the back with me."

Mace's gaze traveled to Ember who watched him with an intensity that made even Kai squirm. She arched a brow in Mace's direction and his shoulders sagged. "Who is going to watch Ember? I can't help keep her magic in check if I'm not with her."

Isa's smile was all teeth. "Then you're in luck; she'll be about fifteen feet away, working the counter. Free ride's over, people."

"But who's going to watch Romero?" Ember asked, frowning as she scratched at the dog's large floppy ear. Kai smiled at Ember's easy acceptance of his name for her dog.

Mace sighed and shook his head at Ember. "That dog won't last the night, luv."

"Nobody asked you," Ember sang.

"She's right," Isa agreed. "Tonight, Neoma can watch him."

The girl giggled and crawled across the floor to the dog. She lay on her belly and rested her chin on her folded hands, giggling again as the dog licked her nose. "You stink. Tonight you get a bath."

"I'll help. He's sort of a lot of dog for one person to handle," Wren said.

"Perfect," Tristin said. "Can we take the Suburban? The Toyota is too small for Rhys."

"Really?" Donovan asked, "He doesn't seem to have any problems fitting into that vintage tin can he loves."

Rhys stared darkly. "I am not cramming into the Toyota."

Isa rolled her eyes. "Fine, take the Suburban, but it better have a full tank of gas when you bring it back."

"Yes!" Quinn fist-pumped the air. "I'm driving."

"Shotgun," Kai said.

"Actually, I'm driving," Rhys said.

Tristin smirked at her brother as they walked towards the door. "Still want shotgun, bro?"

It took an hour to pack and coordinate where they would stay overnight. Just as he closed the back of the Chevy, Ember opened the front door, rushing towards him, red hair flying behind her.

"I need you to do something for me."

Kai hesitated, wondering if this was something Isa would kill him for. Rhys appeared from the driver's side. "What's the hold up?"

Ember folded a piece of paper into his hand, looking at Kai with big eyes. "I need you to go to this address and tell Miller Hammond I'm okay."

"No way," Rhys barked.

If looks could kill, Rhys would be a puddle on the floor. As it was, Ember's jaw tensed, her hair practically crackling as static moved along her skin. Her chest heaved. "You have to. He took care of me for years, made sure I had food, gave me a job, let me do my home-work in his office." Sparks arced across her skin. "I just disappeared. He probably thinks I'm dead. Please, Kai. Please."

Mace appeared at the front door, probably feeling Ember's impending meltdown. He didn't approach, just hung back, waiting to see what would happen.

"Okay," Kai said, placing a hand on her shoulder, jumping back when she shocked him. "What the hell?" he asked to nobody really, shaking out his hand. "I will tell him, but you know I can't tell him where you are. He probably wouldn't believe me anyway. He'll prob-ably try to have us arrested for kidnapping."

"He'll recognize my handwriting, just show this too him or leave it with Alma at the front."

He couldn't take the sad eyes anymore. "Yes, jeez, enough with the puppy eyes, I said I'll do it."

Ember deflated, the storm of energy dissipating as quickly as it gathered. Tristin snickered from the passenger seat, where she'd apparently been eavesdropping. "Suckered by your own sad-eyed stare."

"We need to get on the road," Rhys grumbled, turning on his heel and getting in the vehicle.

As Kai slid into the backseat next to Quinn. Mace gave Kai a jaunty wave from the doorway, ushering Ember back inside. A heavy feeling settled in his gut. He couldn't shake the feeling something bad was coming. Rhys inhaled sharply, looking at Kai in confusion.

"I'm fine," he murmured.

Rhys didn't believe Kai but started the vehicle anyway. Kai was glad Rhys didn't ask, since Kai had no idea what he'd say. Something wasn't right. As they drove away, Kai fought the urge to tell Rhys to go back. Kai ran a hand along the back of his neck, as it hit him like a fist to his gut.

There was really no going back from this thing he'd set in motion. For better or worse, they had to see it through, no matter the consequence.

 232

Chapter 37

TRISTIN

As predicted, the car ride was excruciating. Kai insisted on sitting in the back with Quinn, which left her up front with a cranky-pants, pouting werewolf. Being in the front with Rhys wasn't usually a problem. He didn't insist on filling every minute with unnecessary conversation.

However, his bad mood was contagious, or maybe it was the non-stop running commentary between Kai and Quinn the entire four-hour drive. She tried to sleep, but after the third time her brother woke her with a knee to the back of her seat, she gave up, opting to thumb through her phone instead.

Once they reached the city, yet another argument erupted between Rhys and Kai about whether to honor Ember's request to pass along her note.

"I said we'd do it," Kai said.

"That sounds a lot like *your* problem," Rhys said. "We shouldn't even be in New Orleans. Her father could've had an entire coven working with him. This Eric guy may even be working for him, and you want to dangle yourself in front of him like low hanging fruit."

Tristin rolled her eyes as her brother's mouth fell open. "You can take me there now, or I'll just find a way to go later."

"What if this guy calls the cops or accuses us of kidnapping her or something…weirder?"

"You mean weirder than abducting her and carting her off to a supernatural town where her secret powers are a threat to her existence. Weirder than that?" Tristin added drily.

Rhys gave her his surliest eyebrows. "Listen, I'm in charge and I say no. No way. That's final."

"Fine," Kai told the wolf.

Tristin knew by his tone it was definitely not fine.

Kai proved her right when he said, "I'll just call Isa."

A strangled noise escaped Rhys. "You are such a…child." He fisted the steering wheel until his knuckles were white. "Fine."

Tristin laughed at the smug look on her brother's face, earning her a glare from Rhys.

The address belonged to a two-story building three blocks from the cemetery where they'd first found Ember. It was old but well cared for. A hearse sat parked to the side of the building next to a vintage Mercedes. An old beat-up Buick was the only other car in the lot.

Once inside, Tristin almost gagged on the bizarre energy in the room. She could tell by the way her brother fidgeted he could feel it too. There was no immediate threat, other than the tacky décor, but the place made her skin crawl.

"Do you feel that?" she asked. Kai nodded.

"What? What is it? No supernatural senses here, remember?" Quinn asked.

Kai shrugged. "I don't actually know. Maybe it's all the death?"

"I told you this was a bad idea," Rhys muttered.

An older woman rounded the corner. She had a soft face and half glasses that made Tristin think of Mrs. Claus. She was tiny and plump. Tristin couldn't help but notice how the lady's floral dress matched the carpeting and the table clothes. It was like she'd been there so long the building had accepted her as one of its own.

 234

She looked startled, probably not used to seeing four teenagers standing in a funeral parlor. "May I help y'all?"

They all stared until Rhys shoved Kai forward with a grunt.

"I-I'm looking for Miller Hammond, is he here?"

"No, he's off for the day." She tilted her head. "How may I help you children?"

"Are you Alma?"

She smiled, her hand fluttering to her chest. "Why yes I am, do I know you, sweetheart?"

"No, but I think you know my c—" Her brother was cut off by another quick elbow to the back. "My friend, Ember. She asked that we leave this with you for Mr. Hammond."

Her smile faltered, her eyes going watery. "So she's okay, then? Alive?"

Kai nodded a bit too enthusiastically. Tristin rolled her eyes. He looked like a bobblehead. "Yes, she's fine. Happy."

Alma didn't say anything for a bit, staring at nothing, as if absorbing the information. Finally, she nodded once, saying, "Well, okay then. I'll be happy to pass that on. He will be so relieved. Please, please tell her to come see us. We miss her so much."

Tristin fought another epic eye roll. Everybody loved Ember.

"Well, if that's all, I have a family…" Tristin trailed off, gesturing towards the back.

Shuffling everyone towards the wooden double doors, Rhys looked horrified at the notion of disturbing some grieving family. As they made their way out the door, she noticed the two small portraits on the wall. One was of the woman they'd just met. Underneath it read: Alma Mayweather, Office Manager. The other was of an older black man with large kind eyes and greying hair captioned: Miller Hammond, Owner.

Kai caught Tristin looking. "He has a nice face. At least Ember had one person who was nice to her."

Tristin's cheek twitched. She didn't want to feel sorry for the girl.

Once they piled back in the car, they drove towards their hotel where they had one room with two beds. Tristin dreaded the fight

 235

that was about to ensue. It took approximately six minutes for things to fall apart once they entered the room.

"I'm not sharing a bed with Quinn," Rhys said, arms crossed and jaw set. "No way."

"Wow, man. Rude."

"You sleep like you walk, dangerously. I'm not going to be hit in the face all night by your flailing limbs."

"I don't want to share with you either," Quinn said but still looked hurt by the wolf's rejection.

"Well, I'm not sleeping with Rhys," Kai said, trying to look disgusted but mostly just looking terrified. Tristin didn't have to be a werewolf to know his heart was probably pounding out of his chest.

"Oh, I'm devastated," Rhys snarked back.

"Shut up!" Tristin shouted. "I'll sleep with Rhys, but you two better go to sleep. I'm not going to be kept up all night because you two are giggling like twelve-year-old girls at their first slumber party."

Rhys snickered.

Kai glared at her. "We don't do that."

They proceeded to do just that. Tristin had erected a huge pillow barrier between her and the wolf, but it didn't stop him from tossing and turning next to her, causing the pillows to topple on top of her. She finally flung them to the floor, staring at him in exasperation. He grunted at her in the dark, thrusting a finger towards the other bed.

"Go to sleep. It's after midnight," Tristin snapped. The sound quieted down, and she raised her eyebrows in what she hoped was a happy-now look.

Their peace lasted only about ten minutes before they were laughing again. The wolf huffed air out of his nose like an angry bull but said nothing, instead flopping on his stomach dramatically.

At around two in the morning, Rhys threatened to claw out somebody's vocal cords, letting them know he didn't care which of them it was. The room finally fell silent for good.

The bed was big and comfortable, but Tristin felt like she was sleeping next to a space heater as two hundred pounds of werewolf dozed restlessly beside her. Morning couldn't come fast enough.

She drifted into a restless sleep. She dreamed of Ember and Kai, of their parents on the beach, laughing. Just flashes really. Her dad tossing a small plastic ball to her and Ember. Kai sitting with their aunt, looking at the names of her collected. Tristin and Ember burying their Barbie's in the sand. Tristin crying when hers was carried out to sea. Ember giving up her most favorite Barbie to Tristin because Tristin was sad. Ember said the dark-haired Barbie looked more like Tristin anyway.

Tristin woke with her heart feeling heavy behind her ribs. She was lying with her head on Rhys's chest. His heartbeat thumping rhythmically in her ear. This wasn't okay.

She'd never dreamed of Ember before. Tristin never dreamed of her parents either. Her breath hitched, tears pricking behind her eyelids. She felt Rhys tense beneath her as tears spilt against his skin. She heard his subtle intake of breath and knew he was awake. She didn't even have to look; he was listening for any sounds of impending danger. When he realized they were safe, he relaxed.

He didn't ask questions. The arm that curled around her shoulders flexed, and his hand stroked down her back lazily. She normally wouldn't allow it. She didn't need comforting. She didn't cry, especially over things she couldn't change. It was a waste of her time and energy. Her brother was the emotional one.

Her parents were dead, her aunt and uncle were dead, and whatever friendship happened between her and Ember twelve years ago was dead. Nothing would change that. Tristin could have gone the rest of her life without remembering those things. She didn't want to know. She didn't want to feel like this; it was like losing them all over again.

She pressed her fist against her teeth, keeping her sobs to herself, her skin too hot. Rhys kissed the top of her head once but otherwise didn't acknowledge her distress. She hated this feeling; she hated it.

She didn't know how long she lay there before her tears finally stopped or even if they did. At some point she drifted to sleep, and if she dreamed, she didn't remember.

 237

Chapter 38

EMBER

It was late, or maybe it was early. The others had long since dragged themselves to bed, but Ember couldn't seem to settle. The night hadn't been a total disaster. She'd only sacrificed one plate of French toast to the floor. She almost wore a customer's meatloaf when she went in the out door of the kitchen. Donovan managed to save the dish, kissing her cheek as he slipped past. For once, she wasn't mad. Gravy wasn't her color. She slapped his butt as he walked past, and the wolf howled. It was hard to be mad at Donovan.

Mace didn't seem to agree. He was most definitely mad. Every time the door swung open or she glanced through the pass-thru, he leveled his glare at her, at least until Isa barked another order at him.

It was weird having a job where she interacted with the living. At least the majority of the customers were human thanks to the restaurant sitting just over the border of town. The humans didn't react to her the way they had in New Orleans. Maybe the overwhelming supernatural population dulled the humans to anything unusual. Or maybe it was because humans in Florida were weird too.

She was relieved to find Romero still alive and curled up with Neoma on the sofa in the atrium. She took a long shower, changed into pajama pants and a t-shirt, and grabbed her sketchbook. She skipped the kitchen, heading out the French doors of the atrium to the covered courtyard on the side of the house. Romero watched her with his one sad eye. He heaved a sigh, hopping from the sofa and limping along behind her.

The courtyard was her favorite part of the house. There were big comfortable chairs and a loveseat, even a fire pit. The shape of the house kept it hidden from the street. Gardenia and night blooming jasmine overwhelmed the trellis enclosing the space in a pocket of huge flowers and dizzying fragrance. Tiny white twinkle lights surrounded the perimeter, and a white chandelier hung from the ceiling.

Normally, she wouldn't touch the overhead light; it drew nothing but moths and mosquitos. Not that night, though, that night was perfect. The gentle breeze made the temperature tolerable, and the rustling leaves provided a sort of white noise she found soothing.

Romero flopped himself down with another longsuffering sigh. She curled up on the sofa, tucking her feet beneath her, the soft light making shadows jump around her. She smiled to herself. She was getting used to it, living there, in that space with all those people.

There was always somebody home, somebody talking, people yelling, somebody watching television. Somebody, usually Isa, was always cooking. Even on nights when the wolves would run, Kai and Quinn would commandeer the living room for movie night or video games. They would pop popcorn and order pizza. Neoma would sing. When the run was over, Donovan would barrel through the door and jump on the sofa between Quinn and Kai, snatching the controller and stuffing two slices in his own mouth at the same time.

People lived there, interacted with each other, talked to each other, fought with each other. She didn't think she'd adapt so quickly. It scared her in a way she'd never had to think about before, the fear of having something to lose. Thinking about it made her feel shaky, like it drew her magic to the surface, so she tried not to think about it, tried not to get too used to it. She embraced the quiet moments just to prove she could still be alone if she had to. It never paid to rely on anybody.

She opened her sketchbook to find a blank page but froze at the first image. It was a little girl in a pinafore and a bonnet. She'd drawn the picture months ago, talking to the imaginary girl as she drew.

She'd felt stupid the first time she'd done it, talking to the grave, pretending the occupants buried inside answered back, but her drawing came out with so much more detail, she couldn't see the harm. She chalked it up to artistic process.

She traced the lines of the girl's face, wondering how much of that really was imagination and not wanting to acknowledge the enormity of the answer. Since Ember found out what she was... what she could do...it'd made her throat feel tight. Her mind pulled up images she didn't want to consider. What would this little girl be if Ember called to the girl, pulled her body from the ground like the others? Would there be anything left? Would it even matter? How far past the veil did her reach extend?

Ember shook her head at the thought. She hadn't had her powers then. She barely had them since. It seemed a small consolation, considering how many bodies she'd brought back, only to be slaughtered a second time. Her power made no sense. It seemed vicious and cruel. She sighed; she came out here to not think about this stuff.

She smiled at Romero. "You're going to be immortalized today."

He was unimpressed by the news. She started sketching the dog, her eyes darting from him to the page as she crooned at him, telling him he was a good boy. She swallowed the lump of sadness that seemed to stick in her throat. Was pulling him back mean? She looked at his paw. Was somebody else suffering because of her?

She heard Mace before she saw him, his heavy booted steps clunking along the porch. A full body shiver rolled along her skin, like somebody walked over her grave, her magic acknowledging his. He didn't make his presence known, so she pretended she didn't see him, continuing her masterpiece.

He finally said, "You sure that's a good idea? Perhaps we should ban you from drawing for a bit. I really don't want to stab anybody in the head tonight."

She grimaced. "Relax, lurker, can't resurrect what's already resurrected." She flipped the sketch so he could see Romero's face before turning it back to herself and picking up where she left off.

"You really shouldn't draw in this light. You'll go blind."

"I don't even need the light. I could *do* this blind."

  240

He grinned at her cocky reply, but she wasn't lying. She looked at the dog out of habit, one she'd perfected to appease random art teachers.

"What's got you up so late, beautiful?" he asked.

Her pulse fluttered under the casual compliment, but she snorted. He was beautiful—beautiful and evil. He ate people, deprived them of moving on, crossing over, being reborn.

He gestured, asking to sit; she shrugged, swallowing hard as he jostled her around to fit himself into the small space directly beside her instead of one of the available chairs. Her magic jumped. He felt it too. His cheek twitched, he pressed himself closer. She huffed in frustration. If her power desperately wanting to merge with his wasn't proof her magic was an abomination, she didn't know what was.

"So, just thought you'd sit outside alone in the black of night with your undead dog, drawing in your sketchbook on a school night?"

She blinked at him with mock innocence. "But I'm not out here alone. I've got you."

He smirked but said nothing.

She risked a glance before asking, "Where've you been, out terrorizing the local villagers?"

"I assure you, the villagers are all safe. Well, from me anyway."

His gaze fell to her sketchpad, a gleam in his eye. She tried to slap it shut, but she was too slow. He held the page down, head bent, looking his fill.

"Lovely," he said, his voice close enough to make her jump. "May I?" he asked, holding his hand out.

She took a deep breath and handed him the sketchbook, refusing to look at him while he moved through the images. "These are the pictures you sketched in the cemetery?"

She looked up, startled. "How did you know that?"

His eyes never left the page. "I told you, I saw you."

"You said you saw me the day of the funeral." She stared hard at the side of his face.

"I may have seen you around before then," he said, vague.

 241

She shook her head but said nothing. He was already a killer and a liar, and with his admission, she could confirm stalking as well. She should be mad but why bother. She needed him. The thought felt like a boulder in her stomach.

"Did you know I used to talk to them?" she asked.

She watched him in profile, and he smiled. "I heard you, yes."

"Did you think I was crazy?"

"At the time, a little. Knowing what we know now? No."

"Do you think I saw them, somehow? Like, do you think what I am...do you think I saw them in my mind?"

"You're a reaper," he said with a shrug. "You're always going to feel the pull of the dead. It's who you are. It's tied to the type of magic you have. It's possible you were channeling these people as you drew them."

Ember looked over his shoulder as he flipped each page, sadness sinking into her bones as she thought about all the people whose lives she'd inadvertently invaded. The dead deserved peace.

"Don't you think this is ghoulish? Don't you think it's an invasion somehow?"

She expected his usual flippant answer, but instead he said, "I don't know. There has to be a reason you were given these powers, right? Perhaps some greater purpose."

"If there's a greater purpose, why are reanimators forbidden from practicing what they do?"

He said nothing for a long time. "The people who make the rules, they serve themselves first. Ember, you have no idea what you are. The power you possess..." He trailed off for a minute. "The Grove keeps the reanimators close under the guise of protection—protection of the people, of the magical community—but in truth, they use their powers for their own gain. It's possible they could come for yours as well. It doesn't make you evil, it makes them evil."

"Allister said they're there to protect us. Is Allister wrong too?"

"I don't know Allister, luv, but I do know the Grove."

She rolled her eyes. "Now we are back to luv?"

He grinned. "Do you prefer beautiful, then?"

 242

She scoffed, picking invisible lint off her t-shirt. "I'd prefer the truth."

He turned in the tight confines of the loveseat, his gaze meeting hers with an intensity she'd only imagined in fantasies she'd never dare admit aloud.

"Okay, then. November Lonergan, your hair is too orange, and your eyes are such a strange shade of purple I'm surprised New Orleans didn't burn as a witch. You have too many freckles and that gap in your teeth is…distracting."

Ember's face flushed. It was like she was back in sixth grade listening to her classmates mock her. Her throat tightened, and tears pricked behind her eyes. She didn't need to listen to this. She stood to go.

Long fingers curled around her arm, tugging her down, his voice dropping low, like he was revealing a shameful secret. "Back in New Orleans, I would get lost staring at your face for hours. You always looked so alone and sad and, frankly, a little angry. But then, sometimes, when you thought nobody was looking, you would twirl around or sing in front of your window, and I would find myself thinking about you long after you'd disappeared."

Ember's fingers clenched spastically on her thigh, but he wasn't done.

"I wanted to know what your hair felt like beneath my fingers." He tugged one buoyant curl. "I thought of your lips and if they were that red naturally or because you always seemed to be chewing at them." She was almost positive she'd stopped breathing. "Ember, luv, I've lived a long time, and I've seen tens of thousands of people, but not one of their faces fascinated me like yours. You are strange and broken and more powerful than you could ever begin to imagine, and you were born to force the world to kneel at your feet, so cut the bullshit because one day the world will love you."

She didn't move, paralyzed. "The world will love me?" she asked dully, mesmerized by this pretty boy and his pretty words. She'd be foolish to trust him, but in that moment, she just didn't care.

"I can't love you, Ember. I have no soul. But in the last hundred years or so, you are the first to make me wish I could."

   243

Her gaze rose to his. "You have no soul." Her voice sounded as raw as the words themselves. She cleared her throat and tried again. "Did you ever? Have a soul? Is it true what Quinn says? Were you really so…evil that hell didn't want you?"

He sat back, giving her the space she'd wanted just moments ago. Disappointment flooded through her.

A shadow flickered across his face, before he smiled, but it didn't reach his eyes. "Quinn gets his information from the human internet. The internet gets its facts from old wives' tales and dusty old books written by crusty old professors who like to theorize."

This was the first time she'd ever heard him sound anything but smug. She leaned forward, her hand touching his knee. "So…it's not true? You didn't d-deserve this? Was it like a curse?"

His fingers found another curl, his eyes haunted. "This isn't a fairy tale, Ember. I played my part in making me what I am, but I had my reasons. The why of it really doesn't matter."

She gripped his arm this time. "Of course it does."

He moved forward, his hand at her neck, pulling her towards him. "Don't romanticize me, luv. I'm not some wronged hero. I may not have been born evil, but I became it. Make no mistake, Ember. The things I've done would most assuredly give Lucifer pause to grant me admittance to the underworld now. I've earned the reputation that precedes my kind. I've earned it a hundred times over." He let her go. "Use me, Ember. Let me help you learn control, but don't for one second let me charm you into thinking I can be saved."

His words felt like a slap. "So somehow, no matter how grotesque my magic seems, it must have a higher purpose, but your magic, equally as bad, has damned you forever? Doesn't seem balanced to me."

"Don't let their party line fool you," he said. "The Grove doesn't care about the balance. They don't care about dark and light. They don't care about good versus evil. The Grove cares about power, and you, sweet girl, are powerful."

She said nothing for a long time. They both pretended not to notice as she leaned against him. She let herself imagine it was her magic clinging to his and nothing more.

Romero's heavy panting had a sort of hypnotic rhythm to it. His white fur was clean and fluffy, but his bath revealed his left paw was little more than raw tendon and bone. He didn't seem bothered by it, but it must hurt.

"Do you think he's sad?" she asked.

"What do you mean?"

"He looks sad to me. Do you think he was happy on the other side, and I ripped him from, like, doggie heaven?" She refused to look at him as she spoke.

He looked over at the dog. "He doesn't look sad. He looks pensive, like he's got a lot of heavy thoughts on his mind. Perhaps you just raised an introspective dog."

"You still think he's going to die?" she asked, her stomach clenching at the thought.

"He's already dead," he said. "Your magic should wear off eventually and when it does, he will return to the other side." His voice wasn't unkind.

"You said he would be gone before sundown."

"Yes, I did. It appears I was wrong. As I said, you are more powerful than you know. But, a reanimator's magic will always wear off eventually."

"Is there anything I can do about his paw?"

"Our magic deals with the soul, not the body." His lip curled in a sneer. "For that, you need a witch."

"I don't have one of those handy."

He was quiet for a while, his eyes roaming her features. "Technically, you do."

She wrinkled her brow. "Huh?"

"Your uncle. He'd help you if you asked."

"Even if I'm not a witch?"

"I don't know, luv, but it's worth a try."

She wasn't sure how she felt about the idea of asking her uncle for anything. With her uncle came Astrid and Allister and even Stella. She wasn't sure she was ready for that.

"It's late. Don't you have school in the morning?"

   245

She shrugged. "We both have school in the morning, and also, I'm pretty sure it's morning. Besides, I don't want to go to sleep. I think the sun will be up soon."

He propped his feet up on the table in front of them, and she followed suit. She let herself lean heavier against him, dropping her head against his chest, eyes heavy. It took her a moment to realize that there was no sound.

"You really don't have a heartbeat."

"No, I don't. It's a side effect of being dead."

She sucked in a breath at that information. No wonder his skin was so cool.

"But you breathe, I can feel it."

"Reflex. Habit mostly. If I was to be in a situation where my oxygen supply stopped, I'd be fine."

"Being supernatural is so weird."

"Mm," he agreed. She felt his cheek resting against her hair, and she opted to forget the real world, just for a while. She could be herself when the sun came up. The real world would still be there.

Chapter 39

TRISTIN

Tristin woke before the others, flipping on the tiny coffee maker and hopping in the shower. She woke her brother with a pillow to the face.

"What the hell, Tristin."

"Get up. Shower. We need to somehow make you presentable enough to get the gatekeeper's attention." She wasn't in the mood for her brother's lollygagging about. They had things to do.

Quinn woke, bleary eyed, hair standing on end like a baby chick. He rubbed his eyes. "Coffee," he croaked. "My kingdom for a coffee."

Rhys was quiet, but that was hardly unusual. He stalked around the small room, taking up more space than the others, still shirtless.

Once Kai showered, she forced her brother to sit as she attempted to make him look...well, pretty. When she was done, Quinn whistled, and Rhys refused to look at Quinn, which was the only real confirmation Tristin needed. Tristin pronounced Kai fit for seduction, and they piled into the Suburban once more.

Navigating a college campus seemed much easier in teen movies and television shows. The campus was the size of four Belle Haven city blocks and looked like it should have its own subway line. There were students everywhere, playing Frisbee, riding bikes, clutching coffee cups, and toting laptop bags. They scurried around in ratty clothes and pajama pants.

The global apathy of the student body annoyed Tristin. Kai didn't seem to share her opinion, his head on a swivel as he took it all in, elbowing Quinn occasionally to show him something noteworthy.

They went virtually unnoticed on the large campus, and it took an hour of asking around before anybody knew where to find Professor Denning's old office.

As Ember predicted, a young good-looking man sat just inside the doorway marking the office. A pretty blonde girl leaned over the desk, partially obscuring their view. "So, are you coming to the party tonight?" she asked.

"I doubt it. I can't keep going out like this. Some nights I don't even remember how I got back to my room, if I even wake up in my room."

The girl sighed. "Ugh, fine. Be that way. Text me when you change your mind."

The four of them ducked back as the girl left, staying hidden until she turned the corner.

Tristin stared at the guy. He was tall and lanky with light brown hair, wire-rimmed glasses, and a sad attempt at facial hair. He was wearing a bow tie and a short-sleeved shirt that should have looked ridiculous but instead looked fashion forward. Once he was alone, he clutched a pen between his perfect teeth, deeply engrossed in whatever he was reading. Her brother's eyes were downright predatory as he took it all in. Yeah, Kai faking interest wouldn't be too hard.

"What are you going to say to him to get him out of there?"

"I don't know. He's cute. I'll wing it." Kai shrugged.

"He looks like Quinn," Rhys noted, a scowl firmly in place.

Tristin snickered. "Well then this should be even easier. These two have been secretly in love with each other for years."

Kai smiled at Quinn and winked. "Who said it's a secret?"

 248

"Aw, thanks, buddy."

"Could you get on with it please? We have to be home in time for work," Rhys grumbled.

Kai checked his reflection in the glass, straightening his shirt. He could pass for a college student. He walked past the door as if he was walking down the hallway and then popped back.

"Hey, there you are."

The other man looked up and seemed surprised by Kai's appearance. "Hi?"

"Eric, right?"

Tristin watched the other man's gaze, his eyes lighting up, rake over her brother.

"Yeah, can I help you?"

"I hope so," Kai said, sounding shy. She tried not to snort at that. "I'm Chris. You don't remember me, do you? Six months ago, the thing after that party?"

Tristin cringed at the suggestive nature of her brother's tone. It was a pretty big gamble. There was a long pause. "Oh, yeah, sure, right. Chris. Of course, I remember. How could I forget anybody with eyes as pretty as yours?"

Eric certainly wasn't one for subtlety. Her brother laughed and leaned forward, blocking their view of Eric. Rhys huffed and rolled his eyes. She patted him on the shoulder absently. She didn't have time to stroke his ego.

"Listen, I'm just here for the day. I'm working on a project relating to Celtic mythology and death rituals, and I wondered if maybe you would let me buy you some coffee and pick your brain a bit? You knew so much about it last time we talked."

"I'd love to but..." Eric trailed off, looking around the mess of the front office.

"Oh, no, it's cool. I understand if you're too busy," Kai said, disappointment seeping into his voice. Even Tristin had to roll her eyes at that. Her brother was quite the actor.

"No. No. It's fine. I can finish this up later." She heard the chair scrape back. "I mean, I only have you for one day. I have the rest of the semester to finish cleaning out a dead man's office."

 249

They once again hid as the two left. She couldn't help but feel like she'd stumbled into a Nancy Drew novel as they stood there flattened against a wall in an otherwise empty hallway. Steam practically poured out of the Rhys's ears.

She shook her head.

She sent a quick text to her brother to remind him to text when they were on their way back. They agreed Rhys would keep watch of the hallway. They passed through the doorway to the left of Eric's desk and closed the door behind them.

The professor's office was a disaster. Half-filled cardboard boxes covered every surface. There were papers strewn everywhere. An inch of dust sat on the Tiffany-style lamp on his desk. Her nose twitched at the heavy herbal smell that permeated the room. It was flowery and cloying, like an old woman wearing too much expensive perfume. It made her head swim.

"What's that smell?" she asked.

"It's not one smell." Quinn blinked. "He was doing some serious conjuring in here. Marjoram, patchouli, star anise maybe?"

"I'll take the desk, you start with what's left on the shelves. Will you be able to tell what's real and what's not?"

"I think so." He shrugged, turning away from her.

She pulled open the top drawer of the desk, rifling through pens and random sticky notes with strange cryptic messages. Some didn't even look like English. She put them aside to show Quinn. There was a picture of a little girl with a gap in her teeth and bright red hair shoved towards the back of the drawer. Somebody had smeared a reddish black substance around the photograph. Tristin looked at it for a long time, recognizing Ember's face from her dream.

The second drawer proved just as fruitless: an old magazine, a black binder full of empty loose-leaf paper, and two unopened packs of gum. She pushed the drawer shut with more force than was necessary. It rattled. Something rolled across the bottom of the drawer.

She opened the drawer again, removing everything and examining the bottom. There was a tiny dent in the wood. She used the letter opener to dig at it, cackling when the wood gave, revealing a secret compartment. They really were in a Nancy Drew novel.

   250

Underneath the panel was a vial, a ritual knife, a chalice, a small jar, and a flask. She picked up the vial and opened it.

"Look at this," she said.

He peered over her shoulder. "It looks like the items they give you at the start of a video game." He picked up the black sea salt. She showed him the vial. "Poppy seed? Well, he was definitely using black magic." He opened the flask and inhaled, choking at the smell. "That is not booze. Wow, we know what that smell is. If he was drinking this, he must have had an iron stomach." He tucked the flask in his back pocket.

"Are these anything?" Quinn looked over the sticky notes. "I don't think so. It doesn't look alchemical. It looks like gibberish. Do we know if this guy was, ya know, all there?"

"No idea. Ember doesn't seem real fond of talking about him."

Twenty minutes into their ransacking Quinn let out a triumphant noise, pulling a book from a pile stuffed behind an old leather chair. She watched, fascinated, as he opened the book, scanning page after page with robotic precision. She couldn't imagine a reality where her brain would ever work like that. It was more supernatural to her than her own magic. She barely passed pre-algebra.

She proceeded to continue her search, periodically checking his progress. When she glanced up, he was staring at her. "What?"

"Nothing," he mumbled, going back to his reading.

She stared at him for a long minute before returning to her task. He was so weird. She didn't understand his fascination with her or his insistence that they were fated to be together. Even the wolves didn't believe in true mates anymore. It was simply a myth they'd used to keep bloodlines pure back when that was all anybody thought was important.

She watched as he pushed his glasses up his nose. It would be nice though, to think there was somebody out there fated to love you no matter what. Even if you weren't as smart or funny or beautiful as other girls; even if you weren't happy and bouncy all the time. She watched as his tongue flicked over his lower lip as he concentrated. In another world, she could see staring at his stupid face forever.

 251

He looked up, smiling as he caught her staring. Her breath hitched as her face flushed. Her phone chirped an alert. She thumbed open the screen.

"They're on their way back. Hurry up."

Quinn flipped through ten more pages before sticking the book down his back, tucked into his jeans. He arranged his flannel shirt to cover it.

"What are you doing? We can't take that home."

"We can't take it home, but that doesn't mean we can't keep it somewhere more centrally located. Even I can't read this entire book in one sitting. We'll put it somewhere only we can find it."

She nodded, her stomach knotting in fear. Even holding that book made her nervous, but maybe something in there could save her brother, could save all of them. They were too young to deal with the Grove.

She shook the thought away as they made their way out of the office and back to the hallway just around the corner. Rhys tensed, his lips tightened. Her brother must be close.

Footsteps came towards them. "Can I see you again?" Eric asked her brother.

"Um, honestly, I'm not sure. I can call you the next time I'm in town."

"Well then, I guess I shouldn't waste any time."

There was a startled breathy sound from her brother, followed by kissing noises. Rhys growled low in his throat. She elbowed him so hard he grunted, even if the last thing she wanted to hear was her brother kissing somebody.

"Definitely call me," Eric said, sounding a little dazed. She smiled. Way to go, brother.

Quinn stifled his laugh, biting down on his lip so hard there would be permanent damage.

Her brother managed to mumble. "Yeah, sure. Totally. Thanks for the help."

Chapter 40

KAI

The walk back to the car was awful. Kai stayed close to Quinn, who rolled his eyes as he made absurd kissy faces at Kai, Quinn's tongue lulling in his mouth. "Call me, big boy. I need you," Quinn mocked.

Tristin walked between him and Rhys, eyeing the wolf warily. Rhys kept his eyes forward, his jaw set, in full brood. Whatever. If he was so upset, he should do something about it. Kai was tired of playing this game with Rhys.

Tristin stopped abruptly, her hands on hips. She looked at each of them in turn. "You know what? Quinn and I will sit in the back."

"We will?" Quinn said, startled and confused by her sudden eagerness to be near him.

"Yes," she said.

"Fine, but I'm driving," Kai said, snatching the keys from Rhys's fingers and trudging ahead. He climbed into the SUV and took a deep breath before unlocking the doors for the others. His lips still tingled where Eric kissed him.

His stomach twisted. It wasn't like it was his first kiss. Granted, it was his second and Quinn was his first, but that didn't matter.

Kai should feel happy. It was nice to feel wanted for a change. He thought he'd feel smug that somebody wanted him and Rhys witnessed it, but instead it just felt wrong. He clenched his teeth at the guilt gnawing in his gut.

This shouldn't feel like cheating.

They drove in silence for an hour, Quinn dozing with his head against the window, Tristin drooling on his shoulder, snoring softly.

He glanced over to find Rhys glowering at him.

"What?" he asked, his eyebrows raised.

He wolf snorted, shaking his head as if Kai was the one who was infuriating. "Nothing."

"Of course not," Kai said, mouth twisting, the words sour on his tongue. "Never anything to say."

The wolf hunched his shoulders. "What's that supposed to mean?"

"Seriously?" Kai asked.

"Never mind," Rhys muttered, turning to look out the window.

Kai fumed. Right, just like that. Conversation over, because Rhys decided it was. Kai couldn't deal with this feeling anymore. It was like he lived with a softball lodged under his ribs, making it hard to breathe.

He made a decision, jerking the wheel hard, careening across two empty lanes before skidding to a stop on the soft shoulder of the highway. Tristin screamed, and Quinn's head thunked hard against the glass as the SUV came to a sideways stop.

"What the hell is wrong with you?" Rhys shouted, his eyes wide. "Are you trying to get us killed?"

Kai looked Rhys dead in the eye. "Get. Out. Now."

"What's going on?" Quinn asked groggily, rubbing the side of his head. Tristin looked around, surreptitiously wiping drool from her chin.

Kai ignored their questions, focused only on Rhys. "Get out of the car."

"Is he planning on ditching him on the side of the road?" Quinn whispered. Tristin shushed him, watching the two of them, bewildered.

 254

After a moment, the wolf relented, exiting the vehicle with a huff. Kai climbed out of the driver's seat, slamming the door and stomping past Rhys, not looking back as he broke through the tree line.

Rhys followed. It wasn't just the familiarity of the wolf's heavy footsteps that told Kai so; Kai's body seemed hardwired to know where the jerk was at all times.

Kai waited until they were hidden by the trees before turning on Rhys. He stumbled back at the abrupt change in direction, and Kai suddenly realized he didn't know what he was going to say.

Rhys stood, his arms crossed, brow raised. "In case you were wondering, this is why I don't let you drive."

Kai bared his teeth. "You think this is funny? I can't do this with you anymore."

Rhys sighed, shifting his weight. "What are you talking about?"

Kai shoved him hard. The wolf didn't even budge. "Tell me you weren't jealous when he kissed me?"

Rhys's eyes bulged. "What? Why should I care about your love life?"

Kai wanted to punch the idiot. "You're such a coward. You know that?" Kai shouted. "Do you think I'm stupid? Do you think I don't know what you do?"

"What?" he said again. His tone sounded bored, but his spine stiffened.

Kai growled, throwing his hands up. "Stop saying that."

"Then start making sense," Rhys spit back, raking a hand through his hair.

"I know what you're doing."

Rhys's jaw clenched so hard it popped. "Meaning?"

Kai squinted. "The shoving me into lockers, the brushing up against me for no reason. I've lived with your pack for twelve years. You must think I'm pretty fucking stupid."

At Rhys's bewildered expression, Kai laughed. "You're scent marking me, you dick. Marking me up like I'm yours. I haven't had a guy look at me twice since eighth grade because you've made it so

 255

very clear I belong to you. You've literally marked me as your property, your territory."

Rhys's eyes slid away, his face going red, not denying the accusation.

"Yeah, that's right. You've turned me into a social pariah, dude, and the worst of it is…" Kai sucked in a breath, eyes stinging. "The worst of it is, I wouldn't even mind if you were willing to act on it." He moved closer, stepping into Rhys's space. Rhys stared at his shoes. It made it easier for Kai to say what came next. "I've known how I feel about you since I was twelve years old. I was all in before I even knew what that meant." Rhys swallowed hard as Kai rushed on. "Don't you get it? I would be yours—just yours—if you would be mine too."

Rhys's head snapped up, his golden green eyes flashing bright as Kai's mouth twisted. "But that's not what you want, is it? You don't want me. You just don't want anybody else to have me." Kai swiped at the wetness on his cheeks. Rhys gaped. "You use your scent like a bookmark. You mark me to hold your place. For what? Why do you do this? Do you even know? Why put your scent all over me if you have no intention of doing anything about it?" Kai moved closer, holding his wrist to the wolf. "Do I smell like you? Do you smell like me too? Can you even separate our scents anymore? What are you waiting for?"

Rhys looked poleaxed, every muscle taut. His nostrils flared at Kai's scent. He staggered forward before catching himself with a growl. "You have no idea what you're talking about. You talk so much, but you don't know what you're saying. You don't understand anything. Why can't you just leave it alone, leave *this* alone, before—" He snapped his mouth shut, his hands fisted at his side, words dying on his lips. His eyes darted away again as he hunched over like a cornered animal.

Kai almost felt bad. He lifted his hand, to touch, to comfort Rhys, before letting it drop. Almost. Kai didn't want to play this game anymore. He had to stop pretending this was a movie, and Rhys was going to get it together.

Kai took a breath, his heart breaking. "If you aren't willing to do something about this, about us"—he gestured between them—"then don't touch me. Don't hover over me. Stop growling and snarling when other people notice me. You want me to leave it alone? Okay. Fine. I'm done with you." He vowed, the words like ashes in his mouth.

Kai stuffed his hands in his pockets, curling his shoulders in, finally letting himself think about what was coming. "I don't know how much time I've got before they figure out what I did, but I won't waste them on someone who's never going to care about me." He made sure to meet Rhys's gaze. "I'm not going to waste them on you."

Rhys flinched like Kai punched him, his Adam's apple bobbing.

Kai's blood pounded in his ears. Rhys moved closer before stopping himself with another aborted motion. Kai wanted to scream in frustration. Words were hard for Rhys. Kai knew that; he did. But how long was Kai going to make excuses before he just accepted Rhys would never admit his feelings? How much time did Kai even have, really?

He scrubbed his hands over his face, before throwing them up in surrender. He pushed past Rhys. "Screw you, dude." Kai said, yanking the keys from his pocket, and stalking back towards the truck.

His breath left him in a huff as he found himself shoved backwards against a tree, bark scratching through his clothes. The keys clattered from numb fingers as he looked at Rhys's hands clenched in Kai's shirt.

Kai was pinned. Rhys was partially shifted, his fangs dropped; his eyes were wild, all pupil, like he was the one trapped. He looked feral. He looked hot. Kai's heart jackhammered against his diaphragm, and Rhys made a strange rumbling whine deep in his chest. The vibration shivered through Kai in a not unpleasant way.

He'd seen Rhys shifted; Kai had seen Rhys rip things apart with his bare hands. Although Kai had always known Rhys was a predator, Kai had never felt so much like the prey. Rhys closed the gap between their bodies, and warmth flooded Kai from shoulder to thigh. He forgot how to breathe. When the wolf rumbled, his lips were right against Kai's ear, and he felt it all the way to his toes.

His eyes fluttered closed as Rhys set to work; he rubbed his face against Kai's throat, along the edge of his jaw, back up to the shell of his ear. Kai snorted. The jerk was actually scenting him again. After everything.

Rhys's tongue traced the corded tendon of Kai's throat. Kai moaned, his head dropping to the side thoughtlessly. That was new. He licked his lower lip, his body taut, holding perfectly still.

Rhys growled low and guttural, his teeth sinking into Kai's neck, accepting Kai's submission with enthusiasm. It wasn't the first time he'd had to submit to a wolf, but Kai's body responded differently this time, jerking forward in a way that made them both groan. Rhys let go of Kai's throat, soothing the spot with his tongue before dropping his forehead to Kai's.

Kai kept his eyes shut, listening to the sound of their panting, not ready to break the spell. When he realized nothing more was happening, he finally looked, only to find Rhys's human eyes searching his face for...something.

"What?" Kai whispered imploringly.

Rhys's eyes dipped to Kai's mouth. "You make me crazy," Rhys whispered, and then warm lips grazed Kai's once, twice, hesitant, like he thought Kai would push away. Kai buried his hands in Rhys's hair, pressing their mouths together firmly.

Rhys's hands slid around Kai's waist, fingers playing at the skin under his t-shirt and above the waist of his jeans. Melting against Rhys, Kai's mouth opened beneath the wolf's. Rhys's tongue slipped inside, and Kai's higher thought process shut down, leaving only thoughts like *yes, please, finally,* and *mine.* Kai was screwed. He was a domesticated animal who'd just had his first taste of human flesh, and nothing else would ever do. Rhys was it for Kai.

He'd made a mistake, letting himself have the moment. In his fantasies, kissing Rhys was always perfection. Kai had kissed him in a million different ways and a thousand different situations, each of them amazing in their own way but so very two-dimensional, just moving pictures running through an overactive imagination.

But it was so much different, to know for certain what Rhys's lips tasted like, how it felt to cup his face and feel the scraping of stubble along his palms. Kai could smell him, taste him, feel him, and fuck, if it wasn't better than anything he'd ever dreamed in his fantasies.

 258

He tried to catalogue every single sensation. The way he could feel Rhys's claws pricking the flesh at Kai's hips, the sound of their lips meeting, the way Rhys groaned when Kai bit Rhys's lower lip. Every time Rhys pulled back, Kai's lips followed like a magnet, pulling them back together. He wasn't ready for it to be over, not yet. And it would be over as soon as they left this place. He'd won this battle, but Rhys wasn't surrendering the war.

"Really?"

Rhys jumped back, shoving Kai away at Tristin's indignant shriek.

In that moment, he hated his sister. She had the worst timing of anybody ever. She looked at the two of them like a disappointed mother. He looked over at Rhys's guilty expression, taking in kiss-swollen lips, heavy lidded eyes, and messy hair. Kai must look even worse. He couldn't help but be a little smug. He'd done that.

"We've been sitting in the hot car for twenty minutes so you two can make out in the woods?"

Rhys blushed, snatching the keys from where they'd fallen and stomping off towards the truck.

Tristin crossed her arms, tilting her head. "Well?"

Kai widened his eyes at his sister. "What?"

"What?" She laughed, and then said, "I love you, bro, but I'm not going to hang out in the car staring at Quinn while you lose your virginity against a tree."

Kai glared. "You're a real class act, sis."

She smiled, fluttering her lashes. "I'm not the one dry-humping my boyfriend on the side of the interstate."

Kai's face burned. "Shut up," he said, body checking her gently as he walked past.

"Whatever you say, Romeo."

 259

Chapter 41

TRISTIN

Tristin and Kai walked back to the car in silence. She was surprised
to find the keys in the ignition and Rhys cramped into the backseat
with a bewildered Quinn. Kai yanked open the passenger seat, leaving her to drive. Rhys quickly backslid to his default setting of non-
verbal cave wolf.

She'd endured a lot of awkward car rides with her brother and
Rhys over the years, but none compared to this. Not even music
could dull the tension. Kai alternated between texting Quinn and
staring desolately out the window. Quinn stayed quiet, giving Rhys
plenty of room. Tristin knew the exact moment Kai told Quinn
what happened because Quinn made a noise like a dying cat, staring
wide-eyed at Rhys until the wolf growled at him.

Tristin had never been so happy to be home in her life. She
wanted to fall to her knees and kiss the ground. Once inside, Kai
stormed up the stairs. She flinched as his door slammed hard enough
to rattle the frame. For once, she got his need to be dramatic. The
house was too quiet with the others at work or school. She followed
Rhys into the kitchen, watching as his large form crumpled onto the
bench of the breakfast nook. Rhys rubbed his eyes and sighed.

She snatched a bottled water from the fridge, leaning against the counter as she drank and contemplating her next move. She finished half the bottle before she stalked up to him and punched him on the arm hard enough to make her hand throb. His eyes widened in shock.

She shoved him so he moved over, and she sat down. "You know I love you, right?" His face flushed, and he nodded once.

"Good, because you're not going to like what I have to say." He looked at her warily.

"Stop dicking around with my brother's head."

He looked like he was choking on his tongue. "I—"

"Just listen. I get it. I know you, and I don't really understand all of this touchy feely stuff. The emotional stuff squicks me out too." She looked him in the eye. "But you've been tying my brother in knots, literally since the day he was old enough to realize he liked boys. Why are you fighting this so hard? You have to see you're tearing him apart. What are you so afraid of?"

He looked conflicted, like he was just on the verge of saying... something. But then it was gone, his eyes blank as he shrugged. "What's the point?"

Tristin squinted at him. "What's the point of what? Being in love? Being with somebody? Dating?"

He didn't look at her.

She opened her mouth to tell him what the point was but realized she didn't know, really. The idea of being so dependent on somebody seemed horrible to her. She saw the way Isa looked at Wren, like he was the air she breathed. Isa would never survive if something happened to him. Why would anybody want to be so entwined with another person you couldn't tell where one ended and the other began?

But she certainly wasn't telling Rhys *that*.

She sighed. "The point is to be somebody's person. To be there for them. To make sure when crap gets real you have their back and vice versa. People have been falling in love since the dawn of time, like people die for it and write poems about it. There has to be a reason. My brother wants you to be his person."

"Like Quinn wants you?" he countered.

 261

Tristin's mouth tightened. "That's different."

Rhys huffed. "Really? Why? He's definitely your person. He'd do anything for you. He probably writes weepy sonnets about you in a dream journal tucked under his pillow. He reeks of love whenever you're in the room. You certainly don't have a problem taking advantage of his feelings for you when you need something." Tristin's mouth fell open as Rhys continued, "You know, since we're being honest."

This was not how she intended the conversation to go. She just wanted him to see what he was doing to her brother. She wanted him to understand what he was doing to himself. It had nothing to do with her or Quinn.

She set her mouth in a hard line, glaring at the wolf. Quinn was a good person, one of the few pure souls in this world. He was smart and funny and attractive in a way she tried hard not to think about. Thinking about Quinn was messy and distracting. She couldn't afford any distractions.

She was seventeen. She was fighting monsters and studying for the SATs. Maybe someday there would be room for Quinn, but not at that moment. "Quinn is human. Falling in love with a human is stupid and dangerous. Just ask my dad...or yours."

He looked at her, his eyebrow raised. "That's a pretty cynical view, even for you. Also, you're full of crap."

"Maybe, but it's true. Humans are defenseless in this town. Like baby bunnies."

Rhys snorted. "Quinn is clumsy and spastic, but he's no baby bunny. In fact, he might be the only thing in the world I've actually seen scare you."

Her eyes widened, her heartbeat stumbling. Rhys looked smug. She narrowed her eyes and slapped his shoulder again. "This isn't about me and Quinn. This is about you and my brother. I don't get why you are fighting it so hard. Everybody knows you're in love with him. Nobody hates anybody as much as you two pretend to without secretly wanting to...mate." She smirked at him, waggling her eyebrows suggestively.

His eyes flicked to hers and then back to his hands. His jaw muscle twitched. "Even if I do have...feelings..." He swallowed hard

 262

around the word like it stuck in his throat. "Everybody seems to be forgetting something extremely important."

"Such as?"

"My fiancé?"

Tristin laughed. "Oh my God, you're such a drama queen. She is not your fiancé. You've never even met her. You've never even spoken to her. You were betrothed before you were even born. It's an antiquated tradition. Nobody is going to hold you to that."

"Isa honored her betrothal to Wren," he said.

"One, your sister is an alpha, and it's her job to expand the pack. Two, she's marrying Wren because they are gaga for each other, and you know it. She'd never marry Wren if she didn't love him. That's not who she is, and she wouldn't expect you to either."

Rhys looked at her imploringly. "Marrying a wolf from the Clear-weather pack will solidify our alliances in Oregon, Alabama, and Tennessee. It's what's best for the pack."

"Look, I'm sure this girl—"

"Selina."

"Selina," she continued. "I'm sure Selina is a great girl, but she probably doesn't want to marry somebody who doesn't love her. Pack alliances were for a hundred years ago when werewolf hunting was rampant. It's been a long time since we've had any real threat from the hunters. Most humans don't even know we exist anymore. Even the Grove doesn't get involved in pack mating disputes. Have you talked to your sister about this?"

"No," he said. "And I'm not going to. If my sister can honor her commitments, I can too."

She made a noise of frustration, feeling a sudden need to rip his face off. She turned to look him in the eye. He needed to understand she meant her next words with every ounce of her being. "Fine, be a stubborn ass, but let me make this crystal clear...I love you like my family. I really do. But if you don't stop hurting my brother, I'm going to lace your toilet paper with aconite."

His eyes bulged, his jaw falling open. "Wow, calm down, crazy."

"I'm going to get ready for work. You should probably do the same." She stood, heading to the back stairs. "You should probably also try to sneak in a quick shower. I can smell my brother all over you even without the super werewolf sniffer. Your sister will definitely smell it, and if you think I'm angry, think about how much Isa loves Kai?"

His face paled, and he looked a little sick. She couldn't help her smile as she ran up the stairs. The idea of lacing his toilet paper with aconite, more commonly known as wolfsbane, was her best idea yet. It was a wonderful weapon really. It wouldn't kill him unless he ingested it, but it would give him a rash that made poison ivy seem like a daydream.

She met Quinn at the top of the stairs coming out of her brother's room.

"How is he?" she asked.

Quinn pulled a face. "Not sure. He's staring at the wall, and every now and again he mumbles something like 'Whatever, screw him' and then goes back to staring. How was your conversation with Rhys?"

"He brought up his fiancé."

Quinn burst out laughing, pulling it together when he realized she wasn't kidding. "Wait, seriously?"

"Yep."

"There's no hope for him. He's so desperate to be a martyr we should just change his name to Joan of Arc."

Tristin couldn't help but laugh. Rhys really did seem desperate to be miserable. He needed a therapist.

Quinn shifted from one foot to the other. "Come find me when you get back from work. No matter what time it is. Okay?"

Tristin went cold, eyeing him warily. "Why? What's wrong?"

"Nothing's wrong. I just want to talk, but we don't have time to talk now. So…later, yeah?"

He pushed his glasses up the bridge of his nose and scuffed his shoe across the hardwood floor. It was never a good sign when he couldn't look her in the eye.

"You're lying, but I don't have time to pry it out of you so…sure, we'll talk later. Now I have to go get ready for work so that I can spend all night worrying about whatever it is you want to tell me but can't tell me in fifteen minutes. Thanks for that."

 264

"Dagger."

"Save it. I'm over the men in this house today. Do you hear me?" She shouted loud enough for her brother and Rhys to hear. "I'm done with all of you."

Chapter 42

MACE

In the harsh morning light things seemed much different. He had no idea why he'd chosen to be so honest with her. Maybe this bond with her had even more effect than he'd first believed. With Ember curled up against him, he'd let himself believe his honesty was a ploy to further his own agenda.

He'd told himself she needed to trust him for his plan to work, and telling her not to trust him or others seemed like the perfect way to make her see he was on her side. Besides, it wasn't an entirely unpleasant way to spend an evening, if he didn't dwell on the way her body fit against his or how her hair smelled like lemons.

Afterward, it just seemed like an incredibly stupid move on his part, and he didn't make stupid moves. She'd felt the difference, too. As the sun broke through the tree line, she'd stiffened, pulling away from him and lurching to her feet. Her hair was a mess, her eyes bleary. She'd mumbled something about needing to get in the shower and called the mutt to follow. Their parting of ways felt less like progress and more like the end of the world's most awkward first date.

He stared at the back of her head, fixated on the plastic contraption confining all but the few errant strands of her hair hiding her birthmark. His fingers itched to touch it. He hadn't been lying when he said he couldn't love her. Yet, he was feeling things. It had to be the magic, the invisible noose he'd wrapped around his own throat. There was no other explanation. Her magic was merging with his, somehow making him feel things he couldn't and say things he shouldn't. It was the only possible explanation.

At the front of the room, Ember's uncle was scribbling out their French homework on the board, covering for Madam Krug without explanation. It had been hours, and Ember had barely spoken to Mace. They'd shared several classes and lunch, and the only time she'd spoken to him was when her pen ran out of ink.

She was covertly tapping out a text to somebody on her phone. Probably the boy reaper; they were quite chummy. She most likely wanted to know if they had delivered her message. She seemed oblivious to the way her uncle repeatedly looked to her, as if hoping to make eye contact. She also missed the way the witch—Stella, Mace thought—stared, her eyes narrowed jaw clenched. It seemed hostile for a person he'd never seen interact with Ember.

Mace pulled his phone from his pocket.

What did you do to piss off Snow White over there?

Ember's head shot up. The other girl didn't even have the decency to look embarrassed. She gave Ember one last snotty look before turning towards Ember's uncle, her red lips bleeding into a smile. Alex smiled back, and the girl tapped her pen against her lips in a way Mace found…inappropriate.

She appears to have a crush on our teacher? Don't you think?

Don't know. Don't care.

Her uncle looked up, catching her eye and smiling. "Ember, you want to take a stab at answering this one?"

Ember panicked, her phone clattering against her desk. "Um, sorry, no. Maybe next time?"

A few students snickered. Ember seemed to have all the witches' attention now, not just Stella's. The three students the group referred to as the triplets were now watching Ember with unwavering interest, especially the girl, Lola.

  267

"Put the phone away, Ember, or I'll have to take if from you."

She nodded, sliding it to her lap but not putting it into the pack at her feet.

You seem to be garnering quite a bit of attention from the witches, luv. Careful.

Ember's eyes dropped to the screen for a moment before returning to the board. His phone vibrated against his thigh.

Tristin says the triplets are part of my uncle's pack...coven, whatever...but I think Stella just hates reapers.

You should make nice with your uncle. He could be useful. If the Grove comes, you may find you need as many allies as possible to stand for you.

I'll take my chances.

Will you be so cavalier about your cousin's chances? They may face repercussions from the Grove as well.

Low blow. It's hard to worry about this Grove everybody talks about when literally nobody has ever seen them. Did you ever consider they are just the boogeymen the witches use to keep people in line?

Ember, luv, I assure you, the Grove exists. I've been on the other side of their displeasure. None of you want that, I promise. What is the worst that could happen if you met for coffee? At least give the man a chance?

Why are you campaigning so hard for him? What on earth could you possibly gain from me bonding with my uncle?

This isn't about me. It's about you. It's about keeping you safe. No easy feat. Besides, you can ask him about Romero's paw.

She paused, turning to look at him with narrowed eyes.

Ugh, fine. I'll talk to him, but not outside of school. Not yet.
Fine.

His phone vibrated with another message, but it wasn't Ember this time.

The package is ready for transport.

He flinched at that, suddenly uneasy. He didn't trust the witch could do as he said. He didn't think he'd be able to block the pull of Ember's magic.

Okay. What about the other thing I asked about?

We can talk about that tonight. If you're still looking to talk to a reaper, Cael is in town.

He sighed. Of course she called Cael. Of all the reapers Shelby must know, she chose him. He needed a vehicle and a good excuse to leave Belle Haven.

He fired off a text to the human. *Find what you needed in New Orleans?*

Sort of, but not really. More questions than answers.

Would an audience with an actual reaper help?

There was a long pause before Quinn's response. **Um, I don't know. It couldn't hurt. How would we manage a meeting with a reaper? We are being watched all the time. Kai will never let me go anywhere alone with you.**

Let me worry about the how of it. You just need to make sure we don't get caught by the little alpha.

I'll see what I can do.

He fired off a text to his supplier.

We'll be there tonight.

As Mace sat, staring at the back of Ember's neck, he couldn't help but think this was a terrible idea.

  269

Chapter 43

EMBER

Ember stood outside the door of the classroom with Neoma and Donovan. Mace had excused himself from Ember's meeting with the witch. She was fine with it. She didn't really want to see him anyway, and for once, her magic seemed to acquiesce to her demands. She could still feel the power, pacing inside her, restless, but it didn't flare out of control when he left her sight.

"Sure you don't want us to wait for you?" Donovan asked.

"No, I'll walk home afterwards."

Neoma bit her lip. "What are you going to say to him?"

She shrugged. "Um, hey Uncle Alex, can you fix my dead but not dead dog's foot?"

Neoma stifled a giggle, and Donovan laughed. "I guess that's one way to go about it." After a beat, he looked her in the eye, his mouth hitched in a grimace. "Don't trust him, Ember. I know he's your blood and all, but witches can't be trusted. It sucks, but that's just how it is."

She nodded once. "I'll see you guys at home." Her stomach still flip-flopped at the word. It still felt false on her tongue.

"Not me. I'm leaving for a few days, but I'll be back," Donovan said. They nodded and walked off, Neoma following Donovan as he twirled the car keys in some elaborate spin.

"Well if it isn't the Queen of the Damned."

Ember sucked in a breath, whipping around. Astrid stood in the open doorway, her eyebrow raised, a sneer marring her otherwise perfect face. "What do you want?"

It was so strange to see Quinn's whiskey brown eyes looking back at her with so much hostility. Astrid might have inherited the magic, but Quinn got the personality.

"Astrid, how nice to see you again," she lied, a tight smile in place.

Stella appeared over the other girl's shoulder. There were three others in the room. *The triplets*, Ember thought. She'd learned from Neoma their names were actually Lola, Keegan, and Kieran. Ember had also learned that while the girl wasn't related to either of them, the two boys were cousins. Not as horrifying as dating your brothers but still strange in Ember's eyes. Lola sat on the desk; one boy perched on either side of her like bookends. She pulled a face as she watched Ember. "What's she doing here?"

Ember was already in a bad mood. She didn't plan to cater to Astrid or her bitchy friends. "And here I thought trolls only guarded bridges? Is there a riddle I have to answer to pass?"

Stella seethed, but Astrid rolled her eyes not rising to the bait. "You sound like your idiot cousin."

Stella's eyes lit up then. "Yes, how is your cousin? Has he come to terms with his impending untimely demise?"

Astrid cut her eyes at the girl, shocked. "Stella!"

"What?" the girl asked, blinking wide innocent eyes. "Oh, I'm sorry? Is that insensitive?" She pouted.

The two boys snickered behind her, but Lola said nothing, just watching Ember. She clutched her backpack. "What are you talking about?"

"You didn't think he was just going to walk away from this, did you?"

Ember looked back and forth between the two of them. She had no idea what Stella meant. "Kai? What do you mean?"

 271

Stella cackled and walked behind Ember, forcing her to turn her back on Astrid. Stella was clearly the bigger threat. "Oh my God. Are you really this stupid? No wonder your magic is so out of control."

When Ember said nothing, Stella sighed. "When your cousin saved you, he upset the balance. You were supposed to die. You were fated to die." The other girl spit the words at Ember like bullets. "Now your cousin has sacrificed his life for yours, though I can't imagine it was his plan at the time. That cousin of yours is all heart and no brains." She smiled smugly. "Looks like it runs in the family."

Ember felt sick. Her hands shook, her magic stirring as fear gripped her. "Sacrificed his life?" She swallowed hard to keep her lunch down. "What?"

It made no sense. If Kai had sacrificed himself for her, somebody would have said something. She would have known. Her eyes widened. Tristin's hostility suddenly made perfect sense. Tristin blamed Ember for Kai. No wonder Tristin hated Ember.

Stella wasn't paying her any attention really, pandering to the room like the villain in a movie. "Everybody knows what he did. Everybody. The Grove is coming for him any day now, and when they do..." She sighed wistfully. "It will be the reaper who's collected. If he's lucky."

Ember fought to keep her shaking hands still. She wouldn't give this bitch the satisfaction. Advancing on Ember, Stella's eyes narrowed, a nasty smile on her face, forcing Ember backwards into the classroom.

"How do you think your little pack will hold up without him? Hmm? What about poor Tristin? They say when you lose a sibling you're never the same. I bet it's even worse for twins."

Ember swallowed hard, her throat tight. She put her hand to her collar, trying to catch her breath.

"I bet Rhys will be devastated." Stella ran a fingernail down her own cheek, and Ember swore she could feel the sharp sting on her own face. It took everything not to reach up and feel for herself if there was a welt. "But tell your cousin not to worry, I'll take excellent care of him. I know just what he likes."

Ember couldn't breathe. She was choking, her airway constricting with every word. Her magic flared to the surface, causing a ripple

 272

through the room. The triplets sat, spine straight, eyes snapping towards the door. She didn't have to be supernatural to sense their unease. She just didn't know if they were afraid for her or worried about getting busted using magic.

"Stella, stop." Astrid shoved the other girl hard. Stella's eyes darted to Astrid, only relaxing when she saw Astrid's panicked face. "Anyway…" Stella continued casually, as if they discussed the weather. "The Grove is coming, and they will deal with all of you."

Stella waved a hand, and suddenly Ember could breathe again. She sucked air into her lungs, barely containing the energy boiling under the surface. "Where's my Uncle?" she ground out.

Stella shrugged with a smirk. "Don't know."

Ember flexed her fingers, dropping the tenuous control she'd managed with Mace at her side. She flinched as her magic surged forward, power sparking from her fingertips. A shiver ran through her as she stopped trying to hold back. She was done with girls like Stella. If the whole pack was going down for saving her, did control really matter anyway? She took a deep breath, calling it forth with intention, attempting to control her breathing like Mace showed her. She didn't care anymore.

Pictures rattled on the wall, and chalk jumped from its tray on the board. She held her hands out, sparks building until they formed a pulsing ball of light in her palm. She couldn't help but look at the others, confirming they could see it too. She tried to sound casual as she said, "This looks dangerous. You might want to run."

The five of them gawked at her and then each other. Stella snatched up a bag and shoved it at Astrid, before grabbing a flowery backpack. Stella flung it over one shoulder, never taking her eyes off Ember. "You're crazy. Just like the rest of your little orphan crew. Let's go."

The triplets followed, giving Ember a wide berth as they passed.

Ember stood alone, energy thrumming through her with no filter, staring at the strange ball of light she'd created from nothing. She felt giddy, euphoric. This was so much better than trying to control it. There was no pain. There was just a rush. It just needed an outlet. Just like in the cemetery when she remembered her mother. Her power just wanted to be free.

 273

The door creaked on its hinges, and she looked up to see her Uncle.

"Ember?" He moved towards her slowly, hands up. "What's going on?"

Chapter 44

MACE

Mace held his breath with every step he took. He couldn't remember the last time a simple walk proved this harrowing. Each footstep brought a measure of hesitation. He was wary of the searing agony to follow should the witch not carry out his promise.

He relaxed in increments, as the distance between he and Ember grew, and his skin remained intact. The witch hadn't lied. He was capable of blocking Ember's magic, at least temporarily. Mace couldn't help but smile a little; if the witches could block her magic temporarily, perhaps there was a way to do it permanently. Things were definitely looking up.

He spotted the boy leaning against a tree, fidgeting with his cell phone. Mace shook his head. The human was perpetually restless. He looked up, his eyes widening at Mace's arrival. He pushed himself away from the tree, looking around. He was also a bit paranoid, it seemed. There was little chance of anybody finding them conspiring out here.

Mace met Quinn halfway, noting the dog's still open grave. They hadn't bothered to fill it in due to Mace's assurances that the dog wouldn't survive the night. Clearly, he'd been wrong. Luckily, none of them seemed to be connecting the dots. That worked in his favor.

"So, you managed to sneak away without the banshee or the reaper. I'm impressed. Don't think I've ever seen you alone, actually."

The human rolled his eyes. "They do have names."

"Mm, I'm aware, but there's really no point in learning them."

He perked up. "Really? Does that mean you'll be leaving us soon?"

Mace shook his head. "No, it means, you most likely won't survive long enough to make learning your names a priority."

Mace grunted as two hands hit his chest hard; then he was falling. He hit the bottom of the grave, wincing at the sharp pain twisting along his spine. He had to admit, the hole looked much deeper when looking up from the bottom.

Seems the human wasn't a complete pushover. Quinn looked down at Mace from the edge of the grave. Soft dirt showered in on him. He shielded his eyes, blinking up at Quinn. "I'm going to assume that was an accident. That way I don't have to kill you."

"You know what they say about assuming things," the kid said. "Besides, hard to kill me from the bottom of that really deep hole."

More dirt showered in on him. "What are you going to do? Bury me? I'll dig my way out, and then I'll drain you, slowly and with an exceptional amount of pain."

Quinn regarded him with much less fear than Mace was used to. He found it off-putting. His reputation was really all he had. After five minutes, he finally asked. "I don't suppose you're going to help me out of here?" He kept his tone casual.

"No, you're kind of a dick. I think our talk will go better with you down there."

"Oh, come on, mate. I didn't think you were the type to hold a grudge."

Quinn crossed his arms, giving Mace a long appraising look and a smug smile. "Yeah, well, you just threatened my fragile human life, so I just feel safer with you down there."

Mace sighed, brushing the dirt off his shirt. It was his favorite. "Fine, I'll do it myself."

The hole was just over seven feet deep or so, but clearing it from the bottom was enough to make Quinn's smug expression disappear. Mace placed a palm on the kid's chest, giving him just enough time to realize what was happening before shoving him backwards. He landed with far less grace and a muttered, "Ow."

Quinn lay on his back, wheezing as he tried to force air back into his lungs. Mace waited, impatiently. Finally, he heard Quinn say, "See, I told you you're a dick. I was right."

Mace chuckled but leaned in, offering his hand. Quinn stared at it for a long minute before he sighed, getting to his feet and staring upwards, probably trying to accurately calculate the best route to exiting the situation. He sighed, obviously realizing he didn't have many options. Mace pulled Quinn easily from the pit.

"How did you do that?"

"What? Get out?" Mace raised a brow. "I'm sluagh. I can fly, remember?"

"I do now," Quinn mumbled.

After a minute, he said, "If you think Tristin and Kai are already done for, why are we driving to Georgia to meet this guy? Do you really think he has information that could help Kai? How do I know this isn't just a ploy to get me alone so you can kill me?"

Mace looked around the empty cemetery. "Seriously? I thought you were supposed to be the smart one. Perhaps, I should be talking to the banshee. You just shoved me into a hole, and yet you still breathe air. If I wanted you dead, you'd still be down there."

The human paled a bit but continued, "I'm just saying it seems awfully convenient we've been looking for a reaper, and suddenly one becomes available the same night you go to town."

"I suppose it depends on your definition of convenient. I find Cael's appearance this close to Florida rather inconvenient. We have...history. In fact, my being there may be reason enough for him not to talk to us."

"Then I'll talk to him alone."

Mace laughed at that. There was no way in hell he was letting Cael anywhere near Quinn alone. "Absolutely not. That's not an option."

Quinn frowned. "Why?"

"Have you ever met another reaper other than Kai?"

Quinn shook his head. "Kai hasn't even met another reaper."

"Well, Cael grew up in the in-between."

His brow furrowed. "The in-between? You mean between worlds? Can you do that?"

"Can I? No. Once the Grove took over, those who could flee to the in-between did. Even the Grove's power doesn't stretch that far. But, Cael grew up surrounded by traditional reapers. He wasn't raised to concern himself with the feelings of the living."

"He's not another soulless demon, is he?"

"I'm not a demon," Mace corrected. "But no, he's in possession of his soul. Now his heart? That I'm not too sure of."

"So, why would he be willing to help us at all?"

"Truthfully, I don't know that he will. He may tell you to go to hell. Hard to say really. I'm just warning you, he won't be as kind-hearted as your reaper."

"After the ride home, Kai isn't feeling particularly kindhearted."

Mace snorted. "What did the wolf do now?"

"What?"

"There is only one thing that puts your friend in a bad mood, and that's the wolf. What happened?"

Quinn flushed. "That's personal."

"We don't have time for privacy. What happened?"

"Kai ran us off the road. Rhys and Kai got into a fight, some-body kissed somebody"—Quinn flushed at this information—"and now Rhys is acting like it never happened, and Kai is acting like he wants to kill somebody."

"Lovely." Mace could work with that, a plan already forming in his mind. "This could work in our favor."

"He's not going to let me go anywhere with you alone," Quinn assured Mace.

Mace shrugged. "You're not going alone. He's coming with us."

Quinn inhaled. "How do you think that's going to work?"

It was brilliant actually, Mace and Quinn could talk to Cael, Kai could keep Tate out of Mace's hair for a while, and with any luck, neither would notice his dealings with Shelby. "You leave that to me. Just be ready to go when we are, and no matter what I say, you

 278

make sure to be your tenacious self. He has to believe I don't want you there."

Quinn took a deep breath but nodded. "I'll be ready."

"Brilliant, I'll see you back at the house."

Chapter 45

KAI

Kai sat in one of the two rocking chairs on the wide front porch. He wasn't sure how long he'd been out there. It was still daylight, so it couldn't have been more than an hour or so. He hadn't seen anybody return from school, but they usually came in through the kitchen, so really, anybody could be home. He didn't care anyway. He just wanted to be alone.

He wanted to take his time seething, to let it really sink in how stupid he was. He'd poured his heart out to Rhys, professed undying love like in some sappy romance novel, and he'd just...ugh, he'd just given him the most amazing kiss of Kai's short freaking life. Then he walked away. He just stalked off and went back to pretending it never happened. Kai clenched his jaw until he felt the muscle pop.

He wasn't going to cry. Well, he wasn't going to cry again. His face burned. He'd actually cried in front of Rhys. Luckily, Kai had sailed straight past sad and was well on his way to homicidal. He didn't need Rhys. It wasn't like Kai wasn't an attractive guy. Other guys looked at him, or they would if they didn't think it would get their eyes ripped out. Eric had looked. Eric had kissed Kai. He sighed. Eric's kiss had been nice, but it was nothing like the one Kai had shared with that stupid wolf.

He'd thought about it in every conceivable way. Obviously, Rhys liked Kai. He teased Rhys about being in the closet, but Kai didn't really think that was Rhys's issue. He didn't care about gay or straight. Shifters didn't really think of things that way. Isa said that for wolves it was pheromones and scent signals, not XX versus XY chromosomes. Kai just didn't get it. He growled his frustration and started replaying every detail of the day all over again to see where it all went wrong.

He was just getting to the good part when Mace appeared from the woods on the east side of the house, giving Kai a curt wave and a quizzical look. Mace stalked up the porch steps and leaned against the railing. "I see you survived your trip to New Orleans. Did you find what you were looking for?"

Kai opened his mouth to answer, but realized he had no idea. He'd been so caught up in his drama with Rhys, Kai didn't stop to ask what they'd found.

"So, the sour expression on your face isn't reaper related. That must mean it's the wolf."

Kai's brows shot up.

Mace chuckled. "What? I'm not blind, mate. Besides, I could smell him on you from a mile off. He's marked you quite extensively." Kai cut his eyes at the soul eater but said nothing. "It's very, what's the term, old school? Very prehistoric-mating-ritual. I'm surprised he hasn't left a deer carcass on your front porch. It seems he's all show and no go."

Kai huffed, his chest squeezing hard. It hurt. The only thing worse than what happened between Rhys and him was listening to somebody else reiterate how pathetic it was.

"Where are the others?" Kai asked, changing the subject.

"Donovan said he was dropping the faery at the diner. Ember decided to make peace with her uncle long enough to see if he can fix the mutt's foot, and I'm assuming the little alpha and her betrothed are at the restaurant."

Kai nodded but fell quiet when he realized he'd run out of small talk. For once, he wanted to be the broody silent one. He was entitled to at least one day of wallowing.

"So, what's the plan, reaper? Are you going to sit out here until he comes home so you can glare at him while he walks by and ignores you? Or are you just pouting?"

Kai fumed. "What do you care? Don't you have somebody to kill?"

Mace sighed wistfully. "I promised your alpha I would not kill anybody while I was enjoying her hospitality."

"Wow, you must really be into my cousin if you're willing to starve to survive."

"I don't have to kill to eat. I'm old enough to sustain myself on scraps if need be. In fact, I was just trying to decide what I feel like eating tonight. I'm in the mood for something a little…exotic."

He stared at Kai for so long a sliver of fear crept up his spine. He held up his hands. "Whoa, I might be having a bad day, but I'm not up for being anybody's afternoon snack."

Mace rolled his eyes. "Not quite what I had in mind. However, I have some associates just over the state line who occasionally allow me to feed. I think you might enjoy their company, and I'm absolutely certain one of them would enjoy yours."

Kai scoffed, growing annoyed. "Sorry, not really looking for a rebound, unless maybe you're offering yourself as a replacement."

There was no heat behind Mace's words, but Kai leered at Mace anyway, just wanting to see the soul eater slightly rattled. It wasn't that Kai didn't see the appeal. Mace was sexy in that evil, predatory, is he going to kiss me or kill me kind of way, but Kai was done crushing on emotionally unavailable types.

His attempt to make the sluagh uncomfortable wasn't working anyway. Mace grinned and held his arms up, turning around slowly, allowing Kai to look his fill. When Mace finished his spin, he said, "As I was saying, I think you might like taking a night off from the do-gooder crowd."

Isa would kill Kai. He was already in enough trouble. He thought about the Grove. He swallowed thickly. They were already going to kill him. What did he have to lose really?

"It's a win-win. I get to eat without breaking the rules and you... get to make a few new friends with the added bonus of sending your wolf into an apoplectic seizure when he smells you."

Kai looked at Mace for a long time. "If this place is filled with non-humans, they aren't going to go anywhere near me smelling like Rhys."

Mace laughed. "Trust me, they aren't really the type who respect boundaries. I promise you, they won't care about your wolf or his claim on you."

"How do I know you aren't just luring me out to kill me?"

Mace looked exasperated as he said, "Why does everybody keep saying that? If I wanted to kill you, I wouldn't need to make up an excuse to do so. I'm not looking to anger the she-wolf or your cousin. Ember's powers are too all over the place as it is."

Kai had to give Mace that. Ember's control was tenuous on a good day. Plus, Kai wasn't going to sit around waiting for Rhys to come home and notice him.

Kai took a deep breath and shrugged. "Let's do it."

Chapter 46

EMBER

Ember looked at her uncle, barely containing her panic. "Is it true?"

His brow furrowed. "Is what true?"

That ball of energy grew, and her teeth began to chatter. It suddenly seemed cold and hot at the same time. Her eyes widened. She shouldn't have let this energy free. "Are they going to kill Kai?"

He moved slowly, watching her hands. "What? Who?"

"You know who. Are those...people...the Grove...going to kill Kai?"

He sighed, letting his hands fall to his sides. "Ember, the Grove doesn't want to kill; they want justice. They ensure that people do not tip the balance in any one side's favor. You don't have anything to be afraid of."

She was shaking so badly she felt like she might shatter apart. The walls shook around them, trembling like a small earthquake. "Don't lie to me. I'm tired of everybody lying to me."

"Ember, you need to calm down. I'm not lying. The Grove aren't hitmen. They're scholars. Yes, they punish, but they are primarily about maintaining order. Kai upset the balance, but that doesn't mean what he did is worthy of death. Just calm down and we can talk about it."

"I don't think I can calm down. I don't think I want to calm down. I want people to stop lying to me. Everybody is hiding something from me. People are lying to me about what I can do. What I am. About my mother. Even my father lied. I want to know if I'm the reason everybody is getting hurt. Did I kill my father? Did he die trying to protect me from the Grove?"

"I'll tell you what I know, Ember, I promise, but you have to let me do something first. Okay?"

He moved too fast, startling a scream from her, the ball of light flying towards him. It missed, landing on the desk. Her uncle stared, eyes wide, at the small crater on his desk. "Ember, you cannot let your magic take over. You will never pull it back. It's too much for you. Let me help." He spoke slowly, like a negotiator trying to talk her off a ledge. He moved towards the cabinet against the wall.

"Everything is going to be okay. Just breathe." He turned away from her long enough to grab something. When he turned around, he gave her a sad smile. "Sorry about this."

He blew red powder into her face. She sucked in a surprised gasp, inhaling the bitter powder as she did. Why was everything a powder? She coughed once, and the world went fuzzy at the edges, as if her brain were wrapped in cotton candy. Her limbs felt too heavy, her tongue too thick.

She blinked.

"I promise the effects aren't permanent. It's just a little stasis spell."

He helped her sit in a chair at the front of the classroom, her arms propped in front of her. He walked to his classroom door, looking into the hallway before closing it. He leaned on his desk, mindful of the still smoldering hole.

She opened her mouth, but no words came out.

"It's the spell," he explained. "It will wear off in a minute."

She tried not to panic as he continued, "I lied to you the day we met. I know the wolves told you. I did it because I thought it would protect you. I was wrong. I can't tell you everything because I just

 285

don't know all of it. I'm sure by now you know your father had your magic bound, but what you don't understand is why.

"First, you need to understand binding somebody's magic isn't meant to be a long-term solution. It's a temporary means of containment. The coven binds their magic for a short period, but they must eventually unbind it or remove their magic permanently. Binding one's powers takes an inordinate amount of magic. It's why your mother fought so hard to make sure the council voted against it. She knew it was only the first step in their plan."

"Then why would my father agree to it?" she asked, her voice hoarse.

Her uncle took a deep breath. "Because if he didn't, the Grove was going to execute you and the twins."

Ember felt like her mind exploded. He'd just talked about how the Grove was there for justice, but then said they were executing little kids. "What? Why? What crime did we commit?"

"All three of you were born with the mark of a reaper. Two of you were showing signs of coming into your powers while your mother was still alive."

"That's a crime? They would kill us for something we were born with?"

"You don't know everything, Ember. You don't know what you did."

She swallowed the lump in her throat. "Then tell me."

"Once I tell you, there's no going back."

"Just say it," she whispered.

He nodded, closing his eyes. "Allister said Josephine told you about the council meeting the night your mother died, but they didn't tell you what you did after your mother died, did they?" Ember shook her head, knowing, somewhere deep down, what was coming, but helpless to stop it anyway. "You raised her from the water, called her practically to your front door. If your father hadn't realized you were missing from your bed and gone to look for you...there's no telling what your mother would have done to you."

Her dreams of her mother weren't dreams at all, just more memories resurfacing. Ember shivered as her mind conjured up her mother's distorted face. Ember shook her head, trying to shake the image from her brain. It was awful, horrifying really, but given the amount of people she'd raised in the last few weeks, she thought she was handling it well.

"What does this have to do with the twins? Why would they kill Tristin and Kai? Why not just me?"

He narrowed his eyes. "It's strange that Josephine never mentioned why they met the second time? She never said exactly what caused them to reconvene the council for a second vote. Maybe she didn't know. She wasn't there." He said the last bit to himself. "The council heard what you did and decided they needed to get ahead of things. Tristin screamed for your mother's death, and you raised her from the dead. Two children were now in possession of their reaper powers in one family. The town was leery of your powers, but what happened at the second council meeting changed everything forever."

Ember's head was spinning, but he just kept talking, as if suddenly desperate to unburden himself of these secrets. "Even after what you and Tristin had done, most of the council members stood by your mother's decision. The wolves stood with your mother. A few of the witches, even Quinn's mother, stood with your aunt and your father's decision not to bind your powers, but something happened. People started fighting, screaming. Your father said things got physical, and you and Tristin got confused."

"Confused? What are you saying? Allister said Tristin screamed at the second council meeting. He said her scream predicted the death of her mother," she rasped, her throat like sandpaper. She clenched her fists, feeling finally returning to her limbs as the stasis spell wore off.

"Her scream may have predicted her mother's death, but it may have also set everything in motion."

"What are you talking about? Are you saying you know what this mysterious incident is that everybody talks about, but nobody seems to know about?"

"No, Ember." He met her gaze, looking much older than when he'd started the conversation. "I'm saying the incident nobody talks about...is you."

 287

"Me?" She trembled. "Are you saying I killed those people?" She looked at her hands, thinking about the ball of light she'd almost lobbed at her uncle. "How?"

"You raised an army. Revenants attacked the town. Hundreds of bodies pulled from the ground at the command of a child. We don't even know how you did it. The power it would take…There was no way you could have controlled them."

"Revenants? What are you saying?" She shook her head, unwilling to believe him. That couldn't be true. That would mean she was responsible for the death of her aunt and uncle. She was responsible for Rhys and Isa's parents, Quinn's mom, and so many others. Their deaths were on her head. She lurched from her seat, falling to her knees and vomiting her lunch into the trash can.

He pretended not to notice. "Your father got you and the twins out. He left the others…he locked the doors…and he burned the building to the ground with everybody still inside."

She heaved again, imagining her father making the decision to set the building on fire with his friends and family still inside. She spent her whole life vilifying him. The last time they spoke she'd called him a loser.

"When the Grove came, your father and Allister begged them to show mercy. He said he'd allow them to bind and strip your powers for good. He just asked them to leave the three of you alive. He told the Grove he suspected stripping your power would take Tristin's as well. He said if he was right, Kai would be the sole reaper of the family and the balance would be restored. He never said why he thought yours and Tristin's powers were tied together, but he was right. When they bound your powers, it somehow bound Tristin's as well."

"How do you know all this?"

"He told me. The night he ran with you he told me the Grove was coming back to strip your powers. He told me everything but made me swear to never let on I knew anything, not until you returned. I was too young to be on the council back then, so there was no reason to believe I was there. When the Grove discovered your father had taken you, they took drastic measures to ensure the balance was maintained.

 288

"They gathered everybody in the center of town, both human and supernatural. They wiped the memories of everybody with supernatural ties, even the humans, replacing them with cheap, vague memories of the people they lost. They slaughtered the humans not from supernatural families and cloaked the town from the outside world. Then they started the raids, pulling all books from houses, forcing anybody who wanted to use their magic to register their gifts, and swearing their allegiance to the Grove."

"How do you know all this? How is it you have your memories?"

"I'm immune to compulsion." He lifted his shirt to reveal an intricate tattoo on his side. "A gift from your father. He wanted me to be able to tell you the truth when you were ready."

"Do I seem ready?" Tears streamed down her face, and she could taste her makeup running into her mouth. "Why would you tell me this?"

"Because you need to understand your father wasn't a drunk. Binding powers is a temporary fix because it involves the use of dark magic. Blood magic. To maintain this kind of wall around your magic, he would be ingesting dark herbs on a daily basis. He would be using his own blood to rebind the spell at least once a month. Over time, it would start to eat away at him. Your father was killing himself a little bit at a time to protect you."

Her heart was ripping out. She didn't want to know any more. She couldn't hear anything else. He had to stop. She'd destroyed everybody she loved. She thought she'd wanted to know everything, but she was wrong. All this time she thought Mace was the monster, but really, it was her. She had killed her dad, the council, the humans. She'd robbed her friends of their family, and Kai would have to die for her as well.

"Ember." Alex crouched next to her.

He tried to rub her back, but she flinched away from him. "Don't touch me."

He moved back a bit, handing her a tissue. "I didn't tell you this to hurt you. I told you this so you could see you're a part of something much bigger. Your parents were willing to sacrifice themselves to save you, to save all of you. They did all of this to protect the three of you."

 289

She couldn't even look at him.

"This is where you decide whether or not you throw away everything everybody gave up to protect you. This is where you decide if you are going to fight. I know you're afraid for Kai, but you can't let that deter you." He dropped his voice. "Listen to me. You cannot trust the Grove, but you cannot speak against them either. Ever. Do you understand? Ember, if they think, even for a minute, you and your cousins mean them harm, there will be no way to protect you. Any of you. They are the monsters. Ember and your parents knew it. Your parents saw so much potential in you. You have to trust me; everything we did, we did for you."

She jerked to her feet, stunned. "How can you say that?"

She picked her bag up off the floor, backing towards the door.

"Ember, why did you come to see me?"

She shrugged, numb, her voice dead. "I needed something to heal my dead dog's foot."

"Ah, yes, Romero, isn't it? Allister is impressed with your progress. He talks about you at great length."

She said nothing, watching dully as he went back to the cabinet. She found it strange that Allister thought about her at all. She'd only seen him a handful of times and, most often, not for long.

He took a small jar from the back. "It's comfrey and lavender and a few other things. Wrap it tight for forty-eight hours. If he lives that long, this should fix him."

She tucked the jar in her backpack and walked away. She went home. She didn't know what else to do.

Chapter 47

KAI

Going with Mace was probably a horrible idea. This was definitely probably a horrible idea. They left the house as the sun was dipping low, painting the sky an eerie blood red. They were almost to the car when Quinn appeared, his hands stuffed in his pockets as he gave the two of them an appraising look.

"Just where are you two going?"

Kai blinked rapidly, cursing the fact he hadn't thought of a lie ahead of time. "Uh, we're just going for a drive," Kai said with a stilted shrug.

"Dude, you're so lying." To Mace, Kai said, "He always does that blinky stammering thing when he lies."

"Okay, we're going to meet some of Mace's friends."

Quinn snorted. "Mace has friends?"

The soul eater rolled his eyes, giving Kai a look that screamed for him to hurry this along.

"Just please don't tell Isa," Kai begged.

Quinn adjusted his glasses and stared at him with mock innocence. "I can't tell Isa if I'm with you."

"No. No way." Mace swore, his mouth puckered as if he'd tasted something bad. "Absolutely under no circumstances are we bringing the human."

Quinn grinned.

They left ten minutes later, Quinn in the backseat beaming at the two of them. An hour in, the trip was going smoother than Kai thought it would. The only harrowing moment happened when Quinn called their excursion a guy's night, and Mace looked like he might actually rip Quinn's soul out of his body.

Kai was trying to have the same enthusiasm as Quinn, but Kai lost his nerve sometime around the Florida/Georgia line. Things hadn't exactly gone to plan the last time they'd gone over state lines.

The farther they traveled north, the more Kai felt the need to fill the silence. Quinn was always eager to talk, but Kai was shocked when Mace chimed in here and there. They talked about anything that crossed their minds from the latest video games to the likelihood of *The Hunger Games* ever really happening. They unanimously agreed Tristin would be the only one cutthroat enough to survive without their supernatural gifts.

Kai was grateful nobody wanted to talk about what happened in New Orleans. It seemed there was an unspoken pact to avoid discussing anything too deep or painful. Which left only the most ridiculous subjects up for grabs, often veering them way off topic.

"I mean, really what's the difference between superheroes and the supernatural, really?" Kai asked.

"Spandex, mostly," Quinn reasoned.

Mace nodded, wincing at the idea. "Yeah, I'm not wearing spandex. It looks like it might be...binding."

"I don't know, I wouldn't mind Batman's costume," Kai reasoned.

"Or his toys," Quinn added wistfully.

They fell silent after that. Kai thought about Tristin at work, which led to thinking about Rhys, which led to Kai wanting to punch something. "So, where is this place anyway?" he asked by way of distraction.

"Not far, barely over the state line," Mace supplied vaguely. Quinn and Kai exchanged nervous glances. "Oh, and if you want to say any last words to anybody, you might want to call or text now."

 292

They both looked at him, startled.

"No cell service out there." He grinned.

"Oh," Kai said.

Isa was going to murder all of them when she found out. She had let him borrow the jeep. She never let anybody borrow the jeep. She loved the jeep. He'd said he wanted to go for a drive. She'd never even questioned him, which meant somebody had already filled her in on what happened with Rhys. She'd let him drive the jeep out of pity. Even Isa thought his feelings for her brother were worthy of pity. Sympathy might not get you everywhere, but it could apparently get you a night of exotic dining with a soul eater in the backwoods of Georgia.

"So, what happens if you don't eat? I mean, you are immortal, right? Or undead? Is it the same thing?" Kai asked.

Quinn snickered, Kai assumed at the look of incredulity Mace shot Kai. "You're a reaper, and you don't know the difference?"

"Hey, I'm a reaper who learned reaping from werewolves and witches. I did the best I could. Don't be so judgey."

"Fair point," Mace conceded. "How many souls have you collected?"

Kai wasn't sure why he was embarrassed. "Well, I mean, I don't come into my full magic for another year, so they don't really call on me too often." He could have shown Mace the names, but it would have involved undressing, and it was getting colder the farther north they traveled. "Twenty," Kai finally answered. "Ember would have been twenty-one."

"Strange thing, that," Mace said without clarifying. Quinn's eyes snapped to Mace, and they traded an odd look. Kai didn't want to know what it meant, so he didn't press.

The rest of the car ride passed with him flipping the channels on the jeep's radio as Quinn or Mace vetoed every single song with lengthy diatribes about why each sucked.

Once they exited the interstate, Kai's leg jittered double time. They traveled the back roads on a two-lane highway that gave way to a two-lane gravel road. After a few miles, the road merged into one hard to navigate, barely visible bumpy dirt road. Kai was suddenly grateful for the four-wheel drive. He couldn't help but notice how desolate the area was.

The jeep bumped to a stop in front of what looked like an abandoned granary, and Kai thought he should reevaluate his life choices. It wasn't normal to frequent places only good for shady meetings and body dumps.

An old sign clung to a falling down fence. He could make out only a few letters in chipped paint, the rest was hidden behind layers of oxidized metal. The parking lot was a field of red clay dotted with patches of weeds and the occasional mud puddle. A singular corroded streetlight gave off a sickly yellow glow, making the building look sinister. At first glance it seemed like an average warehouse, all corrugated metal and a tin roof, but a heavy steel sliding door barred the entrance. It seemed overkill for an abandoned factory.

"You're going to feed here?" Kai asked, disbelief leaking into his tone.

Mace squinted, the corner of his mouth tugging to the side in a face Kai had come to think of as Mace's oops-I-may-have-lied face. "About that…"

Kai tensed, his pulse skipping. His hand floated to the knife tucked against his side almost of its own accord. Quinn watched Kai, waiting for an indication things were going bad.

Mace put his hands up, all wide-eyed innocence. "Relax. I'm not going to kill you. I just didn't come here to feed."

"Then what the hell are we doing here?"

"I need to pick up something for a friend of mine, and I thought you'd prefer to get out of the house rather than mope on your front porch like a lovesick puppy. He invited himself." He nodded his head in Quinn's direction. "Besides, the alpha never would have allowed me to borrow the jeep."

Kai rolled his eyes, silently begging for strength. "I can't believe people actually stay here, like, on purpose."

Mace pounded on the steel door. "You know what they say about judging books by covers?" Mace chided.

The door opened, and a shadowy figure stepped back, allowing them inside before floating back from whence they came. Four people peered at them from the right side of the room. Quinn scanned their surroundings, and Kai was sure he was calculating the distance to every visible exit in the place. Kai skimmed over the new faces but couldn't keep his eyes from looking upwards.

A thousand glass jars dangled from the ceiling, each with a single light bulb. Vines crawled along the rafters, making the entire roof look like some modern industrial garden. There was a large conference table in the middle of the space, and just beyond that, a spiral staircase led to the bottom of what must be the grain silo. A large bar stretched along the wall to the right with a fully stocked shelf of expensive booze.

It was the coolest space Kai had ever seen. He fought the urge to take a picture. Just as he opened his mouth to speak, a girl uncoiled herself from her seat at the bar, slinking her way to Mace, her face determined.

Quinn's brows ran towards his hairline, looking at Kai. Kai wasn't even going to guess.

"Until Shelby told me about your deal, I thought for sure you were still in that dungeon being tortured," she said. She had a faint accent. Irish maybe. She had a full figure and dark chestnut hair, and she touched Mace as if she had a claim.

"Hoped would be more like it, Bridget."

"You had it comin'," she said, "Don't steal from the hyenas. They're a nasty lot."

Mace gestured vaguely. "So I've learned," he said dismissively, "I'm looking for Tate."

"Then look no further, friend," came a voice from the doorway.

Kai turned, and his jaw dropped. He couldn't help it. A tall boy lazed against the doorframe. He wore low-slung leather pants, an unbuttoned shirt, a jacket, and a large scarf. He was barefoot.

Quinn's expression said he thought the boy looked ridiculous but not Kai. He thought the boy looked amazing. Kai's tongue shot out, licking parched lips, suddenly having no idea what to do with his hands. He shoved them in his pockets, dropping his head and covertly looking at Tate through his lashes. He had an olive complexion, messy black hair, and abs like an Olympic swimmer.

His eyes glinted solid yellow in the dim lighting, pupils barely visible. He was a shifter. Probably feline judging by the way he moved, prowling towards them with cat-like grace and a calculating smile. He raised the bottle he clutched in his right hand by way of greeting.

Mace rolled his eyes at his friend. "Tate, meet Kai and Quinn. Kai, Quinn, meet Tate."

Tate raked his eyes over Kai, smirking at Mace. "I approve."

"Mm, I thought you might," Mace said, "I trust you won't mind entertaining my friend while I talk with Shelby."

A look passed between the two. "I'm sure I can handle that. Give her a few minutes, though. She's on a conference call. Oh, and be careful...she's in a mood."

Mace grimaced. "When is she not?"

"You." Tate crooked his finger. "Come with me."

"Uh, no way. You're not ditching me to make out with Felix the cat," Quinn said, looking back and forth between the two of them.

Tate smiled at Quinn, measuring him up. "Audrey," Tate called out in a singsong voice. "I have somebody I want you to meet."

A girl their age appeared from the back of the room. She was slight and dainty with blonde hair piled on her head in that messy style that girls wanted people to think was easy but Kai knew from Isa took forever. She had bare feet and wore a loose fitting dress. "Audrey, meet Quinn. I think you should show him and Mace the library."

Her eyes lit up, and she grasped Quinn's hand, dragging him towards the back.

"I see what you're doing," Quinn chided, letting himself be pulled along. "Trying to lure me away with books. It's working... but only because I want it to." Quinn gave one last look over his shoulder at the two, telegraphing his disapproval with his eyebrows.

Kai took a deep breath to calm his nerves, watching Mace follow his friend. "After you."

Tate steered Kai to the spiral staircase below the grain silo, pushing open a tree-house style door and climbing inside. He pulled Kai in after him. Kai stopped short. "I feel like I'm in Jeannie's bottle."

He turned in a circle, taking it all in. Silk and fabric draped from every available surface. No furniture, just pillows. Hundreds of pillows in every shape, size, and color. Tate smiled. "It's a bit decadent, I guess, but once you lie down, you'll understand the appeal."

 296

Kai's stomach turned a little at that. What the hell was he doing here? He didn't want Tate to get the wrong impression. Kai might have come there to forget Rhys but not by sleeping with a stranger in a grain silo in nowhere Georgia. While Kai admitted it would be dramatic, it wasn't quite the effect he was looking for. He was far from home. He glanced at Tate, uneasy.

"Relax, I can smell him all over you," Tate said with a wave of his hand, flopping into the pile of pillows and slugging straight from the bottle he still clutched. "I can keep my hands to myself. As irresistible as you might be." He winked.

Kai's annoyance flashed to the surface. "I don't belong to him. I don't belong to anybody."

Tate cocked a brow, smiling widely. "You don't have to convince me. I'll make out with you if it means that much to you."

Kai rolled his eyes and flopped down next to the stranger, defeated. "What are you anyway?"

"Shifter. Panther," he said, offering him the bottle. "You?"

"Reaper. Collector." Kai drank deeply from the bottle before erupting into a coughing fit. "What is that?" he gasped.

"Moonshine."

"Seriously?" Kai choked out. "You have a house that looks like it belongs in Architecture Digest, but you're slugging back moonshine?"

"You can take the boy out of Florida, but you can't take Florida...blah, blah, blah. Besides, this place isn't mine."

"You're from Florida?" Kai asked, nestling further down in the pillows.

Tate was right; it was comfortable. Kai needed to talk to Isa about doing this to the living room. It would make pack night puppy piles much more fun. He tentatively took another sip from the bottle, wincing at the burn.

"I was born in South America, but I lived in Florida long enough to call it home. Not the panhandle, though. Farther South, near the Everglades."

Kai pulled a face; he didn't ever want to go back to the Everglades. It took him a minute to realize what he said. "How do you know I'm from the Panhandle?"

"Everybody knows who you are," he said, "The supernatural world gossips more than the tabloids."

Kai sat up on his elbow. "What do you mean?"

"You are the boy who saved his charge instead of collecting her. Everybody is talking about what it means."

"What it means? Like how soon will the Grove come flay me alive?"

Tate blinked, his expression quizzical. "I guess. But just what it means in regards to the legend about the curse."

"Legend?"

"Boy, they weren't lying when they said they keep you cut off in that town. Is it true they control all information?"

"Isn't that what it's like here?"

He thought about it for a bit. "Not really. The Grove chooses who they bother and who they don't. Information is available if you know where to look for it. I mean, if you choose to behave yourself, then I guess you're limited in your sources, but those of us with a slightly looser idea of right and wrong can usually find what we are looking for."

Kai chewed on that thought. He laid his head back down, scooting closer to Tate. "So what's the legend?"

Tate hesitated before asking, "Did you know that once upon a time your town was named Necromancy?"

"Necromancy?" Kai repeated. "Catchy. Why the name change?"

Tate smirked at him. "Ritual slaughter tends to leave a need for rebranding."

Kai gawked at him. "What?"

Chapter 48

MACE

Audrey led them down a long empty corridor until they reached a room at the end. She didn't enter, just gestured to the doors. "He's inside."

Mace pushed the door open, gearing himself up mentally to deal with the reaper. They had some unfinished business. He only hoped Cael was willing to see reason. He heard Quinn's gasp, loud in the quiet of the room, before Mace saw the reaper in the corner.

Cael had that impression on people. He'd grown up collecting. He might look young, but his years of experience were written across his skin. Bands of black ink swirled along both arms from shoulder to fingertip. They crawled along his neck, across his bare head and disappearing underneath the black shirt he wore.

Mace knew it was only the beginning. Cael's collections were legendary, as was his reputation for having no sympathy or remorse. He had just enough time to make eye contact before he found himself pulled off his feet by the collector, a large hand squeezing his throat. It was a testament to the reaper's physique. He didn't possess any supernatural strength, just a dedication to violence and an overwhelming need for revenge. He slammed Mace hard against the wall, rattling the pictures residing there.

"You," the reaper growled. "You have the audacity to show your face to me?"

Why was that always everybody's first reaction to him? "Me, yes." Mace managed to choke out. Cael shook him, forcing Mace to remind the reaper. "You realize this is useless, I'm already dead."

"Let's test the theory," Cael growled, reaching for the blade he kept strapped between his shoulder blades.

"You didn't fare so well against me last time," Mace said. "None of you did."

The hand tightened. "Don't," Cael warned him. "Don't you dare talk about that day."

Mace didn't want this to escalate. He needed Cael cooperative and alive. "I'm not trying to start a fight. I just need some information."

Cael flung Mace across the room. He grunted as he slid, his head cracking audibly against the leg of the table. He moved to stand.

Cael was already advancing. "I'm going to enjoy this. After what you did to Rena, did you really think the next time I saw you you'd walk away? Are you really that arrogant?"

"Yes, he is," Quinn answered.

Cael turned on Quinn, noticing him at last. Cael looked the kid over, taking in the crooked glasses, beanie cap, jeans, and Converse. Mace could practically see the wheels turning in the collector's head. Quinn put his hands up defensively, misreading Cael's sudden interest.

"Look, he's a total dick but we need him," Quinn told the reaper. "Well, my friend needs him. My friend needs you."

Mace pulled himself into a sitting position, watching with interest as Cael stared at the human. "Who the hell are you, kid?"

Quinn dropped his hands but still made sure to keep the door at his back. "My name is Quinn Talbot."

The reaper startled. "What?"

Quinn grimaced. "Yes, of the Talbot family. Yes, my father is Allister Talbot. Yes, he's the head of the witches' council. No, I'm not a witch. Can we move on now?"

   300

Cael stood frozen, his forehead furrowed. He looked at Mace and then at Quinn again. "What are you doing here?"

"My best friend, Kai, he's a collector like you." Quinn looked over the reaper before saying, "Well, not exactly like you. We live in Belle Haven."

Cael's eyes darted towards Mace, but Mace stayed quiet, for once letting the human handle things. It was clear Cael still wasn't over Rena, and he still blamed Mace. With reason, Mace conceded, but it was four years ago.

"Your friend is a collector in Belle Haven," Cael repeated like he was testing the words on his tongue. "What do you need from me?"

Quinn swallowed. "My friend, he did something stupid, and now the Grove is probably coming after him."

He watched the clouds roll over Cael's face. The Grove might be the only thing in the world he hated more than Mace. "Go on."

"A few weeks ago, my friend had a name pop up on his arm for a collection. He didn't complete the collection."

Cael's mouth turned down. "We've all had a botched collection. Did he fix it?"

Quinn took a shaky breath. "She didn't die."

"What?"

"He actively prevented her death."

Cael gave one last leery look at Mace before gesturing for Quinn to sit. Quinn thunked down heavily, pulling off his cap and raking his hands through his hair.

"It couldn't have been his first collection?"

Quinn shook his head. "No."

"So, why her?"

"He knew her."

"That's not possible."

"But he did. She was his cousin."

Cael yanked the chair out, spinning it and sitting on the chair backwards. "Tell me everything."

Chapter 49

TRISTIN

Tristin jabbed the end button on her cell phone as her call yet again went straight to voicemail. Quinn said he'd be home. She'd left work early just to talk to him. But there she stood in an empty house, her only clue to Quinn's disappearance a hastily scrawled note on the dry erase board in the kitchen.

He'd gone out with Kai and Mace. She wasn't surprised about Quinn leaving with Kai, but Mace? It seemed impossible. What could the three of them possibly be doing? Had Mace forced them to go with him? Should she be worried?

She heard the creak of the front door opening and stormed into the living room, stopping short when she saw it wasn't Quinn. Ember dropped her bag by the front door and let it swing shut.

Tristin rolled her eyes. "Oh, it's just you."

Her cousin stared at her, her eyes bleary and face blotchy. Tristin had just enough time to process her cousin's emotional state before the girl burst into tears.

Tristin froze. She was excellent at dealing with moody, cranky wolves. She could deal with flesh eating monsters and shrieking harpies, but she did not know how to handle a crying girl, especially one she didn't particularly like.

"Are you okay?" Tristin asked, voice stilted. She took a step towards Ember and stopped. Tristin had no idea what to do if she reached her cousin. The other girl crumpled to the floor and just sobbed.

Tristin opened her mouth to say something—anything really—to console Ember, when the other girl looked up and said, "Did you know? Is that why you hate me so much?"

Tristin winced, she had no idea what Ember was talking about. Tristin didn't hate Ember. Tristin just didn't think Ember's life was worth trading for Kai's. It wasn't fair that Tristin was stuck with the most useless power in the world, and Ember waltzed into an active power like reanimating.

"I don't hate you," Tristin said, begrudgingly. She plopped down on the bottom step of the staircase, keeping a safe distance between the two of them. "I don't even know you."

"You don't want to know me. You never even gave me a chance. Now I don't want to know me either," Ember wailed.

"What happened?" Tristin asked, bewildered.

The girl looked at Tristin, and the floodgates opened. She listened, horrified, as Ember explained everything. Tristin's stomach churned, her insides slippery at her cousin's revelation. Tristin should be furious. She should really hate her cousin. Her actions set in motion the most catastrophic thing to ever happen to them. But Tristin didn't. She wasn't sure what she was feeling, but she didn't hate Ember. Tristin didn't have to. Ember hated herself enough for everybody.

As they sat there, Ember's sobs resolved into dry little hiccups. Tristin finally said, "Listen, we've all done horrible things without thinking. We deal with monsters and magic. None of us is innocent."

"Are any of you mass murderers?" Ember rasped, wiping her eyes with her sleeve.

"You were little." Tristin shrugged. "We were both little. What if you only did what you did because I screamed?"

Ember looked up, startled. "What?"

   303

"It's possible, right?" she asked. "My scream could've been what set everything in motion?"

Ember narrowed her eyes. Tristin could see Ember wasn't buying Tristin's pep talk. She didn't blame her cousin. This wasn't really her thing. Isa was the one who made everybody feel better. Isa, Kai, and Neoma were the heart of their pack. Quinn was the brains. Tristin, Rhys, Wren, and Donovan were just soldiers. They liked orders and absolutes. She longed for Isa or her brother right then.

"What is the Grove going to do to Kai?"

"I don't know," Tristin said.

"I don't get it. If he knew saving me would get him in trouble with the Grove, why did he do it?"

"That's my brother. He'll never save himself to sacrifice somebody else."

"So, now what? They kill him?"

Tristin sucked in a shaky breath. "He upset the balance."

"Does anybody ever get sick of hearing that phrase?" Ember asked.

A smile played at Tristin's lips. "It does get thrown around a lot."

"Why do you think my uncle said Kai would be okay?"

"I really don't know."

They sat for a few minutes until Ember stood up. "Sorry, I fell apart on you."

Tristin shrugged. "It's okay."

"Did you find anything on your trip? Did you find out anything about your banshee powers?"

Tristin looked at Ember then. She didn't know what they'd found. The book was still hidden in the woods, and Quinn was nowhere to be found. The answers they needed could be in that book. Tristin wasn't going to wait around on him all night. "I don't know. Quinn decided to take off with my brother and your boyfriend."

"So, would that make Quinn *your* boyfriend in this scenario?" Ember asked, her brow arched.

"Touché." Tristin sighed. "Want to get out of here? We stashed a book just outside of town. Let's go see exactly what the book has to say about...well, everything?"

 304

Ember looked around as if suddenly remembering something. "Hey, where's Romero?" she asked, hysteria creeping into her voice.

"They took him to the restaurant, even though I'm sure that's violating a thousand health codes."

"Well, technically, if having dogs in a restaurant is a health code violation, they violate that one every night."

"Don't let Isa hear you making dog jokes," Tristin warned.

Ember smiled but seemed uncertain. "So, you're sure he's okay?" Ember asked, distrustful.

"Yes," Tristin said, exasperated. "I promise your smelly dog is still very much with us. Do you want to take a ride with me or not?"

"Yeah, sure. I need to get out of here."

"Okay, I'm going to go get a flashlight. It's getting dark. You should probably go wash your face. You look like a raccoon."

"Gee, thanks."

"You're welcome. Oh, and put on some jeans, or you'll be eaten alive by bugs. We're going deep into the woods."

There was a muffled, "Awesome," as Ember trekked up the stairs.

Chapter 50

KAI

Kai stared at Tate, incredulous. "You're making that up."

"I'm not."

Tate turned so that his head slotted alongside Kai's, both gazing up at the silks waving from the cold air. Kai said nothing. He didn't know if Tate was being presumptuous or if he just wanted contact like most shifters. Tate's hair brushed against Kai's face, and he turned his cheek into it without thought. Tate practically purred in approval, nestling closer. Shifters loved scenting each other. It stood to reason panthers would be the same. It was just a little harmless bonding with a new friend, Kai reasoned, and if he happened to come home smelling like another guy, so be it.

"Tell me more," Kai said. He snagged the bottle from Tate's nimble fingers, tipping it back, embracing the fire as it burned its way down. Kai was pretty sure that was what battery acid tasted like.

"Well, the short version of the story is that about three hundred years ago a coven there slaughtered thirteen virgins in an attempt to summon the Morrigan."

Kai choked, praying moonshine didn't shoot out of his nose. "The Morrigan? The Celtic goddess?"

"Yep, that's the one."

Kai didn't know whether to laugh or balk at the absurdity. "Who would be crazy enough to think they could summon a goddess?" *Witches*, Kai thought to himself, *always witches*.

"It wasn't that crazy, in theory. Your town sits on top of the crossroads of two extremely powerful energy streams. Hell, the entire state is made of limestone. They figured virgins' blood would amplify their magic. Figured with the supernatural signal boost, they might have the juice they needed to summon the deity."

"But why? Why summon her? What did they want?"

Tate tipped his head to look at him. "They wanted access to the one type of magic denied them since the beginning."

"Death magic," Kai said, shaking his head at the arrogance.

"Yes. This coven revered the idea of death magic so much; they named the town after it. They thought their reverence of the dead would be enough to sway the Morrigan to gift them the powers of necromancy. Like the old ones."

"Except those are stories. Necromancers don't exist."

"Dinosaurs don't exist now either, but that doesn't mean they never did." Kai gave a sharp nod, acknowledging the truth of the statement. Tate knocked his head against Kai's. "Shelby says a thousand years ago necromancers weren't that unusual."

Kai pulled a face. He didn't know what to say to that. It all sounded insane. He still couldn't help but ask, "Did it work?"

"Did they summon the Morrigan, or did she give them the knowledge of death magic?" Tate laughed. "The story goes that the Morrigan was so displeased with the town she cursed them and all magical beings so that in order for one to inherit their magic, another would have to die."

"You're saying our town summoning the Morrigan is the reason all supernatural powers come at the cost of somebody else's life? It wasn't always that way?"

He shook his head. "It does have that sort of divine irony the gods are fond of. A rather fitting punishment for people who were so eager to get their hands on death magic."

"So what happened to the town after that?"

"We must maintain the balance," he intoned with mocking.

Kai snorted. "The Grove?"

"The beginning of it, anyway. The gods wanted somebody to be held accountable for the supernatural creatures here on the ground. It took a hundred years for the Grove to become the Grove. That coven set in motion a chain reaction we're all still paying for today. Even after they summoned the Morrigan, the magic in the town stayed amplified.

"The Grove has tried to fix it. They neutralized the coven, salted the grounds, and tried to power down the mystical radio tower broadcasting to every monster out there. It seemed to work for a time, but they set guardians in place just in case something or someone decided to try again."

Kai raised a brow. "I don't know, man. Sounds like the plot of a bad sci-fi movie. Do people actually believe this?"

"Some of us were there when it happened."

Kai's eyes cut to Tate and the panther looked away, realizing his slipup. "Us?" he prompted.

"Yes, us," Tate said, looking Kai in the eye.

"But that would make you hundreds of years old."

Tate laughed. "Yes, it would. Your math skills are amazing."

"But you're a shifter." Kai stared at the side of Tate's face. "Shifters have a normal life span just like the rest of us."

"Mm." Tate looked at Kai. "But that's not all I am."

Tate's eyes bled from yellow to black, the blood vessels around his eyes bleeding dark, like Ember's had in the car. He jumped back, side crawling away, heart pounding as adrenaline thundered through his veins. "Sweet mother of crap."

Chapter 51

MACE

Mace watched as Cael tried to digest Quinn's story. Periodically, he would look at Mace for confirmation, but Mace would only shrug. He hadn't been there, but the boy had no reason to lie. Mace could tell the reaper found the story as bizarre as Mace had. Nothing about Kai's situation made sense.

"So, you're saying he found her in New Orleans?"

"Yes."

"How'd he get there?"

Quinn looked confused at such an obvious question. "He drove."

"Your friend and the girl, his sister, drove out of the city, unescorted?"

"What? Yeah, what do you mean unescorted?"

Cael didn't answer, just leaned back in his chair. "What happened when he saved the girl?"

"They brought her back to Belle Haven."

Cael shook his head, tapping his clothed wrist. "What happened to his mark? The girl's name?"

"It disappeared."

He nodded as if this is what he thought he'd say. "Your friend is being set up."

Quinn sat up straighter. "How do you know that?"

"Collectors don't collect people they know. They certainly don't collect family members, which I'm willing to bet your friend suspected all along. Collectors also tend to work within certain…territories. Long distance travel isn't convenient in our line of work. They wouldn't have sent him to collect her all the way in New Orleans. This had to have been another red flag for him. Had this been a legitimate collection, the name wouldn't have disappeared simply because you rescued the girl. Death will find a way. Just because she thwarted it once doesn't mean it won't try again. The Grove likes to pretend they maintain some sort of balance, but in reality, the balance has maintained itself just fine since the beginning."

"So it's like the movie *Final Destination*? Like, if Ember was really supposed to die, death would have just kept chasing her until she finally did?"

Mace chuckled at the reaper's confused expression, but Quinn didn't notice. He was grinning, his look of relief making him look even younger than he already did. "This is great. If the universe never meant for Ember to die, Kai didn't do anything wrong. The Grove can't come after him."

Cael sighed. "I said she wasn't meant to die. I didn't say they couldn't come after him."

"What? But why?"

"Somebody went to a lot of trouble to get your friend to that cemetery in New Orleans. They obviously wanted the girl brought back to Belle Haven. That doesn't mean the Grove won't make an example out of him. It doesn't mean it wasn't the Grove's intention all along."

"The Grove may be setting up Kai?" Quinn asked, bewildered. "That makes no sense. He's not even a good reaper. He doesn't know what he's doing half the time."

"You said the sister…she's a banshee?"

Quinn looked uncomfortable at the sudden shift in topics. "Well, yeah, sort of, her powers were dormant for a long time."

 310

"Let me guess, until the cousin came back into the picture."

Quinn swallowed hard, not sure how much to tell the reaper. "Um, yes, I guess so. Why?"

Mace watched as the collector started putting the pieces together. He'd say nothing more than he had to, but Mace would love to know what Cael was really thinking. "Listen, kid. I can't say for sure why anybody would go to these extremes to set all this in motion but tell your friends to be careful. If the Grove didn't start this, somebody with a great deal of power did. If the girl's name disappeared off his arm, he can argue she was never meant to die in the first place. If they try to punish him anyway, you know it was the Grove who set this in motion. But I doubt that will be a real comfort once they get ahold of you."

"Me?"

"All of you. You've all been complicit in Kai's perceived criminal act. The Grove, should they see fit, could punish all of you."

"But what if it wasn't the Grove?"

"Then you should pray it's nothing worse." He stood abruptly. "I have to go."

"But, wait—" Quinn started.

Cael held up his hand. "I've said all I can say. I've nothing else to tell you."

Quinn slumped, shoving his hat back down on his head, defeated. "Okay, thanks."

Cael looked at Mace. "You and me…this isn't over. If you survive the Grove—which I'm sure somehow you will—we're going to finish what we started in Nashville."

Mace nodded once.

When Cael reached the door, he looked back at Quinn. "See ya 'round, kid."

 311

Chapter 52

EMBER

Ember cursed as she tripped over another hidden root, her ankle twisting painfully in the dark. It was uncharacteristically cold. Cold enough Ember wore an appropriated flannel shirt from Kai's closet. In her defense, the sudden cold snap caught them all off guard.

"Please tell me whatever we're doing out here is worth it because this is literally the worst day ever."

Tristin whipped around, and Ember squinted against the blinding glare of the flashlight, shielding her eyes.

"Don't you want to know what's in the book we found in your father's office? The book he probably used to perform creepy blood magic on you?"

Ember sighed. She did. She really did, but they had been trudging through the woods for hours. Okay, according to her phone it was twenty minutes, but her feet hurt like it was hours. Even in jeans and boots, she couldn't shake the feeling things were crawling up her pant legs. The sounds of the woods were much louder when a person was amongst them and not just enjoying them from the back porch. The tree frogs calling to each other sounded like thousands of angry crickets. Bugs buzzed past her ears, landing on any available inch of skin. She decided she definitely hated the woods.

She tried to keep up, but Tristin had the advantage of knowing where they were going, so instead she settled for following the beam of light bouncing from her cousin's flashlight. "Is it much farther?" Ember asked, slapping her neck and wiping the corpse of a bug on her pant leg. That was one animal she wouldn't be bringing back. "I thought mosquitos didn't like the cold," she muttered to herself.

"No, you big baby, it's right up here."

She stopped at a clearing surrounded by sand pines and dropped to her knees near a large stone.

Ember cocked a brow. "Really? You hid the book under a rock?"

Tristin pulled a box from the ground and opened the piece of cloth that protected the book. "As opposed to what? Hiding it in a spot that looked like every other spot in the middle of sixty acres of woodlands?"

Tristin sat, parking herself against the trunk of a thicker tree. Ember had little choice but to join Tristin. They looked at each other before Tristin opened the cover. It wasn't as old as Ember would have thought. Somebody had handwritten the text in several scripts with different colored ink. Tristin fanned through the pages rapidly, just to see if it was the same throughout.

Ember propped the flashlight against her knee so she could shine the light on the pages. "What is it?"

"It's a grimoire. A spell book. Probably your families."

It seemed crazy. Somebody in her family had painstakingly labeled each of the pages with the name of each spell, the list of ingredients, and detailed instructions. It looked like an old family cookbook.

Ember supposed essentially it was; except instead of her grandmother's meatloaf recipe, it was a recipe *To Release a Spirit from this Plain*. She and Tristin silently flipped through pages with titles with mundane headings like *To Find a Lost Item* and *To Bond with Your Familiar* interspersed with much darker things such as *To Invoke a Familial Curse* and *To Bind a Witch's Magic*.

"That's it," Ember cried, jabbing her finger at the spell. "That has to be it."

They both leaned closer. The ingredient list read like something from a nightmare. Coffin nails, viper's venom, graveyard dust, blood of the intended, the jawbone of a corpse. There was a list of seeds and herbs as well. The purification ritual was exactly as described by her uncle in excruciating detail. Her father had poisoned himself a little bit every day of the last twelve years to keep her protected.

She sniffed and wiped at her eyes, her cheeks flushing. She was not a crier. Why did this keep happening to her? Especially in front of Tristin. The girl already thought Ember was useless.

Tristin reached into her pocket and handed Ember a tissue. "Here, I brought this in case you started leaking again," Tristin said without looking up.

They flipped a page, and Tristin stopped short at a page entitled *To Protect Yourself from a Banshee's Scream*. Tristin sucked in a sharp breath at the spell.

"Protect yourself? What does that mean?" Ember asked.

"How should I know?" Tristin snapped.

Ember read aloud. "Caveat: This spell will only protect the user from the lethal scream of a fully grown banshee. It cannot prevent the death foretold by the warning wail of the banshee, only the lethal scream she uses to kill her prey. Coat a talisman in the mixture and keep with you always." Ember turned the light towards the girl who was pale under her tan. "Banshees can kill people?"

Tristin said nothing for a long while. "I guess so."

Ember side-eyed her cousin, trying to pick up any emotional cues. She and Tristin were just starting to form an uneasy alliance, and Ember didn't want to take two steps back. Tristin wanted an active power, but one that killed people? They were quiet long enough that all Ember could hear was her own teeth chattering in the quiet of the woods.

"So, you may get an active power after all," Ember said slowly, looking back at the book in her lap before finally asking, "And how do we feel about this new information?"

"We don't. It doesn't matter."

Ember's brows furrowed. "Wait, isn't this why you went to New Orleans in the first place? I thought you wanted to know about what you are."

"No. That's why we told Isa we wanted to go to New Orleans. We actually went to see if any of the books there said anything about how to save Kai from the Grove. I don't care about my banshee powers."

She was lying, but Ember didn't call Tristin on it. What was the point?

They jumped as something vibrated between them, both embarrassed when they realized it was Tristin's phone.

Tristin frowned at Isa's smiling face on the screen. "Hey, Isa. You guys home early?"

She could hear the wolf's frantic tone but not her words. Tristin's already pale face went corpse white. All she said was, "When?"

There was another long stream of conversation from the other end of the phone before she said, "Okay."

She stabbed the end call button and began to flip through the pages of the grimoire with furious determination.

"What's going on?"

Tristin ignored the question, tearing through the pages with so much speed Ember thought Tristin would rip them in two. When she hit the end of the book a second time, she screamed, flinging the book far into the woods.

"Are you crazy? What's wrong? What's happening?" Ember asked, jumping to her feet to retrieve the book. It was all they had. It was all she had left of her father.

Tristin stood, brushing her legs off and heading back towards the car. "Let's go. Hurry."

Ember snagged Tristin's shoulder, yanking her back around. "Tristin, stop. What's going on? What is it?"

Tristin swallowed hard. "They're coming. They're coming tonight."

"What? Who?"

"The Grove."

Ember's body went numb, as if somebody dumped a bucket of ice water on her head. They were out of time. Tristin snagged her phone and tried to dial her brother.

   315

It went straight to voicemail. She made a noise like a whimper. "Let's go."

Ember moved to go, but Tristin snatched her arm. "Are you crazy? Leave that here." She jabbed a finger at the book Ember was holding. "Possession of that book is a death sentence."

Chapter 53

MACE

"Hello, Shelby."

"Are you insane?"

Mace ducked as a stapler sailed past his head. "I'm not the one flinging office supplies at my guests."

"You brought a human and a reaper—you brought teenagers—to my place of business?"

The woman behind the desk glowered at him, yellow eyes luminous in the dim light of her office. If she'd had a tail, it'd be twitching in agitation. She raked long red nails through inky black hair. "You know, you've done a lot of stupid things in the last couple of centuries, but this?"

"Now you're just being melodramatic. They're harmless."

"Don't play with me. You know exactly what I mean. Trying to get my hands on this little item almost got me killed."

So she was angry about the job then. He shrugged. "That's why we pay so well."

She sneered at him. "I don't find you charming. In fact, I loathe you."

"Well then, how about we finish doing our exchange, and then I collect my charges and leave your sight."

She gestured to a small crate in the corner. "What are you going to do with it?"

"I'm not going to do anything with it. I'm a simple courier." He smiled wanly.

"Cut the crap, Mace. What is he doing with Osiris's blade?"

Mace's eyes cut to the box, his smile faltering. The witch had lied. Mace shouldn't be surprised. He was hardly one to talk; he was lying as well, but for good reason. This changed everything.

"He doesn't really include me in the details. I'm more here for the wet work," he said absently, his head spinning.

"You're lying," she growled, revealing razor sharp teeth.

"Not this time. I really don't know his plans," he lied. "What about that little matter I asked you to look into?"

She dropped her elbows to her desk and stared at him as if he was mad. "You must really think I'm stupid."

Mace sighed. "I get that a lot. It's not true though. I think you're exceptionally smart. One of the smartest people I know, in fact. It's just my face, it tends to throw people off."

Her nostrils flared. "Cut the crap, Mace. I know all about your little reanimator. Everybody does."

He forced his face to be expressionless. "Do they?"

"Yes, but I know something they don't; thanks to you."

"What's that?" he asked, boredom dripping into his voice.

She smiled in triumph. "She's not a reanimator."

Mace scoffed. "That's not true. She raised a rather manky look-ing mutt just the other day. Dodgy looking thing, but she loves him. Reapers," he said, with a sad shake of his head. "What can you do?"

She smirked at him, not buying a word he said. "Really? Then why ask about the amulet?"

He shrugged. "Interested third party. Doing a little subcontracting."

"Your employer develops a desperate need for the blade of Osiris just as you've managed to find a reanimator, but I'm to believe it's a 'third party' interested in blocking the magic of a necromancer? Things sure are picking up in the reaper community."

"Did you find the amulet or not?" he asked, losing his patience with the situation.

"No. Nobody has heard a peep about that gaudy bit of jewelry in centuries. Some say it was buried with its owner; others say it was destroyed. Sorry," she said, her tone suggesting she wasn't sorry in the least.

He grunted his frustration, his jaw set. That had been his easiest shot at attempting to block Ember's ability to control him. As long as she held that power over him, they would never be able to move forward. "Nobody had even an inkling of an idea?" he pressed.

"That amulet is long gone, if it ever existed in the first place. Maybe it's a sign you should find better company?"

"I've been around almost two hundred years; I think I'm old enough to know what I'm doing."

"Well, I was dining with kings and sorcerers in ancient Mesopotamia, and I'm telling you that you have no idea what you're playing at."

"And yet here we are in the back room of an abandoned warehouse, both making shady deals. I guess being a feline consort to royalty didn't help improve your social standing by much."

She flicked her hands, her claws releasing with a sinister snick. "You would do well to remember that I'm not one to be trifled with. I'm nobody's consort. I'm the daughter of a goddess. I'll not be talked down to by some parasite."

Mace grinned then. "Calm down. I meant no offense."

He took a deep breath. He couldn't make an enemy out of Shelby. She might look like a twenty-five-year-old law school grad, but she was older than most of the known world and had a temper much like her mother. He'd seen Shelby eviscerate men simply because she was having an off day. Demi-gods were fickle, especially the descendants of Bast. Her offspring had been around so long they were more cat than human. Shelby merely played to her strengths. Sneakiness and curiosity came in handy when acquiring magical objects.

She flexed her fingers, shredding the paper in front of her.

    319

"I used to find you charming. Now I merely tolerate you. I'd hate to send you back to your employer in bite-size pieces."

He bowed his head. "Point taken, I'll mind my tongue. However, I do need the object. It's of great importance."

"Sorry to disappoint, but the amulet is out of the question."

He nodded once and retrieved the package. He had no choice but to take it. He had to keep up appearances. He couldn't let anybody know what he was doing. It would not work out for Ember, and it would certainly not work out for him.

He opened the door. "Oh, and Mace?"

He turned back around with a longsuffering sigh. "Yes?"

"Tell Allister that I'm not going to continue to be the one who gets my hands dirty while he plays the good guy."

He inclined his head. "I'll relay the message."

He turned and walked directly into Quinn who stood just outside the door, a small leather bound book in hand.

"You work for my father?" He shook his head like he should have known.

Mace's eyes widened. "Quinn, I can explain."

"Oh, I just bet."

Chapter 54

KAI

Kai willed his heart back to normal, trying to gauge the distance between the demon and the door.

Tate rolled his eyes. "Relax." He settled back against the pillows. "I'm retired. I'm living out my demon days in obscurity."

Kai stayed where he was. His desperate need to hear the end of the story was currently warring with Tate being a shifter-demon hybrid. Kai didn't know that was a thing. He tried to swallow past the ball of fear knotted in his chest. When had his life gotten so crazy?

Tate's eyes went back to yellow. "Please, I swear, I'm not going to hurt you." Tate gestured back to the pillows.

Kai settled back down, though slightly farther away.

"So, you were in Belle H—Necromancy," he corrected, "when the sacrifice happened?"

"No, but I was there for the aftermath."

"How is it possible that nobody knows about this?"

Tate stared at Kai like he was an idiot. "People do know about it. It's pretty common knowledge in the outside world, and I'm sure it's no secret to some people in your town. The wolves have protected the town for hundreds of years. There are entire legends about the Belladonna pack."

"This is crazy. You're saying people in our town know all of this?"

"I'm saying they should. For years, everything seemed pretty peaceful. But something has changed. Shelby said in the last thirteen years activity has picked up again. Supernatural creatures are wandering into your territory again."

Kai nodded. That much he knew.

"Seems strange that activity would suddenly pick up after being quiet for so many years. You had to have noticed it. Shelby thinks somebody reactivated your supernatural signal booster. Either way, all paranormal eyes are resting on your sleepy little Florida town."

"And this is just common knowledge? Like everybody knows we live in a real life version of Sunnydale?"

Tate laughed loudly, reaching forward and combing his hand through Kai's hair. "Does that make you Buffy?"

"I've been told I'm pretty handy with a piece of wood," Kai said, blushing to his roots at the dirty joke.

"You're kind of adorable," Tate said, leaning forward. His lips brushing Kai's.

Kai sat up then. "Okay, this has been fun and super informative, but I can't do this." Kissing three guys in one day was a limit for him.

"You're really into this guy, huh?"

Kai let his gaze drop, shrugging his shoulders.

Tate narrowed his eyes. "What's the holdup? I mean, he's done everything but piss on your leg. Clearly, he wants everybody to back off, so…why won't you pull the trigger?"

"It's not me," Kai said. "I don't know what the holdup is."

"Closet case?"

"No, I don't think so. He won't tell me what's holding him back."

He sounded miserable and whiny and pathetic.

"Take off your shirt."

Kai's head shot up. That escalated quickly. Tate was on his feet, shucking off his jacket and unbuttoned shirt.

"Whoa," Kai said, hands up. "I'm not that kind of girl."

Tate rolled his eyes. "Shut up. Do you want to make him jealous or not?"

Kai got to his feet, eyeing Tate warily. He came towards Kai, holding out the shirt. "Put it on."

Kai's eyes widened. "Oh." He stripped off his own button down shirt, reaching out for the one offered.

"Yes, 'oh'," Tate repeated, gripping Kai's arm when he reached for the shirt. Tate looked at the swirl of names on Kai's arm. Tate traced the swirl with one finger, dipping under the sleeve of Kai's t-shirt. Kai shivered. "Your cousin's name isn't on here."

"No, it disappeared after we rescued her in the cemetery."

"Odd," Tate said but didn't elaborate.

Kai thrust his arms into the shirt, letting Tate button it up. The panther dragged his hands through Kai's already messy hair and smiled. "That should do it. I can't guarantee he'll act on his feelings, but if he doesn't, his wolf will be seething with jealousy; should make for an unpleasant time for your friend."

Kai struggled to ignore the sharp pain in his heart. Rhys would never act on it. Kai had no idea why, but Rhys was nothing if not stubborn.

"Hey."

Kai looked up.

"You don't have to wait on him. You're gorgeous. You're funny. You're a magical, mystical creature." Kai punched Tate's arm at the joke. Tate continued, "You can have any guy you want. Don't waste your time on a guy who doesn't know how awesome you are."

"The problem is he's the only guy I want."

Tate tsked. "Well, that's a problem, but if you ever change your mind, you know where to find me."

He leaned over and kissed the panther on the cheek. "You're pretty nice for a demon."

"I have my moments." Tate said, leaning towards him again.

The trap door burst open, and Quinn poked his head in, a furious look on his face. "Quit making out, and let's go. Seems Mace has been lying to us...again. Big surprise, right?"

"Huh?"

 323

"I'll explain in the car."

"Okay." Kai looked over his shoulder at Tate. "Hopefully, I live long enough to see you again."

Tate smiled. "Things have a way of working out."

The walk out was awkward; there were five people at the bar. A bald guy covered in tattoos stared Kai down as he walked past. He shivered again. The man was drinking something out of a highball glass. He tipped it in Kai's direction, in a cheers motion.

"Is that another reaper?" Kai whispered to Quinn.

"Just keep walking. We have to get out of here."

Once they were in the car, Quinn lurched forward from the backseat and turned on Mace. "I think it's time you told us everything."

Mace glanced at Quinn and shrugged. "There's so much to tell you; I wouldn't even know when to start."

"How about, when exactly did you start working for Allister?" Kai suggested. Mace was driving but only because Kai and Quinn didn't trust him at their backs. Also, they weren't entirely sure where the hell they were, and they had no GPS signal.

Mace looked at Quinn. "To be clear, I don't work exclusively for your father. I'm an independent contractor. He occasionally hires me to take care of things so he doesn't compromise his...reputation."

Quinn closed his eyes and took a deep breath. "You mean you kill people for my dad."

Mace seemed to consider his options before finally saying, "Yes, among other things."

Quinn went silent, his jaw set, snatching the blue beanie cap off his head and raking his hands through his hair. "This sucks. I knew my dad was a horrible father, but I thought he was at least one of the good witches."

"Did you really?" Mace asked. "Do you really think your father is a good witch?"

Quinn just gazed out the window at the passing scenery.

"We don't know everything, Quinn. Your dad probably has good reasons for doing what he's doing," Kai tried.

"Right, my dad has a soul-eating hitman on his payroll. I'm sure he has the purest of intentions." Quinn looked at Mace. "No

   324

offense, man." Kai risked a look between the two. Why was Quinn apologizing to Mace?

Mace shrugged. "None taken. Listen, I'm not one to point fingers, but your father isn't looking out for anybody's interests but his own. I've known him for a long time. You shouldn't trust him."

"What's in the box?" Quinn asked, gesturing to the back of the vehicle and the crate Mace had stuffed in the trunk.

"That's confidential."

"You don't get to say that anymore," Kai said. "Tell us everything, or we tell Isa."

Mace arched a brow. "Isa is no threat to me. None of you are a threat to me. I'm immortal. Ember needs me. I don't have to tell you anything."

"Does that box have to do with Ember?"

"Look, you don't have to believe me about anything else, but believe me when I say I'll take care of Ember. I have this situation under control."

"My dad hired you to kill Ember," Quinn said, his voice barely a whisper.

Kai's eyes bugged at the idea. "That's right. You tried to kill her. You work for Allister. Allister wanted her dead?" Kai asked.

The two of them stared at Mace, shocked. "I wasn't hired to kill her. I was hired to watch her."

"But you tried to kill her. I saw you," Kai said.

Mace huffed at them in exasperation. "How many times do I have to say this? I wasn't going to kill her. I wasn't even going to hurt her. I was just playing with her. I was bored. I was entertaining myself." Kai scoffed in disbelief. "She started it," Mace said sullenly.

"You just said my dad hires you to kill people, but for some reason, he didn't want you to kill Ember."

"I was surprised too," Mace assured them. "I was told to watch her and report. I wasn't to make contact with her. I wasn't to speak to her. I was only supposed to watch her. My instructions were explicit."

"So, what happened?"

325

"I thought she was human for the first few days. The strangest human I'd ever met, to be sure, but human, nonetheless. She talked to headstones and dead bodies. She always had a sketchbook in her hand. She skipped school all days but one and spent her days in the cemetery. The first time I saw her use magic was at her father's funeral. I had to do something."

"Why?" Kai asked.

"I don't know. She was drenched and panicked and looked so absolutely alone that I just...did."

Kai wondered if Mace could hear the way he talked about Ember. It was strange. "How did he know she was alive? Why would he hire you at all? If all he wanted was a spy, why you?"

Mace took his eyes off the road long enough to look at Kai. "You're asking me questions I have no answer for. If I had to hazard a guess, I'd say it wasn't a surprise to him to learn Ember was alive."

Quinn popped forward again. "What does he want with her? None of this makes any sense. How did my dad know about Ember? Does this mean my dad is responsible for all of this? Why is her magic tied to yours?"

Music erupted from Kai's lap. All three of them jumped. He fumbled, realizing it was his cell phone. Obviously, they had finally returned to a service area. His heart pounded as Isa's face appeared on the screen. He'd left town again without the alpha's permission.

"Isa," he said. "I can explain—"

"Shut up and listen to me," Isa said, cutting him off. "The Grove is coming. They want the entire pack present."

Kai's stomach lurched, his heart pounding so hard he thought his ribs would break. "What? Why? D-did they say why? They are coming for me, right?" He had known this was coming, but he thought for sure he had just a little more time. He thought of Tristin. He thought of Rhys. Kai's mouth went dry. The urge to flee was almost overwhelming.

"I have no idea, but they asked for you, Ember, and Tristin specifically."

"When?" was all he could manage.

"Any time now."

 326

He sat frozen, unable to speak. Mace pried Kai's fingers off the phone, but he didn't fight him. He couldn't believe this. He thought he'd take his impending death like a man, but Isa's words had him fighting the urge to run.

From far away, he heard Mace ask Isa, "What's going on?"

Kai couldn't hear her response, and he was grateful. "We're an hour out," Mace said. Kai heard more shouting and a slight hysteria in the muffled words. "I understand. We're on our way."

"Kai." Quinn shook Kai's shoulder. "What's going on?"

He opened his mouth and snapped it shut again.

"The Grove," Mace said. "They're coming."

"What? When?"

"Tonight. Isa said we need to come home immediately," Kai said, his voice hoarse and his Adam's apple bobbing. He twisted his hands in his lap, not sure what else to do.

After a while, Mace said, "We can keep driving, mate. You can run. Nobody would blame you."

"He's right. Maybe you should," Quinn agreed, his face pinched.

Kai laughed humorlessly. "Run where? It would only make things worse. They would take it out on Tristin and Ember. They're coming for me."

They both glanced at each other uneasily but said nothing.

"Just take me home."

 327

Chapter 55

KAI

There were several cars parked in the drive when they arrived. All lights blazed inside, as if to ward off the evil to come. Like the bad things could only live in the shadows. Quinn bolted for the front door, but Mace hung back, giving Kai a long look. "You sure about this?"

It might well be the last night of his life. He wasn't sure about anything. "Yeah, I'm sure," he lied.

Mace nodded, waiting for Kai to exit the car and walked along behind him. Fear was a gnawing ache in his gut, but he plastered an easy smile on his face anyway.

Tristin tackled him when he stepped through the door, hugging him tight enough to make him stumble. He let his head drop to her shoulder, reveling just a little in a scent he'd always taken for granted.

"I'm fine. Everything is going to be fine," Kai soothed, his hands stroking her hair, trying to reassure her. Her hair and her cheeks were cold and flushed from the air outside. "God, you're freezing."

Quinn slid his jacket off, and Tristin accepted it, burrowing deeper into the warmth. She pressed her nose to the collar, inhaling deeply, and her brother smiled. Quinn ran his hands up and down the sleeves, still trying to warm her up. Quinn would take care of her if things went…badly. She had the pack. She'd get past losing him eventually. She'd be okay here with the others.

Isa took a step away from a very unstable Ember. The alpha hugged Quinn and Kai together, nodding at Mace who nodded back, his gaze going to Ember as if he couldn't help it. He crossed to her, holding her face in his hands and whispering something in her ear. She blinked rapidly, looking up at him, bewildered. Kai couldn't help but wonder what he'd said.

Wren appeared in the doorway of the kitchen, grabbing first Quinn and then Kai in a hug that made Kai pray to breathe. The wolf didn't know his own strength. Kai's heart squeezed. He knew what this was. Everybody was saying their goodbyes. He swallowed the lump in his throat. They weren't sure they were going to make it out of this.

Realization settled over him. They were going to try to fight for him; for all of them. They couldn't do that. They had to let the Grove deal with him, whatever that meant. He looked at Ember, leaning against Mace, and his sister, chewing on her lip. The Grove hadn't asked for just him. They'd asked for all of them. He didn't want to die, but he would rather take the blame alone. He'd had time to prepare for the inevitable.

A shadow from the corner caught his attention. Rhys stood against the wall near the kitchen, hugging himself. Kai's heart flipped in his chest. Dark circles marred the skin below Rhys's eyes, his expression grim, but he was still the most beautiful thing Kai had ever seen.

Rhys looked like he'd spent the last several hours dragging his hands through his hair. Kai physically ached with his need to touch it, to smooth it down, to try to sooth his mind. He couldn't stop himself from wondering if someday he would have taken this for granted. If he had lived to be an old man, would looking at Rhys have ever have stopped feeling like a privilege? Maybe it was good Kai would never know.

His stomach clenched at what he'd done just an hour before. He'd wanted to make Rhys jealous, but Kai didn't want Tate to be the last kiss Kai ever had. That didn't belong to Tate. Guilt gnawed at Kai's insides, and he could barely look at Rhys, who stared Kai down as if trying to telegraph a lifetime of desperate conversations into one hard look.

They didn't have time for this. They didn't have time for any of it anymore. He didn't have a lifetime to play games and fight and breakup and makeup and fight again about weddings and babies. He had that moment. He stalked over to Rhys, determined in a way only desperation allowed. Rhys flinched at the scent of another man as Kai entered Rhys's space. Kai shoved Tate's shirt off, leaving just his own t-shirt from earlier. He ignored the others' freaked-out expressions and delivered what might be the worst line of his life. "If I'm going to die, I want you to be the last thing I taste."

Rhys's eyes widened when Kai kissed Rhys, stiffening in surprise, his breath huffing out through his nose. His hands clenched at Kai's shirt, yanking him closer. Kai slanted his head, wrapping his arms around the wolf's neck. Kai didn't care about the room full of people. All he cared about was trying to sear everything about Rhys onto his soul. He pulled back, palms cupping Kai's face, and pressed their foreheads together. Kai couldn't help but think he would happily stay like that forever.

"You stink like somebody else," Rhys grumbled. "I hate that."

"If I live, you can roll around in my laundry basket and make everything I own smell like you, deal?" Kai laughed softly, hoping the wolf would smile, but he just looked sad and a little desperate. Kai wished he could have gotten just one real smile from Rhys. It was so rare, but when it happened, it was like staring into the sun.

"Don't talk like that," Rhys frowned. "You'll be—" Whatever he was going to say abruptly died on his lips as Allister appeared with four cloaked figures.

Kai's blood chilled in his veins. It should have been cliché. Four hooded bad guys standing in their doorway. If it had been a movie, he would have rolled his eyes, but this was not a movie. This was how he would die, the victim of four movie villains straight from central casting.

Kai tasted blood, and he realized he was biting his lip hard enough to cause injury. The wolves froze, vigilant. The four pushed back their hoods, and Kai finally understood why people used the story of the druids in their fairytales.

 330

The men, if you could call them that, were hairless and pale, their eyes as white as the hooded robes they wore. Ancient symbols marred almost every inch of visible flesh, carved so deeply into their skin the wounds never closed. Rings adorned their fingers, drawing attention to their unusually long slender fingers and razor sharp nails. They stood silent in a line, hands clasped before them in identical fashion.

Allister watched the four anxiously as he made introductions. "Children," Allister said, maybe attempting to drive home how young they were. "These are the brothers sent to represent the Grove." He gestured to each of the four in turn, as he said, "Caro, Hadrion, Maarav, and Macario."

Caro looked directly to Isa, recognizing her authority as alpha. "We thank you for allowing us into your home."

Isa visibly flinched but came forward. They said it as if they'd had a choice, Kai thought, bitterness burning like acid in his stomach. He observed the four as they observed Isa. Well, three of them observed Isa. The fourth, Macario, stared at Tristin, his head tilted, giving her his entire focus. Kai leaned his weight against Rhys, Kai's back to the wolf's front. Kai needed him near for as long as he could have it.

Isa inclined her head, bowing slightly. "It's an honor to host the Grove. Our home is always open to you."

Caro smiled, a monster attempting to blend. "You're well versed in the old traditions for an alpha so young, but I thought you were betrothed?"

Her smile faltered at the statement. "I am," she confirmed, her eyes darting to Wren.

"Congratulations. But, surely, your betrothed has already taken over as alpha in preparation for after you've wed?"

Rhys stiffened, and Kai tried to sooth the wolf by reaching back and squeezing his hand. They were in completely new territory. Isa opened her mouth and closed it again, her eyes wide. "We've yet to set a date," Isa finally answered, avoiding the question.

Wren moved then, standing just behind her. "Wren Davies, blood heir of the Blackthorne pack and beta to the Belladonna pack," he said, inclining his head.

Kai's heart burst with love for Wren. He didn't step in front of Isa or even stand beside her. He stood behind her, making it clear she was his alpha as well. Wren also didn't acknowledge his archaic right to rule because of marriage.

The second druid, Hadrion, stepped forward, his eyes shining, a reptilian smile on his face. "Yes, I believe we had dealings with your pack just a few years back, a rather bloody incident regarding a witch and an omega. Such a tragedy."

Wren's eyes flashed, his jaw clenching. Isa reached back, her hand circling his wrist loosely. They wanted Wren to lose control. Instead, Wren dropped his gaze, regaining his composure. "That's correct, yes. The incident was resolved."

Maarav stepped forward, clearing his throat. "Brothers, we should get to the matter at hand. We have many to see tonight."

Caro held up his hand. "You are correct. Your reaper, if you will."

Rhys growled low in his throat, but it died into a pitiful whine when Kai snapped his head around, glaring at Rhys. "It's okay," Kai promised. Squeezing Rhys's hand once, Kai turned to face his fate.

A sob caught in Tristin's throat, and she stifled it with the palm of her hand. Kai used one arm to hug her, kissing the side of her head. "You'll be okay."

Hadrion looked to each of them, his mouth splitting into what Kai assumed was supposed to be a smile. "You need not fear us. We only seek to punish those who break our laws. Those who obey are friends to us. It's our wish to leave as friends."

Hadrion's words curdled in Kai's stomach. It was as if they were playing at being humans. Their gestures and mannerisms forced and their platitudes empty. When they weren't speaking, they were utterly still, like statues. Kai stopped just in front of the four. The three druids looked at Kai, their expressions blank. The fourth, Macario, still watched only Tristin. A trickle of fear slid down his spine at Macario's unwavering interest in his sister.

"I'm the one you are looking for," Kai said, suddenly hyperaware of everything around him. He could hear Rhys's heavy breaths, could feel the tension in the wolves' bodies; if he pressed out with

 332

his senses, Kai could feel a powerful energy humming through the room. He imagined it was the druids. He prayed it wasn't Ember.

Maarav smiled then, and the effect was chilling. "Yes, but where is the girl?"

Kai's gaze shot to Ember, whose eyes widened at the sudden attention. He could feel her anxiety from across the room. She stumbled forward on stiff legs. She took deep measured breaths as she came to stand near him. He linked their fingers, and he couldn't fight the breath that punched out of him. Her magic was pulling at his. He dropped her hand quickly, and her eyes darted to his, frantic. He willed her to keep it together.

"Look at you," Caro said with something akin to excitement. He reached out and stroked her cheek, one long sharp nail millimeters from her eye. Ember rocked back on her heels but didn't pull away. "So alive."

Maarav spoke next, returning to the reason for their visit. "Christopher Kai Lonergan, you have been accused of failing in your duties of collection and failing to maintain the balance."

Kai closed his eyes and took a deep breath. "It's true. I'll take whatever punishment the Grove feels is sufficient."

The room fell silent. Kai swore his heart was going to beat out of his chest. He felt nervous and jumpy, and he wanted to take Ember's hand again and give her back some of the magic that still tingled where she touched him. He clenched and unclenched his fists, wondering exactly how much time he really had. Would they exact their punishment immediately?

It was Caro who spoke. "Admirable of you to confess, but alas, there was no crime."

Chapter 56

EMBER

Ember gasped, and chatter erupted from the pack. Everybody looking at each other in confusion.

"What?" Kai asked.

"We've investigated the claim. November's name was not in the book. Therefore, she was never to die. If she was never to die, you didn't prevent her death. There was no crime."

"That doesn't make any sense. Her name was right here." Kai rubbed his arm.

Caro shrugged a shoulder, his expression unreadable. "I'm afraid I have no answers for you."

"So, I'm...free to go?" Kai said, blushing when he realized he was in his own house. Rhys deflated against the wall, looking like he'd aged ten years. Ember wanted to laugh and cry at the same time. So much tension. So much pressure and uncertainty, for nothing.

"Unless you'd like to confess to something else," Hadrion asked.

Kai laughed, shaking his head. Quinn clapped Kai on the shoulder. "No, but thank you."

Hadrion inclined his head towards his brother, and Ember flinched, her skin crawling. The four communicated without speaking, the hollow gaze of their white eyes darting back and forth between them. She looked to Mace. She wanted his hand. She wanted his reassurance. What she got was anything but. Mace's expression was dark. Something was wrong.

A quick glance around the room said they all felt it. It felt like the air had been sucked from the room, making her lungs burn with the force to breathe. She registered somewhere that she was just panicking, but she wasn't alone.

"There is one more matter," Caro said. "One we thought handled long ago when we trusted your father to do what was best." Ember froze as he continued, "You understand our concerns, of course. The three of you...your existence is an anomaly, a crime, really. We couldn't let that stand. We allowed the twins to live because only one held an active power. That has since changed."

Ember took a step back, but Kai snagged her hand again. She tried to hold it together as she felt Tristin take her other hand. A ripple ran through the three of them, but they held tight, giving no indication they'd felt anything.

"If you're going to punish Ember, you punish all of us."

Caro waved a hand, smiling, amused by their display of courage. "Again, admirable, but you misunderstand our motives, we don't seek to punish. We're here to keep order. We were going to bind and strip your powers. Your father agreed. We even considered letting the boy keep his powers, but then your father betrayed us. We cannot allow a betrayal to go unpunished."

It was like standing on the edge of a knife blade, waiting for the inevitable. "However, a concerned party has intervened on your behalf. They have convinced us to allow you more time. They said you, of course, acknowledge the Grove as authority over all magic, and that your power will be our power."

The three looked between each other. What were they saying? They had to work for the Grove? The Grove owned them? Ember gripped their hands tighter.

 335

"You have yet to come into your full powers. Once we see what you can do, we will determine how to proceed. You have until your eighteenth birthday. We will return at that time."

Relief flooded through Ember. They weren't safe, but they were safe for some time. She swore she'd lived a lifetime in the last twenty-four hours. Tristin released Ember's hand, drifting towards Quinn. Ember sought out Mace, needing his presence to calm the sudden return of her magic.

"We really should take our leave," Maarav told the others, but Macario held up his hand. "A moment, please," he rasped, his voice so dry Ember thought dust would puff from his lips.

He moved then, gliding forward to stand before Tristin. "Aren't you a pretty thing?"

Quinn moved closer to Tristin, whose mouth fell open, unprepared for the sudden attention. Ember could feel Tristin's panic and confusion as if it were her own, but Tristin stood statue still.

"The book, if you please?"

Hands trembling, her gaze darted to Ember's. How did they know about the book? Could they read minds? Had somebody told? It wasn't possible. She had put the book under the rock herself. Ember swallowed back the metallic taste filling her mouth.

"W-what?" Tristin stuttered.

"The book in your pocket." He gestured to her jacket, to Quinn's jacket.

Tristin looked at Quinn, her confused expression turning into panic as she saw the sick look of dread on his face. Ember felt like the world slid into slow motion as Tristin slipped her shaking hand into the jacket pocket, fumbling twice. Her face crumbled, her eyes horrified as she pulled the small book free.

Quinn exchanged looks with Kai and Mace. Ember had no idea what was going on. Where had that book come from? Why did they all look so guilty?

An elated giggle cut through the silence, causing Ember to jump. Caro looked delighted. "Oh, brother. You've done it again." He shook his head, voice fond as he gazed at Macario. "He has a sixth sense about these things. So clever. He never will tell me how he does it."

It was like time stopped, all of them suspended. Ember didn't know how things had gone from bad to good to horrifying in less than fifteen minutes. Her magic stirred, her hand reaching for Tristin. Since they had locked hands moments ago, it seemed Ember's power sensed Tristin's distress. Mace snatched Ember's hand, his magic forcing hers back with the slightest shake of his head.

"Does the book belong to you, child?" Hadrion asked.

"I-I don't know how…" Tristin looked at Quinn, her voice trailing off. Ember closed her eyes. If Tristin denied the book, she would have to point the finger at Quinn. If she admitted it, the crime would be hers.

Quinn stepped forward. "The book is mine," he said quietly, his face pale but reconciled.

Allister surged forward, stopping a few feet from his son. "Don't be stupid, boy. This girl will never be able to thank you for your chivalry if you're dead."

Quinn ignored his father, instead speaking to Kai and Mace, "Audrey let me look at it. I got sidetracked after…"—he gestured vaguely—"everything." He shrugged, his eyes wide. "I-I just forgot."

Kai nodded jerkily, tears filling his eyes. Tristin looked back and forth between them in confusion, panic setting in. Ember's heart pounded so hard she was sure she might pass out, but it was her cousin's terror she felt, not her own. What was happening? Quinn must be just as scared, but he just stared at Tristin with a sense of resignation.

"Your own son, how disappointed you must be," Macario intoned, sounding bored. Allister flushed, looking more embarrassed than mad. "Much like we were when we found you'd been hiding this girl from us for weeks."

Ember's anger surged, and her magic flared. Mace sucked in a breath and wrapped himself around her from behind. "Do nothing," he whispered against her hair, his voice barely audible. "They will kill every one of you and never look back."

He tangled their fingers together, and she squeezed hard enough that she would have broken the bones of a human. He had to feel this, the raw panic filling her. "Please, Ember. Just hold on," he begged. She was trying. She really was.

"The book belongs to you?"

Quinn looked hard at Tristin, as if he was memorizing every line of her face. He closed his eyes. "Yes."

"Very well," Caro said. "We thank you for your honesty."

Quinn opened his eyes just as Macario flicked his hand. Quinn's head wrenched to the side with a nauseating crack. He had only enough time to look surprised before the light disappeared from his eyes, his body crumbling to the floor.

Chapter 57

TRISTIN

The wail that ripped from Tristin was entirely human, but she felt like her soul escaped with it. She collapsed to her knees, dragging his limp form into her lap. "No. No. No. No. No," she cried. She tapped his face. "Quinn, no come on. Come on." She slapped his face again. "Not him. What did you do? Oh, God. What did you do?" Tristin didn't even know who she was asking. Them? Quinn? Herself?

She stared down at Quinn's face, so peaceful and perfect, as if he was just sleeping. This couldn't be real. They could fix this. This wasn't real. This didn't happen to people like him. He was the good guy. He was perfect. She looked to her brother beseechingly, silently willing him to do something, anything.

Kai stood, tears streaming, disbelief etched on his face as he stared at the lifeless body of his best friend. The wolves stood ready; eyes trained on the druids, watching for further threat.

"Now we may go," Macario told the others, turning away from the devastation he'd caused as if it were nothing, as if Quinn were nothing.

At the door, Macario turned back; face calm. "Keep the book. Your friend clearly thought it was worth his life."

Something exploded inside of Tristin, painting everything in her vision bloody as she launched herself towards their retreating figures, Quinn temporarily forgotten. Two sets of arms, encased her like steel, but she fought anyway. "Let me go. Get off me."

Rage twisted Tristin's insides. She would make them pay. If she could scream for their deaths, she would. She'd scream until they bled, until they burned. She'd scream until they exploded, shattered and bloody, just like she was. But wishing didn't make it so, and her screams were human and sad and not at all lethal, but she fought anyway, clawing and screaming until she had nothing left.

She didn't know how long she stayed like that, how she'd gotten to the floor, still enfolded in Wren's and Rhys's arms. They didn't release her until she sagged in their embrace. She looked at the others through a filter, like she'd survived a terrible explosion. That's what if felt like; she was a bomb victim with a huge gaping hole in her chest. It was the only explanation for feeling like her heart was in shreds.

There was a flurry of motion at the still open door, and Kai gaped. She blinked at the muscled figure at the door. There was no mistaking what he was. Tattoos swirled along almost every available surface, including his scalp. He was no novice reaper. She supposed that should be some consolation. Quinn being crossed by somebody worthy.

"You," her brother said, his voice dull.

The reaper nodded, acknowledging her brother but saying nothing. Tristin blinked at her brother. When had her brother met another reaper? Mace stepped forward, looking angrier than Tristin had ever seen him.

"You knew?" He shouted at the reaper. "You knew and you said nothing?"

"There was nothing to say. It wouldn't have changed what was to happen here tonight."

"But still, you couldn't have said something? You sat across from him for an hour, you talked to him, knowing he was to die? Was this revenge? A way to strike back at me?"

The reaper looked confused. "How would this be getting back at you? Why are you so angry? How are you so angry?"

Mace opened his mouth to respond but came up short.

The reaper shook his head. "It doesn't matter. I have to cross him over."

Tristin was in motion before anybody could stop her, crouching next to Quinn's body. She growled, more animal than the animals surrounding her. They weren't taking him.

"The banshee," the reaper said, looking sad. "You are fierce, but you are wasting your time. I will take him. I don't need your permission."

"Can't you just give us a minute?" Mace asked.

"You know I can't."

"Let me cross him over." All eyes swung to Kai. "Please."

"No."

Once again it was Mace who spoke. "Cael, just let Kai cross him over. He's already dead. He wouldn't leave his best friend's soul in there to rot. You owe him that much."

The reaper, Cael, stared hard at her brother for a long while, measuring him up. "I owe nobody anything. See that his soul makes it across the veil, or you will find yourself joining him."

Cael marched across the room, shoving up his shirtsleeve. He grabbed Kai's wrist roughly, and Rhys growled a warning. The reaper paid him no attention, shoving his wrist against Kai's until Kai hissed in pain. The reaper made for the door. "Remember what I said."

And then he was gone.

Once they were alone, the house erupted in chaos. Kai moved to do what he had to, but Tristin shook her head. "Don't touch him!" She must've looked feral, her hair wild, staring at him like he was the enemy. She didn't care. They couldn't take him.

"Tristin," Kai raised his hand, helpless. "I have to."

"No. Just don't. Don't touch him." She sat cross-legged on the floor, pulling Quinn back into her lap. She fixed his glasses back onto his face, smoothing his hair. "You're okay," she crooned, as if she was soothing a baby. "You're okay."

Rhys turned, slamming his fist through the drywall twice before ripping off part of the doorframe and shoving it to the floor. Kai stared at Rhys, helpless. Then Rhys was crossing the room, folding her brother into his arms.

Wren and Isa moved to comfort Neoma who sat all but forgotten on the sofa. She sobbed quietly into Romero's fur, wrapping her body around the big dog.

Tristin closed her eyes. This couldn't be real. What kind of world did she live in where people died over a book? The Grove ripped her family apart and walked away as if it were nothing. They'd ripped Quinn from this world, from her world, like he didn't even matter. The Grove were fairytale monsters snatching people from their loved ones. Nobody meant anything to them. They didn't value life. They valued magic and order and power. They cared about their precious balance. And they'd be coming back for the rest of them soon.

Tristin opened her eyes, smiling softly as she swiped her tears from Quinn's face. When they came back, she'd be ready for them. They would all pay for what they'd done.

Every last one of them.

Chapter 58

KAI

Kai waited two hours before he tried again. The rest of the pack hovered nearby, sitting vigil around their fallen member. Tristin sat with her back to the wall, keeping Quinn close enough to touch but not actively talking to him anymore. Her eyes were bleary and red, her expression dull. She clutched his blue cap in her hands.

Rhys gave Kai a gentle shove towards her.

"I don't know if I can do this," he whispered, clinging to the wolf.

Rhys sighed and hugged him again, breath against his ear as he said, "You don't have a choice. Would you leave him trapped in his body? His father is coming for him soon, and they will prepare the body for…consecration."

Rhys was putting it kindly. He had to cross Quinn over, or he'd still be in there when they cremated him. Leaning into Rhys, Kai closed his eyes, burying his nose in Rhys's shirt and inhaling deeply, just reveling in the feel of him, the scent of him. Kai didn't want to think about what he had to do. He just wanted to go make out with Rhys and pretend that Quinn was at another forced dinner with his dad. Kai wanted to pretend Quinn would come barreling in the door any minute complaining about how badly his life sucked. But Kai wouldn't do that to his friend.

Kai closed his eyes and prepared for another fight from his sister. He approached her with caution. "Tristin, we're running out of time."

She rolled her head towards him but said nothing. Isa came in from the kitchen, her expression kind but determined. She looked at Kai, her smile flat as she squatted down next to Tristin. "Come on, sweetie, let's get you something to drink. Your hands are freezing. I think we still have that oolong tea you like."

Tristin said nothing, so Isa stood and pulled Tristin to her feet. She didn't resist. She looked down at Quinn one last time, his hat still clutched in her hand, and followed Isa from the room. Kai leaned down over his friend and pressed two figures against his forehead before Kai lost his nerve again.

There was a faint sizzling noise, and Quinn's voice filled the empty room. "Finally. Dude, I really thought she was going to leave me in there."

Kai stood up, turning to look at his friend. A pain cut through him, jagged and raw as he fought the urge to throw his arms around him. It was surreal, seeing him moving and speaking. "You know my sister, man, she's a force to be reckoned with. She's not ready to let you go." He shook his head. "None of us are."

Quinn's mouth drooped, and his eyes slid to his body still lying near the staircase. "That's creepy, right? It seems kind of creepy to talk right here. Can we maybe talk away from my mangled corpse?" He looked around their living room in confusion. "So, is this like purgatory? I thought it would be a big empty space or like a giant movie theatre with my greatest moments playing in the background. Why are we still at home?"

Kai smiled. Quinn had always considered this place his home. "This part of your journey is wherever you decide. Usually people subconsciously choose the place they were happiest."

They walked into the kitchen and out the back patio. "So, you're telling me I'm in the Matrix? Could I turn this place into a fighting arena, or can we be at the top of a building and jump off?"

"Totally, we can go wherever you want," Kai smiled, his lungs constricted. This was it. Once Quinn crossed over, Kai would never see his friend again. What was Kai going to do without Quinn? He was the only one who got Kai's awful movie references. Quinn was the only one who got Kai's sense of humor. He was being selfish, but he didn't care. Quinn was his best friend. Kai didn't know how to do this. He had so many things he needed to say.

Quinn sat on the small stone step that led from the patio to the yard. He looked around, a small smile on his lips. "Nah, this is good. We can stay here. I was happy here." Quinn didn't look at Kai when he said, "Meeting you was the best thing that ever happened to me."

"Me too, bro," Kai vowed, sitting next to Quinn on the step.

Turning to look at Kai, Quinn's expression was more solemn than ever before. "I'm serious. I don't know how I would've survived living with my dad if it weren't for you and Isa and even Rhys. This place was my sanctuary, man. Every good memory I have growing up is here with you guys." He ran his hands through his hair. "You don't know how much it meant to me that you never treated me like I was less important. You guys gave me a purpose. You made me part of the pack. You made me feel important."

Kai blinked the tears from his eyes. "You were important. You are important." He scrubbed his hands over Quinn's face. "Listen, you are one of the most amazing people I've ever met. Meeting you was the best thing that happened to me, too. I was the loneliest kid in the world. You were my friend when everybody treated us like outcasts. Nothing will be the same without you. You are our planner, our mastermind. I know you think you don't have any special powers, but your brain is your superpower. Well, that and your excellent Mario Kart skills." Kai sniffed, wiping his eyes. "Those were awesome too."

Quinn nodded, his eyes wet. "They were pretty excellent."

They sat like that, staring out at nothing, just watching the property line. "So, how does this work? Do we just sit here and wait for my door to appear with its blinding white light. Will I have an angel escort? Is there some kind of protocol in place?"

Kai dropped his gaze to the ground between his feet. "I am the door."

"What?"

"I am the door," Kai said, louder. He couldn't look at Quinn.

"What do you mean?" Quinn stared hard at the side of his friend's face. "Is this a riddle?"

Kai's face turned bright red. "I'm the door." He looked at Quinn then. "You have to go through me."

Quinn laughed but then stopped abruptly. "Wait, are you serious? Like I have to go…inside you?" Kai cringed at the wording, but Quinn didn't stop. "How could you have never mentioned this? How could I have never asked? I'm such an idiot. This is the gold star level of blackmail material."

Kai's face was on fire. "Shut up. I didn't create the process." He chanced a look at his friend and glowered at him when Kai saw Quinn's shaking shoulders. "I should just ditch you here and let your ass turn all poltergeist," Kai pouted.

Quinn tried to come up with a comeback, but he couldn't catch his breath long enough to come up with something. He was hysterical. He waved his hand in front of his face, wiping the tears from his eyes.

After a few minutes, he looked over at Kai's sour expression and said, "Oh, come on, man. You have to see how funny this is. Even that one time we made out in seventh grade has not prepared me for this scenario. I mean, in an unspecified number of minutes, we will be inside each other, merged. For a few brief seconds, we will be one." Laughter racked Quinn's body. "Just let it sink in. Like really marinate. There isn't enough time for all the jokes I want to make right now."

Then Kai laughed too. It was hilarious in a morbid and fatalistic way. "We will not be inside each other. Please stop saying that."

"I can't. I just can't. I am literally unable to stop saying it. Come on, you've never fantasized about this? Even a little?"

Kai buried his head in his hands, still laughing. "Ugh, come on. No. Not even when we made out."

Eventually their laughter died down. Kai knew they were both dragging out the inevitable, but he didn't care. He let it just be. When Quinn was ready, he would tell Kai. He hoped it wasn't soon. He wasn't ready yet, either.

 346

Quinn leaned back on his elbows. "You should try to keep that book away from your sister until she gets through this."

Kai nodded but didn't respond. Quinn died for that book. He would have to pry it from Tristin's cold, dead hands. He winced at the unfortunate imagery, no longer funny. "What is it anyway?"

"It's a book on the origin of banshees. It's what she's been looking for this whole time."

Kai's eyes widened. "Seriously? They had a book on banshees?"

"Shelby has a book on almost everything, Kai. It was amazing. She has books bound in human skin that are so old the years are documented with letters after them. Audrey said that Shelby's related to a cat goddess. Like an actual, bona fide, deity type figure."

Kai couldn't wrap his brain around it. They had fought a lot of crazy things over the past few years, but in the last month, his life had become a constantly evolving lesson in mythological creatures.

"Audrey invited me back whenever I wanted. I think she liked having somebody to geek out with over books. That library, man," Quinn said, wistfully. "I have been looking for a place like that my whole life. Figures I finally find it and—" He made a cutting motion across his neck. Kai shivered.

"I need you to tell the pack that I love them. Tell Isa and Wren that they were great pack parents." He looked at his hands. "Tell Neoma I'll miss our Friday night cartoon marathons." He smiled. "Tell Rhys that he's annoying and stupid and not nearly good enough for you, but that he was an awesome big brother." He huffed out a laugh. "Tell Donovan he can have my Xbox games. Oh, and tell Ember that she has the coolest and scariest active powers I've ever seen, and I wish I knew her better."

Kai bobbed his head up and down, trying to swallow the lump in his throat.

Quinn's voice dropped, choking on his next words. "I need you to tell my sister I love her. I know she won't believe you, but promise me you'll tell her anyway. Tell her that I'm sorry I let our father come between us, and that I know deep down she's a good person. You'll tell her, right? Even if she won't believe you, you'll tell her until she does?"

347

"Of course, man." Kai promised, blinking rapidly, overwhelmed at his friend's desperate need to say the goodbyes he hadn't gotten.

"Tell…tell your sister that she was the best part of my day, every day. Even when she was at her worst, I felt lucky to have her in my life." He sniffed, ducking his head. "Tell her I said to move on. She deserves to be happy. I want her to be happy and to have kids and be a kickass mom." Tears streamed down his face, but he smiled like he was picturing Tristin with their kids. "I really did think we were soul mates, but maybe I was wrong, or maybe people get more than one."

Kai just nodded as Quinn talked, getting it all out. "Don't let this crush her, man. I know she pretended she didn't love me, but that's just how she deals with her feelings, you know? Tell her I knew. Okay? Tell her I knew she loved me, and I understood why she never acted on it."

He raked his hand through his hair. "Please don't let her get herself killed. She's too reckless. Always trying to prove she's good enough even without an active power. She's going to be way worse now. She's going to bury her feelings and pretend she's fine, and she's going to do something stupid or—"

Kai couldn't take it. The desperation in his friend's voice was too much. "I'll take care of her, I promise."

Quinn wiped his eyes, rubbing his nose on his sleeve. "This really sucks, dude. I thought I had more time."

Kai swallowed hard, but the tears came anyway. "Me too. I don't know how to do this without you, you're the Robin to my Batman."

Quinn's smile was watery. "Why am I always the sidekick?"

Kai smiled. "Um, because you're the brains, and I'm the muscle."

Quinn looked out at the tree line. "If we're going by muscle, Tristin is Batman and you're the joker."

"So that would make Rhys Bane?"

"The bane of your existence," Quinn said, cackling at his terrible pun. "Seriously though, man. Rhys is going to come around, and when he does, remember you promised to name your firstborn son after me."

Kai rolled his eyes. "Uh, no, you promised I would name my firstborn son after you, but I'll take it into consideration."

 348

Quinn stood, sniffing loudly and straightening his shirt. "Okay, I'm ready. Let's do this."

Kai stood too, his stomach in knots. He didn't want to do this. He didn't want to lose his friend. It wasn't fair. Kai shouldn't have to lose everybody he loves.

"You're my brother, man. No matter what. I love you," Quinn said.

"I love you too."

Quinn reached out and pulled Kai into a hug. He sucked in a breath as he felt Quinn move through, like the chill someone would get when somebody walked over their grave.

Then he was gone.

When Kai opened his eyes, he was back in their living room. Pain seared his left arm, and he yanked his shirt up to look at his tattoo. He traced his finger over Quinn's name, forever etched into the fabric of other lives Kai had crossed over.

His stomach lurched. He fumbled to get to the bathroom, managing to drop to his knees in front of the toilet before he vomited. His stomach was empty, but that didn't stop his body from trying. He didn't know how long he stayed that way, his face pressed against the seat, his stomach heaving, tears and snot running down his face. He didn't care. He couldn't bring himself to stand, to move.

A cold washcloth moved over his face before large hands pulled him to his feet. "Come on, I'm putting you to bed," Rhys whispered.

Once in Kai's room, Rhys helped Kai get his shoes off and moved for the door.

"Don't go," Kai said, hating the desperation in his voice. "Please? I don't want to be alone."

Rhys nodded once, toeing off his own shoes and lying down on his side. Kai pressed his back to Rhys's front, needing to be the little spoon. Rhys covered them both and wrapped his arms around Kai, saying nothing. There was nothing left to say. His best friend was dead.

Kai should have made Quinn wait just a little longer. Kai had more to say. He had so many more things to say. Two thoughts played in his head on an endless loop. His best friend was dead. His brother was dead.

He turned and buried his face in Rhys's chest while the wolf rubbed circles along his back. Rhys pretended not to notice as Kai's tears started all over again.

Chapter 59

MACE

It took less than forty-eight hours for Allister to remember they had unfinished business, less than two days to forget about his dead son and soldier on with his plans. It took a special kind of monster to be that twisted, and that was coming from him. Allister called his phone every forty-five minutes, but Mace had no way of excusing himself.

Ember clung to him more than ever. She did not know how to grieve with the rest of them. Isa cleaned and fawned over everybody. Tristin was angrier than a pit viper. Kai vacillated between inconsolable and complete denial. But Ember still felt like an outsider, as if she had no right to be upset over his loss, at least not like the rest of them. So instead, she stayed with Mace and focused on learning to control her magic. They'd formed an uneasy reliance on each other.

She seemed to be gaining some control over these powers of hers, no easy feat when you are channeling an enumerable number of magical creatures. He was still puzzling out exactly how her magic worked. He only had bits and pieces of knowledge he'd gathered here and there. Necromancers could restore the soul to the body, they could create hordes of revenants, and they could possess or control any creature who lacked a soul, which, theoretically, meant sluagh and vampire and potentially some species of demon.

What he didn't understand was how she was channeling the old ones. Had she always possessed this ability? Was this her fascination with the dead? Was she channeling magic or souls? The questions were driving him insane. He needed answers.

"Hey!" Ember whacked him on the arm. "You're not concentrating."

He looked at the side of her face as she craned her neck around to look at him. She sat in his arms, back to chest, in the pet cemetery just as they had before. It seemed the more contact they had physically, the easier it was for their magic to do its thing. The more they practiced, the less painful it became. Sometimes, when they were both relaxed enough, it was even rather pleasant.

"Sorry, luv," he said against the shell of her ear, smiling as she quivered. "I'm distracted by your perfume."

He wasn't lying, whatever she was wearing smelled intoxicating. He wanted to bury his nose in her throat and live there.

She looked at him awkwardly, her cheeks flushing. "I'm not wearing perfume. You supernatural creatures and your weird smelling people thing."

"You, too, are one of those supernatural creatures."

"Yeah, but I don't notice smells like you do."

It was true that she didn't let her senses guide her like most of them, but that didn't mean she didn't have the capability. It might be the reason that she had such a hard time controlling her powers. She hadn't learned to trust her instincts or her senses. Somebody needed to teach her.

"No?" He held his wrist to her nose. "Close your eyes?"

"What? No."

"Just do it."

She sighed dramatically and made a show of closing her eyes.

"Now, smell."

She giggled. He didn't blame her; they probably looked a bit stupid. She peeked enough to give him a suspicious look before closing her eyes again. She inhaled deeply once and then again. Her hand

 352

moved over his forearm and pulled his wrist closer. "What is that smell?"

What did he smell like to her? "It's me. Just me."

"Weird," she murmured, her nose grazing his wrist again.

This time he shivered. He leaned forward, smelling her hair. She smelled like coconut and something fruity. He'd never tell her, but he suspected her fascination with his scent was that he was technically dead. Her magic did love its dearly departed.

Ember leaned back against him, relaxed, her thumb rubbing back and forth across his wrist. She didn't seem in a hurry to try using her magic again. He dropped his chin to her shoulder, listening to her heartbeat. She hadn't yet noticed they were simply existing in the same space without any ulterior motive. Maybe she was choosing not to acknowledge it.

His phone buzzed in his pocket again, and he reached between them to silence it.

"Again," Ember mumbled, her head rolling against his shoulder. "Somebody really wants to get hold of you."

"So it seems."

"You could answer it."

"Mm, I could, but it's somebody I need to talk to in private."

"So, go talk to them. I think I can keep from blowing something up for at least a few minutes."

He looked at his phone and the four missed calls from the anonymous number he knew belonged to Allister. He shouldn't make the call. If she overheard him, there was no way he'd be able to explain. Of course, if he didn't talk to Allister soon, Mace might not have any choice but to explain. There was also the added complication of Kai. Mace had no idea why Kai hadn't said anything yet, but the waiting felt like a sword swinging above his head. When that sword broke free, whatever tenuous relationship he and Ember created would be over. He intended to make good use of the time he had with her.

He got to his feet, and Ember crisscrossed her legs and assumed a meditative position. "Try hard not to blow up any freshly dead, luv. It smells awful, and I don't want to pick bone fragments out of your hair...again."

She opened one eye and stuck her tongue out at him. He smiled and stalked off into the woods. He didn't make it more than a couple hundred yards when he hit his knees with a gasp. Pain seared his back, like an iron pressed against his flesh. He fought to suck air into his lungs, his eyes clenched shut, sweat pouring down his face. What the hell?

Ember. This was Ember's magic. He crawled backwards, trying to cross back over whatever invisible barrier he'd inadvertently breached. He pulled himself to the tree, catching his breath and resting his head against the trunk as the pain deteriorated. That hadn't happened in days, and it had not been that painful. Had Allister's spell finally worn off, or was Ember's magic just reminding Mace not to wander too far? He couldn't be sure, but he did know her magic was growing and, with it, her hold on him. It was only a matter of time before she realized it too.

He flicked the lock screen on his phone and jabbed the last number.

"Where have you been?" Allister asked by way of greeting. His manners needed work.

"Consoling a group of grieving teenagers while they dealt with the death of a close friend. Perhaps you've heard of him?"

Mace knew it was nasty, but it irked him that Allister seemed to care so little about Quinn's death. A father should care about the loss of his son.

"Don't presume to tell me how to grieve over my son. I don't need a lecture from a demon."

"Why does everybody keep calling me that? I'm not a demon. I'm a soul eater. It's a subtle distinction, but I feel it's an important one."

"Did you pick up the package from Shelby?"

"The blade of Osiris?" Mace wiped sweat from his eyes, grimacing as he moved. "I did have the blade, yes."

"You had the blade?"

Mace let his eyes close. "Yes, as in I once possessed it but no longer do."

Allister raged. "What the hell did you do with it?"

"I guess that depends on why you want it?"

"It's none of your business. You work for me."

"I'm more of an independent contractor, and since I've yet to be paid for this job, I reserve the right to renegotiate terms at my leisure. So, I'll ask again, what are you going to do with the blade?"

"I'm going to do what's necessary to protect this town. That energy is too much for a girl her age. I'll use the blade to...unburden her."

Mace laughed at that. He couldn't help it. How stupid did Allister think Mace was? "I know how the blade works. You can only take her magic by stabbing her through the heart. Now, I'm no medical professional, but I'm fairly certain that's a fatal blow." There was silence on the other end, which Mace took to mean he was correct. "Now, seeing as how Ember was to be my payment for services rendered, I'm afraid that leaves me feeling as though our business arrangement has run its course. Consider this my resignation."

"You will give me that dagger. I paid a lot of money for it."

He smiled. "And if I don't? Then what? What do you think you can do to me? I'm immortal."

"Ember isn't, and her pack isn't. I have no use for any of them. The Grove will return and they will listen when I tell them about the magic running through her. Do you think they will let her live if she's channeling thousands of dead souls?"

"Either way, she's dead. Why should I give you the blade to ensure her death? You also assume I won't kill you long before you could do a thing to the pack. You're a terrible negotiator."

"You bring me that blade, or I will make sure that Ember watches as every single person she loves dies a slow, painful death, and I will make sure she knows you had the ability to stop it and chose not to."

"You really are afraid of her," Mace said, marveling in this new knowledge. "What is it about her that frightens you? I can't quite figure it out. Is it because she has so much natural magic it just pours out of her? Is it because she can control all things dead? Maybe, just maybe, it's the fact that she doesn't actually need her own power."

He wasn't sure if what he was saying was correct, but the more he spoke, the more sense it made. He thought about his conversation with Kai the other day, and the story Kai had heard from Tate. "You know, a friend of mine recently told me that Belle Haven is a sort

355

of supernatural radio tower. I think Ember scares you because you realize she's a transmitter. She doesn't need her own power because she can literally syphon it from all those dead witches buried here."

"You have no idea what you're talking about."

"Oh, I think I do. Now that I think about it, it actually makes perfect sense. That's why you want her dead. She's an enormous threat even without her own active powers. Imagine the chaos a seventeen-year-old girl could cause with legions of the dead at her disposal. She would have unlimited power."

"Exactly. She's dangerous. We have to stop her."

Mace agreed that Ember untrained was dangerous. Her magic failed more often than it succeeded, but that didn't mean she couldn't learn control. Despite what the Grove said, there had to be a reason why three reapers were born on the same day. There had to be. Maybe it was something awful. Maybe their birth was the signal of some kind of paranormal calamity, but he would let it run its course.

"If it comes to following her or following you, I choose her."

"You only say that because her magic has a hold on you. Don't you see? She's controlling you." The pain in his back told him Allister was correct, but Mace didn't comment. "The more time she stays here, the stronger she will grow, and the more of a hold she will have over you. Don't you find your feelings for her odd? You have no soul, yet you protect her like you love her. Have you ever felt anything like what you feel for her? This desperate need to protect her is her magic. It's not you. You don't want to do this. Give me the blade, and let me end this. You're making a huge mistake."

He stood, wincing as he brushed off his jeans. "That isn't going to happen. Our arrangement is over. You won't find the blade, so don't look for it."

Playtime was over. They needed to kick up her training. There was no way she'd be able to protect herself if she didn't get this under control. He needed to push her. He needed to figure out how to help her. "And so we are clear, if you attempt to harm Ember or the pack, I'll show you why hell didn't want me."

Chapter 60

TRISTIN

A week had passed since Quinn's death. Seven whole days, and she still felt like she had a hole in her chest. She was such a cliché. She slept with his hat. She took her aggression out on the heavy bag. She tried not to hate herself for never kissing him. Quinn had given Kai that message for her with the best of intentions, she was sure, but it just pissed her off. She wanted him here flirting awkwardly, not sending her swoon worthy love letters from the other side.

She stabbed the grape on her plate with a fork and brought it halfway to her lips before she realized she just couldn't eat it. She sighed and let it fall from her fork. She wasn't hungry, but Isa made Tristin eat at least twice a day. She eyed the door; Isa would be back in the kitchen any minute. Tristin wrapped the pieces of orange in a napkin and put them in the garbage, leaving the grapes and two apple slices. She could probably manage that.

The door opened, and Ember and Mace burst in, Neoma on their heels with Romero. Neoma was always following the two of them around lately. Tristin suspected Neoma actually followed the dog. Neoma loved that stupid dog, maybe even more than Ember did.

Tristin didn't get the obsession. He wouldn't eat dog food. He was the size of a small pony. His bark could rattle the whole house. He was constantly under people's feet, following them around, tongue lolling in his mouth, hoping somebody would offer up their scraps.

"...need to concentrate." Mace was saying. "You're all over the place. We have to figure out how to control this."

Ember whipped around, her eyes narrowed. "I'm doing the best I can. I don't go all creepy demon eyes anymore. I haven't blown up anything in two days. I raised Chester without a problem." She jabbed a finger at the mangy grey cat basking in the kitchen window-sill. He hissed at Ember as though he knew she was talking about him. He hated Ember, which made Tristin like the cat just a little bit more.

He was the third animal Ember had brought back from the grave. The second, a bird, had flown away as soon as she'd pulled him from the other side. They hadn't been that lucky with Chester. The cat had a major attitude problem, but Ember refused to leave him to fend for himself. She'd almost blown up the truck when Rhys offhandedly suggested they try reversing the process to see if she could also send the animals back across the veil.

"I'm not going to get any better if you don't ease up," Ember snapped, opening the pantry and snagging the almonds. She flopped onto the bench in the breakfast nook and started munching. Ember didn't have a problem with her appetite at all. She ate all the time, at home, at school, in the car, in the cemetery. She ate more than the wolves. Tristin assumed that yanking helpless family pets from the other side gave her an appetite. She always came back ravenous.

Tristin listened to them bicker.

"I'm just trying to help," Mace retorted back. "I won't be here forever."

Ember rolled her eyes. "Won't that just be a tragedy?"

Mace loomed over her, exasperated. "Why are you being such a...brat today?"

"Just stop pushing me," Ember snapped.

A weird expression passed across Mace's face. "Okay, right," he held up his hands in surrender. "Done."

Isa came in from the family room, glancing warily at Mace and Ember before pulling three defrosted chickens from the fridge and setting them in the sink for dinner. She puttered around the kitchen surreptitiously eyeing Tristin's plate. Looking at Isa, Tristin stuffed a grape in her mouth, chomping obnoxiously.

The alpha sighed and continued dragging things out for their meal. She opened the drawer in the fridge to fish a cheese cube out for Romero when he nosed at her hip. He huffed his contentment, flopping himself onto the mat in front of the oven, forcing Isa to step over him.

The back door opened again as Kai came in, slamming the door hard enough to rattle the glass panels. He threw his backpack on the floor and kicked it. He'd separated from them straight after school. He'd said he had to do something…for Quinn.

Everybody stopped, staring at him.

"What's wrong?" Isa asked, her brow drooping.

"I went to see Astrid."

Ember's gaze slid to Tristin, and Mace hissed as her powers zapped his fingers. "Ow."

"Sorry," Ember said, not sounding sorry at all.

"How is Daddy's little psycho?" Tristin didn't care if she sounded bitter. Kai might have to deliver Quinn's final message to Astrid, but Tristin didn't have to like it. Astrid had been horrible to Quinn. She didn't deserve to be one of his last thoughts. None of them did. Not even Tristin. Especially not her.

"Devastated. I didn't even get to talk to her for more than two seconds and her father was there the whole time," Kai said. "Allister isn't giving Quinn a funeral."

Tristin's fork clattered onto her plate. "What?"

"He said it would look bad for the family," Kai sneered. "He thinks that it's less humiliating for Quinn to not have a funeral because he died a…criminal."

A sharp pain exploded behind Tristin's left eye, and she clenched her fists. "I hate him."

Isa scrubbed her hand through her hair, her mouth drawn. "Everybody grieves differently, Trist."

"Quinn deserves to be remembered. He deserves that. Allister has no right to decide that, he doesn't." She clamped her teeth so hard she thought they might shatter. "He shouldn't get to decide who gets to say goodbye."

"So, we say goodbye in our own way," Wren said from the doorway of the family room. "Let's give him a pack funeral."

Isa's face split into a grin, and she walked up and kissed him square on the mouth. Tristin rolled her eyes. You'd think he was coming back from the war, not a grocery run with Rhys.

"That's a great idea," Isa said.

"What's a pack funeral?" Ember asked around a bite of apple.

"We build a bonfire, we tell stories, we shift and run in the woods. We howl at the moon to honor one of our own. Other packs come to pay their respects. We can invite the town. Hell, invite the whole damn state. Quinn was one of us. He deserves a proper sendoff."

Tristin's head hurt a little less. Quinn would get a proper funeral by the people who really loved him.

Rhys pushed past Wren, dropping twenty bags of groceries on the counter. "Thanks for the help, man," Rhys said, glowering at Wren.

"I don't carry groceries," Wren said, smug smile in place. "Call it the perks of marrying the alpha."

"I call it my sister's marrying a douchebag." Rhys dropped a kiss on Tristin's head and then Isa's. He'd been much more affectionate in the past week. It was weird, but in a good way. He seemed younger without that constant scowl on his face. He even almost smiled occasionally.

Kai made a beeline for the groceries. He loved to rifle through the food before they put it away. Rhys snaked an arm around Kai's chest and tugged, causing him to stumble backwards into him. Kai opened his mouth to protest, but Rhys just kissed him hard once and let him go.

Kai practically floated to the counter, a dopey smile in place. Tristin's heart clenched. It wasn't like she wasn't happy for her brother. He'd been waiting years for Rhys to get it together. He helped Kai cope with Quinn, and that was great, but she didn't know how much

 360

more of the touchy feely stuff she could take. She was being selfish, but she just didn't care. Watching them physically hurt her.

"So, when are we doing this?" Rhys asked.

"Doing what?"

Tristin's lip curled at the new voice. She couldn't believe the audacity. Who just walked into somebody's house like that? She spun around on her stool and stared down Quinn's sister. "Don't you know how to knock?"

Astrid looked at Isa, hesitant, half-turning towards the door like she might bolt. Isa glared at Tristin. "She doesn't have to knock, she's family." Isa walked over and hugged her. "How are you, sweetheart? We haven't seen you in forever."

Tristin rolled her eyes. Of course, they hadn't. She'd decided she was way too good for them years ago.

"Tired. Sad. Trying not to hate my dad."

Ember eyed the girl from the table, clearly still not over their run in at the school. Tristin pushed her plate away. No way was she eating now.

Astrid flopped herself onto the stool at the opposite end of the counter as if she did it all the time. There was a time when Astrid had practically lived there. She was at their house as much as Quinn until it became clear Astrid would be the only one to inherit any magic. After that, her father hadn't allowed her over anymore.

She looked terrible. The girl hadn't left her house without full hair and makeup since she was twelve, but there she sat in a pair of grey sweatpants and a flannel shirt Tristin knew belonged to Quinn. She had her glasses on, wore no makeup, and had her hair piled sloppily on her head. She looked like she hadn't slept in days. Good, Tristin thought meanly, she wasn't the only one sleep deprived.

"What are you even doing here?" Tristin asked, exhausted.

Astrid pointed to her bag, her eyes haunted. "I was sleeping in Quinn's room, and there were a couple things I thought you might want."

Tristin looked at the bag, startled.

She blinked back sudden tears, her chest squeezing so hard she felt like she was dying. She hated this. She spent every minute on the verge of tears. She bit her lip hard enough to draw blood. She was

 361

not going to cry in front of Astrid. Tristin didn't think she'd ever feel whole again.

"We're giving Quinn a pack funeral," Kai told Astrid as he licked something off his finger.

She looked at Isa, unsure. "Can...Can I come?"

"Of course you can," Isa said. "It's for anybody who wants to say their goodbyes."

Ember's head snapped up, and she looked at Tristin with dread.

"Except Stella." All heads turned at the venom in Tristin's voice. "You tell that witch to stay away. She's not allowed here after what she did to Ember."

Heads swiveled to look at Ember, their confusion obvious. Ember shrugged but said nothing, her expression relieved. Ember got on Tristin's nerves, but Stella was a nightmare. Besides, Tristin could dislike her family, but it didn't mean anybody else could.

Astrid looked contrite. "I'm really sorry. I didn't know she was going to do that. I promise it will just be me."

Ember nodded, and Astrid turned back to look at Tristin. "Can we talk? In private?"

Tristin narrowed her eyes at her. "Porch?"

Astrid nodded. When she stood, Romero lumbered up to her staring at her with big soulful cow eyes—well, eye—probably hoping to scam a new person out of food.

Astrid's eyes widened, and she looked to Ember. "Wow. He's huge. Is this...is this the one you..." Astrid gestured at Ember vaguely, unable to say it. Ember nodded, stuffing a cookie into her mouth.

"Ember," Isa said. "Slow down. Dinner's in an hour."

"I'll eat," Ember promised, reaching for another cookie. Isa shook her head.

Astrid stared for a long time at Romero, fascinated. Finally, Tristin said, "You wanted to talk?"

"Oh. Yeah."

Once on the porch, Astrid turned calculating eyes on Tristin. All traces of that sweet, sad girl in the kitchen were gone. "How long has that dog been around?"

 362

"Oh, hello Astrid," Tristin said. "I wondered when the real you would show up."

Astrid scowled. "Just answer my question."

Tristin eyed the girl, wary of her sudden personality change. "I don't know, a couple of weeks."

"And he's okay?"

"Yes, I guess for a horse-sized zombie dog who's a non-stop eating machine. What do you care?"

Astrid folded her arms across her chest, looking Tristin in the eye, a smile playing at Astrid's lips. "Cause we're going to bring my brother back, and Ember's going to help."

Chapter 61

MACE

Mace watched the front door, his foot tapping. He hadn't expected to see Astrid. Things were complicated enough without her showing up. Ember had herself convinced she was doing better but only because she didn't see how much hold her magic had over him right now.

Pushing her had backfired on him. He was now more of a prisoner than ever. If he went more than a block, her magic retaliated. It wasn't just the pain. He could deal with pain, but she was snapping orders at him with alarming frequency, and he had no choice but to obey.

She still had no idea. She was so preoccupied with the Grove's threat to return, she hadn't stopped to wonder why he wasn't putting up a fight, acquiescing to even her most ridiculous demands.

Worse still, his recent house arrest was making it impossible to feed. He needed to feed to control his…impulses. If he couldn't sustain himself, there would be no way to keep her in check, and nobody wanted her power on the loose; they could all just trust him on that.

If Astrid told Tristin about working for Allister, Mace was screwed. They were all screwed. *If* Astrid knew. Did she know? He raked his hands through his hair. What was she even doing there? He'd like to think he'd been lucky Kai had yet to talk, but the reaper had a reason. Kai wanted to talk to Mace first, he could tell. There was no mistaking the looks from Kai when they were together. A conversation was imminent.

Mace wasn't sure how he'd lost control of everything so quickly. For once, he had no plan, no scheme. The amulet had been his best chance at gaining the advantage, and that was lost. The only way he could break Ember's hold on him was to give into Allister's request, and Mace couldn't do that. All he could do was try to stay one step ahead of Ember and the witch.

He popped his neck, first one way and then the other, trying to ease the tension in his shoulders.

"Could you not do that, please?" He turned to look at Ember, who leaned against the doorframe of the kitchen, her expression pained. "The sound, Quinn's neck…"

"Sorry, luv," Mace said, unable to hide his exhaustion.

"What's wrong with you?"

"What?" he tensed. All it would take is her demanding he tell her everything, and he'd have no choice. "Nothing, I'm just tired."

A small smile played at her lips. "Big, bad, evil soul eaters get tired?"

She leaned her head on the doorframe, and he could see she was tired too. Her hair was a riot of frizzy flame curls, and she still had a leaf in her hair from outside. Her eyes looked haunted since Quinn's death. Mace had to remind himself she wasn't like the others. They'd hunted; they'd had to take out living things. Until recently, Ember only viewed death once the victim had passed. She'd never watched the life drain from somebody's eyes.

She chewed on her bottom lip, thoughtfully, as she watched him watch her. He was pushing her too hard, but he couldn't do anything else. This was all going to fall down around them. The pressure building in his chest when he looked at her was just this side of too much. Was it all her magic as Allister said? Sometimes he didn't think so, even though anything else was impossible.

He must have stared too long because her eyes became uncertain, and her hand fluttered to her cheek. "What? Is there something on my face? Is my hair a mess?"

He shook his head. "No, sorry. Like I said, I'm just tired."

He glanced again at the front door, wondering what Tristin and Astrid could possibly have to talk about for this long. Their only commonality was gone. When he looked back, Ember was close enough to tilt his chin up and turn his head with gentle purpose. "You look pale. Are you sick? Is that a thing that can happen?"

He put his hand over hers, pulling it from his face. He didn't let go. "I'm fine."

He licked his dry lips. He was definitely not fine. If he didn't eat soon, the side effects were going to get much worse.

"When did you eat last?" she asked, narrowing her eyes at him.

Fantastic, could she read his mind now? This just kept getting better. He looked down, shrugging. "A few days ago, I guess."

"A few as in three?"

He could lie, but it was too risky. If she demanded the truth, he might spill everything in his magic's pathetic attempt to appease hers. Finally, he just decided on honesty.

"Seven."

She pulled him out of the living room and into the dining room, pushing the doors shut and turning on him.

"Seven days?" she whispered. "Are you crazy? That's a long time to go without eating."

He crossed his arms, trying not to be himself. "Listen, luv, I know lately you can't go four minutes without stuffing a cookie in your mouth—and I adore that about you—but when you are as old as I am, it's not necessary to eat constantly."

It was sort of a lie but not exactly. He didn't *have* to eat. It wouldn't kill him. He'd go crazy. Possibly go on a brutal murder spree. He would eventually shrivel up into a mummy-like state, forced to endure no company but his own horrid thoughts for all eternity...but he'd still be on this side of the veil.

She arched a brow at him. "So, now you have a problem with my weight?"

 366

His face contorted in disbelief. "What? That's what you got out of what I said? I don't care what you weigh, Ember. Eat your body weight in cookies, eat carrots or string beans, gain a hundred pounds. It's all the same to me."

The tension leached from her shoulders, and she flopped into one of the dining room chairs. He shook his head at her defeated look. He crouched down in front of her chair, his magic wanting to be nearer to hers. "I'm just saying that I don't need to feed. I'm stuck on this plain whether I'm well fed or starving. Just call it another perk of being immortal."

She gazed at his face for a long time, her gaze roaming over every feature. He fought not to squirm under her scrutiny.

"You need to eat."

He couldn't help the frustrated groan that escaped as he looked up at her. "No, I don't."

"Yes, you do. I know I'm doing way better, but what if something happens, and you need to help me? How are you going to do that if you don't have any strength left?"

Mace struggled around her twisted logic, opting to divert her from her current train of thought. "Do you think it's a good idea for me to be feeding off people in or near town after what just happened? Do you think the Grove won't notice a few of their faithful followers missing?"

Her eyes slid away from his, and he stood to pace.

"I understand you're trying to help, but I think the best thing we can do is try to keep a low profile until we get you fully under control."

"How do you do it?" she asked suddenly.

He frowned. "Do what?"

"Feed."

He did not want to go down that rabbit hole. "It's hard to explain."

"But you can feed without killing somebody. You said so."

He wanted to be done with this conversation, just talking about feeding made his teeth hurt and increased the gnawing ache in his stomach. His magic stirred; it wanted to feed. He clenched his jaw, trying not to think of how much he needed it. "Yes, can we drop this, please?"

"Feed off me," she offered, so quiet he almost missed it.

His breath punched out of him. "What?"

She stood, crossing over to him. "What? You need to eat. I can afford the power loss."

"Ember, it's not the same thing. It's not power; it's your soul."

She crossed her arms, her jaw set. "I don't care. Better me than some defenseless human out there. Besides, my magic allows me to defend myself if you take it too far. Nobody outside of this town can say that."

He wanted to fight, but his power wasn't interested in his feelings. It was hungry. He was hungry. He swallowed hard, stepping towards her. He was so hungry. He wanted to say yes, to push her against the nearest wall and sate himself on what she offered so freely. His magic slammed around inside him like a rabid dog trying to free itself from a cage, but he wouldn't do it unless she knew the truth. "Do you know why I kill my victims?"

She looked at him, startled. "W-what? Don't your kind feed on the dying?"

He smiled slightly. "Did Quinn tell you that?"

She nodded. "Isn't that what your kind does? Feed on the souls of the dying before they can cross over?"

"Some, but not me." He turned away. He didn't want to look at her when he said this. "I told you I'm not a victim to some curse. I've spent years feeding off the souls of the healthy. Sometimes for money. Sometimes for fun. Sometimes I even go for the strongest ones, to make more of a sport out of it. It's why I eventually stopped hunting humans and started hunting people like us. I like the challenge of the preternatural." Ember watched him but said nothing. "I could leave their bodies alive, leave them soulless."

Ember's brow was furrowed, lips tight. "Like zombies?"

"Worse."

Ember snorted. "Worse than zombies?"

"Yes, far worse." He turned on her. "The soul is like your conscience. It's the metaphysical reason for all our emotions. Imagine legions of humans and super-humans out there with no conscience,

 368

people who take whatever they want without any concern for them-selves or others. Imagine unleashing your zombies on the world but completely able bodied and looking just like everyone else. That is what happens when I take the soul of a living person. Had I left them alive, I could have bred a race of serial killers the size of a small country." He turned to look at her, hoping she understood why he couldn't feed. "That is why I kill my victims."

"Then isn't that the more humane way to feed?" she said.

"What?"

"If leaving them alive means they would hurt others, aren't you doing the right thing by killing them?"

Mace paused, staring hard at Ember. She just didn't get it. The girl was mad. A thought occurred to him then, and it made him go cold. What if Allister was right? What if his feelings for her were just a side effect of their link? More importantly, what if it wasn't a one-way street? Could she be losing her empathy? She mourned the loss of Quinn but not like the others. Could he be stealing Ember's soul in an entirely different way? Ember's powers were already too much. The only thing that kept her in check was her compassion.

Ember without her soul was a terrifying prospect.

"They wouldn't need to be killed if I wasn't feeding off their souls. Ember, I'm a murderer."

She shook her head. "You have to eat. You didn't ask for this. Did you?"

He had, actually, sort of, but that was hardly the point.

"Ember…"

"No," she said, putting up a hand. "You're going to feed on me and that's the end of it."

He was moving before he could stop himself. He couldn't deny her. She made a face that showed she was pleased with herself. She shouldn't be. He could make it so it didn't hurt, but there was no way of knowing how much of who she was would be lost if he fed.

He reached out and cupped her face with both hands, stepping farther into her space. She sucked in a surprised breath, her magic jumping at the contact, thrilled with whatever it was that led her closer to him.

"What are you doing? Is this how you f-feed?"

 369

"Just hold still," he whispered. He was close enough to feel her heartbeat rabbiting in her chest.

She trembled as his magic took control. Her mouth opened, and she whimpered as a piece of her became his. To anybody else, it looked like an intimate embrace, a couple just on the verge of kissing, one hand at the back of her neck, the other on her cheek. Nobody could see the soul. They couldn't see him pull it from her lips and into himself.

He didn't need to touch her to feed. It was better for them both if he didn't. He needed to concentrate, and it was so much easier if he wasn't touching her, but she was so close and smelled so good he could find no reason why he couldn't do both. When his lips touched hers, she gasped, but she didn't pull away. Her hands slid to his shoulders, letting him press her gently against the wall of the dining room.

He took it slow. Somewhere in the back of his mind, he reasoned this was probably her first kiss. He'd kissed many people in his lifetime, but few without wanting something in return. A feeling like disgust curled inside him. He was even robbing her of that. Ember deserved better. She deserved everything.

He tried to make it good, tried to make it about her. His fingers slid into her hair, tilting her head and deepening the kiss. He tried not to take too much, to be aware…but the noises she was making were distracting; her tiny breathy sounds made him care less about feeding and more about seeing what other noises he could pull from her.

But something wasn't right. He could usually feel the soul slipping, could feel as it drained away, but that wasn't happening. If anything, it seemed Ember's soul was an endless supply, constantly replenishing. It took longer than it should to make the connection. He wasn't accessing Ember's soul at all. All that power Ember channeled daily was right there, hundreds of old and powerful souls his for the taking. It shouldn't be possible, yet it clearly was because he could feel their essence appeasing his hunger.

He tried to pull away, to break the connection. He didn't go far, his lips trailing over her jaw to her ear. She made a sound, pulling him closer. He could still feel them. He was still feeding. It seemed once

  370

Ember allowed the connection, he had access until she rescinded the invitation.

He groaned against the shell of her ear, and her breath hitched, offering more of her throat for exploration. There were so many of them. He felt drunk. He couldn't think of anything better in the world than exploring Ember and all those souls.

He wrenched himself away from her, attempting to put some space between them. Ember stared at him, her eyes wide, her chest heaving. Her violet eyes glowed, and her hair seemed electrified. She seemed electrified. She looked like a goddess. In a way, he supposed she was the goddess of destruction, wreaking havoc on him and his entire world. She was a walking disaster, and all he wanted was more. More of her lips, more of her souls, just more. He wanted it so bad he wasn't sure he could stop himself.

"Did that help?" she asked, her voice raw.

He nodded wordlessly, his eyes roaming her face. His fingers itched to touch her. "We can't do that again."

Something akin to disappointment flickered across her face, and her hand unconsciously reached for him. He had no choice but to move closer. Her hands roamed his chest. He could no longer feel the souls as he had moments ago, just that thrum of magic constantly humming between them. He wasn't sure if he was relieved or disappointed to see she'd severed the connection.

She seemed conflicted too. Her face flushed red at the way her hands moved over him seemingly of their own accord.

"Is this me or the magic?" she asked, frustration leaching into her tone.

"Touching me?" he asked. "I don't know. Does it matter?"

Her arms wound around his neck, breathing shallow. "I don't know."

"I told you, luv, we shouldn't do this again?"

"The feeding or the kissing?" she inquired before she leaned forward and pressed her lips to his throat. He felt her smile as he swallowed hard. She liked the effect she was having on him, that much was clear. She let her lips drag along his throat, across his jaw, behind his ear just as he'd done to her. *She's a fast learner*, he thought.

He let her explore every muscle in his body, straining to control his instincts.

This was a terrible idea. This was the absolute worst thing to do in this situation, but he wouldn't tell her no. He placated himself by reasoning he couldn't tell her no. It was much easier to think he was powerless to stop her than to think he didn't want to.

The door opened.

"Ugh, yuck. There isn't enough bleach in the world to un-see that." Kai stood, his arms folded, a smug expression on his face.

Ember stepped away, her face flushing. "I'm gonna go."

As Ember made her way out, Kai looked at Mace. "We need to talk."

Chapter 62

TRISTIN

Tristin stood, her mouth open, attempting to process what Astrid said. Tristin glanced at the front door and back again. She wasn't sure what scared her more, the others overhearing or being out there alone with Astrid. She was clearly unstable. "What are you talking about?"

"We…are…bringing…him…back," she repeated, her jaw thrust forward, her eyes daring Tristin to contradict the statement.

"The coven?" Tristin whispered, again looking around to make sure nobody was within earshot. "That's crazy, witches can't do death magic." She couldn't imagine Allister or Alex ever agreeing to such a thing.

Astrid rolled her eyes, pulling a face. "Of course not, stupid. You, me, and your idiot cousin."

Tristin grit her teeth, praying for patience. Astrid was grieving too. She'd just lost her brother.

She stepped closer. "Are you going to say something, or do I need to talk even slower?"

Tristin gaped at Astrid. Even when she was asking for a favor, she was horrid. Tristin wished Isa could see the real Astrid. "Well, gosh, when you put it like that, how could we refuse?"

Her lip curled. "I'll kiss your ass when my brother is back safely; until then, I'm not interested in anybody else's feelings."

Tristin's stomach clenched, her eyes dropping to stare at her feet. She hated Astrid for even hinting at the possibility. It's not like Tristin didn't want him back. There wasn't a single part of her not aching for him to be there. She didn't know how to be her without him. She hated herself for that, but it was true. He forced her to be stronger, harder, and more self-aware. Bringing him back wasn't an option. He wasn't a puppy. He was a human.

"Please tell me your whole plan doesn't revolve around Ember because she is the worst reanimator ever."

Tristin didn't know if that was true or not, but she would say anything to stop her insides from shaking right now. Ember was the only reanimator, but given her track record, Tristin was probably right.

"Ember is the plan."

"You're nuts. It'll never work. Ember blows up as many animals as she reanimates. Besides, reanimators can't bring people back permanently."

"Then it's a good thing she's not a reanimator," Astrid snapped, losing her patience.

Tristin's head snapped up. "What?"

Astrid smiled, her expression smug. "Don't you think it's weird that none of the animals she's returned have crossed back over?"

Sure, Tristin thought it was a little odd, but Mace insisted it wasn't permanent. Reanimators lack the ability to anchor a soul to a body. It was only a matter of time before the magic wore off, and they crossed back. It's why he didn't want Ember getting so attached. Yet, all the animals were still here, none of them slobbering corpses.

"I guess," Tristin said carefully. "So if she isn't a reanimator, what is she? Witches can't bring somebody back from the dead."

"A necromancer can."

Her heart sank. Astrid really was crazy. Necromancers? Tristin thought Astrid was smarter than that. She'd put all her hopes into a fantasy, a witch-reaper hybrid with god-like abilities. They talked about them in mythology class along with Loki and Icarus. They weren't real. "Necromancers don't exist."

Astrid shrugged. "Neither do banshees, and yet here you are."

Tristin chewed on the inside of her cheek. She wanted to believe it was possible so badly, but it just couldn't be. "What makes you think Ember is a necromancer?"

"I overheard my father talking. He's planning something, probably something super horrible. He told somebody on the phone that she was a necromancer. My father doesn't throw words like that around easily. If he thinks she's a necromancer, then so do I."

Allister had more information than any of them. If he believed it...It made more sense than anything else currently happening in her life. Still, she couldn't help but remind Astrid, "Ember might be able to restore the souls of dead animals, but the last time she tried it on a human it didn't go so well."

"You mean her mother?"

Tristin narrowed her eyes.

Astrid just smiled. "Yeah, I know about that too. My father is far too casual about the conversations he has in our house now that Quinn's gone. She was five years old. Imagine what she can do now?"

"I don't have to imagine. I'm not talking about Ember's mom. I'm talking about Ms. Carlton, our math teacher, and Mike from the garage. Ember accidentally yanked them back too...well, their bodies anyway," Tristin said. "Her powers are out of control. She blows up a dead animal at least once a week. It's pretty gross."

Astrid's face contorted. "Well she can't blow my brother up because he's currently occupying our mantle in a tacky cardboard box marked temporary while waiting for the gaudy urn my father purchased. Now, some would call that box ironic but I consider it a sign from the other side that they aren't quite ready for my baby brother yet. Either way, she can't do much more harm than that."

Tristin stared at Astrid, annoyed for even entertaining this crazy idea. "Just suppose I said I'd consider this. You just said Quinn's been cremated," she said, choking on the last word. "Where do you plan on putting his soul once Ember yanks him back from the other side?"

 375

Her eyes shifted to the left, and she tapped her manicured nail against her temple. "I've got that all figured out. All that's needed is an empty vessel, and I know exactly where to find that."

A chill crept up Tristin's spine. Astrid was as smart as her brother and way more cunning. Tristin didn't want to know why the witch looked so pleased with herself. "So, let's pretend everything goes according to plan, then what? Quinn spends the rest of his days masquerading in somebody else's body?"

Astrid rolled her eyes. "Oh buck up, Sourpuss. One little glamour spell from me, and all you will ever see is the face you fell in love with. Consider it an early wedding present."

Tristin felt like she'd been kicked in the stomach.

"The rest of the world will see someone else. It's the only way we can get away with this."

"We will never get away with this. This is insane. We have the Grove coming back. This is going to get us all killed. We don't have a spell, we don't have a coven, and we don't have any idea what we're doing."

"Just leave the details to me. You just need to get your cousin to agree to this."

"She's not ready," Tristin said. "She'll never agree to this. Not only that, she'll rat us out to Isa, and we'll all get in trouble."

"Then we'll just have to give her some incentive."

"What does that mean?"

Astrid shrugged. "I'll think of something."

"Nobody will ever agree to this."

"I have some of the things I need in place. You just need to make sure Mace keeps Ember under control."

Tristin side-eyed the girl. "Mace? Didn't realize you two were on a first name basis."

"We are now. He works for my father."

"What?"

"You think you know what a jerk my dad is, but you haven't even scratched the surface. He's not the person people think he is, but I'll worry about him when I have my brother back."

"You're crazy," Tristin said.

"Maybe," Astrid smiled. "But if we get my brother back, does it matter?"

 376

Chapter 63

KAI

Mace eyed Kai warily. It wasn't like he was eager for this conversation either. He'd allowed himself to ignore the problem for the last seven days because, honestly, he just didn't have it in him. As long as Mace and Ember were where Kai could see them, where was the harm? But now they were making out? He definitely couldn't handle that.

"It's been a week. When are you going to tell Ember you work for Allister?"

Mace scrubbed his hand across his face. "It's not that simple."

"Why? Because you're developing a thing for her?"

"No. Because she needs me right now."

"She's been fine."

"No, she hasn't."

"She's not blowing things up...well, as much. She hasn't knocked any pictures off the wall or boiled her own blood, relatively speaking, isn't that better?"

Mace sighed. "No, it's not." He stared at Kai for a long moment, as if gauging something. "She hasn't learned control; her magic has just found a way to...divert her excess energy."

Kai looked at him. "Huh?"

Mace sat down on the dining room chair, his elbows on his knees as he rubbed the heels of his palms across his eyes. Not for the first time, Kai noticed Mace looked terrible. He had black circles smudged under his eyes, his cheeks sunken in. He looked tired.

"Your cousin is channeling her magic through me. She's tethered our magic together."

Isn't that why they had allowed him to stay in the first place? Kai must be missing something because Mace looked freaked out. Considering Mace was immortal and hundreds of years old, Kai could only assume it was bad, exceptionally bad.

"So, what does that mean?"

"It means instead of Ember learning control of her magic—to call it at will—she is just on full juice all the time and diverting it to me so as not to cause any mishaps like blowing up birds or raising an army of revenant zombies."

Kai let that information sink in. "Is this a side effect of the binding spell wearing off? I would have thought by now that the magic would have, I don't know, righted itself?"

"Right, we never did get to that part of our story, did we?" Mace said, almost to himself.

Kai's pulse quickened. "What part?"

Mace waved him off. "The point is our connection is having some rather unfortunate side effects."

Kai smirked. "Like you ramming your tongue down her throat in the formal dining room?"

Mace gave Kai an epic eye roll. "Like she has bound our magic together, both literally and figuratively."

Kai waited for Mace to continue but he didn't. He just stood there staring expectantly like he was waiting for Kai to comprehend how catastrophic this news was. Finally, Kai said, "Seriously, I'm trying to get why you are so spooked, but you're going to have to spell it out for me."

"Your cousin has me on a supernatural choke chain. I can't go more than a few hundred feet without her magic yanking me backwards, painfully, horribly, grotesquely backwards."

Kai's lips twitched. He couldn't help it. Mace had been terrorizing people for two hundred years only to be magically neutered by a seventeen-year-old girl.

"Laugh if you like, mate, but I can't leave. If I can't leave, I can't feed. No feeding for me equals bad things for everybody around me."

Kai narrowed his eyes, his smile fading. "Yet you look just slightly better than you did this morning."

Mace's eyes slid away from him, checking a spot on the floor.

"Is that what I walked in on? Were you feeding off her? What the hell, dude?"

"She offered," Mace grumbled. "Besides, it wasn't her I was feeding on."

Kai looked around the room, the hairs rising at the back of his neck. There was nobody else there. He was so tired of feeling as if he didn't get it. He would like everybody to stop being so enigmatic. "How so?"

"Look, she's not what you think she is," Mace said, dropping his voice, "She's channeling a ton of ancient magic, and that magic has decided that I need to be...close."

Kai arched a brow at him. "You looked pretty close to me, and it sure didn't look forced."

"It's complicated."

Kai snorted. "I bet," he said, before his brain registered something. "Wait. What do you mean Ember is channeling ancient magic?"

"Your cousin is somehow tapped into whatever frequency the dead in this town appear to broadcast."

"Huh?"

"She's all souls radio, mate," Mace growled in frustration. "She's playing all the souls of the eighties, nineties, and today."

Kai's brain hurt. "Can reanimators do that?"

"No," Mace huffed. "But necromancers can."

"Necromancers?"

  379

Mace faced him. "Tell me it hasn't occurred to you?"

Kai flushed. It hadn't occurred to him. Even with everything he'd talked about with Tate, it'd never occurred to him. He was an idiot.

"Does Ember know?" Kai asked.

"No, but Allister does."

"You told Allister? Seriously?"

Mace scrubbed his hand along the back of his neck. "Allister already knew. He's had plans for Ember this whole time."

"The whole time? Did he know she'd come here?"

Mace shrugged. "I don't know. I'm not really part of his inner circle. I was hired to watch and report...and to retrieve that package."

"Right, the package," Kai said, digging his thumbs into his eyes with a sigh. "What was in that package anyway?"

"The blade of Osiris," Mace said. "It's a transference device."

"Transference?" Kai chewed that over. "Well, it obviously doesn't transfer anything good. How does it work?"

Mace winced. "When you plunge the dagger into the victim, the handle pierces the flesh of the user. It will transfer the power from the victim to the killer."

"Killer." Kai took a deep breath, trying not to panic. He wasn't losing any more people. "So, it kills the person whose power you want to take?"

"Yeah, it's a nasty little bit of blood magic. It's not for the faint of heart."

"And he plans on using that on my cousin." Kai's anger flared, and he let himself entertain the idea of punching Mace in the throat. "And you were going to help him do it?"

"No," Mace said, before reconsidering. "Well, yes. Kind of. I didn't know he planned to kill her when this started. I mean, I suspected it was his intention, but I didn't really care because it didn't pertain to me."

Kai gaped at Mace. Seriously, was this his defense? Hope he didn't end up going in front of a jury. "Oh, save the judgment, Reaper. I'm the bad guy. It kind of goes with the territory. Besides, I wasn't exactly privy to his plans until I saw the knife."

"So what did you do with the knife?"

"It's in a safe place," Mace answered.

"Forgive me if I don't believe you."

"Having that knife could put all of you in danger."

"Dude, we are already in danger. The Grove will be back, and I don't believe for a second they will wait until we turn eighteen. If we haven't gotten our crap together, we're all going to die…just like Quinn." His name stuck in his throat, and he swallowed convulsively, trying to calm the sudden storm of feelings his name evoked.

"Listen, mate, I understand what you're saying, but this is more than just Ember. Allister isn't a good guy, and if he gets ahold of that blade and Ember's magic, he'll be more powerful than anything out there."

"Won't the Grove step in at that point?"

"Do you think they'd believe us? Allister has been their lapdog for a long time," Mace reasoned. "Besides, think of the damage he could do in the meantime."

Kai didn't want to think about that. "Ember deserves to know the truth. She deserves to know you've been lying to her."

"You don't know what you're asking. This is all going to go sideways posthaste."

Kai shook his head, determined. "No. You're going to tell her. You have until the bonfire, or I'll tell her myself."

Mace looked at Kai with tired eyes, shrugging his shoulders. "Don't say I didn't warn you."

Chapter 64

EMBER

She couldn't believe he'd kissed her. She couldn't believe she kissed him back. She ran her thumb across her lower lip. She thought about it all night. She thought about it in the shower that morning, when she brushed her teeth, while she stuffed her legs into her shorts and dragged her t-shirt over her still damp body.

All she did was think about him. It was crazy to think of him as anything but a monster. He enjoyed the suffering of others. He'd said he killed people for sport. He'd killed them because he was bored. But she'd killed people too. Maybe killing people was more than the average five-year-old was capable of grasping, but it didn't make them any less dead. Who was she to judge?

Mace clearly didn't agree. He was acting weird, not bad weird, but nervous weird. He wasn't talking to her, looking away any time she smiled at him. He didn't try to leave when she entered a room; he just stood there awkwardly. Any time she turned around, he was just there, hovering in her periphery, watching.

It was making everybody nervous. Tristin said it was because the wolves could smell people's emotions, and it made them edgy. Ember didn't want to make any more trouble for anybody, but that didn't seem to matter. It felt like the entire house took turns staring at her. It was unsettling. She wanted to believe it was just the tension between her and Mace, but she couldn't help but wonder if maybe it had to do with Quinn.

She flopped back on her bed, bolting upright again as a demonic screech emanated from beneath her, and a mangy grey ball of fur flew out from underneath her pillows. "Chester," Ember growled, trying to bring her pulse back down to normal.

She hated that cat.

Tristin stuck her head in the doorway. "Isa says breakfast is ready."

Ember nodded once, not making eye contact. It didn't matter; Tristin disappeared as fast as she'd arrived. Ember still found it hard to look at Tristin. She was hurting, and it was Ember's fault. Everything was her fault.

She tucked her feet into her flip-flops and snagged her backpack. If she ate fast enough she could sketch on the back porch for a bit before school. Ember filled her plate with eggs, bacon, fruit, two pancakes, and two pieces of sausage. She just wasn't hungry.

"Wren's already at the restaurant. I'm late. Tristin don't you dare be late for your shift," Isa said over her shoulder, as she bolted out the door with a careless wave. At the counter, Kai fed Rhys a piece of bacon, dangling the food above his head. Kai laughed when the wolf bit down on Kai's finger. Tristin rolled her eyes at the two, shoving between them to grab her food.

Tristin's appetite appeared to be returning. She ate everything on her plate at dinner and was piling all kinds of food onto her plate now. She'd never seen Tristin eat anything but vegetables and protein. She wasn't sure she even knew what carbs were. Neoma sat on the ground feeding bacon to Chester and Romero, her feet filthy, as if she'd already been outside in the dirt.

Once Ember stuffed the last bit of bacon into her mouth, she grabbed her bag and headed for the back porch. She tucked herself into her chair and pulled out her sketchbook. She didn't stop to think about what she drew and just let the pencil glide along the paper.

"That looks just like me."

 383

Ember's head shot up, her heartbeat pounding hard enough to make her lightheaded. She blinked twice. "Holy shit," she said, before clapping a hand over her own mouth. "Quinn?" she whispered.

"Potty mouth," he said by way of greeting, a smile playing on his lips. His gaze flitted through the kitchen window. He faded out like an old television searching for a signal before returning stronger. She could see through him if she looked hard enough.

"Are you real? Am I hallucinating?"

He laughed at that, pushing his glasses up his nose. "Um, I'm real, well, real enough."

"What are you doing here?"

"Uh, I didn't call this meeting. You did."

"I did?"

"I do not have the powers necessary to pierce the veil so…yeah. This is all you. Which is still so awesome."

She looked over her shoulder at the others. "I should—"

"No. Don't," he said. "I don't want to do this to them again. I said my goodbyes." He gazed into the house, sadness obvious even as he flickered in and out.

"Quinn, I'm so sorry. I don't know why I did this. I was just thinking about you, I guess." She looked at the picture of him. What if he hadn't been cremated? She shuddered.

"Aww, that's sweet," he said, tone teasing as he dragged his gaze from the window.

"I'm really, really sorry," she said, tearfully.

He looked confused. "What? Oh, God, don't cry. Sorry for what?"

"For everything. This is my fault. Everything that happened to you is my fault."

He was flustered, fidgeting even in death. "Please stop crying. If I try to comfort you, I'll just fall right through you, and it will be super embarrassing for both of us."

"Huh?" she wiped at her eyes.

"I just mean, I appreciate the martyr thing you have going, but I don't blame you for anything. If anybody is to blame, it's my father. You need to stay away from him, Ember."

 384

Ember frowned. "Your father? Allister? What does he have to do with me?"

Quinn laughed humorlessly. "Everything, Ember. I don't know how, but I'm almost positive he's the reason you're here."

"Here? Here, as in the town, here as in with you guys, or here as in this situation?" He faded out again until she could barely see him, and her heart stopped before he popped back into view. She let out a breath she didn't realize she was holding. "Here how?" she asked, feeling stupid.

"I don't know. I just know you can't trust him anymore than you can trust Mace."

"Mace?" What did Allister have to do with Mace? "I don't understand."

"Kai didn't tell you?"

"Tell me what? Kai knows something about Mace?"

Quinn's gaze skated back to the window where Rhys was attempting to load the dishwasher while Kai sat on the counter squeezing bubbles out of the bottle of soap. Mace sat at the end of the table, looking right at her. She turned around quickly, giving her attention to Quinn.

"Mace works for my father. He's been working for him the whole time."

Ember wanted to be shocked or surprised, but she was numb to it. "Why? What does that mean? What does your father want with me?"

Quinn shrugged, mouth flattened. "I don't know. I'm sorry. I don't really know anything. I only know you can't trust him."

Ember sat, her mind reeling; she was so stupid. Of course, Mace was lying to her. Of course, he worked for Allister. He'd been against her this whole time and she'd just believed everything he'd said blindly. He was a killer, an assassin. He was a soul-eater. She was so stupid. But Kai, why would he keep this from her? Why would he take Mace's side?

"Is it terrible over there?" Ember asked, in a failed attempt to distract herself.

 385

"Nah," he said. "It's kind of weird. My mom's here. Everybody is here. I expected more harps and angels, fluffy clouds and stuff. It's peaceful, I guess." He began to fade out. "Do me a favor?"

Ember nodded. "Anything."

"Don't call me back again if you can help it. It's too hard." He looked back at Tristin who was now feeding her pancakes to Romero.

Ember nodded, swallowing past the lump in her throat. "I won't. I'm sorry."

He shrugged again. "It's cool. Be careful, Ember. I don't want to see you over here."

This time when he faded he stayed gone. The door opened and everybody piled out, bags in hand.

"Ready, luv?" Mace asked, giving her a half smile that didn't reach his eyes. He picked up her bag for her, holding it so she could put away her sketchbook.

She stared at him hard. No wonder he was acting so strange. What would he do if she called him on all of his crap right then? Would he leave her to fend for herself with her magic? She was doing fine. She felt good. She hadn't had a single power surge in days. She didn't need him. She should tell him to screw off…but she didn't. Instead, she pushed her book into the bag and zipped it closed, taking it from him.

"I guess we'll find out."

Mace stared at her in confusion, but she didn't care. Nothing was making sense. How could he work for Allister? How could Allister have brought her here? Kai brought her here. Her name on Kai's wrist had brought Kai to her and her to Belle Haven. But who put her name on Kai? Her uncle's face flashed in her memory. Why had he been so sure that Kai would be fine when the Grove finally came? Did Alex work for Allister?

She sighed. She needed to have another talk with her uncle.

Chapter 65

TRISTIN

Tristin wasn't alone four minutes when someone grabbed her by the arm, yanking her into an empty classroom. She shook the hand off her arm, glaring at Astrid before rushing to the door to make sure nobody saw them. The last thing Tristin needed was anybody thinking they were spending time together.

She closed the door quietly before dropping her bag on the counter. Five sets of long tables sat in the middle of the classroom, each with their own stools, microscopes, slides, and petri dishes. They were in the chemistry lab.

Astrid went to grab Tristin's arm but she sidestepped away. "Do you mind?"

"Did you talk to her?" Astrid demanded.

Tristin narrowed her eyes at the girl. Tristin had hoped Astrid would've come to her senses. "No. I told you, she would never agree to do this. Nobody would agree to this."

"It's amazing anybody ever gets anything done in your pack, such do-gooders." Astrid huffed a dramatic sigh and dropped her book bag on the desk to open it. She pulled out a huge book with a battered leather cover and worn yellow pages.

"What is that?" Tristin whispered, dread sinking into her bones. The last time she'd seen a book like that Quinn had died.

"A grimoire, stupid."

The insult barely registered as Tristin stared at the book. "Quinn said all grimoires were digital now."

Astrid just shrugged, carefully opening the book to a page marked by a red ribbon. Tristin's fingers moved of their own volition, running over the faded black ink. "Is that Latin?"

"Yes."

"I thought your family grimoire was written in Gaelic."

Her head snapped up. "Did Quinn tell you that?"

Tristin returned Astrid's vague gesture but said nothing else. If Astrid wasn't going to give Tristin answers, two could play at that game.

"This isn't our grimoire. I bought it."

Tristin's stomach lurched. "What do you mean, you bought it. Bought it from whom? How?"

Astrid smiled. "My father has a friend. Shelby. She's in the magical import/export business. I asked where I might find the spell I needed. Turns out, she has a whole library hidden in the middle of nowhere."

"Are you crazy? What if she tells your father? He will kill us. The Grove will kill us. They will snap our necks just like they did Quinn's. You're losing your mind, Astrid."

"She hates my father as much as I do," Astrid said venomously. "Besides, business is business. I gave her every dime I had in my savings account for this book."

Tristin rubbed her temples, closing her eyes and trying to slow her heart rate back to a normal pace. Before, it seemed like a possibility, bringing Quinn back, having him whole and healthy again. After everything, she saw it for what it was, the fever dream of a sickminded girl. There was no way it would work. It couldn't. Witches couldn't do death magic. Witches had never been able to do it. The fact the spell existed at all showed how futile their attempts were.

But Ember wasn't a witch, a voice nagged at the back of Tristin's mind. Ember was a necromancer. Tristin's heart squeezed hard. She thought of Quinn, smiling, joking and laughing with her. She wanted to feel his arms around her. She wanted to hear him call her Dagger. She just wanted him. It was cruel to even let herself think about it.

"What does it say?" Tristin couldn't help but ask, reading over the witch's shoulder. "*Os ex mortuis?*"

"Bone of the dead," she translated absently.

"Sanguine?"

"Blood," Astrid said. "To perform the ritual we need blood and bone from the dead."

Tristin paled. "From our dead? Well it's a bit late for that."

"No. It isn't. I managed to get what I needed before my father sent him to the incinerator," Astrid said, her tone clipped, almost professional.

Tristin was going to be sick. Somewhere, Astrid had Quinn's bones and his blood. What kind of monster could hack up their own brother? Why was Tristin even entertaining this? Why was she letting Astrid torture both of them this way? Tristin didn't know, and she couldn't stop.

"What else?" she heard herself ask.

"Belladonna, mistletoe, graveyard dirt, snake eyes, and an empty vessel."

"This," Tristin pointed to the two words. "*Stigmatium malifica. Malifica* means witch, doesn't it?"

"Yes."

"*Stigmatium?* Like stigmata? You aren't nailing her to a cross are you?"

"Don't be stupid. It simply means branded."

Tristin froze, hunched over Astrid's shoulder. "What?"

"The witch performing the spell must bear the mark of Osiris."

"The god?"

"No, the shoe designer," Astrid sneered. "Yes, the god. This is blood magic."

"This is death magic," Tristin reminded Astrid.

"Yes, and she's a necromancer, so it has to work."

"How do you propose getting Ember to brand herself with the sigil of Osiris?"

389

"I have that all worked out," Astrid said, sliding the book back into her bag. "When Ember comes to you later, you're going to tell her the answer to her problem is a simple tattoo to ward off compulsion." She brandished a small scrap of paper and held it out to Tristin. "And then you are going to take her here. Ask for Rune."

Tristin looked down at the name of the only tattoo place in town. The place was run by Tibetan shaman, well-practiced in the art of magical tattoos. Tristin ran her thumb across her hip, where she'd gotten a tattoo six months ago. It felt like six years ago. They were neutral; they wouldn't ask questions.

"You want me to trick my cousin into branding herself with the sigil of the god of the underworld? Astrid, listen to yourself. This is crazy."

Astrid, her eyes wild, turned on Tristin then. "Crazy? You haven't even begun to see crazy yet. I am the daughter of Allister Talbot, granddaughter of Briona Talbot. I have magic in my blood going back over a thousand years. We are descendants of the goddess." Astrid's nostrils flared, advancing on Tristin. "You *will* do as I say. I'm getting my brother back, and you're going to help me, or I swear I'll make sure your brother joins him."

Tristin's mouth hung open. "What happened to you, Astrid? You used to be a human being."

Astrid wiped the spittle off her chin delicately. "I evolved. I adapted. I embraced my true nature. Witchcraft is neither black nor white. In order for a balance to be maintained a witch must be both dark and light."

Goosebumps broke out across Tristin's skin. Astrid said this as if someone had forced her to say it again and again, as if she were brainwashed. Given what she knew about Allister, she probably had been.

"I am my father's daughter. I always get what I want, and now I want my brother back."

 390

Chapter 66

EMBER

Ember was starting to feel like a prisoner. Knowing Mace worked for Allister made his constant vigilance oppressive. She silently questioned everything he did. Every time she thought about kissing him, her face flushed with embarrassment. He wasn't interested in her. He'd never been interested in her.

Her brain was wild with theories. Was he somehow controlling her magic? Was he somehow keeping her from controlling it? Everything she thought had been a lie. Maybe she only thought she needed him. After all, they'd been setting her up all along. He'd said it himself. He said not to fall for him. He said he could never love her.

The thought of his betrayal festered, her hostility increasing with every class. She sat glaring at the side of his face as he doodled on his paper, paying little to no attention to the lessons. She guessed when you were hundreds of years old you didn't really have much left to learn about American history. She amused herself by fantasizing about the various ways she could use her new powers to torture him, only feeling a little guilty when he caught her staring and grinned at her.

Her stomach fluttered. Why did he have to be so damn attractive? *It's his job*, she reminded herself. That was why Allister hired him. He doesn't care about you. Maybe if she said it repeatedly her traitorous heart would get it. When the bell rang, he grabbed her bag for lunch. She yanked it back and glowered at him.

"Somebody's in a mood."

Her lip curled, that lilting accent she'd thought so sexy made her want to punch him in his stupid English face. She fought the urge to mock his accent, knowing she was acting childish, even if it was in her own head.

"What has you so cross, luv? Is it about the kiss?"

Heat crawled up her neck, turning her chest and cheeks an unattractive bright red. "Ugh, don't remind me."

Mace's eyes went wide, watching her intently. She could see him trying to figure out what he could have done to anger her. *Go ahead and wonder*, she thought. She stopped at the entry to the East corridor. "I need to go find my uncle. I'll see you at lunch."

"Alone? Do you think that's a good idea?" Mace asked, his voice edged with what almost sounded like panic. "I'll go with you."

"No. Go eat lunch. I'll see you in class."

His face paled, but he nodded. He looked queasy. Did soul eaters get sick to their stomach? She really didn't care. She hoped he puked everywhere. She turned on her heel and made her way to the government classroom. She was ten steps into the room before she realized something was wrong. When she heard the door close behind her, panic gripped her. She turned to see Stella standing in front of the only exit.

Ember's magic flickered, and she dug her nails into her palms. Pain was still the only thing that kept her magic in check when Mace wasn't available. Stella looked Ember up and down, sneering at her clenched fists.

"Are you following me?" Ember asked.

"Yes, as a matter of fact I am." Stella moved farther into the room. Ember backed up, not willing to take her eyes off the witch.

"What's your problem?"

"You're my problem," Stella said in a singsong voice. "Girls like you. You're weak. Your powers are all over the place. You have to

 392

rely on a boy to take care of you. You're pathetic. You have an active power most witches would literally kill for, and yet you turn your back on your witch side and instead choose to associate with mutts and demons."

Ember smirked, heat curling in her belly as her magic began to flow. "From what Tristin tells me, you're just mad because the mutt you were practically begging to associate with is now happily cozied up with my cousin, Kai. Very happily," she reiterated.

Stella's nostrils flared, and Ember's hand flew to her own neck, squeezing. Stella smirked as Ember began to choke, the victim of her own hand. She tried to drag in a breath, but she couldn't. Her lungs seared as she tried to use her free hand to tear the other free.

Panic climbed her throat as her body fought to make use of the miniscule amounts of air in her lungs, shutting down the supply to her extremities. They weren't supposed to use magic at school, her brain supplied unhelpfully.

"I guess nobody told you about my active power. I believe humans call it telekinesis. I prefer mind control. Neat trick, right?"

Her face felt tight and bloated, tears streamed from her eyes. Her magic surged, struggling to break the witch's hold, but nothing worked. Dread pulled at Ember like a lead weight on her chest as her vision began to go black at the edges.

She was going to die. Stella was going to kill her.

Stella flicked her fingers, and Ember's hand dropped to her side. Ember doubled over, sucking air into her abused lungs. Her pulse throbbed in her head, her own blood pounding in her ears. She swallowed hard, wincing at the pain. It felt like she'd gargled razor blades.

"Why are you doing this?" she asked, her throat hoarse.

"Cause I can? Because you're the reason my best friend's brother is dead. Because you ignore Alex when he's so eager to do anything for you?" Stella shrugged. "Take your pick."

Stella's gaze strayed to Ember's uncle's new desk. "Want to have a little fun?"

Ember blinked, trying to clear away the white sparks floating before her eyes. Stella waved her finger, and Ember's hand snatched the letter opener off the desk, gripping it tight. Her eyes widened, darting from the letter opener to Stella and back again. "What are

  393

you doing?" Ember tried to calm the hysteria in her voice, but her magic writhed, making her edgy.

Stella tapped her nail against her lip. "Hmm, I don't know. What shall we do?" She swayed on her feet, Ember's hand began to spin the blade. "I could have you shove that letter opener through your hand. How many nerves would it sever? Reapers don't have advanced healing, do they? Oh, or maybe you could slit your wrists? I'd love to watch you bleed." She wiggled her fingers, delighted with herself. "No, I know. Maybe I'll just have you gouge out one of those pretty...purple...eyes."

Ember's hand moved, and she had only enough time to gasp, flinching as the blade stopped barely a millimeter from her pupil. Ember felt lightheaded, like she was on a roller coaster, her pulse thundering at her throat. She tried in vain to put her arm down, but she was completely under the witch's control.

Stella chuckled and again waved her hand, the letter opener clattering to the floor. "Not so mouthy now, are you?"

She paced in front of the door. "The Grove left the witches in charge for a reason. Our powers are far superior to yours. We can get to you anywhere. We can get to anyone, anywhere. Wouldn't you rather be on a winning team instead of those losers you associate with?"

Ember assumed the question was rhetorical.

"You should talk to your uncle, Ember. Family is important."

Ember clenched her jaw to keep her teeth from clattering together. The combination of adrenaline and magic made her want to use that letter opener to tear her own skin off, but she wouldn't dare give this bitch the satisfaction of thinking she'd won anything.

"Kai and Tristin are my family too," Ember said. "And they've never threatened me. Did my uncle tell you to do this?"

Stella tsked. "Of course not. Alex wouldn't dream of hurting you. He talks about you all the time. Ember this. Ember that. Blah, blah, blah." She stopped to stand close enough that Ember could smell Stella's sour breath. "But I don't recommend tattling on me, or you might wind up accidentally cutting out your own tongue, and wouldn't that just be a shame?"

 394

Ember didn't have anything to say. She sensed the danger had passed, but Stella still blocked the exit.

The door opened, and Mace poked his head in, his hair damp, his face pale. He looked awful. "What's going on in here?"

Stella's lip curled as she turned on Mace. "Oh, it's the demon."

Mace sighed. "Why does everybody keep calling me that?"

Stella rolled her eyes and looked at Ember. "Remember what I said."

The minute Stella disappeared her legs gave out beneath her. She expected to hit the floor but found herself in Mace's arms. She wanted to tell him to back the hell off but instead wrapped her arms around his neck, burying her face in his throat. Her magic found his, and they both sighed. She didn't know why Mace looked so beat up, but she just couldn't bring herself to care. Life was so much easier back when her only friends were dead people.

"What happened? What did she do to you?"

"Shh," Ember said, her mouth finding his. "I don't want to talk," she mumbled against his lips.

He lifted her to sit on the desk and buried his hands in her hair, tugging her back enough to look at her, concern etched across his face. "Are you all right, luv?"

"Shut up," she said, reeling him back in. "And kiss me."

He gave in, lips sliding over hers, and she lost herself in the feel of his kiss and the scent of his magic. Her hands gripped his t-shirt uselessly.

He tore his mouth from hers. "Not that I'm complaining, but I can't help but think that maybe you're using this as a way to deflect talking about your feelings."

She growled in frustration, allowing herself the satisfaction of biting his lower lip hard enough for him to flinch. "I'm sorry, are you my school-appointed therapist? When did you start caring about my feelings?" When he looked like he might actually answer, she gripped his chin and looked him in the eye. "If you say one more word, I promise you will never kiss me again." *You'll never kiss me again anyway,* she thought silently.

His eyes roamed her face, a smile tugging at his lips. "Well, when you put it that way..."

 395

She sighed into his open mouth and let her mind go numb and float away. She just needed to forget about everything for a little while. She'd be stronger later. She would deal with Mace's betrayal later. She would deal with Stella later.

Ember would deal with everything, she promised herself as Mace's hand found its way under her shirt, just...later.

Chapter 67

TRISTIN

Lunch was almost over by the time Ember and Mace made it to the table. Tristin couldn't help but notice her hair was a mess, and she was sporting an obscenely large hickey on her neck. Were they in seventh grade?

Ember dropped into the seat between Kai and Donovan, forcing Mace to sit next to Tristin. Ember's refusal to make eye contact with anyone told Tristin she was definitely doing dirty things with the demon.

Donovan wordlessly pushed his food towards Ember, who looked at him like she could kiss him.

"Where have you been?" Ember asked, looking at Donovan with suspicion.

Donovan laughed, plunging his hands into the pockets of his hoodie. "I'm an omega. I need my me-time. After what happened to Quinn...I just needed some space. Isa gets it."

Ember frowned but said nothing. She loaded her plate with people's leftovers. As she ate, she told them about her encounter with Stella. Tristin was both horrified and impressed by Astrid's evil ploy to get Ember on team Osiris.

"What am I going to do? How do I protect myself from… myself?" Ember asked nobody in particular.

"It's because you're not warded." Tristin volunteered.

All eyes swung to her.

"Warded?" Ember asked.

"Wards. Enchantments. Magical spells for protection?"

"You can ward yourself from mind control?" Ember asked, voice wary.

"Yes and no. You can protect yourself from undue influence. It's not foolproof, but it can take the edge off of compulsion."

"What do I have to do? How does it work?"

Tristin stood and dragged her shirt up, revealing the tattoo on her hip. Donovan whistled through his teeth. Tristin ignored him. "This is a sigil, a magical symbol."

"I know what sigils are," Ember sighed. "They were all over my house. Guess that should've been my first clue something was up."

Tristin shrugged. "This is to make me invincible to my enemies."

Ember, her face pinched and her brow raised, looked at Tristin. "That makes you invincible?"

Tristin pulled a face. "It doesn't make me bulletproof, but yeah, it helps me get by. This has as much meaning as you give it. A talisman only works if you believe in it."

"Do you all have…wards?" Ember asked.

Everybody nodded except Neoma. "I don't. I don't need them," she said cryptically. Ember's gaze slid around the table, probably hoping somebody would elaborate.

Instead, Kai tugged down his shirt to reveal the seal of Solomon he had on his chest. Donovan stood, dragging his shirt up over his stomach like a striptease to reveal two runic symbols etched into the cut of each hip, just above his jeans. He patted his belly for good measure. Ember looked at Rhys expectantly. He heaved a weary sigh and stood, turning around to pull his shirt up. Tristin watched as both her cousin and her brother gaped at the bare expanse of Rhys's back. It wasn't like Kai hadn't seen them before. Inked along the ridges of his spine were the phases of the moon. Tristin wasn't

   398

sure if Ember was impressed with the tattoos or the back on which they'd been applied, but she knew which currently held her brother's fascination.

"Why aren't you shirtless more often?" Kai asked Rhys. The wolf huffed in embarrassment, yanking his shirt down and shoving a fry into Kai's grinning mouth.

"So, I just find a design, go to a tattoo parlor and think happy thoughts while the guy tattoos it on my body and bam, instant talisman?" Ember sounded cynical.

"No. You go to magical tattoo shop, like the one here in Belle Haven, where shaman practiced in the art of ink magic apply specially chosen symbols imbued with spells to give them power," Tristin explained impatiently.

"Oh." Ember sucked her bottom lip into her mouth, chewing on it absently. Tristin watched as Mace stared. What was his deal anyway?

"What about you, Mace? You have any magical talismans?" Tristin asked, genuinely curious about whether demons felt the need to shield themselves.

Mace dragged his gaze away from Ember with a grimace. "You could say that."

Ember perked up at that. "Where?"

"Everywhere," Mace said vaguely. "But I can assure you, the person who applied mine took some…artistic license."

"Let's see 'em," Tristin prompted. He glanced at the few stragglers left at the tables surrounding them. "Oh, come on. You don't strike me as the shy type. We showed you ours; it's only fair you show us yours."

Tristin didn't know why she wanted to see them so badly except maybe for his increasing level of discomfort. He should squirm. He was working for the enemy…but, to be fair, so was she.

"It's not very appetizing," Mace promised, making no move to show them.

They all watched him. "I'm sure we'll live," Rhys said, staring down the soul eater.

399

Mace's mouth turned down in an expression that said you-asked-for-this and he stood, sliding his shirt up until it sat just under his arms.

Ember gasped. Neoma's hand flew to her mouth. Tristin just stared. Archaic symbols marred almost every available inch of flesh, not in ink, but in puckered pink scars that could have only been created by burns. Some of the symbols were shiny, as if they were the newer scars; others appeared hardened like leather as if someone had burned him repeatedly with the same symbol. The hours of suffering one would have to endure for that type of scarification was inconceivable. She thought of the druids, and the symbols carved into their bodies.

Tristin shivered. Who did this to him?

Stagmatium malifica, Tristin thought to herself.

Mace smirked, but there was no amusement in his eyes. He had their attention, and he made point of slowly turning so they could see the damage carried around to his back. Ember looked like she was going to be sick. Kai and Rhys both looked spooked.

"Who did that to you?" Ember whispered, her fingers reaching out to touch before she caught herself and dropped her hand. Mace dropped his shirt as people at the other tables started pointing and whispering.

"Not important. But Tristin is right. I can't imagine living in this town and not having protection of some kind in place."

Tristin stared hard at Mace. Did he know? Was he in on this? Had Astrid told Stella *and* Mace? She hated this crap.

"I'll take her tonight," Tristin volunteered.

"Um, you're working," Kai reminded his sister.

Crap. She'd forgotten. "Can't you cover my shift?"

"Sure," Kai said. She felt her stomach unknot a fraction before he said, "But who's going to cover my shift while I'm covering yours?"

Her heart sank.

"I'll do it," Rhys sighed.

"But you're already pulling a double on Saturday." Kai reminded him.

 400

"It's fine. More time with you," Rhys muttered, taking a swig from his water bottle, his face in direct conflict with his words.

"Aw, baby," Kai crooned.

Rhys choked, sputtering, "Baby?"

Kai furrowed his brow. "What? No? I was just trying it on."

"Um, no. Definitely, no. No calling me baby."

"Whatever you say...baby."

Rhys snorted. "I take it back, I'm not covering your shift."

"Okay, okay, not baby." Kai pouted.

Rhys dipped his head and nosed at Kai's ear. "At least not in public," the wolf said softly. Kai went pink to the tips of his ears, grinning to himself.

Tristin wanted to gouge out her eardrums with her plastic spork. What was wrong with these people? There was paranormal craziness happening everywhere, and she was trapped in an endless episode of *The Newlywed Game.*

"Anyway," Tristin said, bringing everybody back to the situation at hand. "Now we're free to go and get your ward"

"I don't even know what I would get," Ember said.

"I know just the thing for you," Tristin promised. "Besides, I have a friend who's working tonight."

"You have a friend?" Kai asked, surprised.

She threw a cherry tomato at his head. "More friends than you."

Tristin glanced at Ember who smiled, looking relieved. Tristin's stomach soured. She was a horrible person. She was going to hell for this for sure. She would risk hell for Quinn.

This had better work.

Chapter 68

EMBER

Ember wasn't sure exactly what she'd been expecting from a magical tattoo parlor, but it certainly wasn't the brightly lit storefront with black and white checkerboard floors and lime green paint. Flash art hung on flip boards on the wall, and elaborately drawn artwork hung lit from above. There were two artists currently working on clients, bent over, their faces masks of concentration. It didn't look magical to her.

"Can I help you?" a voice asked from her left.

Ember looked over to see black Converse and a pair of long legs in black jeans disappearing behind a display case. She looked at Tristin in confusion before edging closer. Behind the counter, an Asian boy around their age stood on his head, using the wall for support, his eyes closed. His shirt was rucked up under his arms, the victim of gravity, revealing a series of intricate tattoos.

"We have an appointment," Ember said, pushing a strand of hair behind her ear.

The boy let his feet hit the ground and hopped, his hazel eyes bright as he swayed. He ran his hand through his black hair and smiled. "Great, who are you seeing?"

"Rune," Tristin said.

The boy's smile faltered. "Sure. He's finishing up with another client."

Tristin stalked over to the chairs lining the front window and yanked out her cell phone, her thumbs flying. Ember hovered near the counter, not sure what to do with herself. The car ride over was filled with awkward silence. She wasn't eager to return to it.

"First magical tattoo?" the boy asked.

"First any kind of tattoo."

"Nervous?"

"Is it that obvious?"

He shrugged. "A little. It'll be okay. Wait, want to see something cool?"

Ember nodded. "Sure."

The boy pulled up his sleeve, revealing a serpent tattoo around his bicep. Ember leaned in to look at the detail. "Wow." He waved his hand, and the snake appeared to move, slithering across his skin and down his arm. The mouth opened, and it hissed. Ember jumped back, her eyes wide, laughing.

"How'd you do that?"

"He's a wizard," Tristin said, without looking up from her phone.

"Like a male witch?"

"No, male witches are called male witches. He's a wizard."

Ember blushed. "Sorry, I don't know the difference."

"A witch works with elements under the blessing of their deity. A wizard manipulates magical energies and bends the laws of science. Think alchemy versus holistic magic," he tried to explain.

"There's just so much I don't know." She groaned. Tristin snorted and reached for a magazine, pointedly pretending to ignore them. Ember gave Tristin a long look. Ember had briefly thought that their cold war had ended when Tristin had volunteered to bring Ember there, but no. She turned her attention back to the cute boy with the pretty eyes.

He grinned at her. "You must be new around here."

His teeth are perfect, she thought. "Very."

He held out his hand. "I'm Aaron Yi."

 403

She took his hand. "Ember."

His eyebrows shot up. "Lonergan?"

"Yes?"

"So, you're what all the fuss is about," he said, scrutinizing her. "Yeah, I get it."

"Shut up," Ember laughed. Tristin looked up and sighed, flipping the pages of her magazine loudly. "Does it hurt?" Ember asked, nodding her head towards the artists.

"Depends on the placement. Some spots hurt more than others."

"Does it hurt more or less because it's...magical?"

He laughed, and she blushed. That was a stupid question. "No. No more, no less."

He leaned forward on his elbows, dipping his head to ask, "Rune was working on your design yesterday, I think. I have to ask, what made you choose that?"

"Oh, I don't think that was me. I only decided to do this today. My cousin picked out the design. She thinks it will keep me safe."

Aaron opened his mouth but never had the chance to speak.

"Ember," Tristin snapped. "We don't need to be telling our business to the magical community." To Aaron, she said, "Mind your own business, Harry Potter."

He held his hands up. Ember gave him a look of apology and flopped herself down, crossing her arms and shooting a look at Tristin.

"Don't pout. You can flirt with him tomorrow. He goes to our school."

Ember's eyes darted to Aaron, hunched over the counter, charcoal pencil in hand, sketching on a small piece of paper, tongue poking from the side of his mouth as he concentrated. He went to their school?

"I've never seen him before."

"He's in the gifted program."

"Our school has a gifted program?" Ember mumbled.

The beaded curtain at the back rattled, and a rail thin middle-aged man emerged with cellophane wrapped around his bicep. He was riddled with tattoos. A large bald Polynesian man lumbered in

 404

next. "You keep that ink clean, Hanley; if that thing gets infected like the last one, don't come crying to me."

The man—Hanley—dug the heel of his hand into one bloodshot eye, making a disgusting noise at the back of his throat. "Yeah, yeah. I hear ya."

As he passed by, he looked at Tristin with interest. He smiled, revealing a set of broken, yellowed teeth. "Hey, beautiful."

"Keep walking, dirt bag," Tristin said without looking.

"Feisty," he said, laughing to himself as he walked out the door.

"I'll be with you girls in a minute, just let me get set up," Rune called from the back.

"Sure," Tristin said, glancing sideways at Ember. Tristin's leg started to jiggle.

"Why are you so nervous?" Ember joked.

Her leg stopped. "What? I'm not. I'm just ready for this to be over so we can go home."

Ember nodded, her eyes falling to the beaded curtain. She chewed on her thumbnail. This might be a bad idea. She wasn't good with needles. She hated medical procedures. She didn't think this necessarily qualified as a medical procedure, more a religious rite. She'd never been good with those either. Of course, if the alternative was cutting out her own tongue or stabbing herself in the eye, what was a little pain?

The curtain moved, sounding like pearls scattering on hardwood. "Come on back, girls."

As she walked by the counter, Aaron snagged her hand. "Here you go, new girl. A present."

He handed her a folded up piece of paper. She held it carefully, assuming it was whatever he'd been working so hard on moments ago. She smiled. "Thanks, you're sweet." She went to move, but he held on, looking at her with such intensity her heart knocked off-beat. He looked...worried.

"You're welcome," he murmured, his gaze shifting to the paper in her fingers and back to her eyes.

She looked at the paper in her hands, not sure what he wanted.

 405

"Ember, let's go." Tristin tugged Ember away. He let go, his gaze falling to the man at the back.

Once they were behind the curtain, Ember's nerves ratcheted up a notch. She wiped her palms on her jeans.

"Where do you want this?" He held up a stencil with a series of complicated lines and circles.

She hadn't thought much of it. "M-my hip, I think."

"Back or front?" he asked, not bothering to look at her.

She looked at her cousin. Tristin's was in the front, but Ember didn't have the amazing abs that her cousin did. "Back, I think."

"Roll over and lift your shirt."

She did as she was asked. He tucked what looked like a paper towel into her jeans and prepared the area, applying the stencil. He poured ink into tiny paper cups and pushed the trigger on the tattoo gun to test it. Ember shuddered. It sounded like a dentist's drill.

"I know you're nervous, darlin', but you gotta calm down. Can't have you shaking while I'm working."

Ember nodded jerkily, folding her hands under her cheek before remembering the paper. She leaned up on her elbows as he rubbed something greasy on her back. She unfolded the paper and smiled as she saw the tiny lifelike rabbit. Her breath caught, smiling as the rabbit began to bounce across the page, darting from one side to the other. She glanced up to see if she could see Aaron through the curtain, but he was gone. She looked back at the picture in time to see her rabbit twist and transform, the lines rearranging themselves to form a single word.

RUN.

Ember didn't question it. She jerked into a sitting position, just as he dipped the needles into the ink. "I'm not doing this. I can't. I want to go home."

She yanked the paper towel from her shirt, wiping the goop off her back. "Thanks for your time, but I'm not ready yet."

Bolting through the curtain and sprinting for the front of the store, she didn't wait for Tristin.

Ember didn't stop until she reached the car; Tristin hot on Ember's heels. "What the hell is wrong with you?"

   406

Ember turned on Tristin. "What's wrong with me?"

Tristin stopped short. "Yeah, what's your problem? You said you wanted protection."

Ember couldn't believe her friend. "You are unbelievable. What's really going on?"

Tristin's eyes skirted away. "I don't know what you're talking about."

"You're lying. Mace is lying. Everybody is lying to me, and I don't know why." Ember felt herself getting hysterical, her magic bubbling to the surface.

"Ember, calm down," Tristin begged. "Please, nobody is lying to you. Just relax, you don't have to get the tattoo if you don't want it. It was a stupid idea. Just forget it."

Ember felt like she was on fire. Sweat trickled along her back, and sparks shot from her fingers. "I'm not doing this anymore. People need to start telling me the truth."

Ember squeezed her eyes shut. She felt like she was going to explode with all this pent up magic and frustration.

"Ember."

"Oh my God," Tristin said, gaping at the corner of the building.

Ember turned at the raw sound of her name. "Mace?"

He hit the ground on his knees, and she ran towards him.

"What happened to you?" She cupped his face in her hands. He was dripping with sweat.

"You did, luv," he rasped and passed out cold.

 407

Chapter 69

MACE

Mace blinked swollen eyelids, colors swimming before his eyes as he tried to focus. His skin burned. He felt like he'd been put through a meat grinder. He let his fingers roam under his shirt, relieved to find that his scars were no longer burning. Ember's magic was far more sadistic than he'd imagined. She hadn't been gone five minutes when the pain started, steadily increasing until his skin felt as if it was blistering under his clothes.

It wasn't like Mace had never experienced pain. He'd been tortured by people who considered themselves experts in such matters. This was different. It was like reliving every injury at once.

He tried to sit up, but the world tilted. He lay back, his stomach lurching. He was hungry, ravenous even. His teeth ached, and his mouth was dry. He felt horrid. He felt...human.

What was she doing to him?

He lay there, curled into himself, only snatching pieces of angry conversations as he fell in and out of consciousness.

"What were you thinking, Trist—" Sounded like Kai.

"What about you? How could you not tell us about Allister?" Rhys, maybe.

"Everybody needs to calm—" Donovan? Mace thought before fading again.

When he came to a second time, it was to Isa's furious voice. This time when he opened his eyes, his vision was clear enough to see the alpha's mutinous expression. "You're all going to tell me what the hell is going on. It seems like every time I come home from work, somebody is unconscious or bleeding. I'm done with the lying. I'm not sure why you people have all decided I'm stupid—"

"That's not—" Kai tried.

"Shut up," Isa shouted. "The next person who says so much as one word without my permission is going to get their asses kicked. Are we clear?" Heads bobbed with enthusiasm. "Good. Sit down."

He blinked as Isa's shadow loomed above him. His eyes fought to focus on her. "How about you? You ready to start talking? You look like crap."

"Thanks," Mace said, dragging himself to a seated position on the sofa.

"What happened to you, anyway?"

Maces eyes darted to Kai whose gaze slid away. Guess that was his way of saying he wasn't getting involved.

"I have no idea, really. Maybe it was Allister making a show for power?"

"You said it was Ember's fault," Tristin supplied, an ever present scowl etched on her face. He flexed his jaw. He really disliked her. He knew she was going to be a problem the minute she hit him with that shovel.

He looked at Ember warily. "Only in the sense that my life hasn't been the same since we met, luv. I was out of it."

Isa stared him down, and Ember looked suspicious, but he expected nothing less. He'd said he couldn't be trusted and proved himself right again and again. He'd proved it once more. There was a tinge that felt suspiciously like regret. He couldn't wait to sever the connection so he could stop all these feelings.

Wolves and reapers dotted the living room. The little faery was the only one to escape the wrath of Isa, as usual. Neoma sat in the corner of the room, a hundred and fifty pounds of dog in her tiny lap, oblivious to the tension. What was her story?

Wren was the only one to remain standing along with the alpha, his arms crossed and looking like a disappointed father. Ember sat at the opposite end of the couch, near Mace but not near enough to touch. It was a pity. Perhaps her magic would quell the shaking. He felt strung out.

"Now," Isa said, standing in the middle of the group. "Which of you wants to start?"

Eyes darted away from her. "Volunteer or I'll pick somebody."

Kai caved first, singing like a canary. He spoke of Ms. Josephine and what they'd really learned about Ember, including the part she played in the deaths twelve years ago. The alpha and her mate took the news well. Kai told, again, the legend Tate described about the history of the town attempting to summon the Morrigan, and how it changed the course of magic as they knew it. This was news to Donovan who wasn't there in the days following Quinn's death.

The reaper clearly took the alpha at her word because he divulged everything, including hiding a book in the woods just outside of town. Isa growled low in her chest at that.

Ember stuttered out what she'd learned about her childhood from her uncle and how she and Tristin had found the spell her father used to bind Ember's magic. She told Isa about her run in with Stella, and then, her voice shaking, she talked about inadvertently summoning Quinn's spirit.

That got Mace's attention. How much had Quinn had divulged in his time on this plane.

"I don't even know how I did it," Ember told Tristin, who looked as if she'd been slapped in the face. "I was just drawing him, and he was there."

"Drawing? Ember you can't—" Wren started, only to be cut off by Tristin.

"W-what?" Tristin stumbled forward. "How could you not say anything? What's wrong with you? What did he want? What did he say?"

Ember swallowed hard. "I didn't tell you because he asked me not too. He didn't want you to have to go through it again. Any of you."

"Is that all?" Wren asked.

Mace sat up straighter. He was also interested in what Quinn had to say. Ember's gaze found Mace's before sliding to Kai, her tone accusatory. "No. He said I couldn't trust Mace or Allister and seemed surprised I didn't already know this since Kai did."

All eyes swung to Mace and then Kai. Isa stalked into Kai's space. "Now, why would Quinn think you had some knowledge of Mace and Allister?"

Kai sucked in a breath and said, "Because Quinn overheard Mace and Shelby talking about how Mace worked for Allister."

The room erupted. "You work for Allister?" Wren said just as Donovan asked, "Who's Shelby?"

"Ember, I'm sorry—" Kai started, but Ember just shook her head.

There was murmuring and side conversations until Isa hollered, "Enough."

"You. Talk," she growled at Mace.

"What would you like to know?"

Isa flexed her jaw, and Mace had to admit watching her partially shift was fascinating. Her teeth elongating, eyes glowing, and claws extended as she advanced on him. "I'm done playing with you, Soul Eater. Talk, now."

"I worked for Allister. Past tense. I have since terminated our arrangement."

"What did you do for Allister? He sent you to Ember? What is he after?"

"Ember's powers."

Isa's brow furrowed. "What does that mean?"

"Allister thinks Ember's magic is too dangerous, and he is hell-bent on unburdening her of said magic, good humanitarian that he is."

"Why would Allister want the powers of a reanimator? How would he even go about that? He's not a reaper. Even if he wanted her skills, he couldn't take them."

"He could with the blade of Osiris."

"What the hell is that?" Wren asked.

"A transference device," Kai mumbled.

Isa spun on the boy. "You knew about this too?"

Rhys was staring, his expression dark.

"I just learned about it. Besides, Mace isn't telling you everything. He's not telling you why Allister really wants her powers. Allister doesn't think she's a reanimator."

"What does he think she is?" Donovan asked.

"A necromancer," Kai murmured.

They all looked at Ember, who took a step back. "A what?"

"Necromancer," Mace said. "Allister thinks you're a necromancer."

"What exactly is that?" Ember asked warily.

"A fairy tale," Wren muttered.

"No," Neoma said from her seat on the floor. "They used to exist. They just don't anymore. Or, they didn't until Ember."

"What does that mean? What's a necromancer?" Ember said again, a tinge of hysteria creeping in.

"The most powerful creature ever to walk the planet," Mace said, "Necromancers have abilities that rival the gods'. They have complete and total control over the soul. They can control the soulless, restore a soul, and resurrect the dead."

"Is it true?" Isa asked, staring him down. It made sense but there was no way he could be sure.

"I hope not because if Ember is a necromancer and word gets out, she's going to have a target the size of Mars on her back. There will be no creature living or dead who won't want to kill her or control her."

He heard Ember's shaky gasp, and he could feel the heavy weight of her betrayed look but couldn't bring himself to meet her eyes. Isa snatched him from the couch with one hand, claws digging into the back of his neck. "I extended my hospitality to you. We took you in, and you've been plotting against one of my pack this whole time?"

"I didn't intend to hurt her. I didn't know about the knife. He wanted her power. That's it. I didn't know he planned to kill her. Honest. As soon as I knew, I quit and hid the blade." He kept his voice calm, resigned to his fate. He couldn't die, but that didn't mean she couldn't make him long for death.

"Right, because you felt guilty? Soul eaters being known for their conscience and their strong emotional bonds," Rhys huffed. "Sure, that seems believable."

"I had a vested interest in Ember staying alive."

"Meaning?" Ember asked bitterly.

"If she was dead, she was useless to me," Mace said, deliberately vague.

"What were you getting out of this?" Ember demanded, her voice unsteady.

"Ember…" he started.

"What! What was in it for you?" She yelled, with a choked-off sob.

Kai moved to comfort her, but she put her hand up. "Don't you touch me."

To Mace, she said, "What did he promise you? Just what exactly was it you thought powerless me would be doing for you?"

Mace could tell by the look on her face she was taking her thoughts to a far different place. He didn't know which answer would provide more comfort. He could tell her the truth. He could tell her he hadn't known what he was doing since the moment he laid eyes on her. Instead, he said, "What do you think I wanted? I wanted your soul, luv. It's who I am."

Her face fell, tears brimming until she blinked them away. "Don't you dare call me that." With fierce eyes, she turned on Tristin then. "Did you know?"

Tristin thrust her chin forward. "About him working for Allister? I only found out the day Astrid came by."

"Wow. You really do hate me. What did I ever do to you?" Ember said, looking shell-shocked before asking, "Why did Aaron tell me to run?"

Tristin's eyes went wide, and she sneered. "Is that why you bolted? Ugh, that little weasel. This is why nobody likes him."

 413

Isa shoved Mace back onto the sofa, turning to the girls. He wiped at the blood seeping sluggishly where her claws had pierced his flesh.

"Answer her, Tristin," Isa growled. "Why should a simple warding tattoo illicit a warning?" To Ember, Isa said, "What did you choose for your sigil, Ember?"

"Tristin picked it. This." Ember lifted her shirt, showing Isa the stencil.

Isa's eyes flashed red, and she lunged for Tristin. "What were you thinking? What were you doing?"

"What is it?" Kai asked, moving forward.

When Ember spun to show him, Mace's eyes widened. "Osiris. Again."

"What? Why?" Kai was looking at his sister. "Tristin what the hell. Are you working for Allister too? You were going to put that on Ember permanently? Why would you open that...link?"

Ember panicked. "Is this bad? Is it bad?" She started frantically scrubbing at the stencil, erasing it from her skin with her shirt. "What does it mean?"

"You tell us everything, Tristin. Now."

Tristin burrowed deeper into the armchair. "We were going to bring him back."

"Who? Bring who—oh, Tristin," Isa said, desolate. "You didn't think you could bring Quinn back, did you?"

"She's a necromancer. It's what they do." Tristin's face burned red, and a single fat tear fell from her eye. "She brought back that stupid dog. She brought back a bird and now that demonic cat. Why not him?" Her voice cracked as she pulled her knees into her chest. She looked at Ember accusingly. "Why not him? How is it fair you get to see him and I don't?"

Ember looked at her, hands spasming uselessly at her sides. "If I could do that, if I could bring him back, I would. I don't know how."

Tristin looked at Isa imploringly. "Astrid says the spell will work. She says because of what Ember is, the spell will work. She's sure of it."

Isa looked sick. "Astrid put you up to this? Is Allister a part of this too?"

 414

Tristin shook her head. "I don't think so. She said it was just us. I didn't even know about Stella's plan for Ember. Astrid just told me when prompted to make sure Ember ended up at the tattoo parlor."

"But why?" Ember asked.

"The spell calls for a branded witch," she muttered.

There was stunned silence. Mace didn't know if they were shocked at the lengths to which Tristin would go to bring back the boy or if they were contemplating the consequences of Ember having the tattoo. It didn't pay to bind yourself to a god, especially the god of the underworld.

"Anything else?" Isa asked, making eye contact with every person in the room. "Does anybody else have anything they wish to confess? Because after this, the next person to keep anything from me is on their own. You can only push me so far. I cannot protect my pack if I don't know what we are fighting. Speak now, or forever hold your peace."

"What about you?" Tristin asked quietly, tears streaming freely.

Isa turned on Tristin. "What?"

"What about you, Isa?" Tristin repeated. "Do you have anything you want to tell us?"

Isa stared, her arms crossed and head tilted. "Clearly you have something to say, Tristin. Now is the time to speak."

"I overheard you talking to Allister. You said, 'They don't know they're prisoners.' Who are they, Isa?"

Isa's gold eyes bled red again, jaw tense. "There are things I can't tell you. You need to trust that I know what's best for you and the pack."

"You said you worked for the Grove," Tristin whispered the words like saying them aloud would somehow invoke the druids.

Everybody stared at the alpha, except Wren who kept his eyes lowered. "You're taking that out of context."

"But you sent Kai and Rhys to deliver a message to the witch in the swamp. You must know something. Sending them went against Allister's orders. You clearly don't trust him. Did the Grove tell you to send a message to the witch?"

Kai was staring at Rhys, who didn't seem surprised to learn of his sister's association with the Grove. In fact, Rhys looked guilty. Kai

415

seemed to think so as well. Kai looked at Isa. "Is this true? Do you work for the Grove? Do you work for the people that killed my best friend? Do you?"

Isa snarled. "I don't answer to you. I'm the alpha. I make decisions for the good of the pack."

Ember got to her feet, tears in her eyes. "You're all liars. Every single one of you. You said you were my family, but you are all just looking out for yourself. Every one of you is just using me for your own selfish reasons. You work for Allister, too? The Grove? The people who killed Quinn?" Ember shook her head, as if embarrassed to have believed they could ever really care for her. "I'm leaving tonight. I'm better off on my own."

"I'll go with you, luv," Mace said, trying to keep his voice even. Without Ember, he was done for. He couldn't let her leave him again. "I can help you control your magic, and you need protection."

Ember scoffed at him. "You're a liar too. I'll be fine on my own."

Isa's eyes shifted back to green as she put a gentle hand on Ember's shoulder. "I can't let you do that, Ember. I'm sorry."

Ember threw her shoulders back, squaring off against the older wolf, all bravado. "You can't keep me here."

Isa looked hard at Wren, and he nodded his head, resigned.

"I can, Ember. In fact, I have to." She turned to Tristin. "You want to know who I was referring to when I said they don't know they're prisoners?" She gestured at the reapers. "You. You are the prisoners I was talking about."

"P-prisoners?" Tristin asked. "How are we prisoners?"

Isa looked away, like she was trying to figure out what she could explain. It was Rhys who spoke. "Don't think of it as being prisoners. Think of it as you being under the Grove's protection."

"You knew about this?" Kai asked.

At Kai's betrayed expression, Rhys mumbled, "It's not as if we had a choice either."

With tears forming, Kai jutted his jaw forward, looking at Rhys like he'd sprouted horns. "Like Quinn? Was he under your protection? You knew about this? We leave without permission one time and Allister has us branded prisoners? We only went to New Orleans."

Isa sat hard in Ember's vacated chair and scrubbed her hand across her face. "You've been prisoners of the Grove since you were five years old. The Grove needed to keep a close eye on you."

The pack stared at Isa, shocked. She shrugged at them, palms up. "You have to understand, I was barely sixteen years old. Allister came to me and showed me a piece of paper signed by my parents saying they'd signed a treaty with the Grove years ago, and that, as the new alpha, I was to honor the agreement or face imprisonment myself. He said they'd take Rhys from me. They said I was to keep you safe. They said keep you close, but you were never to leave and never to know. They said you were safest here in town, but they never said why."

Kai and Tristin just stared, but Isa continued. "I didn't have a choice. By the time I was old enough to even consider why you were so valuable to the Grove, it didn't matter. I love you guys, you are pack, and you are my family. If I had refused, they would've taken you with them. What do you think they would've done to you then? What kind of upbringing would you have had with them?"

Everybody was silent for a long while before Ember said, "This is insane. You can't keep me here against my will."

Isa made a frustrated noise, her gaze hardened when she looked up again. "I can, and I will. I'm doing what I think is right." Mace had to admire the way the tiny alpha commanded the room even dwarfed in the oversize chair like some child queen.

"Now we can do this two ways. One, everybody continues to get along with a few added security measures so nobody has to be... uncomfortable. Two, we do this the hard way where I show you what it really means to be prisoners. So, show of hands, who's up for option one?"

All hands shot up, Mace's included. He had to hand it to the alpha; she knew how to get what she wanted. However, by the look on her face, she was realizing being a good leader sometimes meant being unpopular.

"Anybody else have something to say? No, Good," she said without waiting for an answer. "Now this is what happens next. Everybody is on lockdown. Curfew is at sundown. If you aren't home, you are at work or at school. Nobody goes anywhere alone, especially Ember."

"What about Quinn's f-funeral?" Tristin asked, stumbling over the word.

"That's still on...for now. You," she pointed at Mace. "What did you do with that blade?"

Mace shook his head. "I'm not telling you that. It's safer for everyone if I'm the only one who knows."

"That's not an option." She was still partially shifted, flexing her claws. "Tell me or leave."

Even though Mace had made it through this fiasco without revealing his predicament, leaving would indeed be a fate worse than death. He couldn't think of anything worse except maybe the way Ember was looking at him right then.

Finally, he pretended to cave, trying to look like it physically pained him to do so. "Behind the property in the old pet cemetery, in the mutt's grave."

Isa's eyes widened, shocked, he was sure, that he gave in without a fight. Isa would keep it safe. Allister would never expect Mace to give it to the wolf, so Allister wouldn't think to go looking there.

"Let's take a walk." She hauled him up by one arm. "Let's all take a walk."

They trekked the property in a line, Isa and Mace leading the group. Wren followed along the back like an infantry soldier guarding prisoners of war or a preschool teacher chaperoning errant toddlers. It took Donovan and Rhys shoveling furiously for fifteen minutes before they reached the package. Isa moved forward, looking into the box.

She pulled a piece of paper from the box, reading it before turning on Mace, already partially shifted. "Is this some kind of game to you?"

She thrust the piece of paper at him, and he unfolded it, dread making him sluggish.

"You lose," He read aloud. He crumpled the paper and tossed it into the darkness.

The wolves shifted, alert, scanning the perimeter for danger. Tristin and Kai flanked Ember.

Rage coursed through Mace. He growled, bringing his foot down on the empty container, gaining no satisfaction as the wood

 418

splintered beneath his heel. He would tear Allister apart, slowly. Mace would make the man sorry he ever uttered Ember's name.

He continued his destruction until nothing but splinters remained. He stood, examining his handiwork, panting. Ember didn't even look fearful. She looked numb. Maybe it was a trick of the light, but he could swear there was the slightest hint of a smile playing at her lips. What was happening to her?

Allister had the blade. Allister was mocking Mace. Allister was coming for Ember.

Was there enough of the real Ember left in there to care?

Chapter 70

KAI

Kai found Ember in the courtyard, sitting alone with Romero at her feet. She didn't look up when he approached. He was grateful, as he didn't know yet what he would say. How could he explain his actions? If it had just been him, maybe she'd get past it, but they'd all lied to her from the beginning.

"Can I sit down?"

She shrugged. He figured it was as good as he was going to get.

He took the seat to her left, trying to give her a little space, fighting his instinct to touch. He'd been pack for too long. Except he hadn't, not really. He wasn't pack at all. They'd lied to him too. It made what he did to Ember worse somehow. "Please don't hate me. I know you won't believe me, but I was trying to protect you."

Her lip curled at that, disbelief etched across her face.

"I know you think I'm a dick. But I swear, I thought if I could watch him, keep a close eye…he could help you, and you'd still be safe because you were surrounded by the pack."

He could see the tears in her eyes. He risked moving closer, sitting on the table in front of her and forcing her to meet his gaze.

"Ember, please. You're my family. I would never intentionally hurt you. I was freaked out over Quinn's being…you know, and I thought if you lost Mace you might self-destruct for real this time. I couldn't lose you too. We just got you back."

She was crying now.

"Please don't cry. I know this sounds insane, but I don't think Mace wants to hurt you. I think he might even love you a little."

"That's impossible. He has no soul," she muttered.

He smiled a little. "Well, since you've arrived, we've all had to reevaluate our idea of impossible. If there is any way he could love you, he does. Ember, I know you think we're all selfish jerks out for ourselves, and maybe Tristin was being selfish, but it was for the best possible reason. She's grieving. She's heartbroken. We all are. I'm not asking you to excuse our behavior, but please don't think we don't care about you."

She nodded once but didn't verbalize her acceptance. Kai threw his arms around her. "I love you, cuz."

She nodded, her face smooshed against his shoulder as she said. "I'm not ready to forgive your sister."

He nodded. "I don't speak for her. She'll have to make her own apologies. I'll leave you alone."

He trudged upstairs, feeling a bit better but not really. He wasn't ready to deal with Rhys. Kai had no idea what he would say. He felt like somebody had drilled a hole in his stomach.

When he pushed open his door, Rhys was sitting on the bed. Kai scoffed, pulling off his plaid shirt and yanking open his dresser drawer; it was really too early for bed, but he didn't know what else to do. He rifled around, looking for sweatpants and a t-shirt. He watched Rhys watch in the glass of the mirror. "I don't know what you think is happening here, buddy, but whatever it is, you're so wrong," Kai assured him.

"Are you even going to try to let me explain?" Rhys asked, dropping his gaze and staring at his hands as if they were to blame for this mess.

"Explain what? How you and your sister have lied to me pretty much my whole life? How you've been kissing me and making out with me"–Kai dropped his voice—"and doing what you did in the

 421

truck with me…" His face burned as images flashed in his mind. "And this whole time I was a prisoner? This whole time you worked for the Grove. Even after what they did to Quinn, you still said nothing. You stood there and watched and said nothing."

Rhys's reflection swallowed hard, his jaw popping. "It's not that easy."

Kai snorted. "It's not that difficult. Not if you'd trusted me. Not if you really cared about me."

"You've never lied to protect somebody you cared for?" Rhys asked, arching a brow. Kai knew the wolf was talking about Ember, but it wasn't the same thing. Kai had lied to Ember for a couple of days to keep her magic from boiling over and killing them all. Rhys had lied to Kai for years. What if Tristin had never overheard Isa? What if he'd never found out?

"Would you have just lied forever? Was there an end to this prison sentence, or was I doing life? Would I still be oblivious if Ember had never arrived?"

Rhys growled, standing. "You're being crazy. It wasn't like that at all. You weren't prisoners to us. We never treated you like prisoners. I have never done anything with you that I wouldn't have done either way. Have you ever even asked to go anywhere outside this town?"

"That's beside the point. What if I had? Would Isa have found an excuse for you to follow me like usual?"

Rhys stepped closer; Kai still couldn't look at Rhys. Strong arms wrapped around Kai's waist, pressing his face against the wolf's throat. "Isa made excuses for me to follow you because she knows how I feel about you. How I've always felt about you."

Kai stiffened in Rhys's embrace. No, he didn't get to get out of this with cuddling and a convenient declaration of affection. Kai wiggled out of Rhys's arms. He let Kai go. "No. I'm not doing this. Not now…maybe not ever. I should be able to trust my pack. I should be able to trust you. I don't know who you are. I'll play my part for the visiting packs, but after that we're done."

Rhys met his gaze in the mirror, gutted. "What?"

Kai blinked rapidly, his eyes burning. "You heard me. I don't want to be with somebody I can't trust, and I can't trust you. I don't know why I ever thought I could."

Rhys stood statue still for a long minute, a myriad of expressions passing over his face too quickly to catalog. He gave one stilted nod, turning on his heel and leaving. Kai waited until he was sure the wolf was gone. Then, Kai changed his clothes and curled up on the mattress, burying his face in his pillow.

He missed his friend.

 423

Chapter 71

EMBER

Ember sat there long after Kai left. She didn't know why she'd felt his betrayal the most. Maybe because Tristin hated Ember, so using her to get Quinn back made sense in a twisted logic kind of way. She didn't feel the sting of Isa's betrayal like the others because Ember believed the alpha had the best of intentions.

"Can we talk?"

Ember's eyes flicked dully to Mace. He lounged against the side of the house. He tried to look indifferent, but his shoulders were just a little too stiff. She supposed if she let herself feel it, Mace's betrayal would have hurt the most. If she chose to feel it. Which she didn't.

Maybe it was her magic attempting to keep its anchor. Maybe it was her amazing denial skills. She didn't know. She didn't care. When she looked at him she just wanted. She wanted his magic, his kiss, his body, his scent. She just wanted him for however long she could have him. She could deal with the pain when she was more herself.

"What is there to talk about?"

"You have to know…when this whole thing started, I didn't know his plan. I really was hired just to watch you. I didn't know his plan to take your power, and I certainly wanted nothing to do with killing you."

"No, you just wanted my soul," she said, standing and moving towards him.

"It's not like that, not really."

She didn't want to hear his excuses. She didn't care anymore. Everybody lied. Every one of them wanted something from her. She would bide her time, play the good girl, and when she could, she'd run.

She dragged her hands along his chest, feeling the scar tissue beneath his t-shirt. She let her nails dig in just enough for him to grimace. She nosed her way along his jaw to his ear. "Hungry?" she whispered.

She took the way his breath hitched as a yes.

"Me too," she said, catching his bottom lip between her teeth.

"I told you we can't do that again." He pressed the words against her open mouth, his hands sliding into her hair. She dragged her tongue across his lower lip. "Are you sure?" she taunted, her hands sliding around his back, dipping below his shirt. He flinched as her fingers traced the layers of scars.

He flipped Ember so she was pressed against the side of the house. "You are playing a treacherous game, luv," he murmured.

She worried at his lip with her teeth before soothing it with her tongue. "I thought you liked danger? I have to say, you aren't really living up to your bad boy reputation." Her gaze met his, and his eyes flashed silver. His hands were at her thighs, lifting her, giving her no choice but to wrap her legs around him. This time he kissed her how she wanted to be kissed, hard and punishing, with no empty platitudes about sorry. He walked them backwards, setting her on the railing. She didn't unwind her legs, just pulled him closer, her magic snaking around them both, offering herself to him in every way.

He gasped into her mouth as he realized she was the one who'd opened the connection for him to feed. She smiled. He pressed against her harder, practically crawling inside her. He couldn't get enough.

She shivered as he fed. His hands were everywhere. His lips everywhere. She liked this feeling of control. The big, bad soul eater

 425

helpless to resist what she offered; what only she could offer. She could do this forever.

She could hear herself making whiny, needy little sounds, but she didn't care. His hips were pressing into her in the best possible way, and the sensations seemed to reverberate through her in a way she didn't think she'd ever be able to describe.

Her magic severed the connection when it decided he'd had enough. He pulled back, stumbling, slack jawed and intoxicated, his eyes glassy. "Yeah, you love that, don't you?" she purred at him. "Just because we are stuck with each other doesn't mean we can't both get something out of it. You don't even have to lie to me anymore."

"Ember," he slurred. "That's not—"

"Shh, be good and you can have some more," she promised.

His lips found hers, and she tried to ignore the way her power gloated. She could keep him if she wanted to, soul drunk and so very pliant. She could. She mentally shook the thought away. She couldn't get cocky. Her magic was only happy when Mace was near. She couldn't lose sight of what they were doing there. She needed him, if only for a bit longer.

Chapter 72

TRISTIN

Tristin lay curled against her pillows, Quinn's black frames on her face and his hat scrunched in her hand. It hurt more this time. She couldn't say why. The first time it had felt like somebody sawed her open while she was still awake, a pain so acute she knew it couldn't last forever. This time, it was like she'd lost a limb but could still feel the pain of it, this phantom empty agony with no hope of ever resolving.

She pressed the hat to her nose, tears soaking through the knit cap. His scent faded more every day. Ember had gotten to see him. She'd gotten to say goodbye face to face. Tristin felt like if she could just see him, touch him one more time, maybe she could see her way around it. Like maybe she could honor his request to move on.

But the idea made her sick in her soul. She didn't want to live her life without him in it. She didn't want to get married and have kids if he wasn't there in some way. Even if he'd come to his senses about her and met the real girl of his dreams. One capable of talking about her feelings and taking care of him like he'd deserved. Even if he'd met that girl, Tristin could have resigned herself to the work of living as long as Quinn was just…there.

But he wasn't. He never would be.

She jumped as something tapped against her window. She gaped at the shadow perched just outside on the roof. She stared until Astrid gestured to open the window, a scowl fixed in place.

Tristin hopped to her feet, rushing to let the girl in. "What the hell are you doing here? Isa and the pack know everything, if they catch you here…"

Astrid laughed. "What? If they catch me, what are they going to do?"

"Tell your father? Unless he already knows."

"Are you kidding? Don't be stupid. Of course not."

"How did you get up here anyway?"

"Easy, I cloaked myself from the wolves and climbed right on up. Speaking of climbing, did you know your cousin is outside climbing your soul eater like a tree? Looks like he's enjoying every minute of it too."

Tristin winced. That was a mental picture she didn't need. She could not understand her cousin's fascination with Mace. He was evil. He lied at every turn. He tried to kill her. Ember was pathetic.

"So, did you get her to the tattoo place?"

Tristin nodded. "I got her there, but she spooked and ran."

Astrid's face flushed red. "What?"

Tristin met Astrid's gaze. Tristin's tongue stuck to the roof of her mouth as she said, "She didn't get the tattoo. The plan is off. We can't bring him back."

Astrid shoved Tristin hard enough to knock her into the mattress. She sat down before she fell, looking at the witch with wide eyes. "What is wrong with you?"

Astrid gaped at Tristin. "What's wrong with me? What's wrong with you? You claim you love my brother, but you give up so easily."

"I did—I do love him, but what you want can't be done. Death magic won't work."

"You're pathetic. I don't need you for this. I'll figure out another way, and when I get my brother back I'll make sure he knows how you lost your nerve. I thought you were the fighter."

"You're crazy, Astrid. There's nothing left to do, just let him go."

"No. I won't be stuck alone in this place. I can't be in this family without him. I'll figure out a way to get him back. I swear it."

Tristin just stared helplessly as Astrid left the way she came.

When Tristin felt like she was truly alone she finally gave in and just let herself be miserable. She carefully placed his glasses on the table and spread his hat across her pillow. This time when the tears came, she didn't try to stop them.

She didn't even know if she could.

Chapter 73

KAI

The morning of the bonfire, Kai woke panicked, wrenched from a nightmare where he lay trapped beneath a steel beam in a burning house. He woke up sweaty, weighed down by two hundred plus pounds of overheated werewolf. Rhys snored, tightening his grip when Kai made a halfhearted attempt to push the wolf off.

Kai hadn't wavered since their conversation, but Isa said it was essential the other packs believed Kai and Rhys were together. If the packs thought there was any dissention among their ranks, they would be a target for a bigger pack to try and take over. Belle Haven was prime territory, and Kai knew why. Who wouldn't want access to all the extra magical juice pumping from the ground? Isa insisted the only way the others would believe they were still a couple was by scent.

Isa had suggested the two cohabitate for the night, which showed just how desperate the alpha was. Kai couldn't think of a time when Isa would ever have agreed to her brother and Kai sharing a bed. He knew he had to play the part; he just wished it wasn't so painful. He pressed his nose against Rhys's shoulder, inhaling deeply. Kai could just go back to sleep. Sleep was his friend. He lived for those tiny moments in between sleep and waking where he forgot, for just a while, how much it all sucked.

He shoved at the wolf one last time. Rhys grumbled, burying his face deeper against Kai's neck. Goosebumps broke out along his skin. Even sleeping, Rhys knew how to make Kai squirm. He just wanted a few more minutes to pretend, but it was a terrible idea. He wiggled, trying to dislodge Rhys but only succeeded in letting him settle in more fully. Kai clenched his eyes shut and tried to think about baseball or that sound the wolves made when they shifted, anything to keep himself from taking advantage of the way his hips were flush against Rhys's.

Rhys's body tensed above Kai, suddenly fully awake. He waited, knowing his own bounding pulse gave him away. Rhys slid his hand over the bare skin of Kai's arm, threading their fingers together. Rhys moved his hips in a way that had Kai's vision going white at the edges. Kai opened his mouth to protest, but Rhys ran his tongue along the space where Kai's neck met his shoulder, and all that came out was an undignified moan.

This was exactly how things had gone too far in the truck. Oh, God, thinking about what they'd done in the Suburban was doing exactly the opposite of calming his hormones. Rhys growled at the scent of Kai's obvious arousal, pressing his pelvis against Kai's to show interest in the proceedings. Kai gasped. It would be so easy to let things go there again, just one more time.

Rhys's mouth found Kai's and his lips parted instinctively, letting Rhys in. Kai couldn't think with Rhys and his touching, kissing. Kai pressed himself closer, rubbing himself against the wolf's sweatpants-clad thigh.

It took Kai too long to realize Rhys was speaking, muttering, "I miss you. I miss this. This is stupid."

It was like cold water in the face. Kai's feelings weren't stupid. Rhys had lied, and he still didn't get it. Kai turned his head away, shoving against Rhys. "Get up. We aren't doing this. I think we stink enough of each other for people to believe we're still together."

Rhys pulled back, sitting on his knees. "Why are you being so stubborn about this? About us? You forgave Isa. Why not me?"

   431

Kai pressed his lips together. "It's different with you. For years, I've followed you around like an idiot. I confessed my undying love to you, and you just stood there, letting me, and it never once occurred to you to say anything about my sister and me being your prisoners?"

"You aren't my prisoners," Rhys muttered, looking put out.

Kai could feel his face turning red. "I can overlook the fact you can't express your feelings. I can overlook this Neanderthal instinct to mark me as your property. I can even overlook how you jump to defend me even when you know I'm fully capable of defending myself." Kai took a breath to calm himself. "But I can't overlook you lying to me, especially when you make it look so easy. You'll constantly have the advantage of knowing everything I feel for you. You can smell when I want you; you can hear when I'm lying. The only thing I have is what you give me. If you won't talk to me about your feelings, I have to guess. If you tell me something, I have to just trust that you wouldn't lie. If we're together, there can't be any lies between us. You just proved you have no problem lying to me, especially if you think it's for my own good. You would've lied to me forever."

"That's not true," Rhys said, but the color rising in his cheeks gave him away.

"Are you sure?"

Rhys looked away, frustration etched across his face.

"That's what I thought. I'm going to go shower. Don't be here when I come back."

He didn't look behind him as he grabbed his clothes and left.

In the shower, he leaned his head against the tiles, letting the water cascade over him, not really even trying to wash.

The house had become their prison. Nobody went anywhere alone. Tristin was spiraling since there was no hope of getting Quinn back. She rarely got out of bed. She wouldn't eat. She barely spoke. She hadn't been to school since everybody made their confessions. Kai didn't know if she was avoiding Astrid, or if the reality of knowing Quinn wouldn't be there was more than she could take. Losing the chance to bring Quinn back broke her in a way he hadn't seen when it first happened.

   432

He was worried...and not just about Tristin.

Ember seemed to have lost her mind. She barely spoke to anybody except Mace. You would think finding out Mace hand delivered a weapon designed to kill her would make her hate him, instead it seemed to only drive her further into his arms. She was even still feeding him, a thought that skeeved Kai out to no end. Kai kept apologizing to Ember, and each time she smiled and said it was fine, but it wasn't. Something was wrong. He could feel it.

He was hardly one to judge, he supposed. Every day he missed Quinn more, not less. Quinn always knew what to do. He could tell Kai how to fix things with Ember and whether he should forgive Rhys. Quinn would rationalize why Isa wasn't really trying to hurt Kai and make everything seem okay. He wished he'd never known of his sister's plan because then he wouldn't constantly wonder... what if. What if Ember had been able to bring Quinn back? What if it could've worked and they'd stopped it?

Kai swiped at his eyes, feeling like an idiot, crying in the shower. He turned off the water and toweled off quickly, throwing on his clothes. It was a school day, but it was closed for the Thanksgiving holiday. Nobody even thought to celebrate the holiday. Instead, Isa had closed the diner and focused on Quinn's funeral.

Even if they'd had school, it wasn't unusual for the wolves to skip it the night of the full moon. Full moons for the wolves meant heightened senses, increased aggression, and for the bitten wolves like Donovan, the inability to control his shift. Donovan usually did okay when he ran with the pack, but Isa worried about him being around so many other shifters, given his past.

That night, the town would be crawling with shifters from packs all over the state. Seven packs confirmed they were sending members to pay their respects. Quinn would be thrilled to be remembered as pack, but it added an unknown threat level to their already contentious situation. It made everybody nervous, Kai could tell. Not that they'd ever admit it.

Downstairs, everybody congregated in the kitchen. There was food everywhere. The restaurant closed every full moon, a novelty that even the non-in-the-supernatural-know customers found amusing; an idiosyncratic quirk of the Howl at the Moon Café.

 433

Isa was already on a tear. "Everybody listen up. Today is going to be insane, so you have one option and one option only. You help. If you don't pick a job, I'll assign you one. So, everybody start calling 'em out."

"Firewood," Rhys barked. "I need to hack something to pieces."

Kai rolled his eyes but said nothing.

"Food," Donovan called, flipping the knife in his hand, already prepping trays.

"I'll do whatever you want me to do," Ember said with a shrug.

"You'll stay with Mace, and Mace will help Rhys with the bonfire," Isa said. "Wren's already at the site getting everything ready for the grill. Nobody goes anywhere alone, and nobody loses eyes on Ember." Ember flushed. "Are we clear?"

"Crystal," Mace said, walking in and snagging a tomato from the platter. Donovan slapped Mace's hand with the flat edge of the blade. He glowered, popping the tomato in his mouth and chewing loudly. Donovan flashed his eyes, growling.

"Enough," Isa sighed. "Tristin, you'll stay here with me. I'm going to need some help getting the house ready."

Tristin looked wrecked. Her eyes were bloodshot, her hair greasy beneath Quinn's hat. She even wore his glasses. Isa didn't need Tristin, Kai knew; she just needed to keep an eye on her. She looked docile enough, but given her state, she was more unpredictable than the wolves lately. And tonight, they couldn't handle any more unpredictability. All of their lives might depend on it.

Chapter 74

EMBER

Ember sat next to Wren, watching as the others built the bonfire and dragged wood for seating. She hated this. They'd turned her into some helpless maiden, sitting idly by while others protected her. She didn't understand it. She had more power than any of them. If they would just let her try her magic out, she could take care of herself just fine. Feeding Mace was really helping her. When he fed, their magic hummed, making her feel more in control than she ever had before.

They just didn't get it.

It wasn't like she didn't recognize Mace was a problem. She hated herself for not being stronger, but she needed him. He kept her from coming undone. He kept her from hurting anybody. She didn't have to keep feeding him for that. She certainly didn't have to keep making out with him, but she was weak. She wanted him there. She wanted his arms around her. She just wanted…him, and she hated herself for it. She'd become the movie cliché she swore she'd never allow herself to be.

Isa still had no idea what to do about Allister. He had the weapon. He could come for Ember any time. Mace's suggestion of tying Allister to a chair and slitting his throat was met with a hearty level of acceptance, but Isa vetoed it. She said their best bet was to wait and be ready to fight, and confronting Allister could be seen as an act of war against the Grove. The pack didn't want to draw their ire for a second time.

"We'll figure something out, kid," Wren said.

Ember looked up startled. "What?"

"Full moon," he said pointing up at the sky as if it were already visible. "I can smell the frustration on you from here."

"I can't live like this forever, you know?"

"Well, you won't live at all if Allister gets hold of you." He dropped the top on the grill, or smoker, whatever it was. "I'll be right back."

He glanced over to where the others were working, ensuring she was still within their line of sight. She set her jaw, flexing her fingers as a strange feeling settled in her chest. It wasn't her magic, or if it was, it had never felt like this before.

Anger flared in her gut, a raw burning agitation like an itch she couldn't scratch. Her magic didn't like this feeling. She could feel it unfurl as her tension grew, making her stretch her muscles. She jumped to her feet, shaking out her hands, breathing deeply. She hadn't felt like this in so long, like somebody had yanked all of her magic to the surface at once.

She needed a distraction. She paced. She scratched at her skin. Nothing worked. That energy slithered, making her want to scream. Rhys put his nose in the air, turning to look at her sharply before saying something to Mace.

Mace cut his eyes to her. Stupid wolves and their stupid noses.

"What's wrong, luv?"

"I'm fine," she growled, rolling her shoulders.

Mace eyed her warily. "You don't look fine. In fact, you look exceptionally...unfine."

"Wow," she sneered. "You say the sweetest things."

"Ember, I know—"

"You don't know anything. You don't know what this is like. You don't understand this at all."

His brows shot up. "Oh, well aren't you pissy all of a sudden."

She bared her teeth at him, rolling her head along her shoulders. "This is all your fault."

It wasn't his fault, the logical part of her brain said, not really. But she was mad. She was just so mad.

"My fault. How, pray tell, is this my fault?" he asked, incredulous.

"You were the one who started this whole thing. Maybe if you hadn't been in the cemetery that day, my powers would have stayed asleep."

"Oh, that's rich. Let me ask you, luv, how long do you think you would've lasted in that cemetery if my magic hadn't soothed yours? How many people do you think you would've taken with you in that cemetery if I'd done what Allister told me and just stood by and watched?"

"Gosh, I don't know. Maybe we should ask him. He's your boss, after all."

He stared at her. "How long have you been waiting to play that card, hmm?" He asked. "I chose you, remember. Much to my own peril."

"Peril? You're immortal. What's he going to do, take you off his Christmas card list? You act like you've done me some big favor by not helping him murder me." She laughed. "Should I thank you?"

His brows shot up, and he gaped at her. "As a matter of fact, perhaps you should. You'd already be dead by now if it wasn't for me."

"And if it wasn't for me feeding you, you'd probably be a shriveled-up husk because you haven't sucked the life out of anybody."

"I'm sorry, is this news to you? I'm a soul eater; it's what I do. You knew that when you kissed me the first time, and you knew it when you climbed into my lap and kissed me this morning."

Ember's face flushed, and her magic sparked off her fingers. She fumed. "Get away from me."

He backed up two steps, his face falling a bit. "You say you want me to back away, but your magic doesn't feel the same. I can feel it pulling me closer."

"I don't care what my magic wants." Ember clenched her teeth. "I want you gone. Now. I don't care if I take this entire town down with me."

 437

The scowl on his face smoothed out. "Ember, don't be like this." He advanced, stopping short. "I didn't mean it. I just thought you needed a distraction. A way to burn off some of your excess magic." He raked a hand through his hair. "Come on, luv. You're just going a bit stir crazy. I bet if I ask nicely I can get the little alpha to let us go to the pet cemetery and work off some of this power. It's obviously making you crazy."

Her rage was instantaneous. "Crazy? My magic is making me crazy? Right, because I can't just be tired of this. I can't just be completely done with this whole absurd situation. It has to be my power. Ember can't possibly be feeling her own feelings."

"Ember, luv, I didn't mean it like that."

Anger twisted inside her, like a spring coiling tighter. "I want you gone. I don't need you anymore."

He skin looked as grey as his hair. "Ember," he pleaded, his voice soft and sweet like that morning when he'd pushed her hair behind her ear and kissed her forehead. It just made her angrier.

"Go," she said again, catching on a sob.

He looked sick, defeated. "Fine, but I think this is a horrible idea."

"I don't care what you think," she said meanly, blinking back tears. She had no idea what she was doing, but it was too late to turn back.

"If you change your mind, I won't be far."

Her power was furious, her skin practically sizzling, but she was done caring.

She was done letting her magic control her.

She was just done.

 438

Chapter 75

TRISTIN

The packs arrived as the sun set. Isa took one look at Tristin in her ratty shorts and old t-shirt and banished her upstairs.

"Don't you come back downstairs until you've showered and brushed your teeth," Isa said. That was fine by her; she would just stay upstairs.

"You know, Quinn would never dishonor your memory or this pack by looking so slovenly."

"Well, he was always a better person than me," Tristin fired back, but there was no heat behind her words. She showered and brushed her teeth. She pulled on clean jeans and a black t-shirt, but that was as much as she could manage.

When she came back downstairs, it was dark, and people were everywhere. Isa was mingling with Wren, making introductions and following pack protocol. She'd put Rhys and Kai at the front door to greet guests as they arrived. Kai charmed the pants off the arriving packs, and Rhys was the epitome of diplomacy, shaking hands and giving a curt nod to each arriving member. Donovan was smiling, happily feeding the crowd.

Tristin hung back, avoiding the throng of people. They didn't need her to be social. The newcomers were content to stare at her as they walked past, fascinated by a pack with not one but three reapers. She couldn't help but notice their disappointment when they saw she looked so…normal.

Neoma flitted about in her long black dress and always bare feet, showing off Romero and Chester while the visitors would gasp in wonder.

Welcome to the Belladonna Pack and our Supernatural Side Show, Tristin thought bitterly. These people weren't there for Quinn. They were there to spy. They were voyeurs cashing in on their chance to see three active reapers in one pack. That had to make people nervous.

Tristin couldn't think of anybody who wanted to be there less than her, except maybe Ember. Ember too sat away from the people. She sat and moped, staring into the abyss. She was probably lamenting about sending her soul eater packing. It was the first smart thing she'd ever done as far as Tristin was concerned. He just couldn't be trusted.

She lost track of the people traipsing through their house. It was a sea of foreign faces laden down with food offerings. She wasn't sure who started the tradition of bringing food to funerals, but it was safe to say they would be able to feed the entire town for over a week.

She was about to head for the stairs when she noticed a guy standing against the open back door, watching her intently. He was a shifter, feline of some sort. His eyes were shifted, but with the moon rising, it was to be expected. Periodically, howls pierced the sky, and if she squinted, she could see the flames of the bonfire almost to the edge of the property line.

"Tristin, there you are," Isa huffed. "Please go grab more ice from the garage?"

"Sure," Tristin sighed. "Why not."

She had just pulled two bags from the deep freezer when a voice asked, "Need some help?"

She turned, warily observing the shifter from the kitchen. "Sure," she said, smiling snarkily and shoving both bags at him as she pushed past and kept walking.

 440

He laughed at her, following along obediently. "Guess your brother got all the manners in the family."

She let him catch up, narrowing her eyes at him. She knew all her brother's friends. The pack consisted of all her brother's friends. "You know my brother?"

"Yeah, we met a while ago. I'm Tate."

She whipped around to look at him. "Tate?" she gasped. "Georgia Tate?"

He grinned. "You've heard of me."

She hadn't until recently. Not until her brother spilled everything about the trip at Isa's impromptu pack meeting. "You're the jerk who helped make my friend insane with jealousy after you did…whatever you did with my brother." Tristin pulled a face. She so didn't want to know what happened.

"Guilty as charged, I guess." He picked up the bag of ice and followed her to the coolers. She stood by while he dumped the ice. All around them people laughed and joked. Animals roamed, both foreign and domestic.

It certainly didn't look like a funeral to her. She swallowed the lump in her throat. This wasn't honoring Quinn at all. Everything about this was so wrong. She wanted to cry or scream or hit something.

A glimpse of tawny-colored hair drifted past in her peripheral, and for a minute, she thought Astrid had made good on her promise to come. Would Astrid still try the spell tonight? Maybe she would. Maybe by some miracle it would work and Tristin could have him back. She didn't realize Tate held her arm until he tugged her towards the end of the clearing.

"Walk with me? I'm not much for crowds."

She nodded absently. She wasn't much for crowds either.

"I knew your friend. He was a good guy," he said, sounding like he meant it.

"We were going to get married," she said.

His eyes widened. "Really? You were engaged?"

She laughed, her mouth crooking in a bitter half smile. "Nope, we weren't even dating."

He eyed her queerly, but said nothing as they walked. The noise from the party dissipated the farther they went, and she breathed a little easier. She could hear people moving in the surrounding trees, but nobody in the woods would bother them tonight.

"Was that book any use to you?" Tate asked after a bit.

"The book?" Tristin asked. The book. The. Book. She stumbled, stomach lurching. She was grateful she'd skipped food today.

She could see him wince, his feline eyes glowing in the dim light. "Sorry. That was tactless of me. I didn't mean to upset you."

"You didn't do anything," she said, her voice hoarse from the bile still burning at her esophagus. It was her. How could she have forgotten the book he'd died for? How had she not even thought about that? What was wrong with her?

"Did you give him the book?" she asked, wanting him to say yes. If he said yes, she could hate him. It would be wonderful to have a face to put to this constant burning rage that seared her heart.

"I'm afraid he stole it. Though, I think it may be more the case he forgot to put it down in the excitement. It seemed finding out Mace worked for Allister threw everybody. From what I remember, neither he nor your brother took too kindly to that information. They left in a hurry."

"Do you know what book it was?"

"Yes. Expensive. My boss was intent on selling it for an enormous price when the time was right."

Tristin looked at him. "Why would Quinn care about some fancy book?"

"I suppose because it was on banshees," he said. "And, if the rumors are true, you're a banshee."

Her pulse thudded in her throat. He'd died for her. He'd sacrificed his life because of a stupid book he'd seen about her kind. She wanted to bring him back just to kill him again for being so stupid.

"So, did you come here to steal back the book for your boss?"

"The book has been paid for. My boss said a third party paid for the book and then paid Shelby a rather large sum to procure another item of great value."

 442

"Third party?" she snorted. "Aren't you the mysterious one?" She was suddenly acutely aware of how far they'd drifted from the others.

He didn't seem to notice. "Yes, they wanted to ensure there wasn't any bad blood with Shelby. It doesn't pay to piss off a demi-god. They were kind enough to pay Shelby triple the amount she would've asked."

Tristin couldn't keep the scowl off her face. "Oh, I just bet." It had to be Allister. Who else had that sort of money? "So, now what? You came to get the book back for this third party?"

"No, they don't really care about the book. I'm here for the other item."

Tristin shook her head in confusion. "What is this other item?"

He smiled sadly. "You."

He hit her then, just once but it was hard enough to stun. She stumbled backwards. "I'm really genuinely sorry about this," he said, snatching her and hauling her over his shoulder. The ground turned upside down as her world went fuzzy at the edges. "But I have people to answer to as well. Truthfully, I would've preferred your brother, but we need him for later."

She opened her mouth to say something, but then her world went black.

Chapter 76

MACE

Mace had no idea where he was. They'd chased him from the woods. He'd tried to stay downwind of the shifters, but it was only a matter of time before they caught the scent of him. Without Isa there to call him friend, he'd had no choice but to flee.

Every muscle hurt. It felt like the atoms in his body were attempting to rearrange themselves simultaneously. He stumbled, tripping along the old railroad tracks. He couldn't think. He could barely keep his feet underneath him. He had no idea where to go.

He wasn't sure how long he walked, shaking and sweat blinding him, before he realized he no longer felt the tracks beneath his feet. He lurched along the empty paved road in the blackness. He wiped the sweat stinging his eyes, but it didn't matter; his vision was fading in and out, this world a hazy shadow realm of looming shapes and utter silence. There were no streetlights, no headlights of passing cars. It appeared the world had abandoned this place just like Ember had abandoned him.

He collapsed in the street on his back. The full moon was a blurry orb overhead. Most of the wolves would be fully shifted by now, prowling the woods and looking to hunt. Was he far enough away?

He groaned, his body twisting as another wave of pain hit him. It was almost unbearable. Nothing made it better. He was sure he was in flames, his skin blistering and cracking until the flesh peeled from his body. But when his hands skimmed over the battered surface, there was nothing wrong, just the same layers of scar tissue. It didn't stop the pain. Nothing could stop this pain. It was the worst type of hallucination. He closed his useless eyes and prayed for a death that could never come.

"Oh, brother, what have you done to yourself?"

Somebody jostled his head, and gentle hands petted through his messy hair. It was his sister's voice. Another sadistic fantasy from Ember's magic, but he embraced it anyway. He opened his eyes, afraid of what he might see. Who knew what horrors all that power could create? But his sister looked exactly the same as she had hundreds of years ago with her pale blue eyes and that waterfall of blonde hair. She was always the beautiful one.

"Asa?" he mumbled.

"It's all right, Balthazar, I'm here." She kissed his forehead. "I'm right here."

He sighed, letting her comfort him. "Mace, it's Mace now."

A giggle escaped her lips, so much like when they were children. "You always were one for the dramatic. Mother would have a seizure if she knew. She named you after grandfather."

"I-I know. Hated him. Still hate him," he panted, staring up at her face. He just wanted to look at her for a while.

As he watched, her eyes bled silver, and her blonde hair went grey. "No. W-what's happening?"

"I took my true form, just like you."

He shook his head, retching as his world spun violently. "No. You're not real. Th-this isn't real. You aren't like me."

She smiled wistfully. "I know, but does that matter?" He supposed it didn't. He tried to answer her, to tell her he missed her, to tell her he wanted her to stay. He hadn't seen her face in so long. Her face contorted above him. "You abandoned me. You abandoned us. Left us defenseless in that place. The truth of what happened to us is far worse than this."

"No. I did this for you, to keep you safe. To keep you both safe."

 445

"Safe? Did you really think he'd honor his word? He was a soul-less monster just like you, like me."

"Please, Asa. Don't say that," he begged. He wasn't even surprised when her grey hair became a mass of orange curls, and Ember's face appeared, a sneer across her face. "Look at you. What a mess you've made. This is what happens to liars, Mace. This is the price you pay."

Another delusion, he told himself. She wasn't real. They weren't real. His sister wasn't like him. Ember wasn't cruel. She was kind and sweet and everything he wasn't.

Spasms racked his body, his teeth clacking together violently. What the hell was happening to him? Ember disappeared as a white light seared his tender vision. Headlights. He prayed they ran him over. He longed for just a few moments of peace.

Tires screeched as the vehicle lurched to a halt. He couldn't move. He just lay there as two pairs of jean-clad legs swam into sight, and rough hands hauled him to his feet.

"Holy shit," a male voice said. "Just look at him."

Another male voice said, "I told you the spell would work. She did exactly what I said she would. Poor guy didn't stand a chance."

A female voice, chimed in, "The spell only worked because she's not warded. She'd never have kicked him out of the pack if she was immune to compulsion."

"I don't care why it worked, as long as it worked," the original male crowed.

The second male snorted. "Yeah, yeah, you're a genius, get him in the van."

They sounded familiar, but Mace couldn't place them. He hit the floor of the van with a grunt, grimacing at the scent of the dirty blanket beneath him. It smelled like blood and motor oil, a combi-nation his stomach couldn't tolerate at that moment. They'd spelled Ember. That's why she'd sent him away. It made whatever came next a little easier to take.

A low, throaty chuckle came from somewhere above him. "Hold him down." He recognized the voice immediately.

He gathered every ounce of strength he could muster to growl, "When I get my strength back, I'm going to drain your whole coven, you bitch."

 446

Stella laughed again as two hooded figures yanked his arms behind his back. The coven. One of their hoods fell back, revealing icy blonde hair. One of the triplets. How many of them were there in the van?

Stella's face came into view, and her cold hands yanked up his shirt. There was a loud snick, and then his vision went black as razor sharp steel cut through the layers of scar tissue across his abdomen, the scent of his own blood making him sick.

"Bind him," she barked at the two.

"Why? Look at him. He's not going anywhere," the girl said, giving voice to his own thoughts. He was hardly a threat.

"Do it anyway," Stella snapped. "Don't question my orders, Lola. Astrid might like you, but I think you're an idiot."

Even in the state he was in, he couldn't miss the look Lola threw at the back of Stella's head before Lola did as she was told, binding his hands roughly with some kind of plastic pieces.

Stella didn't notice, shoving his head roughly. "Yeah, you definitely don't look like much now. Killing you will be a kindness after this."

"Go to hell."

"Ooh, burn." She laughed. "I'm going to assume your girlfriend's magic has thrown you a little off your game."

Mace tried to swallow what felt like wadded sandpaper in this throat. "What are you even getting out of this?"

Stella laughed and slapped his face. "We all have our parts to play." She looked at somebody else. "Let's go, it's getting late."

As they drove, he swam in and out of consciousness. Doors slammed and another opened. Hands yanked him free, catching him under the arms and dragging him along, the toes of his shoes scraping for purchase along concrete until they entered a darkened building. He tried to pick his head up but lacked the strength.

As his eyes adjusted, he caught glimpses of rows of grey metal lockers. The school. Why the hell were they at the school? Blood oozed from the wound on his stomach, splattering on the floor as they pulled him along.

They tossed him roughly into a wooden chair in the center of the room. He fought just to remain upright in the chair. Stella's face

 447

appeared as she squatted in front of him. She yanked his head back, rolling it around, laughing as his eyes fought to track her. She held up what looked like a paintbrush of all things. That couldn't be right.

"This part is going to be a bit uncomfortable for you, I'm afraid but given the state of you, I don't think it really matters much."

He barely had time to register what she aimed to do before she jabbed the brush into the wound on his stomach. He grunted.

"Normally," she said, conversationally, "this part of the ritual is done by the witch who will perform the spell, but given the fragile state of our little necromancer, I think it's best we try to do as much for the poor dear as possible, don't you?"

She moved to the floor, using his blood to paint a circle, frowning when his blood didn't go as far as she'd hoped. "Hmm, this won't do."

She pulled the knife from her belt and went for his stomach before stopping short. "I wonder…" she started, a cruel smile spreading across her face.

He looked at her in confusion, before he lurched to his feet. He only made it two steps before he came up short. Unable to move. He looked at her. "What are you doing?"

"I'm not doing anything." She cut his hands free and handed him the knife, twisting her hand in the air. He grunted as his hand turned the knife on himself. He was too weak to resist the compulsion. The knife dug far deeper this time, the blood pouring freely.

"Much better. Now be a dear and draw this for me, will you?" She shoved the drawing in his face.

"Careful, Stella, my brother has to live in that body," Astrid cautioned from the doorway, waving in somebody carrying what looked like a body over his shoulder. "Put her over there."

"You'll fix it later," Stella said, brushing off Astrid's concerns. "Now that we have the decorations under way, maybe it's time to invite our guest of honor?"

The newcomer dropped the girl on the floor in the corner and stopped, looking hard at Mace and the blood pouring at his feet. His vision cleared. "Tate?"

Tate's face twisted into a frown, and he gave Mace a long look before he left.

He groaned as the witch plunged her hand into his stomach, not sure if it was blood pouring from his lips or saliva. He couldn't die, but if he could, he imagined this was what it felt like. Stella waved her hand, and he hit his knees. "Get to work. You have a lot to do."

Astrid gasped. "What are you doing?"

Stella walked towards the hallway door, both hands coated in his blood. "Leaving some breadcrumbs."

Chapter 77

EMBER

Everywhere Ember went, Kai and Rhys were two steps behind. She was restless. She couldn't stop wandering. She knew it irritated her new bodyguards, but she just didn't care. She was tired of people staring at her, whispering about her. She just wanted to be alone. It was New Orleans all over again.

She scanned the crowd, looking for any signs of Mace. She'd texted him three times but still nothing. She wanted to apologize. She had no idea why she'd acted the way she had. She couldn't even remember what made her so angry. She thought for sure he would have come back by then. It wasn't like he couldn't take care of himself, but she couldn't shake the feeling something was really wrong.

Maybe it was just that night. The full moon. A funeral that seemed more like a college frat party. Her magic rolled along beneath her skin, letting her know it was displeased. She needed Mace; her magic needed his. It itched to touch him. It wanted the coolness of his skin beneath her fingertips. It wanted the taste of him on her tongue. Somewhere deep down, in a dark place she didn't want to acknowledge, she knew it wasn't her magic at all. She was so screwed.

She found herself navigating through the sea of bodies, gyrating together to music booming from the speakers Wren and Mace wired earlier. It was surreal. Animals she'd only seen on the nature channel prowled the woods of her backyard. It was like she'd rolled a four in a game of *Jumanji*. She'd seen wolves, panthers, and even a jaguar pad silently out from the tree line. They all watched her warily, giving her a wide berth as if she were somehow the predator in their midst.

She found a seat on a log far enough away from the crowd but close enough to appease her security detail. She knew they didn't want to be babysitting either.

They did their part to pull the focus from her. Kai was drinking, tossing back the last gulp of what she'd counted as his third beer. She wasn't sure if he was drunk, but he was drunk adjacent, giggling too much, occasionally losing his footing. Rhys would steady Kai, letting a hand linger on her cousin's lower back for just a little too long.

The music changed from a loud rowdy song to one with a slow throbbing bass beat, and Kai stumbled again, falling forward into Rhys's lap and whispering something in his ear. The wolf looked startled and aggressively shook his head. Kai only laughed.

She watched dumbfounded as her cousin climbed into the Adirondack chair Rhys currently occupied. Kai wrapped his arms around the wolf's neck, moving in time with the music, hips rotating suggestively in a sloppy version of a lap dance. It was painful to watch, but Rhys didn't seem to share her opinion. As always, he watched her cousin with a single-minded intensity, glowing green eyes hungry.

The shifters watched too. Kai said it was because they couldn't believe somebody as high ranking in the pack as Rhys would waste their time with a reaper, but Ember wasn't so sure. Both her cousin and Rhys were attractive, and they both seemed to draw an equal amount of attention.

In most circumstances, Kai was level-headed, but that night he didn't appear to be himself. If he saw another shifter watching the two of them for a little too long, he'd hold their stare, laying down a challenge he had no way of winning. Each time her cousin challenged another shifter, Rhys stepped in, partially shifted, accepting the challenge Kai issued.

 451

Isa was forced to step in each time, issuing hasty apologies and hollow excuses about heightened emotions. It was a funeral after all. They had just lost one of their own. The injured party had accepted the alpha's apologies and shaken hands, but Isa was losing her patience with the two of them.

Her phone vibrated against her leg, and she cursed the way her stomach flip-flopped, hoping it was finally Mace. It was a text message from an unknown number.

Do not react to this message. Tristin's life depends on it.

Ember's brow furrowed as she tried to puzzle out what it meant. She looked around, realizing she couldn't remember the last time she'd seen Tristin. Ember thought her cousin must have escaped upstairs to her room.

Ember tried to compose her face into some semblance of normal. She could already feel her magic thrumming to life, beating against her veins. She hoped the heavy base music masked the violent pounding of her heart. Texts came in one after another.

You are cordially invited to the resurrection of Quinn Talbot.

Actually, it's not an invitation. It's a summons.

In fifteen minutes, there will be a distraction. You have forty-five minutes from now to get to the school, or we start severing body parts.

Reapers don't have advanced healing, and your cousin will have a hard time reuniting with her beloved if her ring finger is missing.

Her phone vibrated again, and a picture of her cousin appeared. She lay on the ground, unconscious, blood trickling from a wound at her hairline.

If that isn't enough incentive, we have your soul eater too, but he's not quite as photo ready as your cousin.

They had Tristin. They had Mace. Ember had sent him away, and they had him. She clenched her jaw, willing her body not to show any of the panic she felt. She couldn't do anything to mask the scent of her distress. She just had to hope that the amount of sweat and pheromones in a group of people this big would take care of that for her.

Time slowed to a crawl. One minute seemed like ten. Kai stood as a stranger approached. He was tall and lean with dark hair and yellow eyes. He seemed to know Kai, smiling and running a finger along Kai's cheek. Ember stood as Rhys sprung to his feet, placing himself between the stranger and Kai. Kai ran a soothing hand over Rhys's arm, but the wolf was too far gone, partially shifted and advancing on the other guy who danced back on agile feet, laughing in delight.

The music was too loud to understand what they were saying, but whoever the guy was, he was the distraction. Rhys lunged, taking the guy to the ground. There was the slick sound of bones moving under skin and a panther broke from Rhys's hold. Kai yelled for Rhys to calm down, but Rhys shifted, his wolf going for the panther's throat. Kai yelled for Isa, standing frozen as a crowd began to form.

This was Ember's chance.

She turned and ran for the path. Getting there on foot was her best chance. There would be no way to get into the house, grab the keys, and get the car out of the driveway without being caught. She had no idea what she was walking into. She willed herself to calm down. She really couldn't afford to lose control. Tristin and Mace were counting on her.

Chapter 78

EMBER

She was ten minutes early. She stood outside the school, wiping her shaking palms against her jeans. It seemed a bitter sort of irony that this was the place they'd chosen to battle it out.

She'd always found school intimidating, a dangerous labyrinth she was forced by law to navigate five days a week. In New Orleans, it was awkward stares and whispers about her appearance. Here, it was actual threats of violence and death. She honestly wasn't sure which was worse.

The doors to the main hall suddenly looked more intimidating than a maximum security prison. Behind those doors was nothing but darkness. Of course, they'd killed the lights. She took two steps forward before she lost her nerve again. Just do it, Ember. She took a deep breath and stepped through the doors.

How had it come to this? She had just wanted a place she belonged. She'd wanted a family. She'd wanted to be normal. She leaned against the closed doors, blinking her eyes, needing them to adjust to the darkness. Why couldn't that have come with her super-human powers? She fumbled with her phone, jolting when her flash-light app flared to life, blinding her.

She swept the phone back and forth, half expecting for a lumbering monster to come bolting from the shadows. Her heartbeat slammed against her ribcage, offbeat and stuttering like she'd had too much caffeine. She wanted to turn and run. She couldn't do what they wanted. Nobody could.

Her footsteps echoed like gunshots in the empty hallway, holding her phone before her like a talisman, hoping it would somehow ward off the anxiety ratcheting higher with every step. Would anybody notice she was gone? Would anybody come to look for her? They wouldn't even know where to start. Could they track her scent?

She was such an idiot. She was holding her cell phone. They had said not to tell anybody, but what else would they say. She didn't want to get anybody hurt, but she couldn't do this alone. She stopped and pounded out a text on the keys, making her words as succinct as possible. She hit send and quickly deleted the text.

Tristin and I are at the school. Witches. Help.

She hoped she didn't just get her cousin killed. Ember was afraid for her cousin, but a thought nagged at Ember. Was Tristin really in danger? She had gone to a great deal of trouble to bring Quinn back once. Had this been her and Astrid's plan all along? Ember licked her bottom lip as fear clawed at her lungs. Could Tristin have set this whole thing up? Would she knowingly sacrifice Mace to save Quinn?

She took two steps forward, stumbling in the dark. Her hand shot out blindly to steady herself, landing on the warm metal of the lockers. As she walked, she dragged her hand along the metal, using them to steady herself.

Sweat trickled from her hairline down her spine. Somebody had turned the AC off, or maybe it was off for the holidays. She pushed damp hair away from her face, recoiling as a foul scent hit her. The smell of copper clung heavy in the air, so thick she could taste it. Slowly, she turned her flashlight towards the floor, dreading what she'd find. Along the floor, a rust-colored smear stained the linoleum as if something was dragged down the hall and around the corner.

That was blood. That was a lot of blood. Could somebody lose that much blood and live? Mace couldn't die but Tristin could. Whose blood was that? This time when Ember's magic came to the surface she didn't even try to stop it. She welcomed the feeling. Instead of

 455

slithering just under the surface, it curled around her, swaddling her in a hazy warmth, temporarily dampening her anxiety.

On some level, Astrid had to know Ember wasn't capable of doing what Astrid asked. She wasn't crazy like Stella. She had to be able to see reason, right? Ember swallowed as a thought had her frozen in her tracks. What if Tristin was already dead? What if this was simply a trap? What if this was Allister all along?

Ember had to try, though. She had to believe Tristin was alive. Besides, they still had Mace. Ember let her thoughts linger for just a moment on those quicksilver eyes and that predatory smile. It would serve him right if she left him there. She couldn't believe he was forcing her to do this alone.

All he had ever done was tell her she wasn't ready, and when he needed her to save his stupid ass, she wasn't ready. She so wasn't ready.

What if she killed everybody…again? Why had he gone so far away? Why had he listened to her when she told him to leave? He said he'd be close. He lied. All he ever did was lie.

She wanted to be brave. She really did. She wanted so badly to be the hero she'd thought she could be just a couple of weeks ago. Before she knew what her magic did; what it was capable of. Heroes didn't die. All the books and movies said so.

But she wasn't the hero; she was the villain, responsible for an entire town's unhappiness. A villain who was a crying, sweaty mess with snot running down her face. She had done everything wrong, and because of it, more people were going to die.

She wiped her face with her shirt. Breathing in and out, in and out. Sparks shot from her fingertips. She had to get it together. She had to do this. She had to go in. She couldn't be the reason that any more people died. She looked at her phone. She was out of time.

She grabbed hold of the door handle and pushed, stepping through the doors and stopping short. The scene before her was like a horror movie. Six figures stood shrouded in blood-red robes, faces cloaked in shadow. A thousand candles lined the bleachers of the gymnasium.

Once upon a time, she probably would have laughed at the theatricality of it all. Maybe even made a snarky comment about it. Not anymore.

Somebody had painstakingly painted a large circle in the center of the room, that same brownish red blood from the hallway, a dozen runic symbols embellishing the inside. She shuddered as she contemplated the amount of blood required to make something that big, that elaborate.

Mace sat in the center of the circle. A noise escaped her at the sight of him. He wasn't tied up, but he sat unmoving, head down, blood pooling beneath him from a wound Ember couldn't see. Tristin was nowhere in sight.

The doors clattered shut behind Ember, and she jumped with a yelp. All heads turned to her, and a figure stepped forward from the shadows, pushing back the hood of their robe. Astrid. Ember felt herself relax just a bit. It wasn't Allister. There was the slightest chance Astrid might see reason.

It wasn't Astrid who spoke, however, but Stella, stepping forward. "Excellent, you showed. I knew you would come for one of them, though for the life of me I can't imagine why. Astrid didn't believe me, but I knew. It's kind of sad, really."

Ember searched the room for any sign of her cousin, fear turning to anger when there was no sign of her. Ember's sudden fury caused a ripple in her magic, and she let it ride. If that melodramatic bitch touched one hair on her cousin's head, Ember was going to personally rip Stella's fingernails out. Ember could reason with Astrid, but there was no reasoning with Stella. She was insane.

The girl stood, patiently waiting for a reaction, like a true psychopath. Ember didn't take the bait, her gaze tugging back to Mace. She knew this would be easier for them if she was mad, but they couldn't begin to know how little control she would have if she let her power go unchecked. The last thing they wanted was to see her when she lost control.

She closed her eyes and took a couple of deep breaths, imagining herself sitting with Mace in the woods, trying to remember the way his hands would run up and down her arms, how he'd whisper for her to just focus on him. Why was he here? They couldn't kill him. Was he part of their plan all along, or had they seen an opportunity and taken it? Had she done this to him? She angrily swiped at the tears on her cheeks. Where the hell was Tristin? Ember prayed this wasn't all for nothing. *Please don't be dead, Tristin*, Ember begged silently.

"Astrid, what are you doing? I can't do what you want. I don't know how. I'm not a witch." Astrid set her jaw, looking to the floor. Ember took a wobbly step forward. "I know you get that. I know somewhere deep down you know what you're asking of me is impossible. I would do it if I could, but he's gone. He told me he's happy. He said he's with your mom."

Astrid's head snapped up then. "You're lying. You shut the hell up."

Stella stepped forward, putting a comforting hand on her friend and saying to Ember, "We can do this one of two ways. One, I drag your cousin out here, and we all watch while she cuts her own organs out one by one until she dies. Or two, you can do the spell exactly as we tell you, and we all win." She looked at Mace, his face falling in mock sadness. "Well, except your little soul eater boyfriend. I'm afraid his role in this production has come to an end."

Ember's hands sparked, and she clenched them into fists. "Why are you doing this? You know better than to mess with this sort of thing. Tristin had to have told you what happened last time? What I did."

Stella rolled her eyes. "We don't have time for this. Search her and let's get started."

Astrid looked uneasy but resigned. "Ember, you're out of options."

Chapter 79

TRISTIN

Tristin woke to tearful shouting, her head pounding and her mouth so dry she had to peel her tongue from the roof of her mouth. It took her a minute to remember. Her hand went to where Tate had hit her, wincing at the tender spot. Allister had sent Tate to kidnap her. She lurched to her feet, only to have her arm snagged. She tried to keep her feet under her as her assailant dragged her a short distance before shoving her back to the floor. She hissed as pain shot through her shoulder.

This time she moved slowly, struggling to sit up. They were in the school gym. Was that Mace? He sat, his head down, his hands hanging limp at his sides. Shadows flickered over the walls, candles the only light. She hoped nobody had to read for this little ritual, or they were all in trouble. She doubted anybody had bothered to consecrate a flashlight.

She heard Ember's voice then, shaky and tearful, pleading with somebody. Tristin blinked to clear her vision, wondering absently if she had a concussion. She expected to hear Allister's voice echoing in the empty gym, but instead it was just Astrid…and Stella.

Astrid was really going through with it. Tristin pushed down the momentary elation she felt. It wasn't real. The ritual couldn't work. *But what if it did?* A voice whispered in her head. What if she could have Quinn back?

A thousand butterflies fluttered in her chest. They were quickly squashed as she watched one of the hooded figures shove her cousin into the circle of what Tristin could only assume was blood.

Astrid noticed her then. "Oh, good, you're awake. Glad to see you made it for the show."

"Astrid," Tristin said. "Maybe everybody's right? This isn't going to work."

Astrid looked at Tristin like she was stupid. "Why? I have everything I need for the spell. I have the necromancer, the blood, the bone, the ingredients"—she pointed at Mace— "and the empty vessel."

Tristin's eyes darted to Mace and then to Ember, who looked at them in confusion. "Empty vessel?"

"There was no way my father would have left Quinn's body intact. I took what I could, but his soul needs a body." Astrid pointed at Mace. "His body has no soul. It's kismet."

"No," Ember said, face contorting. "No. You want me to jam Quinn's soul into Mace's body? You're sick."

"No, I'm practical. I really don't understand your fascination with this...creature."

"I n-need him," Ember said. "I can't control my magic without him. Do you have any idea the damage I could do? Do you understand what I'm capable of?"

Tristin couldn't do this anymore. She liked her cousin, hell maybe someday Tristin might even grow to love the girl, but she was absolutely clueless. This whole time the information was right under Ember's nose, and she just wouldn't see it. All anybody had to do was look at Mace's condition to know how wrong Ember was.

"Don't be stupid, Ember," Tristin said, all eyes swinging to her. "Don't you get it? Even now he's lying to you. He had the opportunity to come clean about everything but chose not to."

"What do you mean?" Ember asked, shooting Tristin a look so filled with dread it made her heart hurt. She stuffed the feeling away. Ember needed to know this.

Tristin pulled herself to her feet, shuddering as she swayed. "Meaning, you don't need him." She took two steps forward. "He needs you. Do you understand? He's the parasite, and you're the host. Your magic controls him. Your magic feeds him. You order, and he obeys. Your magic bound him to you like a slave."

Ember shook her head. "You're wrong. I can't control my powers without him."

Tristin growled in frustration. "Look around, Ember. You're controlling your powers, and it's not because he's here; it's because you've had control all along." Ember stared at Tristin, mouth agape but Tristin charged on. "Outside the tattoo parlor, your magic started to spiral out of control, but as soon as you were distracted, poof, it disappeared. You've had control this whole time. The binding spell has worn off. These flares you have are nothing more than...supernatural panic attacks."

"No. You're wrong. That can't be true."

Mace's head jerked upright as Stella came forward. "Why don't we ask him?"

Mace blinked heavy lids at Ember, grimacing as he swallowed.

"Speak, sluagh," Stella commanded. "Tell her the truth."

"Is it true?" Ember asked.

"Yes," Mace said.

"So, you don't care about me at all?"

"Of course I do," Mace rasped. "Just because your magic holds me to you doesn't mean you control my feelings."

Stella rolled her eyes. "Please. He has no soul. He's literally incapable of feeling anything for anybody. He's a liar. He is beholden to you." Ember flinched at the words but said nothing, staring at Mace with a sad sort of longing. Tristin knew that feeling.

Stella wasn't finished. "I know that sounds like a pretty word, but all it means is that he only feels what you want him to. He only does what you tell him to. He's a shell. Sluagh have no feelings because they have no soul. They're monsters. Anything he feels for you, he only feels because you want him to. Any emotions he has he only has because you give them to him."

 461

Her cousin nodded her head as if Stella's answer made too much sense. Tristin knew then the witches had won. Ember would do what they wanted.

Chapter 80

EMBER

It made sense in a way that crushed her heart. She had created this whole thing in her mind, a three-dimensional delusion. She'd created a supernatural boyfriend to protect her and keep her safe. It was the cruelest sort of joke. She wanted to curl up in a ball and just die. She didn't even try to stop the tears this time.

Mace spoke, his voice raspy and so weak. "Ember, that's not true. If I only did what you wanted, if I only felt what you wanted, I wouldn't have been able to lie to you. The very fact that I kept this from you proves that I care for you."

She wanted to believe his twisted logic, but how could she? How could she trust herself or her magic? Everything was so upside down.

"I don't know what to believe," she said.

"You do what you need to do to get out of here. Do the spell, save Tristin, bring back the human if you can, but don't ever believe I wanted to hurt you, or that my feelings weren't my own. I don't know how I feel what I feel, but I know the feelings are mine."

"You can't be sure. There's no way for you to know," she said. He had to know that.

"Ember, please," he begged, the look in his eyes almost too much.

She pushed the sweaty mass of hair out of his face. "I don't want to do this," she whispered.

"Well, nobody cares what you want," Stella snapped. "We need to get started; we are losing the moon."

"Gather the ingredients," Astrid ordered.

"Wait, we almost forgot the most important thing," Stella said, tapping her nail on her temple. "I was so caught up in our little teen drama that I forgot about this."

She waved her hand, and Ember's eyes grew wide. She tried to run, but Stella's magic held Ember firm. A figure approached with a long piece of iron, smoldering at the end.

"No, no, no, no," Ember gasped, shaking her head. "Stella, no. Oh my God, don't do this."

"You should've just gotten the tattoo," Stella murmured.

Astrid's eyes widened. "I thought you were going to find another way?"

"Do you want your brother back or not," Stella snapped. Astrid dropped her gaze, nodding.

Fear engulfed Ember's body, metallic taste flooding her mouth. "Don't move," Stella said, laughing at her own joke. Ember could only stand there as Stella circled her. She yanked down the sleeve of her shirt, revealing her shoulder.

"I'll try to make this quick," was the only warning Ember received before pain exploded throughout her body, and the smell of burning flesh permeated the air. Adrenaline thundered through her veins, her knees going weak.

"There, all done," Stella said, her voice chipper.

Ember could see the brand. She could see it no longer touched her skin, but it felt like it was still there, burning through layers of fat and muscle.

Astrid moved forward and pressed her fingers against Ember's neck, muttering something in another language. The relief was instantaneous.

"Thank you," she whispered, unable to help herself.

 464

"I need you functioning," Astrid muttered. "Get everybody in place."

There was a flurry of motion as they placed a small table, a bowl, and several ingredients in the middle of the circle.

"Close the circle," Stella barked.

The circle flared to life, glowing red. The robed figures took their place around the perimeter, but Astrid spoke only to Ember. "Put everything in the bowl, starting left to right. Use them all. When I tell you, say the incantation."

Ember's hands shook. "It's not too late to stop this, Astrid. I don't want to do this. I don't care if he's lying to me. Nobody deserves this."

Footsteps fell heavy outside the circle, and one last robed figure took his place. His robe was black, a heavy piece of metal hung from his neck. He didn't even try to hide his face. Allister. Ember stumbled away, almost tripping on the table.

He raised his hand with a smile. "Relax, everything is going to be okay, Ember."

She looked at him like he was insane. "Right, you only want to kill me and steal my power."

"I may have been a bit…hasty in my quest for power. I simply want my son back."

"Don't any of you care that he's happy where he is?"

"You shut up," Astrid screamed. "You don't get a say in this. You will bring my brother back."

"Calm yourself, dear. Ember's going to help us. Aren't you?"

He moved to Tristin, gripping her shoulder tight. Tristin flinched, and Ember looked to Mace again. Even if he didn't care about her, she cared about him no matter how stupid that sounded.

"Ember, I know this is confusing for you, dear, but he doesn't love you. He can't love you. He's evil. A killer." Allister looked to Mace. "Does she know? Have you told her the truth?"

"What truth?" Ember asked. What now? She didn't know how much more she could take. "What are you talking about?"

Allister shook his head. "I knew you couldn't know. Nobody would be that blindly devoted to the boy who killed her father."

 465

"What?" Ember gasped, the breath punched from her lungs at the weight of his words. That wasn't possible. It just wasn't possible. She shook her head. She turned on Mace, forcing his head up. "I'm not even going to ask if it's true. You'd just lie to me anyway."

Mace looked to Allister before Mace turned his gaze to her, his eyes soft. "I was doing my job. I didn't know he was your father. I didn't even know you."

She slapped him hard, twice, before stumbling back like she'd received the blow. She head jerked to Tristin. "Did you know?"

Tristin's eyes widened. "What? Ember, no. I swear."

Mace looked up at her like it took every bit of strength he possessed. "Just start the spell, Ember."

Chapter 81

MACE

This time she didn't fight them, Allister's revelation effectively burning away the last of her resolve. It was Mace's own fault. He should have told her. He just never knew how.

That wasn't true.

He hadn't wanted to tell her. He could have done the right thing, but she would have pushed him away. He was a lot of things. Selfish. Soulless. Evil. What he wasn't was a hero. If he'd told her the truth about what he'd done to her father, she would have made him go, and he'd chosen to save himself. He always chose to save himself.

Even now, he still used her. Being in her presence lessened his pain. Her magic had called off its attack on him since he was returned to his rightful place by her side. Her power couldn't do much for the wound at his abdomen, but for once all that scar tissue had protected him, keeping Stella from forcing him to watch as he lost his entrails to a dirty gymnasium floor. He could deal with the physical pain. It was a relief compared to the way Ember looked at him just then.

He wouldn't die in agony. He wouldn't die at all. Dying implied moving on; he would simply...cease to be. Blinking out of existence was preferable to her look of betrayal. He didn't want that look to be the last thing he saw. Yes, he was selfish, but he'd rather leave the world with her forgiveness.

He watched her sink into herself, letting her power take her. He didn't blame her for hiding; the world betrayed her at every turn. Her features softened, her expression vacant as her magic wound around her. His magic valiantly tried to rise to the call of hers, but Stella still held him bound by her witchery.

Outside the circle, the chanting began, old and archaic. Latin. Ember's motions were jerky, stilted. She fought to do as she was told while keeping her magic at the surface. He could feel her power pulling, tugging at her. It didn't like this. It felt…off. This was not soul magic. This was death magic, and her magic knew the difference.

But as she worked, her movements became more rhythmic, the coven's chanting more frantic, until Mace was certain Ember was no longer in control. The energy shift was palpable. Each ingredient added seemed to suck more oxygen from the room. The witches swayed on their feet, and Ember's eyes fluttered. He'd only seen things like this in hoodoo rituals.

Whatever they had invited into that circle had accepted Ember's invitation sevenfold. By the time she reached the last ingredient—Quinn's blood—she no longer needed Astrid's whispered instructions.

When Ember's eyes opened once more, the words flowed from her lips without hesitation or uncertainty, those perfect violet eyes becoming solid black. Mace went cold. That was not Latin. It was older. Much, much older. Sumerian? Aramaic?

His chest felt tight. He couldn't breathe. Was this the spell? It made no sense. He didn't need to breathe. He didn't need air in his lungs. Shock, like electricity, coursed through him as he finally gave name to the feeling overtaking him. He was afraid. This was fear, not for himself but for Ember, wherever she was in there.

She walked to him, a bowl in hand, yanking the remains of his shirt apart. He didn't know if it was the layers of scarring or the gaping wound across his abdomen, but she blinked as if her body rejected the sight. She hesitated, swallowing hard, fighting whatever force worked within her.

     468

When she looked at him again, he almost thought he saw her, but then it was gone, taking with it any hope of this ending in any way but him gone and Ember lost to whatever evil force had accepted her invitation. He only prayed she hadn't invoked Osiris as Astrid had hoped.

Ember's face contorted, and she broke through this other magic's hold, misery etched across her face. She couldn't hold this force at bay for long, but she faltered, just for a moment. Hand stuttering. Her hesitation was enough. It was enough for him to know she cared enough to not want to do this, to fight this power. But she had to do this. It was the only way for this to end. If she failed, everybody died.

"It's okay, luv."

Her fingers moved lower, hovering over the jagged cut before she pressed her fingers inside, her face pale, her eyes haunted. He tried to mask the grunt of pain, but her gaze shot to his again as she dipped her bloody fingers into the bowl, mixing his blood with Quinn's.

He closed his eyes, letting himself enjoy the feel of her fingers as she began to paint the mixture across his chest, fingers far more gentle than any others ever were. She painted his forehead, his lips, and his left cheek. She paused when she reached his right. It was the last step before the final incantation.

Her hand shook, and he knew this entity, this power squatting inside Ember was playing with her. It wanted her to suffer. To see this sacrifice. It even let her magic open their connection. Her face crumpled, tears spilling down her cheeks.

"I could have loved you," she whispered, just for him to hear. "I think I did love you. How could this not be real?"

The bewilderment in her voice hurt like a physical blow. Tears filled his eyes. The feelings weren't his, couldn't be, but somehow that made it worse. He'd done this to her. Was still doing this to her. Suddenly, he was talking, words spilling from his lips without his permission. "Who's to say what's real, luv?" He wanted to touch her so badly. "Maybe you do love me. If you do, then I'm lucky, because there is nowhere—in this lifetime or any other—where I've ever been deserving of it, but I'm still selfish enough to take it."

 469

He took a shaky breath. "Maybe everything I've felt for you is just an illusion. I've spent hundreds of years feeling nothing. I gave my soul away so I could feel nothing. But you come along, and you're all feelings: guilt, doubt, pain, love. Everything I tried to avoid."

She flinched. "But, Ember, if I had to spend eternity feeling another person's feelings, it would be you...just you. That must mean something, right?" Her breath caught, her hand so close to his cheek. "But this was never a redemption story. The bad guy doesn't get the girl. Monsters don't get happy endings." He smiled a little. "The universe is quite strict about these things."

She was sobbing now. "I don't know what to do."

"Of course, you do, luv. Finish the spell. Bring back your friend. I know you'll never truly understand this, but I feel it's true. If I was capable...if I am somehow capable of loving anybody, it's you."

With that, he turned his cheek. He wasn't going to make it any harder on her than it had to be. She stood frozen. "Go on, then."

She swallowed hard, nodding jerkily. She painted the last symbol and looked at the others before grabbing his face and pressing her lips to his.

He'd kissed her many times before, but this time it was different, like somebody pouring water into his lungs, the pressure so great he was choking on it. He could still feel it even as she pulled away.

She stepped back. "Unum quod que—" Her body convulsed, eyes bleeding black again. Ember was no longer Ember. This time the voice that fell from her lips was not hers at all, it was a male voice, and the words were that same ancient tongue spoken moments ago. It was nothing Mace had ever heard before.

Panic filled him in a way that could only be described as human. He fought Stella's compulsion as he stared at the thing squatting inside of Ember. He couldn't leave her like this. But it was too late. His vision was fading; Ember's face was all he could see. He tried to take her in. There was no place to go from there, no heaven, no hell, no in-between. He would simply cease to exist. He wanted to remember those violet eyes and her wild hair. He wanted to see her smile. But the slick grin that split across her face was not her own.

"I'll take excellent care of her," it whispered.

Then nothing.

 470

Chapter 82

TRISTIN

Ember fell to her knees, and Mace's body went limp. Ember buried her head in his lap, sobbing hard enough to make her whole body shake. Tristin had no idea what she just witnessed, but that strange bubble of power drained from the room so quickly, she felt woozy. Everything just felt wrong.

"Did it work?" Astrid questioned.

"Break the circle," Allister demanded.

Astrid rushed forward, shoving Ember to the floor and slapping Mace's face. "Quinn? Quinn!"

Mace exploded off the chair, knocking it backwards, hitting the floor and crawling backwards to the wall, gaze darting around the bizarre scene before him. "Astrid? Tristin? What the hell is going on?"

Astrid wrapped herself around Mace's body. "Quinn?"

"Yeah." He shoved his sister back. "Astrid, what did you do?"

She looked confused and then hurt. "What do you mean? I brought you back."

"Oh, God, Astrid," Quinn said. "You shouldn't have done this. What were you thinking?"

He stood, doubling over and covering his abdomen—Mace's abdomen—with both hands. He looked down, eyes roaming the scars along his belly and chest and the huge wound there. He looked horrified.

"This isn't me. Oh my God. This isn't my body. Whose body is this? Oh my God." His face blanched white, his chest heaving. Tristin was almost positive he was having a panic attack.

Astrid came forward. "You're hurt, let me fix this, okay."

He jerked back. "Don't touch me." He was reeling, unsteady, looking around in horror.

Tristin stumbled out of Allister's loosened grip, dropping to her knees and grabbing his face. "Hey, Quinn. Listen to me. Listen. You have to breathe. Okay? Please. Just breathe with me, okay?" He was sweaty, his eyes unfocused, but he nodded. "Astrid has to fix you, okay? I'm right here. Just breathe with me." To Astrid, Tristin said, "Do it."

This time he didn't protest as she laid her hands across the gouge in his flesh. Tristin watched as the skin pulled together, not fully healed but better.

Quinn looked at her with dread. She met his gaze. She'd helped them do this. She'd been so eager, so desperate, to see him again that she'd never stopped to consider Ember was right, and he was happy. She never thought he could be at peace without her. She'd been so selfish. She deserved to watch him suffer for what she'd done.

"I can't look at you like this," Stella said, stalking up to Quinn and waving her hand. He lurched to his feet against his will. Tristin jumped up to step between them, but Stella was already whispering a spell.

As Tristin watched, Mace's features shifted, merging and morphing until it was just Quinn standing there, whiskey brown eyes and messy hair, minus the glasses. He looked at himself like he didn't trust Stella's magic, but Tristin couldn't help herself. She flung herself into his arms, wrapping herself around him. He pulled her close, and she felt like she could breathe for the first time in forever.

 472

"I'm so sorry. I didn't know what else to do. I'm so sorry," she told him, kissing his cheeks, his forehead.

"I know," he said, his voice resigned, his hands roaming her back. "I know."

Allister stepped forward, and Quinn stiffened in her arms.

"I should've known you'd be here," Quinn said, pushing Tristin behind him. "How could you have agreed to this?"

"I didn't. Not at first."

Ember stood, swaying on her feet, taking in the scene.

"Ember, dear," Allister said. "Come to me, please?"

"I don't think so," she said, drifting closer to Tristin. Tristin grasped Ember's wrist and didn't let go, even when her magic sparked.

"It wasn't a request. Stella, the blade."

Astrid looked to her father and then to her friend. "What? What are you doing?"

"I'm doing what I intended all along."

Astrid stood in front of her father. "This wasn't part of the plan. We got Quinn back. Let's just go home."

Allister sighed. "You're completely incapable of seeing the bigger picture."

Astrid's mouth fell open like she'd been slapped.

Stella came forward, a wicked looking dagger in her hand. The blade was black, but the handle was white with sharpened spines that looked to be made from shards of bone. There was no way that bastard was shoving that thing in Ember's heart. Tristin wasn't losing another person.

"You'll never get away with this," Tristin promised.

"This isn't an after school special, dear." Allister laughed. "The coven would never turn against me. My children would never speak against me, especially since one of them is technically dead. What are you going to do? You don't even have an active power. With Ember's power, there isn't a force in the world that can stop me. Ember, come here. I won't ask again."

Ember fought, but there was no getting past Stella's freaky mind control. Ember staggered towards him. Tristin made to follow

 473

Ember, having no plan at all, just a need to help, but then the gym doors burst open, startling everybody. The pack poured in, partially shifted and snarling. There was only a heartbeat of hesitation before they went for Allister.

Tristin's chest lightened. Allister was no match for four wolves. There was a bright light and a sound like an explosion, and everything went still. The wolves were frozen in place, victims to one of the witch's spells, though Tristin couldn't say which one.

Nobody moved until a blur of motion came from the gym door and her brother slid to a halt, his eyes falling on Quinn's face. Kai hadn't been there for the glamour spell, but she could swear he recognized his friend anyway.

Kai looked to the others, realizing he was the only one not affected by this magic. He rushed forward, stopping only when Ember whimpered. Allister held her against him, the blade to her heart.

This couldn't be how it ended, not after everything they'd been through. After everything they'd lost. Allister would win, and they'd die? The moment Allister killed Ember Isa would give the order to challenge the coven. The wolves would lose.

Allister laughed at Isa. "You're too late."

Quinn pressed against Tristin from behind. She closed her eyes, waiting for him to say goodbye. Instead he simply whispered, "Scream."

And she did.

Chapter 83

EMBER

The sound that pierced the air was unlike anything she'd ever heard before. It had no impact on the reapers in the room, but the others reacted as if electrocuted. They fell to the ground, clawing at their ears. The wolves howled, the spell broken, bolting back out the gym doors, trying to protect themselves from the soul-splitting shriek.

The knife clattered to the gym floor, Allister apparently not immune to a banshee's scream. His face contorted, blood trickling from his ears. Ember took two steps back.

Tristin went silent, the echo of her scream bouncing in the giant room. Tristin's face drained, her legs giving out. Kai rushed forward, catching her as she fell. This time when the doors opened, the wolves were in human form, shaky and bleeding, but all in one piece. Ember let go of the breath she didn't realize she'd been holding. Her people were okay. Her people were alive.

Everybody but Mace.

That brought her up short, the pain slicing through her chest, sharper than any knife blade. Mace was gone, and she had killed him. She'd blinked him out of existence. *He killed your father*, a voice nagged. Even knowing that, she would have saved him if she could have. Did that make her a terrible person?

"Ember!" Isa screamed.

Ember's head jerked upwards just as Allister grabbed the knife from the floor, lurching to his feet. Ember had no time to react. She was going to die.

"No!"

The cry wasn't hers, but Quinn's. He rushed his father, shoving him backwards in a blur of limbs and movement. Allister still held the knife. "Quinn, stop," Ember cried, but it was too late. The slick sound of steel slicing through flesh filled the room, and blood poured to the floor.

Astrid screamed. Quinn stumbled back, looking at the knife protruding from his father's heart. "Dad?" he whispered. "I'm sorry."

Allister wrenched his own hand from the blade, reaching for his son. Quinn took his hand, his expression softening. "I'm so sorry," Quinn said again.

Allister's face bled into a look of disgust as he forced Quinn's hand around the blade, squeezing until he cried out.

"What's happening?" Astrid asked, reaching for her father.

"No," Isa barked. "Don't touch him."

They all stood there, suspended, as the knife did what it does, Allister's magic pouring into Quinn. His father's eyes drained of life, his body falling to the ground. Ember had this horrible sense of déjà vu.

Quinn still held the knife.

"What just happened?" Quinn asked.

"Dude, did you just absorb your father's magic?" Kai asked.

"I don't know," Quinn said, shaking the spines of the knife loose with a shudder. It fell to the floor. They stepped away from the knife like it might come alive and attack them.

Tristin raced forward, tugging Kai's flannel shirt off his shoulders so she could wrap it around Quinn's hand. Ember stood frozen. Not sure what she should do.

"Do you feel any different?" Tristin questioned, her eyes wide and still so pale.

  476

"Nope," he said, staring at his father's body. "That just happened, right? I just did that? I killed my father. That wasn't some magic trick or optical illusion? He's—he's dead. Oh, God."

Ember gaped at Allister's body. Blood, so dark it looked black, oozed from the wound over his heart. So much blood. How had this happened? She looked to the members of the coven. They would tell everybody what they'd done. Nobody would be safe. The Grove would come back, and this time they would kill all of them.

She sank to her knees next to the older man, feeling for a pulse she knew wasn't there. "I'm sorry," she said, sincerely. "I'm so sorry, but you have to wake up."

"Ember, what the hell are you doing?" Kai asked warily.

"I don't know," she said, hoping Tristin was right, hoping that all these magical power surges were nothing more than psychic panic attacks; because if Tristin was wrong, Ember was going to kill everybody. But if Allister stayed dead, they were all dead anyway.

"Ember, I know what you're thinking, but you can't," Isa said. "If you try to bring him back, you have no idea what you'll get."

Ember looked at her alpha. "I don't care what I get as long as he comes back, Isa. He just has to come back." She glanced at Quinn, wincing at her insensitivity. "Sorry." He shrugged, his expression blank. To Isa, Ember said, "If Allister is dead, the Grove comes back now. Right now."

"This is a really bad idea," she heard Donovan say from the doorway. But it was too late. She'd already made up her mind.

She took a deep breath and dropped the wall between her and her magic, shaking off the fear and the anxiety. She let her magic take over, power surging through her. This time it settled around her like a blanket, thrumming through her with a steady warm pulse. She was fully herself and yet also her magic when she saw the sparks arching off her fingers. She could do this. Just like the bird. She pressed her hand to the center of Allister's chest. Nothing happened. She tried again.

"Come on. Come on," she whimpered to herself. "Just do it."

"Ember—" Tristin tried, but it was too late. Ember slammed her hand against his chest and gasped as the energy left her body.

 477

The force hit like the shockwave of a bomb, knocking everybody backwards. Allister's eyes flew open, and he sucked in a breath, violently forcing air back into his lungs. He stared at Ember in horror. "What did you do?"

"Holy fucking shit, dude, I think my cousin just resurrected your dad," Kai said.

Arms engulfed Ember as Astrid chanted, "Thank you, thank you, thank you."

Ember nodded slightly, shoving Astrid away just in time to puke everywhere. Would Ember ever stop vomiting? Thick black goop and something like dirt poured from her mouth. Was she dying? Was that what dying felt like?

"Ember," Kai yelled, but she threw her hands up. "Stay away from me, I don't know what this is," she managed before she vomited again.

The gym doors opened once again. Two figures stood shadowed in the doorway, and for one terrifying second, she feared it was the Grove come for them months too soon.

"Josephine?" Isa asked.

The swamp witch, Ember recalled, not able to keep her head up long enough to see the woman. Rhys nudged Kai. "Isn't that Ember's boss, what's his name?"

"Miller," Ember managed, her head snapping up to see if it was true. It was another bad idea. Another wave of nausea hit her. Ember watched the little old woman teetering along next to her former boss and wondered if she was dead and this was purgatory. Behind them were a group of partially shifted wolves.

Ember tried to look for her own wolves to know whether these new wolves were friend or foe, but she lacked the strength.

"Well, it appears we did not arrive in the nick of time," the witch rasped. Cane tap, tap, tapping on the floor.

"What is going on?" Quinn whispered.

"I have no idea," Kai said, his mouth barely moving.

 478

Chapter 84

TRISTIN

Tristin stared between the old witch and the tall well-dressed old man, Tristin's confusion growing by the minute. So that was Ms. Josephine. She didn't look like much to Tristin, but the woman obviously wielded a great deal of power because the seven wolves standing behind her stared at her like she was their alpha.

She wore a purple and blue housecoat, white tufts of hair standing on end as if she'd rolled out of bed. She looked crazy to Tristin.

"Well, y'all have created some kinda mess here."

Isa came forward. "Josephine? What are you doing here?"

Josephine smiled at Isa, patting her cheek. "Donovan sent for me. We were…delayed. Full moon," Josephine said, as if that explained everything.

"Donovan?" Isa's eyes turned to the young wolf who'd all but melted into the shadows. "What does Donovan have to do with this?"

Josephine waved away the question.

"Edgar," she told the oldest wolf, pointing to the coven members still lying on the ground. "Take these children outside," she scoffed. "But don't you let 'em leave." She pointed at Allister, still sitting on the ground, dazed. "And this one, you lock him up good 'til I know exactly what's what."

"Can you help her?" Kai asked Josephine, gesturing to Ember. Tristin's lip curled at the growing black puddle beneath her cousin. That was really disgusting.

"She almost done," Josephine assured him. "This is the consequences of bad magic. All that darkness gotta get out somehow. You're already feeling better, ain't ya, child?"

Ember nodded weakly.

She wiped her mouth on her sleeve, sliding away from the mess on the floor. She was white as any ghost Tristin had ever seen. Ember's eyes were still glassy, but she didn't look like she was dying anymore.

The witch huffed. "Good, cause I need to sit down." She tottered towards the bleachers with enough wobbling momentum that Tristin feared the witch might topple over face first. As she walked, she waved a hand, and the overhead lights flared to life, temporarily blinding the room.

They all followed along behind her, unquestioning. The old woman used her walking stick to knock the witches' candles out of her way. Tristin couldn't fathom how the woman held so much power. She looked like she had one foot in a retirement home and the other in the grave. Josephine plopped herself down with a heavy sigh. Ember's boss took a seat beside her.

Once settled, the witch turned her gaze to Tristin and then to Ember. "What were you two thinking? Blood magic?" Josephine snorted. "After all the things I put in place…years of planning, and you two manage to muck it up in a matter of weeks."

"Josephine, what are you talking about?" Isa asked, her bewilderment apparent.

"I'm talking about setting up these children to inherit their birthright."

"Our birthright as reapers?" Tristin asked, annoyance creeping into her voice. Kai winced, giving her his wide-eyed, shut-up look. She rolled her eyes, unimpressed by the old bat.

"She's talking about your birthright as the Morrigan," Miller answered.

 480

Josephine slapped the man's arm, her eyes fond. "There you go, stealin' my thunder."

"The Morrigan?" Kai gasped.

Tristin's anger flared. Oh, of course. "Ember's a goddess? That figures."

The old woman crooked a finger, and Tristin lurched forward, hitting her knees before the older woman. Tristin's pulse slammed against her throat as she realized she was unable to get away. The old woman held Tristin in place with something...swampy witch magic.

Josephine placed a palm against Tristin's cheek, and she felt her unease slipping away. "Child, you are, by far, the feistiest of my three, my little warrior, fightin' the world."

Josephine addressed all three of them then. "Do none of you know your history? What do they teach you in this town? The Morrigan wasn't one person but three. Three separate reapers, each with their own gifts and abilities. Each powerful in their own right. But together...together they were unstoppable."

Ember stood, unsteady as a baby deer, moving to sit on the floor near her old boss, placing her head on his knee. The elderly man startled at the touch, but then began to comb his fingers through her hair. "You've become a bit of a wolf yourself, Ember," he said. She nodded against his leg, looking exhausted.

"You're saying we're gods?" Kai asked, his face flushing. He blushed so easily, but Tristin admitted it sounded crazy. He reached for Rhys's hand but then Kai stopped, as if remembering it wasn't his to hold anymore. Tristin's eyes found Rhys's, and he stepped closer to her brother, his huge hand encircling his wrist. Kai looked relieved but so sad Tristin had to look away.

Josephine smiled. "I'm saying the magical world has waited a long time for you."

"Not the entire magical world," Kai quipped, looking at the bloodstain where Allister's body had lain.

When Ember could muster the strength, she turned her face towards her old boss. "Miller, why are you here? How do you know Donovan or Josephine? How does Donovan know Josephine? I'm so confused."

"I'm here because my sister said you needed me, and I've been looking out for you your whole life."

"You're Ms. Josephine's brother?" Tristin asked.

The man nodded. "I am."

"I don't understand any of this," Ember groaned. "What is this?"

Ms. Josephine chuckled. "I had a vision the night the three of you were born, and I knew we had to protect you no matter what the cost."

"A vision? You're a psychic witch?" Quinn asked, moving closer to Tristin like she had her own gravitational pull.

"No, child, I'm an oracle."

"No way," Quinn blurted.

"Like in *The Matrix*?" Kai asked. Tristin hid her face. He was so embarrassing.

"Perhaps." Josephine laughed. "But I knew, just as your mothers knew, that you had returned to save us."

"Save you from what?" Tristin asked.

"From the curse. From the Grove."

"From the Grove?" Ember gasped. "How could we ever save you from them? We couldn't even save Quinn."

"That's not important now. That comes later. It's clear we have much to do. First, we have to clean up this mess." Josephine looked at Quinn. "How you feelin'?"

He flushed as all eyes turned to him. "Okay, I guess. A little weird. I look like me, but I don't feel like me, exactly?"

"That's what happens when a reaper uses witch magic to try to restore a soul."

Tristin's heartbeat stuttered. "Are you saying it won't last? Is he going to disappear?"

Josephine quieted Tristin with a gesture. "Nah, it'll hold, but there will be consequences. Big ones."

Ember lifted her head, her eyes guarded. "Like what?"

Josephine didn't answer right away, as if trying to decide what to say. "I've been waiting for this for so many years. I knew you three were destined to change our world, but no amount of planning can control how things come to pass." She frowned, her eyes haunted. "Your father knew the only way for you to truly be free of his spell was for him to die. He'd always known it had to be this way. We knew when we dropped the cloaking spell that hid you and your father that

 482

Allister would come." She looked to Kai, a hint of a smile on her face. "It's why I put your name on Kai's arm. It was a gamble, but from what Donovan told me, Kai wouldn't be able to resist seeing if it was really Ember."

"That was a pretty big gamble," Wren said.

"So, you knew who I was the whole time? You knew everything when we came to see you? You lied to us," Kai said.

"I didn't tell you nothin' that wasn't true. I just didn't tell you everything. You didn't tell me everything neither. You coulda' told me Ember was alive. You coulda' told me her powers were out of control. Let's not talk about coulda'.

"I didn't count on the soul eater. Given what I knew of Allister, I should've, I suppose. He'd never do his own killin'. But I never saw him in my visions. I never figured you'd find a way to bind yourself to somebody so quickly. I didn't figure on you restoring his soul."

"Restoring his soul?" Ember repeated sluggishly, like the words were fighting her. Tristin thought her cousin might puke again. "He didn't have a soul."

"Not until you gave it back the night you met him in the cemetery. You remember?"

Her cousin swallowed hard. "That weird ball of light?" she whispered.

"It took a while for him to really start to feel human again. You both blamed it on the bond, but Donovan said Mace's soul seemed to be anchoring a bit more every day. Had you not tethered him to you, he might have realized it eventually, but you were still dealing with the effects of the binding spell wearing off. You did better with the critters."

Tristin could see the exact moment the enormity of what the witch said hit Ember. "So, if Mace had a soul..." Tears formed in her eyes. "Was what we felt real? He...sacrificed himself...his soul..." Her eyes widened, horrified. "Oh, God, what did I do with his soul?"

Josephine shook her head. "I don't know, child, but I expect we'll find out soon enough."

Ember swiped viciously at her eyes before suddenly asking, "So, you're saying my dad knew he was going to die?"

 483

Miller nodded. "As long as he lived, your powers would never truly be unbound. Without your full powers, Tristin and Kai's powers could never advance."

"Advance?" Kai asked.

Miller chuckled. "Oh, yes. You haven't even begun to see what you're capable of. But you will."

Ember shook her head. "This is crazy."

"We have time to explain everything to you, but not tonight."

"I have one more question that will need an explanation. Tonight." All eyes turned to the alpha who'd stayed silent until now. "Who is Donovan to you?"

Donovan moved to sit next to the older lady, kissing her cheek. "Donovan is my grandson. His mother was my daughter, Deja. His father is Edgar. I sent him to you but not with any ill intent. I needed to know Kai and Tristin were okay. Miller was taking care of Ember as best he could. I knew if you saw an injured wolf, you'd take him in. You gotta big heart, Isa. It's why I chose you to watch over the twins."

Isa looked conflicted. "Allister brought them to me. He said it was under orders of the Grove."

"A man so desperate for power is easily manipulated. It only took a little nudge to get him to see keeping you three alive was a far greater benefit to him than having you dead, at least until you grew up."

"Donovan was near dead when we found him. We could have killed him. You injured your own grandson so he could infiltrate our pack?" Wren asked, sounding more spooked than Tristin had ever heard him.

"My grandson is resilient. He understands what's at stake. Soon you will too."

Miller stood. "I think that's enough for tonight. You need to get some rest. From here on out, everything changes."

"That's it?" Tristin asked. "That's all the explanation we get? We're supposed to save the world with this information?" She gestured to herself, Ember, and Kai.

Quinn pulled Tristin from her knees. "Tristin, I'm tired. I want to go home. I'm sure Ms. Josephine will give us more answers soon, right?"

"Course, child," she said.

Tristin shivered as Quinn wrapped his arms around her. She returned the hug but gasped as she felt Mace's scars. "What is this?"

Miller stood, stretching. "That glamour spell that girl used is glitchy. You children have no training whatsoever."

He waved a hand, Latin pouring from his lips. Tristin pulled up Quinn's shirt, earning a yelp from the boy. "Hey, handsy, no means no," he said, yanking his shirt down. "Buy me dinner first or something."

"Better?" the old man asked.

Tristin nodded.

Everybody began making their way towards the door. Everybody except Donovan. "What about me?" he asked quietly, looking to Isa.

Isa looked at Josephine. "Yes, what about him?"

"Donovan's father may be an alpha, but Donovan was born human. He took the bite by choice. He will always be a beta. He's earned the right to choose his pack. If he's still welcome in your pack?" Josephine smiled at him.

He kept his head down, his eyes to the ground only daring to glance at Isa when it became apparent they were waiting on him.

"What do you want, Donovan?" Isa asked.

He risked a look at his grandmother. "I want to stay. I want to stay with Isa but not as an Omega. I want to be permanent." He looked at Isa. "If-if that's okay with you?"

Isa stared at the boy for so long he withered under her gaze. Finally, she said, "Fine, but that means no more running off whenever you feel like it; you cannot answer to two alphas. If you're mine, you're mine. No more secrets. How's your father going to feel about that?"

"It's my choice. I promise, no more secrets."

She looked to Wren who nodded. Rhys looked leery but nodded. "Okay, let's go home."

 485

Chapter 85

KAI

Kai felt like he'd aged a hundred years in one night. They'd taken two vehicles to the school, the Suburban and the Corolla. Ember, Quinn, and Tristin rode home with Donovan in the Corolla. Kai and Rhys rode back with Wren and Isa. Kai was a little disappointed he didn't get to ride home with Quinn, even though Kai pulled in the driveway only two minutes behind them.

He smiled a bit as he made his way up the stairs. His friend was back from the dead. Kai couldn't be sad about that, but it was strange to see Quinn in reality when mirrors reflected Mace. Isa spent two hours working hard to ensure the other packs knew an attack on Mace—Quinn—Mace, ugh, was an attack against their pack.

The other packs begrudgingly accepted the soul eater. Kai suspected it was because they were wary of a pack that now contained four wolves, three reapers, a faery, and a soul eater.

He didn't care as long as they were gone.

He pushed open his bedroom door to find Rhys sitting, once again, on the bed, staring at the floor.

"I never wanted to lie to you," Rhys said.

Kai was too tired for this but couldn't help but say, "Then why did you?" Rhys opened his mouth but closed it. So, Kai finally asked the question he'd been afraid to ask that first night. "How long have you been my personal guard? That is why Isa never let me go anywhere without you, right? She knew how I felt about you, so she thought it would be easier? That I'd want you around me all the time?" Kai couldn't look at Rhys. Since he'd said it out loud already, he kept going, letting his imagination fill in the blanks. "Is that why you had a sudden change of heart about us? Did you decide I was easier to control if you just pretended you cared about me too?"

Rhys's head jerked up at that. "What?"

Kai swallowed the lump in his throat. "What? Makes sense. Makes way more sense than you having feelings for me. Why else would you suddenly just give in?"

Rhys shot to his feet, grabbing Kai by the shirt. "You almost died. I almost lost you. You stood before the Grove, and I thought they were going to take you from me…twice." Pressing against Kai's neck, Rhys inhaled deeply like he was trying to soothe himself. "I gave in because I couldn't stand not doing this, not touching you. I couldn't stand seeing that look in your eyes every time you wanted me to touch you and I'd disappointed you…again. I'm always disappointing you."

Kai snorted. "You felt sorry for me?"

Rhys pulled back, his hands on Kai's face, forcing him to meet Rhys's gaze. "You're so stubborn. I fought my feelings for you because I couldn't stand the idea of being with you when you didn't know the truth. I didn't want it to be like that. I don't want there to be lies between us. Isa said if you knew about the Grove making you prisoners, we'd all be in danger."

This time it was Kai who couldn't summon any words.

Kai was positive his heart seized when the wolf said, "You told me you've wanted me since you were twelve. I've known you were mine since the moment we met. From the first time I saw you, you smelled like mine."

Kai stared, his mouth open. Rhys could hear Kai's pulse. Hell, Rhys could probably see it throbbing in Kai's neck. He tried to say something, anything really. "I—"

  487

"No, you wanted the truth, here it is. I love you. I've never loved anybody but you. I will never love anybody after you. You're my home. We're bonded. Do you get what that means? Wolves mate for life—" Rhys stopped abruptly, stepping away. "But you aren't a wolf. This doesn't have to mean to you what it means to me. I mean, that's a big commitment at seventeen? Are you ready to promise me forever now that you know so many better options are out there for you?"

Kai was nodding before he even knew it, his mouth finding Rhys's, mumbling against his lips. "There are no other options for me, you big stupid wolf. I told you that. If we are mated, bonded, whatever you want to call it, I'm totally on board." Kai pulled back suddenly, staring at Rhys dubiously. "Wait, is this a marriage proposal? Cause I would have liked a little more fanfare. A ring. A fancy dinner. Perhaps a sonnet or two?"

Rhys rolled his eyes but then was kissing Kai again, walking him backwards, pressing him down into the mattress. His heart felt like it was bigger than it was ten minutes ago, and he knew that was stupidly romantic, but he didn't care. Rhys loved him. Rhys said they were mates. "Oh God, we are those stupid kids who get engaged in high school."

"Technically, I've been engaged since before I was born."

Kai pulled back. "Oh, yeah. Selina right? Is that going to be a problem?"

"They can't fight a mating bond," Rhys promised, kissing his way along Kai's throat. Rhys pressed his body closer to Kai, biting along his jaw and doing that hip rotation thing that made him temporarily lose his ability to process rational thought. Pulling Rhys's head back, Kai looked at his wolf. "Hey, you think if we tell Isa we're engaged, we can start having like actual sex?"

"What we did in the truck wasn't actual sex to you?"

"Well, I mean, yeah. Sure. Like, um depending on your definition of sex," Kai mumbled.

Rhys snorted, but Kai threw his leg over the wolf and twisted, letting surprise and momentum flip them so Kai was on top. He bit Rhys through his shirt. Rhys's eyes glowed green, his fangs dropping.

Kai couldn't help the laugh that escaped. "Uh, maybe we should have you declawed first before we break into the advanced sex stuff."

Rhys rolled his eyes again, but kissed Kai's nose.

He bit the end of Rhys's nose in return. "I love you too, you know?"

Rhys turned bright red. "Yeah, I know."

"If we're going to spend the rest of our lives together, you're going to have to stop blushing every time I say it. Here, let's practice. I love you." Kai laughed louder as Rhys's face went purple. "Nope. Didn't work. I love you."

Rhys buried his face in Kai's neck, making a weird growling sound and then Kai was twisting, trying to squirm away from the fingers digging under his ribs. It was useless. "Stop. Stop. I hate being tickled. Stop it."

"Then stop making fun of me."

"Okay," Kai shouted. "I'll stop. I'll stop." He sucked in a much-needed breath. "I do love you."

"I love you, too, though I have no idea why."

"Stay with me tonight?"

"Isa will kill me."

"Nah, she's way too busy dealing with all that information Ms. Josephine dropped on us."

Rhys looked at Kai. "So you're a god, huh?"

He rolled his eyes. "Oh, yeah, that's me, behold the mighty god of reaping. Ms. Josephine is an old lady. She's crazy."

Rhys pushed a strand of Kai's hair out of his face. "I don't know; I could see it. There's always been something about you."

Kai was the one who blushed this time. He didn't want to think about that. "Come on, sleep in here with me."

"Fine, but we're just sleeping."

Kai brought his knee up to press between the wolf's legs, biting his earlobe. "Just sleeping?"

Rhys groaned. "Well, mostly sleeping."

Kai laughed. "Best…fiancé…ever."

Chapter 86

EMBER

The ride home seemed longer than the ten minutes it took to get there. So much tension. Tristin watched Quinn like he might disappear at any moment. Quinn indulged her, letting her press herself against him the whole way home, letting her rest her head on his chest to listen to him breathe, to listen to his heartbeat.

Mace had no heartbeat. Ember's rational self knew Mace no longer existed. She knew it was Quinn. But while the others only saw Quinn—thanks to Miller's spell—Ember saw something different. She didn't know why it hadn't worked on her, but when she looked at Quinn, it just wasn't right. It was as if somebody had double exposed old film, superimposing Quinn's face over Mace's. It was unsettling, and it made her ache in a way she didn't think she could.

Every time Quinn would catch her looking, he'd give her that same sad smile, like he knew somehow. Or maybe he just didn't know how to feel either. He'd been happy on the other side. Then he was back there where people wanted to kill them pretty much every day. He'd killed his father, possibly absorbed his magic, and watched two werewolves haul his resurrected father off to who knows where. He only seemed happy when he looked at Tristin, and even that seemed…bittersweet. Her cousin finally seemed herself again. Maybe better than herself. She seemed happy.

Nobody spoke of Josephine or her predictions or what it meant for them. People had sacrificed themselves for Ember, Tristin, and Kai all based on this idea that they were some mythical incarnation of the Morrigan. Ember couldn't begin to imagine anything so stupid. They were all going to get themselves killed waiting for her and her cousins to come into their imaginary superpowers.

If they made it that far.

It was only a matter of time before the Grove found out what happened. Allister was alive, but was he on their side? Was he even still alive? What had Josephine and Miller done with Allister? What had they done with any of the coven? Her uncle would notice if a large number of his teenage witches went missing. He would notice if Allister went missing. Where did her uncle's loyalty really lie? With the Grove? With Allister? With her?

Ember excused herself as soon as the car hit the driveway, going in through the garage. She stopped, her hand on the doorknob. She didn't want to go inside. Inside were Romero and Chester and a million other reminders of Mace. She knew she didn't need Mace to control her powers. She'd proven it. She could call her power; she could control it. She didn't need Mace.

But she wanted him. She wanted him more than she wanted anything. She missed him. Josephine had said Mace wasn't soulless. She'd said he was capable of feelings. Did that mean he'd loved Ember, or was it always just the stupid magical bond she'd created between them? Did it change anything? Did it really even matter? Mace was dead, and she had killed him. She had sacrificed him to save Quinn.

The walk to her room felt like a walk to the electric chair. She wanted to forget everything. Maybe she would do what Tristin did and just hole up for a week. Ember didn't want to feel her feelings.

She shoved open the door to her room and stopped short, her mouth falling open at the strange orb of light pulsing against her window. She moved forward as the image stretched, morphing into something almost human, almost recognizable. Her whole body trembled. She'd seen this before when Quinn came to see her.

 491

She still couldn't make out much detail, but she saw silver eyes and a swoop of grey hair. She shook her head, almost like she couldn't take a full breath. She closed her eyes and opened them again, but it was still there. Mace was still there. She didn't know whether to laugh or cry. She moved closer, her hand reaching out towards the apparition as it took a less amorphous form.

"Mace?" she whispered.

Even though he wasn't solid, even though he flickered in and out like a bad television signal, there was no missing the grin that split across his face.

"It would appear you owe me a new body, luv."

Book Two in the series, "Dark Dreams and Dead Things," is available now!

Dark Dreams and Dead Things

17-year-old November Lonergan spent her whole life feeling like an outsider; like she was different. She was right. She's a reaper like her mother; like her two cousins, Kai and Tristin. The supernatural world believes they are part of a prophecy to save them from an evil known as the Grove. Ember just wants to survive high school and fix the fallout from bringing back her friend.

Old enemies are lurking; waiting for their opportunity to strike but the pack has a new problem. A group of legendary hunters has resurfaced, threatening the reapers and anybody who stands with them. They are making good on their threats too; attacking those closest to the pack.

Their only hope of defeating the Legionaries involves trusting a stranger to perform a dangerous spell to advance Ember and her cousin's powers. But Ember has a secret; a secret she can't tell the pack. One that leaves the pack vulnerable.

An attack on pack allies, leaves one member of the group injured and another missing, along with a mysterious girl named Evangeline who may play a bigger part in this than any of them realize. As the Legionaries are closing in, the pack must trust their enemies, enter hostile territories, and play a dangerous game of cat and mouse with a psychopath. Their entire plan lynches on a dangerous bargain, but rescuing one member of the pack could mean losing another in their place…possibly forever.

About the Author

Martina McAtee lives in Jupiter, Florida with her teenage daughter, her best friend, two attack Chihuahua's and two shady looking cats. By day she is a registered nurse but by night she writes young adult books about reapers, zombies, werewolves and other supernatural creatures. When she isn't working, teaching or writing she's reading or watching shows that involve reapers, zombies, werewolves and other supernatural creatures. Visit her website for playlists, excerpts, deleted scenes and other fun extras.

www.martinamcatee.com

Made in the USA
Middletown, DE
09 November 2017